CASIDDIE WILLIAMS

Hazel's Harem

To all the single moms, curvaceous moms and good girls, enjoy!

Contents

Preface

CONTENT NOTICE: This work contains explicit content and is written for adults. (18+) This is a Why Choose romance meaning the female main character has more than one love interest and does not have to choose between them.

Acknowledgement

If you've reading this, YAY! You've picked up my book! Thank you so much, and please know I appreciate you.

I need to give a big shout-out to my Alpha and Beta readers, Amy, Beth, and Veronica. Without them, I would have spent hours talking to my dogs about plot lines and character development and many, "Oh, what do you think about this?" texts and phone calls. The three of you helped me take an idea and grow it into my debut novel, all in 8 weeks. And you're still listening to me talk about them, along with the newest characters to pop up in my mind.

To my many ARC readers, you were invaluable in finding the many mistakes that I don't know how I missed in the dozens of times I read and edited my book. No one's perfect, and that's why authors rely on you to give your amazing feedback and funny comments.

To my children, who hopefully never read this book, thank you for hanging out with me and even sometimes letting me bounce the tamer ideas off of you. If you liked Mac and his story line, you can thank my personal 12 year old daughter for that. She said Wynnie's dad needed to be in her life, and so it became.

A final thank you to everyone who follows me on TikTok and Facebook. Every like on a post and comment of encouragement has helped me drive this book home. I documented my journey of writing, editing, and even arguing with my characters. It's been an amazing ride, and I can't wait to continue it will all of you in my next books.

<3 Casiddie

1

Hazel

13 years earlier

"Has it been 3 minutes yet?" I asked my best friend, Dellah, as I paced the small bathroom in her dorm room. The space has white walls, a white tub, and white floors. Who decided white was an appropriate color for a college dorm room? It feels sterile here, which is ironic because I may see the inside of many doctor's offices soon.

How is this happening? It was a random party with one gorgeous guy and a few too many red cups of punch. Well, duh, Hazel, I think you just answered your own question. I just wanted to have fun and let loose for one night. Depending on what that test says, it may have been my last night of fun for the next nine months. Hell, probably the next 18 years.

"Hazel, stop pacing. It's not going to make the timer go off any sooner." Pfffhh. Easy for her to say. She's not the one who's a week late for her period during her senior year of

1

high school.

Dellah, my petite blonde spitfire of a best friend, graduated last year and has been living her best life at college this fall, getting started on her graphics design degree. Thankfully she's only an hour away and took my panicked phone call this morning when I looked at my calendar. In true Dellah-style, by the time I drove to her dorm, she had a test waiting for me. She also had tissues, ice cream, and a few wine coolers that she bartered from her roommate. She's prepared for either outcome.

"Which guy was it again?" she asked. I shot her an incredulous look, and her hands raised in surrender. "No judgment, girl, there were some hot as fuck guys at that party. I was just trying to remember who it was."

"Well, it sure sounded like judgment." I stop pacing and assess the girl looking back at me in the mirror. Do I look different? I don't feel any different. Same auburn hair and hazel green eyes. Same freshman fifteen I managed to earn four years ago during my freshman year of high school instead of college.

I glance at the reflection of my best friend, anxiously waiting for the timer to go off. She's the reason I got into this mess. She invited me to spend the weekend at her dorm, and of course, we ended up at a party. What else is there for an 18 and 19 year old to do on a college campus?

"The Mad Hatter," I replied.

"The who?" she asked, eyebrows raised.

"The Mad Hatter from *Alice in Wonderland*. He had a tattoo on his forearm of the Mad Hatter's hat with a playing card and a pocket watch. You know how much I loved that story growing up. It's what made me spark up a conversation with him in the first place. Well, that and the liquid courage." Besides his obvious tall, dark, and broodiness, of course. Dellah stared at the wall momentarily, brows pinched, trying to remember my mystery guy.

"I never got his real name. I kept calling him the Hatter. In fact, when I walked up to him, that liquid courage took hold of me. I grabbed his arm with the tattoo, looked right into his cornflower blue eyes, and asked, 'Why is a raven like a writing desk?' Without hesitation, he looked back and said, 'I haven't the slightest idea, Alice.' "

Our conversation flowed easily. We talked about my mother and his grandmother and little sister and our collective love of *Alice in Wonderland*. He was so excited to be able to talk about it to someone who had as much of a passion for it as he did. Many drinks later and we're bouncing off of walls, mouths fused, trying to find a room with an unlocked door.

My mystery man, my Hatter, had me panting his 'name' while calling me Alice and turning our one night stand into the strangest evening of role-playing. And before we parted ways for the evening, he kissed me one last time and whispered, "Fairfarren, Alice."

I shake my head, bringing myself back to the present. It was all too easy to fall back into the memory of those piercing blue eyes as my nameless Hatter wooed me with our mutual love of a fairy tale. I never expected I'd have a memorable and meaningful conversation at a college party.

Now here I am, five weeks later, impatiently waiting for the longest three minutes of my life to pass. The timer goes off, and Dellah and I stare at the test, neither of us brave enough to look at it. With a long sigh, I finally turned it over. Dellah doesn't need to see the two pink lines I'm staring at to know it's positive. My collapse to the floor and immediate sobs give her all the answers she needs.

"Now what?" Dellah asks as she crouches down to the floor embracing me in her arms. "We can go back to the house where the party was and see if anyone knows who he is. He looked older, so someone must know him."

"No. No. I made this mistake, and it's my burden to bear. I'm going to be a mother, and you're going to be the most kick ass aunt in the world." We both chuckled slightly because what else was there to do in this situation?

"You better believe I am, bestie! We will get you through this together, and this baby will have the best life he or she will ever know."

2

Hazel

Present day

"Wynnie, I promise you the world isn't ending. It's only a few hours drive back to Spring Ridge to visit your friends. This move is a great opportunity for us-"

"You, Mom," she interrupts. "This is a great opportunity for *you*. You get to be back with your best friend while I'm leaving Nora behind. Don't get me wrong, you know I love Aunt Dellah but the two of you living together is not my idea of a good time, and Nora is the only best friend I have."

She's not wrong. I know this will be more of an adjustment for her than for me. We've spent the last 12 years, her entire life, only her and I living four hours from my hometown, Mountain Pines, Georgia. But you jump on the offer when your best friend calls to tell you that a nursing position has opened at the local pediatrician's office. Higher pay, regular hours, and more time with my daughter was an easy sell for me.

"We aren't living *with* your Aunt Dellah. It's an apartment above her detached garage. It's just like being neighbors." Her cornflower blue eyes shoot me a look from the passenger seat that I know all too well as my own. She's not buying my attempt to tamp out my excitement of being with my best friend again.

Driving down the tree lined highway in my little red sedan littered with fast food and snack wrappers from our trip, I get lost in a memory. Finding out I was pregnant during my senior year of high school completely rocked my world. I had a lot of decisions to make quickly. After the shock wore off, I confessed to my parents that I was pregnant, and we had a long talk. I wanted to move away to my mom's sister's house to give me and my unborn baby the best chance of living without criticism. My aunt lived just far enough that my parents could still be there for me when I needed them.

Within two weeks of my positive test, I moved to my aunt's and enrolled in a GED program to finish high school. Leaving everything I knew behind was hard, but my life wasn't just my own anymore, and I knew I was making the smartest choice for our future. I wanted to give my baby everything life had to offer, even if they didn't have a father in their life.

My baby girl, Rowyn "Wynnie" Juniper Gibson, was born that summer. And that fall, I enrolled in an online CNA certification class and worked to become an LPN over the next few years.

"How about we stop for more road food before getting to your aunt's house?"

"Mom, are you trying to bribe me with greasy food in an

6

attempt to convince me that this move isn't all for you? You know I'm not 6 anymore, and an ice cream sundae with a cherry and extra sprinkles doesn't hold the same weight, right?"

Damn, why do they grow up so quickly? She is too mature for her age. I can't decide if it's a good thing or a bad thing. Being a single mom for her entire life has made her grow up quicker than she needed to. Gone are the days that I'm her hero simply for buying her a new pack of crayons, and hello to the days that a $125 pair of sneakers earns me a half smile and a "Thanks, Mom."

"What about a large fry and extra bacon on a burger? Does that get me into your good graces, any?" My questions catch me a side eye and a little huff.

"It's a start, I guess." I smile and shimmy my shoulders. I'll take it as a win, even if I can almost hear the eye roll from the other seat at my little happy dance.

My personal party is interrupted by my phone ringing over the radio speakers. "Hola? Has visto mis pantalones?" I answer with a giggle knowing it's Dellah on the line.

"Bitch, you left your pants back at that part-"

"SPEAKER PHONE!" I interrupt before she can finish wherever she plans on going with that sentence.

"Hi, Aunt Dellah," Wynnie chimes in.

"Sorry, kid. I should have known better." You can hear the slight amusement laced in her apology through the speakers. "Just checking in on your ETA. I was planning to order pizza to arrive when you get here."

"Mom is bribing me with greasy fast food, but I know 'pizza' is code for wine and gossip. The GPS says we have about 45 minutes until we arrive." She certainly knows me and her aunt well. It's been far too long since I've been back home to see my best friend, and we have a much needed girls night planned for tonight.

The squeals of joy have both Wynnie and me wincing. "See you soon, Dells. Love ya."

"Love you too, Hazy. I can't wait!" The phone disconnects, and I'm left sitting in silence while my preteen plays on her phone.

3

Hazel

Pulling into my hometown never gets any easier. The trees, bare from winter, lining the streets look taller, and the awnings on the stores seem faded from age, but everything stays the same in this town. By now, everyone knows why I left my senior year. Getting pregnant at 18 was never as much of a scandal as my juvenile mind made it out to be, but hindsight is 20/20.

A few years after giving birth, my parents moved closer to be near Wynnie and me. and her sister, whom I was living with. It was sad to say goodbye this time, and they would all miss seeing Wynnie, but my mom loved being closer to her family again and had no plans to return to Mountain Pines. Ultimately we all know this move and the new job opportunity would help advance my career.

Getting closer to Dellah's house had me doing a mental checklist of everything I needed to take care of over the next two weeks during winter break. Unpacking, making sure

Wynnie is fully registered for her new school, finding the local gym, and preparing myself for my new job, to name a few.

To no one's surprise, my best friend was waiting for us in her driveway, jumping up and down at our arrival like someone had lit her shoes on fire. I barely put the car in park before she opened my door and flung herself at me into a huge hug.

"You're heeeeeeeeeere!" Dellah screamed into my ear.

"Holy shit, woman. I think you just broke the sound barrier with that greeting. Dogs everywhere are probably wincing at the pitch you just screeched at me."

"Don't be dramatic, Hazel. You know I save my best notes for karaoke night." Who could forget karaoke nights? I love this woman to death, but she can't hold a tune to save her life. I'm given a moment of reprieve from the screeching when Dellah hurls herself over my lap, half across the center console, to grab my unsuspecting daughter into a hug.

"How's my favorite niece? Any boys in your life? Never mind, of course not. You're only 12. Do you even like boys yet, or do they still have cooties?" Dellah's rapid fire questions have my head spinning.

I give my best friend a big shove trying to remove her from my lap. "Dellah, your ass is in my face, woman." She continues to bombard Wynnie with questions as I get out and round the front of the car. Rolling my eyes, I open the door, grab Dellah's petite frame in a bear hug and drag her away from my daughter. "Give the poor girl a breather."

"Hi again, Aunt Dellah. Nice to see you, too. I think you might want this back." With a chuckle, Wynnie passes Dellah her sandal that fell off in her exuberance of flinging herself across the car.

"Thanks, girl," she says to Wynnie before returning to me. "Alright, come on. Let me show you your new humble abode. It's got everything you should need for tonight. Feel free to make yourself at home however you like. We can go shopping in the morning to stock the fridge and hit up any local stores that you might need to make this place your own."

To the left of the driveway stands Dellah's magazine-worthy two story white house with your typical black shutters and red door. We follow Dellah to the right through a side door in her detached garage. Inside we climb a flight of stairs to another red door. Walking in, I'm in complete shock.

"Um, Dellah, I think you may have undersold this place when you were describing it." In front of me is a fully furnished two bedroom apartment that looks like you walked off the beach. The cool blue walls make the entire space seem impossibly larger. The accents in the room are white and coral.

"It's nothing much," Dellah scoffs. "This first bedroom on your right is the master. You have your own bathroom and a full tub." She looks over her shoulder at me and winks. "Wynnie's room is the last door on your right." She points to a door at the end. "The one in the middle is the main bathroom with a shower."

The entire left side of the apartment is the living room and an open concept eat-in kitchen. There's so much light in the room from large windows and skylights.

"Unfortunately, the laundry is downstairs in the garage, but it's a full top and bottom set, and it's all yours to use. I have my laundry room in the main house." Main house? I don't even have words for these accommodations.

"Remind me what your husband does again?" I ask as I look around in awe. I know Collin well, and it's a running joke between us since we both know Dellah's graphic design business makes enough money to support whatever lifestyle she wants.

"I told you, girl, I married up." She winks at me. "Besides, this apartment came with the house, and it's just been sitting unused. We finally get to live out our childhood fantasy of being sisters and living together. Well, close enough together." She's bouncing on her toes and clapping like a fairy.

"Shh, don't say that too loudly. It's been hard enough to convince the preteen that we *aren't* living together. If she hears you say it, there will be no convincing her otherwise. Speaking of which, where is said preteen?" I turn in a circle in the middle of the large living room, not seeing her. I walk to her new bedroom and find her sprawled across the bed with her headphones in her ears, playing on her phone. Dellah and I look at each other, laugh and simultaneously say, "Teens."

4

Phoenix

Keys, wallet, water bottle: Check, check, check. Getting ready to head to the gym, I run down my mental checklist of things not to forget before I leave.

I love school holiday breaks, but the disruption in my daily schedule always throws me off for the first few days. Although, a break from school is never really a break for me. Teaching Auto Shop at the local high school means if I'm not in the classroom teaching teens to fix cars, I'm either working on my own car or helping a friend with theirs.

The drive to the gym is quick and routine, and I'm walking into the building on autopilot when I open the door and walk right into the intoxicating smell of peaches.

"I'm so sorry," says a female voice.

"Are you alright?" I ask as I look down at the contents of a small purse that has spilled on the floor.

"I'm totally fine. I wasn't paying attention while looking

for my license in my purse. I must have left it in the car or at home. I'm trying to sign up for a membership and apparently didn't come prepared." She's rambling as we attempt to pick up her items from the floor.

I look up and come face to face with the most stunning woman I've ever seen. She's lost in her train of thought while I'm lost in her eyes. They aren't quite green like mine and there's a subtle honey color mixed into them, making them hazel. A warm and inviting hazel color that I want to swim in.

"...Hazel."

Her word shocked me back into the present. What? Was I speaking out loud? Did she just read my mind? Shaking my head to regain focus, "I'm sorry, what did you say?"

With a shy smile, she repeats herself. "Hazel, my name is Hazel. Nice to meet you, and I'm so sorry for rudely walking into you." So I didn't lose my internal monologue. That's a relief.

"It's alright," I say while handing her the items I retrieved from the floor. "It's nice to meet you, Hazel. No need to apologize. I wasn't paying attention either."

"Oh, well, thank you for these." She gestures to the hand sanitizer and nail file I handed to her from the floor. "Hopefully, I'll get my life together today and try this membership thing again tomorrow." She smiles again, but this time it's brighter.

"Good luck, Hazel," I say, still half hypnotized by her eyes. "Maybe I'll see you again here soon, without such a grand entrance." We both laugh. She gives me a nod of thanks as I hold the door open for her to leave.

As the door closes behind her, I can't help but linger a little longer than I should, watching her walk away. Her auburn hair, high on top of her head in a ponytail, is swaying back and forth in time with her hips. Hips that aren't slim and bony. These are well-rounded, broad hips. The kind of hips that make me want to grab hold of them from behind and-

Phoenix. I internally chastise myself. I need to stop thinking about her hips before I walk into the gym sporting a semi. That's not a pleasant gym look, nor is it easy to hide in these athletic pants.

5

Hazel

"It was completely embarrassing," I groaned into my glass of wine, having just recounted to Dellah what happened this morning at the gym.

"It couldn't have been that bad. You said he was hot!" She whisper-shouted while tucking her legs under herself on the couch, leaning in to get all the juicy details. We are sitting in my living room, drinking wine and gossiping.

"He was, but it could have been so much worse! What if I hadn't just packed the essentials in the small purse I had brought to the gym? Can you imagine if it was my actual purse? We would have been picking up god knows what from my bottomless pit. Definitely a tampon or two. Maybe some sugar packets. Hell, there may even be a condom floating around in there." I lower my voice on those last words to avoid letting them carry into Wynnie's room.

"Hazy, relax. He probably won't even remember meeting you." She tucks a strand of her blonde hair behind her ear like she didn't just insult me.

"Gee, thanks, Bitch. Glad to know you think I'm so easily forgettable." I shove her shoulder, almost knocking her off the couch. We explode into a fit of giggles. I missed having a friend close by. It's been so long since I've been able to relax and let go like this. Almost 13 years too long.

"Well, if he knows what's good for him, he won't ever forget a hot piece of ass like you. Tell me what he looked like again."

"He was tall and built, and it felt like I ran into a wall when we collided. I saw some tattoos around his shoulders under his tank. He had the shiniest jet black hair, the brightest green eyes, and a five o'clock shadow that I wanted to lick."

"Girl! Do you think he goes there often?" She pauses and makes a sour face. "Wow, what a cliche question." We burst into another fit of giggles at her statement.

"Mom." We both abruptly stop laughing at the reminder that we aren't irresponsible teenagers and I, in fact, have a child of my own. I look at Dellah wide-eyed before turning towards Wynnie.

"Yes, dear," I reply, the sarcasm dripping through the words. I swat at Dellah, who's sitting beside me with barely contained laughter.

"Ouch," she exclaims. "You hit my tit." Another fit of laughter ensues.

Wynnie walks over to the coffee table in front of us and grabs the almost empty wine bottle. She takes it to the kitchen, puts the cork back into it, and puts it in the refrigerator. Illuminated by the light from the open door, I can see the "mom look" she's giving us with her piercing blue eyes. Dellah must notice it, too, because her laughter erupts even louder, and she grabs my shoulders and shakes me.

"Oooh, we're in trouble now. I think it's time to go to our rooms." She turns to Wynnie. "Do you want to give your auntie a big hug and kiss goodnight before I go?" Dellah is really pushing her luck now. If looks could kill, Wynnie would be writing her obituary.

"Good night, Aunt Dellah. See you tomorrow morning and bring coffee and donuts. You two are trouble together." Wynnie rolls her eyes at us as she walks away. One more fit of giggles and Dellah's out the door, back across the driveway to her house. After I watched through the window and saw her go inside, I walked back across the living room and knocked on Wynnie's door.

"Come in," she says.

"Just wanted to say good night and tell you you're my favorite kid." I sit at the end of her bed on her navy comforter and give her a big smile while she gives me an exasperated scowl. "The room looks nice with the new bedding and curtains. It feels more like you than the coral colors that were in here." The room was pale blue, white, and coral, like the rest of the apartment. Changing out the corals for blues and reds made this room seem more like a teen room than a beach house.

"I feel so honored to be your favorite out of all your other options." She sticks her tongue out at me, and I return the gesture before we start laughing.

"How are you doing with all the changes? I know this isn't the easiest for you, and you've been such a trooper with everything." I grab her hand and give it a gentle squeeze.

"I'm doing okay. I'm a little nervous about starting a new school. Making friends isn't always the easiest for me. I miss Nora."

18

"I know you do, kiddo. Have you put any more thought into joining the softball team like at your old school? I know that's something you enjoyed, and it might help you make friends easier."

She looks down at her bed and picks at an imaginary piece of lint. "I'm still thinking about it. I haven't made a decision yet. I still have some time before tryouts at the end of January."

"Okay, hun. You let me know if there's anything I can do to help you make a decision. I want this transition to be as easy for you as possible. Aunt Dellah and I are going out tomorrow for some shopping and a lunch date. I don't start work until you go back to school. Would you like to join us?"

"Hmm, I'll decide in the morning based on the donuts that she brings." She gives me a genuine smile, and I see the twinkle in her eyes, knowing the truth. There isn't a donut that Wynnie doesn't like.

6

Jude

Two weeks of winter break went by far quicker than I expected, and the next eight weeks aren't going to go by any slower. I have to take a continuing education class twice a week for the next eight weeks after school to stay updated with my school counselor certification. I've spent the last four years opening this office door daily for the middle schoolers in this town, and I love what I do.

Sitting at my desk, I turn on my computer and sip my coffee while it boots up. I check my email and see an attachment from my principal. We have a new transfer student joining the 7th grade class. As the school counselor, it's my job to have a few sit down sessions with transfer students. Initially, to introduce them to the school and a few follow-ups to ensure they are acclimating well. I briefly look at her transfer files and spot exactly what I need to connect with this new student.

About 20 minutes before the first bell rings, there's a knock at my door. I look up to see a young lady standing in my doorway. Rising from my seat I wave my hand at the chair in front of my desk.

"Come in. I'm going to guess you're my new transfer student. Welcome."

A slight nod and smile let me know my assumption is correct. I sit at the opposite side of my desk and open her file on my computer.

"Miss Rowyn Gibson, correct?" I ask.

"Yes, Sir," she replies quietly.

"So nice to meet you, Rowyn. My name is Jude Sanders. The kids call me Mr. S. I like to keep a casual but respectful atmosphere in my office. Do you go by Rowyn, or is there another name you'd prefer?"

"Nice to meet you, too, Mr. S. I prefer Rowyn. My family has a nickname for me, but I go by Rowyn at school."

"Sounds great. Rowyn it is. Have you had a chance to look over your schedule from the office? Are there any questions I can answer for you?" Assuming her first stop was to the main office, that's the only way she would have found her way to my office.

"Everything looks good. All the classes look basically the same as my old school. The electives are a little different, but I'm happy to have an Art class over a P.E. class." She gives a half smile at that admittance, and I smile back.

"I agree. Art is much more fun than a physical education class any day." At that, her smile widens, and I see some of her first day jitters relax.

"So, Rowyn, I was looking at your previous school records," I start and immediately see her stiffen. "Nothing at all to worry about." I look up and give her a warm smile, and she relaxes again. "I see we have something in common."

21

"What's that?" She looks at me inquisitively.

I plastered a big smile on my face. "Softball. I'm the coach here at the middle school level. Is that something you would like to pursue here? We have spring tryouts soon."

"Oh," she says. I've clearly surprised her. "I haven't fully decided yet." I can hear the hesitation in her voice.

"Okay, well, if you have any questions or if you'd like to come out to watch or participate in an unofficial practice, the girls like to get together after school and work on their skills in the backfield. You're welcome to join at any time."

"Thanks. I'll talk to my mom and see what I can work out." She stands and starts to leave my office.

"Miss Rowyn." I stop her at the door, and she turns around. "As a transfer student, the principal likes to have you check in with me once a week for the first few weeks. I'll see you this time next week?" It's not a question, although I phrased it as one as a courtesy, but it's mandatory.

"Oh yeah, sure. See you next week, Mr. S."

"Or sooner if you'd like to come to a practice. Backfield, number 6, right after school. Have a good first day, Rowyn. My door is always open." I smile at her, and she nods back and leaves my office.

7

Hazel

The first day in a new office after being off work for over two weeks was refreshing as much as it was stressful. I'll have a few weeks of training with the early morning shift before I move into my permanent position as the mid-shift nurse. I hated leaving Wynnie this morning to get to school on her own for her first day, but Dellah assured me she would take care of everything. Once I complete training I'll be able to drive her myself to school, and I'll be home by 7:15 PM in time for dinner. That will be a vast difference from my 3-11 PM shift at my old job. I felt like I never got to see Wynnie, which was heartbreaking for me.

Before heading home, I decided to stop at the grocery store to grab the supplies for tacos, our favorite meal. I'm mindlessly wandering the aisles, picking up anything else we might need. I stop in front of the canned tomatoes trying to decide which brand to grab, when I'm jostled by the crashing of my cart. I look up to see the most apologetic cinnamon colored eyes under a mop of dirty blonde hair attached to a beautiful specimen of a man.

"I'm so sorry, ma'am. My nose was in my cell phone, and I wasn't even paying attention to where I was going. Please forgive me, ma'am." I can hear the anxiety in his words and I cringe at his use of the word ma'am not once but twice in his apology.

"My name is Hazel. No need to call me ma'am. It makes me feel like an old lady, and I'm barely 30. Okay, well, I *am* 30, but only by a few months, so that's practically 29." *Enough, Hazel, no need to spill all your insecurities to a complete stranger.*

"Of course, Miss Hazel, but you don't look a day over 25. And I truly am sorry for crashing into your cart." The smile that he's giving me could light up a city block.

"It's no problem…" I let the sentence hang in the air, hoping that he will take the opportunity to fill in the blank with his name. He does.

"Jude." His smile brightens.

"Nice to meet you, Jude. You didn't cause any harm running into me. It just startled me out of my own train of thought. It seems we were both distracted." He's giving me a look I can't quite describe.

"Miss Hazel, I was wondering if I might be forward?" Might be forward? Who still speaks like that these days? I hesitate a moment to take in the man in front of me. He's tall and lean, but I can tell by the straining buttons on his light gray dress shirt that he's hiding some muscles under there. His shaggy but styled dirty blonde hair gives him a boyish charm, and his khaki pants look like they were molded specifically for his amazing thighs.

"Um, sure?" I replied with apprehension. "Go ahead, Jude." Where could this be going?

"Miss Hazel, you have the perfect name to match your beautiful eyes." And he seems to have the most perfect gaze into these eyes of mine. It's like he's staring into my soul, devouring my innermost secrets. I feel my cheeks flush pink. When was the last time I received such a sincere compliment, or blushed for that matter?

"Oh, um, wow, Jude. Thanks." Five single-syllable words were all I could manage to get out of my muddled brain at the moment.

His smile grew impossibly wider. "May I be forward once more?" Still, without words, I nodded. "Could I interest you in going out to dinner with me?"

How did I go from pondering tomato brands to being asked out on a date? I moved my right hand towards my left and gave my wrist a little pinch to make sure I wasn't dreaming. Nope, that hurt. Definitely awake. Jude watched my hand movement, and I watched him dip his head in a soft chuckle. Yep, I'd be laughing at me, too.

"Maybe that was a bit too forward. How about I offer you my phone number? You don't even have to give me yours if you don't want to. That way, the decision is all in your hands." He gives me a reassuring smile. It takes several blinks of my eyes to come out of my brain fog.

"Let me see your phone, Jude." I extended my hand out to him. He unlocks it and hands it to me, and I call myself from his phone. "Now we have each other's numbers." I offer him back a warm smile.

"Thank you, Miss Hazel. That sounds like a fair compromise."

"Just Hazel."

"Excuse me?"

"Please just call me Hazel. No need for the 'Miss' part. We've exchanged phone numbers. We're more acquainted now, and there's no reason for the formality of miss or ma'am for that matter."

A sheepish smile forms on his face. "Of course, Hazel. I look forward to speaking to you. Enjoy the rest of your shopping trip." With that, he veers around me and continues down the aisle. 20 minutes later, when I'm leaving the store, my cell phone buzzes.

Unknown: Little Dove. It was so lovely to meet you. I hope we can get to know each other better and you will agree to a date in the near future. <3 Jude

Little Dove? And did he just "less than 3 me?" Wow, Jude is a different brand of man, and I think I'm here for it. But also, what's with all the hot men and them literally crashing into my life? Oh, well. Who am I to look a gift horse in the mouth and question fate? Let me save his number before it gets lost.

Me: It was my pleasure, Jude. I'd love to go out with you on one condition. During that date you have to tell me why you just called me Little Dove.

Jude-Grocery Crasher Guy: Deal, Little Dove. I'll be in touch soon to make plans. Enjoy your evening.

Well, this was undoubtedly the most interesting grocery store trip I've ever taken.

8

Phoenix

Me: Hey man, are we still on for lunch? I've barely seen you at all this week.

Jude: Absolutely. I'll meet you in the quad after 4th period. Gotta tell you about this goddess I met!

Me: A goddess. I'm intrigued. See ya soon.

This has been the longest first week of school. There are more freshmen in my Auto Shop classes this year than in previous years. I'm not used to going back to the basics, teaching the kids about tools. But it's worth it when they get excited to learn.

The end of 4th period finally arrives. As I walk through the quad between the middle and high school, I see Jude sitting at a picnic table, pulling out his lunch. I bow my head and chuckle to myself.

"What are you wearing? Are those faces on your tie?" He lets out a sigh. "You lost another bet, didn't you?" He drops his head between his shoulder blades, staring at the sky, and it's all the answer I need. "When will you learn that making bets with middle schoolers never ends well?"

"Sometimes I have to play hardball to motivate these pre-teen guys," he said exasperatedly. "You teach high schoolers how to get greasy and catch all the girls."

"Hey, the second part of that just happens to be an added bonus sometimes. But, okay I'll bite. What kind of a bet did you lose?" This better be good because I can't imagine the embarrassment his day has been wearing a hot pink tie, with mini faces of, I assume, one of his students, all over it.

"Listen, I made this bet at the end of the last school year, and I had no idea they'd remember."

"You should have known better." He never learns.

"Yeah, you would think I would have learned by now that bets and I don't mix. These kids can't remember to turn in their homework assignments, but you make a ridiculous bet with them six months ago, and they won't forget. And that's the exact reason I made a bet with them."

"Them? There was more than one bet?" He's got himself in trouble this time.

"Thank goodness, no. It was a collective bet. I had a group of four students that seemed to end up in after-school detention weekly. The principal asked me to talk to them and see if I could motivate them to straighten up over the summer and return to have a better school year. So, I brought them into my office before summer began last year. I bet them if they had no more than two detentions each between the beginning of the school year and winter break, they could choose any tie for me to wear, and I'd wear it for a week when we got back." I'm watching him in amusement as he strokes his tie like a loving pet. The laugh I've been holding in finally spills over.

"Okay, two questions. Why did they still get two detentions, and why did you agree to wear it for an entire week?"

"It's called compromise. They drove a hard bargain. They wanted five detentions each and a month of wearing the tie. I gave them free rein of the tie as long as it was school appropriate, and we agreed on the two detentions because no one is perfect. And one week of tie-wearing because that was all the embarrassment I was willing to endure. And here we are." He's gesturing to his tie with an apprehensive look on his face. I can see now that there are four different faces on the tie, not just one, as I had previously assumed.

Oh no. "You made them another bet didn't you." He nods. "What now?"

"No detentions and two weeks with a school appropriate hat next year."

"But we aren't allowed to wear hats in school."

He raises his brows in amusement. "Exactly." He gives me a devilish grin. "But I'll wear it before and after school and any sporting events I attend during those 2 weeks. And I'll let them take selfies with me to commemorate the occasion. Whatever it takes."

"Whatever it takes." I agree. "So, how have your night classes been going? And then tell me about this girl."

His face lights up, and it makes my stomach flutter. Hmm, weird. "Classes are going well. Just the typical refresher course." He pauses, seemingly for dramatic effect. I roll my eyes.

"And the girl?" I ask.

"She's a woman, my Little Dove." He's got this strange far-off look on his face.

"Your what? Little Dove? You're gonna need to give me more than that, man. And get that goofy look off your face." I give his shoulder a light shove from across the table. Checking my watch I remind him, "We've got ten more minutes for you to spill all the details. Get your head out of the clouds."

"It was a clandestine clash of destiny."

My forehead lands in my hands as I groan. "I swear you need to quit reading those romance novels. Who says 'clandestine' anymore?"

"Okay, fine. Have it your way, but it was a literal crash of our shopping carts. I was checking my schedule on my phone and crashed right into her cart in the canned food aisle. When I looked up, it was like the clouds opened up and-"

"Nope. No figurative angels singing or fireworks raining from the sky. You were at the grocery store. So you crashed into some woman's cart at the grocery store, and…?"

"And I was mesmerized."

Rolling my eyes, "Here we go again. Okay, you were *mesmerized*, then what? What's this Little Dove thing about?"

"Phoenix, she was the most amazing woman I've ever seen. You know, growing up in my household, doves stood for purity, peace, and a new beginning. That's what I saw when I looked at her." He's got it bad. That far-away look is back on his face.

"So you asked her out?" Did he grow some balls?

"Yes, but she didn't answer. I think she was still a little shocked by our cart crash. So instead, I suggested I give her my number. We ended up exchanging numbers, and have been texting all week. We're going out Saturday night."

"Nice! Good job, man. I'm proud of you for putting yourself

out there." We fist bump across the table.

The warning bell rings, and we head back to our respective buildings. I love the second half of the day. I've got three more periods to get through, and they are all juniors and seniors. It feels more like leisure than work when we all work together to fix up their cars.

I'm struggling a little to stay focused through these last classes. The image of Jude's smile keeps flashing through my mind. Was that a flutter of excitement for him meeting a girl? I try to shake it off and get through the day.

After school, I decided to head to the gym. I've been trying different times of the day to see if I can catch a glimpse of the little vixen I almost ran over a couple of weeks back. So far, I've had no luck. Maybe she didn't end up getting a membership after all.

9

Hazel

"What am I supposed to wear? I haven't done this in forever. Dellah, you aren't helping. Stop laughing at me."

"Babe, I'm sorry. It's like we're back in high school again. It's just a date with a guy. Stop freaking out." Of course, she would be calm. She's married. When was the last time she went on a date with a stranger? And that's precisely what he is. We've had fun, light banter this week through text, but I still know nothing about him.

"You're right. I'm a 30 year old woman," I say with conviction. "I can go on a date with a gorgeous man that's way out of my league." I spin around to my best friend, who's relaxing on my bed while I'm having a mini meltdown in front of my closet.

"Gah! Why did I agree to this? What was I thinking?"

"You were thinking with your lower lips." She wiggles her eyebrows at me. "Ouch! What's with you and the titty hitting?

32

It was a joke. Guys can use the excuse that they were thinking with their dicks. Why can't we use the same excuse?" She shrugs. I guess she's not half wrong.

"There's no way I'm putting out on the first date, so you can just get that thought out of your pretty little head, Dells."

"But Hazy, you gave me the cutest little niece, and I want more- Oomph!" This time I whacked her with a pillow.

"No. Nope. Absolutely not. You take that back right now. I don't need that thought floating around in the universe. Get the sage, and a rosary, and some holy water, and get all that juju out of this room." I love Wynnie to death, but the thought of starting over at 30 scares the shit out of me.

"Listen, Dellah, if I get knocked up again, you better be prepared for me to actually move into your house, and become my sister wife. I've done the middle-of-the-night feedings and diaper explosions alone once, and I won't be doing that again."

"Alright, alright. No first date hookups, got it." Glad we are on the same page about that. While she didn't actually change any diapers, she got plenty of middle-of-the-night phone calls from me with a crying baby in the background. She isn't a complete stranger to life with a newborn. "Now, what do I wear?"

"Little black dress, jean jacket, and chunky white sneakers. Go with the classic. Wait, is your date inside? Do you even know what you're doing?" Great question.

"I have no idea. I'm gonna text him and ask what the attire should be. I'd hate to freeze my butt off during a first date. It's one of my favorite assets." While there are many things about my mom bod that I'm insecure about, the booty that I was left with after childbirth is one of my favorite things.

Me: Hey, can I get a hint at what we are doing tonight so I know what to wear? Indoor/Outdoor activity?

Jude- Grocery Crasher Guy: No hints, Little Dove, but I'll tell you it's indoor. See you in an hour.

"He said it's indoor, but won't tell me anything else." Dellah gives me a pondering look.

"Stick with my original plan. It's cute, flirty but not too over the top. A chunky necklace and some fun earrings, and it's the perfect look." She smiles at me, seeming satisfied with her decision.

An hour later, we see lights pulling up in the driveway. He's right on time. Before he can get out of his SUV, I text him that I'll be right down.

"Wallet?" Dellah asks.

"In my purse," I reply, holding up my purse in display.

"Keys and cash?"

I nod, "In my purse."

"Pepper spray and condoms?"

With an eye roll, I reply, "Yes, woman, I'm always prepared, just in case."

"Good," she says. "Lube?"

"Dellah!"

"What? You said you're always prepared. You never know when you might find yourself in a *tight* situation."

"Oh my god, I have to go. You and Wynnie are good?"

"Yes, we are wonderful. Not that she needs me here, but we have a date with a big bowl of popcorn, some ice cream, and some clowns with red balloons. Now go. Don't do anything that I wouldn't do."

"Well, that leaves the door wide open then."

"Exactly." She winks at me. "Have all the fun and come home and tell me about it. I expect you out late. Or maybe early tomorrow morning." She wiggles her eyebrows. She's incorrigible. I groan, and with a quick goodbye to Wynnie and a warning to go easy on her aunt, I'm out the door.

10

Jude

I see Hazel walk through a door in the garage, and she looks breathtaking. She's in a little black dress, and I trail my eyes from her white sneakers up her exposed milky legs to her luscious curves that I want to dive into and lose myself in. Before I jump out of the SUV, I turn on her seat warmer. I want to make sure she stays toasty warm in her little dress. I open the door for her when she approaches me.

"Thank you for picking me up, Jude." She could say my name over and over again until it had no meaning anymore, and I'd still listen to it coming from her lips.

"It's my absolute pleasure, Little Dove. You look beautiful." Is she blushing? That's going to be trouble. I didn't think she could get any more beautiful, but that pink tint on her cheeks proved me wrong.

"Thank you. You look great yourself. Glad to see the hot pink tie stayed at home." We both laugh. I sent her a picture of the tie over text yesterday, promising an explanation during our date. I chose to wear khaki pants and a dark blue button-down shirt. I have something fun and casual for us planned tonight, and I hope she enjoys it.

"You ready?" I ask.

"Well, seeing as you wouldn't tell me what we are doing, I hope I am."

I helped her get into my SUV, and shut the door behind her. Climbing back into the driver's seat, I look at her and ask, "How do you feel about shopping?"

"Shopping? Are you taking me back to the scene of the elusive cart crash?" She smiles, and it's radiant.

"Not quite. I was thinking more like Target. Have you heard of the Target date challenge?"

She narrows her brows at me. "A Target date challenge. Can't say I've heard of that, but I'm intrigued. Can it start with a coffee because I can't Target without Starbucksing first?"

"The plan was for the coffee to come at the end of the shopping. Think you can hold out? Although it isn't Starbucks that I was planning to go to. I promise it's better."

"You promise? That's a bold statement going up against Starbucks, but okay, I'll trust you. Tell me more about this challenge.

"You'll see." I give her a big smile.

We get to Target and walk inside. I grab a cart for her and take one for myself. I hand her a piece of paper. She opens it and silently reads the list. Looking back at me, I can see the question in her eyes as I hand her a Target gift card.

"The gift card is loaded with $75. The list in your hand has five categories that you need to fulfill. Unlike the actual challenge where you normally pick out things you think the other person would like, I want you to pick out the things *you* like." I can see she's unsure of what I want her to do.

"For example, number 1 is a treat you like. That could be anything from a candy bar to a lotion or a favorite nail polish color. The purpose is for us to get to know each other without the typical first date nervousness. Shop the list for yourself." She nods at me.

"Okay, I think I get it now. This seems like fun." I'm blessed with a big smile.

"Good, that was my hope. Now, there are two stipulations," I warn her.

"Oh no, already changing the rules on me?" She gives me a big exasperated huff and an eye roll as she plops her hands on her hips.

Smiling and counting on my fingers, I tell her, "You can't go over budget, and you have a 45 minute time limit. Think you can handle that?"

"You're only giving me 45 minutes to get lost in Target? I might not even make it past the dollar spot in that short amount of time?" I can see the mock horror on her face as she pretends to clutch her pearls.

"Ready. Set."

"GO!" she yells and takes off before I get a chance to finish the last word myself.

45 minutes later, I meet her at the front of the store with a big smile on my face that's being eclipsed by her own.

"How'd you do?" I ask.

"That was harder than I thought. I don't usually think about myself when I go shopping. How about you?"

"I'm all set. Let's head out to our next location." I'm the

most excited about this part.

11

Hazel

That was so much fun. Who would have thought shopping alone on a first date would be exciting? We are heading towards town when Jude pulls over onto a side street.

"You ready for the next part of our evening? Grab your bag," he instructs. I grab my bag, and I'm about to pull on the handle to get out of the SUV when he lightly grabs my wrist.

"Don't you touch that handle. A gentleman always opens the door for a lady."

Without thinking, I blurted out, "I haven't been a lady since I gave birth in front of a room full of doctors at the age of 18." *Oh shit!* I hadn't mentioned yet that I had a kid. Well, this was a nice date while it lasted. I already suspected that he might be a little younger than me, but now adding the baggage of a kid onto the first date seems like a quick way to end things.

I'm staring at my lap in silence when his hand touches my chin, urging me to look up at him. I give him a shy smile, and he returns it.

"Hey, I know we haven't known each other long, so I don't think I've told you what my career is." His face reveals nothing of his feelings, so I can't anticipate what he might say next.

"Hazel," oh no. He said my actual name, not Little Dove. This can't be good. Here it comes. "I'm a school counselor. I love children." Okay. I didn't expect that. I finally look up into his eyes and see nothing but sincerity.

"Oh, well, that's a bit of a relief." I sigh. "I wasn't trying to hide it. It just didn't feel like a first date conversation when we didn't know each other."

He nods in understanding. "How many children do you have?" Before I can answer, he adds, "Not that the number changes anything."

"Just my daughter. It's just the two of us." He gives me a warm smile as he slides his hand from my chin to my cheek.

"Do you need to get home to her? I don't want to keep you out too late." My eyes snap up to his. Did he just put my daughter above himself? He doesn't even know her. Or me, for that matter.

"No, she's completely fine. She's at home with her aunt, my crazy best friend." I laugh, thinking it's more likely Wynnie is watching over Dellah than the reverse.

"Okay, if you're sure. But I want you to know one important thing. She will always come first, no matter what. Alright?"

I have to blink a few times before nodding in response. I don't trust myself. I already kid-bombed him on the first date. Crying might be the straw that breaks the camel's back.

"If you're ready to let me open that door for you, could we continue our evening? I know I'd like to if you're still up for it. Or, if you'd prefer, I can take you home. The choice is yours."

And even though I barely know this man, I know he's telling the truth. The choice is mine to make, which is why it's the easiest choice. "Let's go compare our lists."

He kisses me on the forehead before removing his hand from my cheek and coming to open my door.

12

Jude

I led us down the cobblestone street of downtown Mountain Pines with my hand on the small of her back. It took all my willpower not to pull her into my arms back in my SUV. No woman should ever feel like she has to hide her child or be scared of a negative reaction from a man. I could tell she thought I would reject her when she slipped that she had given birth at 18. I already knew that she was a strong woman by the way she carried herself, but I only have more respect for her now, knowing that she's raising a child all on her own.

I'm excited about the next part of this date. She has already mentioned she's a coffee lover, so I got that part right. I hope I've also guessed correctly that she's a reader. I'm unsure if I'd call this place a coffee shop with a book addiction or a bookstore with a coffee addiction. Either way, it's the perfect mix of both, and I thought it would be a great place to share our shopping purchases while enjoying more of the evening.

I direct her to the door of The Book Beanery. As I open it, our senses explode with the delicious aroma of coffee beans and paper. Her eyes widen as she spins towards me.

"This place smells like heaven. What is it?" Her face looks like pure bliss as she takes in the stacks and tables full of books scattered around. To the left is a small coffee counter and display case with homemade pastries. In the middle of the room are several mismatched tables and chairs. The entire right side is floor to ceiling book shelves.

"This is my favorite little secret in town. I know I'll win you over with the coffee because I have a promise to keep, but are you also a book lover, Little Dove?" Her facial expressions tell me I couldn't have brought her to a more perfect place.

"I absolutely love to read. However, my Kindle is usually my go-to, because it's just easier. But I love the smell and the feel of a book in my hand.

"Good. That's the answer I was hoping for. Now, there's one more item not on the list to purchase. Go find your favorite book and meet me back at the coffee counter. Be quick."

She lets out a tiny squeal and gives me a huge smile before she turns on her heels and disappears down an aisle.

Tucked in a little table in the corner, coffees in hand, and a few pastries to share between us, I pull out the list I handed her at Target, and we prepare to share our purchases.

"You ready to learn more about each other?" I know I certainly am.

"Absolutely! What's first?"

ITEM 1: A treat you like

I fish around in my bag and prepare to pull my "treat" out, and she does the same.

"On the count of 3, we will both pull out our item. Got it?" She nods. "One, two, three." We both pull out our purchases and put them on the table.

She places a greeting card beside my excessively large bag of Reese's pieces. She's giggling at my chocolates when she looks up and must read the curiosity in my expression.

"Okay, let me explain," she says.

"I'm all ears," and I am. It's an interesting choice for a treat.

"Growing up, I thought I wanted to be a writer. I loved reading the greeting cards at stores because I thought that the simple little poems were the epitome of great writing. People write full-length novels to get their point across, but these writers could convey their messages with a few heartfelt, meaningful sentences. Feeling sad, here's a card. Monumental life event, here's a card. Someone passes away, here's a card. Have a baby, card. You get my point. Even after I decided that writing wasn't my career path, I still loved the meaning behind the messages. When Wynnie was a baby, sometimes we would walk to the store on a nice day, and I'd stroll down the card aisle and read all the happy greeting cards to her. I have several boxes at home filled with blank cards I've purchased." I'm so engrossed in the beautiful sentiment that a simple greeting card can bring her when I realize she has revealed another piece of herself to me without meaning to.

"Wynnie?" I question. "Is that your daughter's name?" She looks up at me shocked, for a moment. I don't think she realized she had spoken her name.

"Oh, yes. That's her." She looks away quickly, and when her gaze returns to mine, she says, "So you prefer the pieces over the cups, huh?"

Shocked at the quick topic change, I realize she no longer wants to talk about her daughter, and I respect her wishes.

"I'm a pieces man all the way. I much prefer the chocolate-to-peanut butter ratio. How about you?"

"I also prefer pieces over cups, but not because of the ratio. Because they mix so much easier in my ice cream." We laugh together. "Okay, next."

ITEM 2: Something in your favorite color

"This one was hard." She let out a little moan at her statement. Why did that sound go straight to my cock. *Damn.*

"What was hard about it?" We really need to stop saying "hard."

"Because I could choose ANYTHING in my favorite color. No rules or exceptions, just anything."

"Alright, well, I can see you agonized over this decision, so let's get it over with. One, two, three." We place our items on the table.

I put down a blue dress shirt, similar to the one I'm wearing because I can always use more shirts. She places down blue eye shadow. I look up at her, and she's red with embarrassment.

"You left me unsupervised, and it was the last item I needed to get, and I panicked. Don't judge me."

"Well, first, it's nothing to be embarrassed about. I bet the color would look beautiful with your hazel green eyes. Second, I see that we both have the same favorite color." Clearly, in her embarrassment, she hadn't noticed our matching color choice.

"Well, that's convenient." She has a devilish little smile on her face.

"How's that, Little Dove?"

46

"Because if that's *your* favorite color, there's a good chance I'll get to see you wearing a lot of *my* favorite color." She has a very valid point. I look down at the blue dress shirt I had picked, and imagine her wearing nothing but that shirt.

"Next item," before I think too hard about her being mostly naked.

ITEM 3: An item you use daily

"One, two, three." I place down a deodorant, and she places down toothpaste.

"Well, thank goodness for good hygiene," she giggles. "Do you mind?" She picks up my deodorant. I nod, not exactly sure what she's asking for. She takes the cap off and inhales.

"I thought I liked the smell of your cologne, but I guess I like the smell of your deodorant." She shrugs and places the cap back on. She likes the way I smell. That makes me smile, and my heart beats a little faster. She's incredible.

"Two more items left. You ready for the next one?"

"I'm ready." She sits up a little straighter in her seat.

ITEM 4: Something that reminds you of your childhood

"Can I confess something first?" She bites her lip, and damn, I want to pull it out from between her teeth.

"Sure, should I be worried?" I ask hesitantly.

"No, but I feel like I cheated on this one. The first thing that came to mind when I read this one was those ice pops with the double sticks you pull apart. My summers were full of them. But for obvious reasons, I couldn't buy something frozen."

"I'm not sure where the cheating part is."

"Well, I took some creative liberties. I bought something that I use now that, in a way, reminds me of those summer days."

"Do you feel like you stuck with the spirit of the item?" She's taking this challenge very seriously.

"I do. And I hope you see it, too."

"Alright, well, let's see how much trouble you're in. One, two, three." We pull our items out. On the table sits my Tamagotchi and her hard raspberry seltzer. I burst out laughing.

"Alcohol reminds you of your childhood? Where's my pure, innocent Little Dove?"

"Your what? Pure and innocent might be the last words I'd use to describe myself." She looks taken aback by my question.

"I guess that's one explanation I owe you isn't it?" How to explain this without sounding like a complete creeper? Big breath in, "The day I crashed into your cart, you mesmerized me with your beauty. When I asked you if I could be forward, it was because I'm not usually the outspoken type. My family was and still is very religious. That's how I grew up. The dove symbolizes a new beginning as well as pureness and innocence. Your beauty reminded me of all those things. It's why I was so bold to ask out a stranger that I just tried to run over in the grocery store." I look up after giving my explanation to the table. Her cheeks are flushed pink, and there are unshed tears in her eyes. Oh no, I've gone too far. "I'm so sorry. That was probably way more than you bargained for." I've put my foot in my mouth again.

She gives me a big smile and shakes her head. "No need to apologize. That was beautiful. I'm touched by your sentiment. While I'm not entirely sure I agree with your assessment, I understand that perception is reality, and who am I to judge what you see." We sit in silence for a moment until she bursts out laughing, breaking the tension between us.

48

"I'm glad one of us can find humor in this situation," I say through my embarrassment.

"You bought...a...Tamagotchi." She barely manages to get the words out through her fit of laughter, and I start to laugh along with her. "I could never keep those things alive. And they always shit so much." The mood is officially back to light and fun.

"I think you still owe me one more explanation." I wrack my brain trying to figure out what I could still need to confess to her. "Pink tie," she reminds me.

"Ah, yes. The lost bet." I spend the next few minutes recounting the events leading up to my hot pink tie.

"That's... classic." She's laughing at me, and I can't even be upset about it. "Do you plan on losing the subsequent bet with the students?"

"Honestly, I hope I do, for their sake. But truthfully, I'm terrible with bets, and I've lost enough at this point in my life that I should know better than to make any more."

She looks highly intrigued. "It sounds like there are some juicy stories that you have to share." She rubs her hands together and leans in, waiting for the gossip.

"Oh, I have some stories, but they are absolutely not first date material." I give her a wink. "You might have to give me a few more dates before you learn all my deep dark secrets, Little Dove."

"Hmm. That could probably be arranged. But first, let's see what your last item is.

ITEM 5: Something you'd like to do together

She beats me to the countdown. "Three, two, one." In front of us is a deck of cards and a box of jelly beans.

"Jelly beans, Jude. That's the best you could come up with

as something you wanted to do with me. I'm disappointed." She's teasing me.

"You have little faith in me. Did you even look at the box, Little Dove? These are no regular jelly beans. These are Bean Boozle beans."

"Okay," she stretches out the word, still not understanding what they are.

I shake my head chuckling. "This is an experience in a box. Every color jelly bean has two different flavor options—"

"—Oh, that sounds interesting," she interjects before letting me get to the interesting part.

"—but one of the flavors isn't favorable." Now I've thoroughly confused her.

"Not favorable?" She questions. "Oh, like black licorice? No one likes that flavor."

"Not exactly." I flip the box over and show her the pictures. "Let's use a green jelly bean as an example. It could be juicy pear or… booger flavored."

"What?" Her eyes widened in shock. "Boogers? How could a jelly bean taste like boogers?" She paused for a moment, waving her hands in front of her face before I could answer. "More importantly, who was the taste tester for that jelly bean that determined the actual flavor of a booger?"

She continues looking at the back of the box at all the different flavor choices. Her head snaps up, and she shoots me a skeptical look. "If I didn't already know that you had no idea I was a mother before you bought these, I would have considered this a cruel joke. Spoiled milk, boogers, barf, and stinky socks sound like an introduction to the first five years of motherhood. These flavors must have been created by men.

"So, did I earn some brownie points? After all, you just grabbed a deck of cards. Where's the fun in that?" She's once again clutching her nonexistent pearls with a look of shock and horror.

"First of all, I'll give you credit for the jelly beans. Although I'm not looking forward to that experience, I imagine it will still be fun. Secondly, a deck of cards is so versatile," she raises her hands to start counting off her list. "There's Spoons, Speed, War, Egyptian Rat Slap."

"I've never heard of half of these card games. I think you're making these up to inflate your ego." She moves to shove my shoulder playfully, and I grab her wrist. Bringing it to my mouth, I place a soft kiss in the palm of her hand. She inhales a small breath before she leans in closer.

Unsure of what she might be thinking, I pause a moment. I look down at her mouth and see her lips part. They look so soft and inviting. Before I can think any more tempting thoughts, she leans close to my ear and whispers, "But don't forget the best card game of them all. Strip poker."

She gives me the most devilish grin with heated eyes and leans back in her seat, crossing her legs. She knows exactly what she's done as she watches me shift uncomfortably in my seat, trying to make room in my pants for my inflating cock.

"Well, well, Little Dove. It seems I've underestimated you. You will definitely be trouble for me." So, so much trouble.

We finish our coffee and collect our items, with me sneaking several of the things I bought for myself into her bag and heading back to her house. Pulling into her driveway, I give her a side glance so she knows not to open her door. I grab her bag and head over to her side of the SUV.

Opening the door, I extend my hand to help her out. She

stumbles over herself when her feet hit the ground, and I catch her before she falls. She ends up flush to my chest with her arms pinned between us. I'm sure she can feel my racing heart under her hands as much as I can feel her quickening breath on my chest.

I look down into her eyes, getting lost in the green being reflected by the moonlight. "I was planning on being a perfect gentleman tonight, Little Dove, but you're making it very difficult being pressed up against me like this."

"Sometimes it's good to be bad, Jude."

Before I can respond, she shifts closer to me and locks our lips together. I have a split second of hesitation from shock at her closing the gap between us before I move my lips in sync with hers. She sighs, and her lips part. I take that as my invitation to sweep my tongue into her mouth. She tastes the faintest of caramel left over from her coffee. Her hands snake up my chest, around my neck, and to the back of my head. Her fingers run through the hair on the nape of my neck, and I melt into it. My hands find the soft curves of her hips, and I give a light squeeze loving the feel of them in my palms.

There's no rush in our kiss. It's soft and sweet and so much like her that I don't want to stop, but I pull away before either of us gets out of hand. I place a kiss on her forehead and pull back just enough to see her entire face in focus.

"I'd like to see you again." I'd rather not leave.

Placing her head on my chest, she giggles, "I'd like you to see me again, too."

"You are most definitely trouble for me, Little Dove. I had a wonderful evening. Thank you for the pleasure of your presence. I'll see you again soon." One more kiss on her luscious lips, and I step away from her before I lose my will to leave.

"Will you do me a favor, Jude?"

"Anything for you." Down boy, that was a little eager.

She blushes, and I know her thoughts went somewhere dirty as well. "Will you text me and let me know when you get home? It's a total mom thing, I know, but it's a hard habit to break, and it would make me feel better to know you got there safely."

"Of course, Little Dove. I'd love nothing more than an excuse to text you goodnight. Now go upstairs so I know you got inside safely."

"Good night, Jude. Thank you for an amazing evening and all my goodies." She gives me a small wave before she unlocks the garage door and disappears inside.

13

Hazel

I did that. I really did that. I kissed him first. Where did that come from? I wasn't sure if he would do it, and I couldn't stand the thought of not kissing him before he left. His intoxicating smell of citrus drew me in. *Oh my god!*

As I'm unlocking the apartment door at the top of the steps, the doorknob gets ripped from my hands, and I stumble inside. Dellah is standing there with a Cheshire cat grin on her face.

"I'm gonna take a wild guess that you just saw everything that happened in the last five minutes?" There's no need to guess.

"Uh huh, uh huh. Squeee!" She's clapping her hands and nodding her head so hard I'm worried it will fall off.

"Shhh, don't wake Wynnie up. I don't want to scar my 12 year old for life with your antics."

She scoffs at me. "You know that girl is wise beyond her years, Hazy. She could probably teach you a thing or two herself."

"Eww, Dellah, that's your niece and my daughter you're referring to. Let's not even go there. First off, how was *your* evening?"

She gives me an impatient huff before responding. "You know it was completely uneventful, or you would have heard otherwise by now. We ate terrible, junkie food and watched creepy movies. Then about two hours ago, she retreated into her room like a good little preteen who's spent too much time with her annoying aunt. She loved every minute of it. Now, what's this?" She impatiently grabs the large Target bag from my hands.

Snatching it back, I explained, "This was part of our date night. We did the Target date challenge with a twist."

"A twist? Okay, you sit. I'll grab the wine and be right back. I want all the details, including that steamy kiss I witnessed." She heads off to the kitchen, giving me her back.

"Yes, mother." I draw out the words in a whine. I'm sure she could hear my eyes roll as she walked away.

Rummaging through the bag while she gets our glasses, I notice there's more in here than just the items I purchased for myself. Included are the Reese's pieces, jellybeans, and the Tamagotchi. Also in the bag is the last item we didn't exchange, the book. Except it's not the book that I chose. I wonder if there was a mix-up. He was trying to make sure we didn't give away each other's books when we purchased them with our coffee. I'll have him check his receipt. I pick up the book and laugh at the title, *"Who Moved My Cheese."*

Dellah returned with two overfull glasses of wine as she looked over all the goodies on the coffee table. "Okay, spill all the gory details."

I pull the list from my purse and explain all my purchases and the extras Jude snuck into my bag. Midway through, my cell phone buzzes.

"Is that him?" She is far too excited for my first date.

Jude- Grocery Crasher Guy: Little Dove, as requested, I'm letting you know I arrived home safely. I truly had the most wonderful evening, and I can't wait until I can see you again. Sweet dreams.

Me: I had a wonderful evening as well. There seem to be a few extra things in my bag. Was that an accident, or should I be saying thank you? Also, the book in the bag isn't the one I chose. There may have been a mix-up.

The three bouncing dots appear right away. Dellah is anxiously watching over my shoulder.

"Hey, give those back. These are mine!" I grabbed the bag of Reese's pieces that she somehow silently opened while I was responding to Jude.

Jude- Grocery Crasher Guy: No mix-up at all. Everything in the bag was meant for you, including the book. I switched them out. That one was my pick for you. We can discuss it next time we go out. Sweet dreams, beautiful. I know I'll have them thinking about you. ;)

"Wow. Did you find yourself a book boyfriend? He's got total Cinnamon Roll vibes. Oh my god, Hazy. You know what all the best book boyfriends have, right?"

"Oh god, there are so many different directions that you could go with that question. I'm not touching it with a 10-

foot pole. Keep those thoughts to yourself. It was a first date, an incredible one, but still a first one."

"Well, there sure could be ten of something..." I groan and shake my head.

She leans towards me on the couch and puts her head on my shoulder. She lets out a heavy sing-songy sigh. My mind is doing the same thing.

"He obviously wants to see you again. We can talk about his *assets* next time." I shove her shoulder with my own, and before she can fall off the couch, she grabs my arm and takes me with her.

We're laughing on the floor like two teenagers when I blurt out, "I told him about Wynnie."

She pauses her laughter and looks directly at me. "And?"

"And he was so sincere about it not being a deal-breaker that I almost cried. I can't decide if he's even real. OUCH! What the hell was that for Dellah?" I look at her in shock, rubbing my arm.

"I pinched you. If you felt it, then obviously, this is real, and so is he. Did you feel it?"

"Obviously." She pinched me hard. I stand and clean my mess on the coffee table. "I don't know Dells, but he really does seem too good to be true. He said all the right things. He set up this beyond sweet date." My mind wanders to all the fun I had tonight.

"That kiss?"

"That. Kiss." My hand comes up to my mouth, remembering his lips on mine. So tender and sweet, there was no rush or urgency. It's like he had all the time in the world to stand there and kiss me until he had his fill. To memorize every crevice of my mouth.

"Girl, close your mouth before you start drooling." Her words snap me out of my little memory bubble.

"Shut up." I roll my eyes at her. "Like I said, there's no way I got it right on the first try. He probably still lives in his parent's basement or collects his cut toenails in a jar on his nightstand."

"Oh, are we ready to talk about his assets now?" I let out an audible groan. I give up on this woman.

"You're incorrigible."

"And you love me despite all of my amazing flaws." She looks up, fluttering puppy dog eyes in my direction.

"You know I do. Now go back to your *main house* and leave us peasants to our lil 'ol apartments above the garage. Some of us need our beauty sleep to stay this fabulously beautiful." I gesture to my body.

"And fabulous you are." She smacks my ass on her way out the door. "Girl's night soon. G'Night, bestie."

"Night, Dells. Thanks again for keeping an eye on my kid for me."

"Always."

She walks out the garage door, and I watch her through the window, as I always do, until she disappears into her back door. I walk across the apartment to Wynnie's door and give it a light knock before I open it.

"Still awake?" I ask as I peek inside.

"Yeah, hey, Mom. Come on in. Did you have fun?" She pulls out one of her earbuds to talk with me.

"I did. Did you have fun with Aunt Dellah? Was she well-behaved?" We laugh because we understand that Wynnie babysits Dellah more than the reverse.

"She was on her best behavior. I'm glad you had fun. You

58

need to hang out with an adult that's a little more adultier than Aunt Dellah sometimes."

"You're a smart cookie, Rowyn Juniper Gibson. Love you, girlie." I lean in and give her a big hug.

"Love you, too, Hazel Jane Gibson." I pull back from the hug and give her a mom look. "What? I thought we were being formal." She shrugs and smiles. I roll my eyes. "G'Night, Wynnie."

"Night, Mom."

14

Jude

This is different from the type of book I would have thought she'd buy. I fully expected some romance novel with a half-naked man on the cover. Maybe a fantasy book of some sort. But a middle school required reading book. I couldn't have predicted that.

There's a soft knock on my office door. "Come in." The door slowly opens. and I see Rowyn standing there.

"Come on in, Rowyn. Have a seat." I gesture towards the chairs in front of my desk. Placing the book down, I give her my full attention.

"How are things going? You're three weeks into the school year. Are classes going well?" She's staring at the book that I put down.

"I'm doing good. Classes are fine." She gestures toward the book. "Have you read that, Mr. S?"

I pick it up and hand it to her, *The Giver* by Lois Lowry. "A friend recommended it to me but I haven't started it yet.

60

Have you read it?"

She shakes her head. "I haven't, but my mom keeps trying to get me to read it. Apparently, it's one of her favorites. She was required to read it in middle school, but it's on the banned book list now." She flips it around a few times, scanning the synopsis on the back.

"Banned book list? That makes me want to read it even more. I'll let you know what I think once I finish." I smile at her, and she nods.

She places the book back on my desk. "I wanted to let you know that I've decided to try out for the softball team. I've been watching the practices, and I think it would help me to get involved with something. I've been missing my friends back home." She drops her head to focus on her wringing hands.

"That's great, Rowyn. I know change can be hard, especially as you get older. They are a great group of girls. They haven't mentioned seeing anyone new around the field, though." I haven't seen her either the few times I've gone out to see how everything is going.

"Oh, yeah. I've kind of been hanging back. I didn't want to bother their practice."

"Well, there's no need to hang back, but if that's what you're comfortable with for now, that's alright. Tryouts will be at the end of next week. Unfortunately, I won't be around for the entirety of the tryouts. I'm taking a night course for the next few weeks, but I've left you girls in capable hands. Mr. Graves, the other coach, is the Auto Shop teacher at the high school and a good friend. I trust his judgment to help me build the best team."

"Sounds good, Mr. S. Thanks." She stands and walks to the

door.

"Enjoy your day, Rowyn. I look forward to seeing you on the practice field soon." She gives me a small smile and a wave as she leaves my office.

I picked up *The Giver* from my desk, where Rowyn had left it, and opened it to the first chapter. *"It was almost December..."*

Some time passes by with my nose in the book when my phone buzzes.

Phoenix: Wanna grab beers at the Tipsy Penny on Friday and talk about the tryouts for next week?

Me: Damn, we need to do that but I promised my folks I'd come home this weekend and help take down the Christmas lights since the weather will be nice enough. Sunday night?

Phoenix: That'll work. Tell your parents I said hi.

Me: Sure thing

15

Phoenix

I check my reflection in the bathroom mirror one last time before heading out: black hair perfectly gelled to the messy look, my favorite pair of black boots, dark denim jeans, and a black v-neck shirt. Oh, and I can't forget my panty-melting smile and green eyes. Jude may be unable to hang out tonight, but it's a Friday night at the Tipsy Penny. There's bound to be someone there I know. Or someone I'd like to get to know for the night.

Walking into the bar, I do a quick scan and don't immediately see anyone I care to say hi to so I head to the bar. Finding an empty stool, I sit down and nod toward the bartender, Scotty.

"Hey, man. The usual, Nix?" Scotty and I have known each other since high school when I thought it was cool to have a nickname and only introduced myself to others as Nix. It stuck for some people.

"Yeah. Thanks, Scotty. Add a shot of fireball on the side."

He nods his head in acknowledgment.

A few drinks in, I'm playing on my phone when I hear hysterical laughter behind me. Rolling my eyes to myself, I figure a bunch of college girls have just walked in. I turn my head to see what the commotion is all about when I spot my vixen. She walks in the door with a petite blonde by her side and both women are in a fit of hysteria.

I find myself smiling as I take in the women before me. Her friend looks cute in a green dress that looks like a long sweater with boots. But my vixen, oh my vixen. She's wearing a denim skirt that stops just above her knees and a black lace top showing a hint of cleavage. I wonder if there's more lace under her clothes? And fuck me, she's wearing red stiletto heels, with her lips painted to match her shoes.

My mind is battling between imagining those red lips wrapped around my cock and her red heels wrapped around my back while I'm buried deep inside her. I don't care which image wins because, in either scenario, I win.

They sit at the other end of the bar, and Scotty approaches and takes their drink order. I feel like an animal stalking its prey as I watch them talk and laugh while I plot the perfect time to make my move.

When their second drinks are almost empty, I see this as my opportunity. I stand up and walk towards them. Both women are so lost in their conversation that they don't notice me when I approach them.

I lean into my vixen's ear, "Can I call you Angel because the last time I saw you, it was like you fell from heaven?"

Having heard what I said, her friend looked at me, half shocked and half in awe. My vixen turns around, her eyes rolling in full force.

"Yeah, sorry. Not inter-" She finally sees me and pauses. The exasperated look on her face from my cheesy pick-up line turned into a full smile at the recognition.

I returned her smile, "Hi, again." We stare into each other's eyes, locked for a few long moments.

"Hi, I'm Dellah. This is Hazel. Nice to meet you." Her friend, Dellah, as she's just introduced herself, smiles sweetly at me. Her words snapped us both out of our daze.

"Oh yeah. Hi again, I'm Hazel, in case you've forgotten." I could never forget her beautiful name.

"How could I forget?" I turned to her friend, "Nice to meet you, Dellah."

"Do you two know each other?" Dellah looks between the two of us several times, trying to figure out the connection. Hazel doesn't respond to her friend immediately so I fill in the blanks for her.

I look over at Dellah. "We had a little *run-in* at the gym a couple of weeks ago." My eyes flash back to Hazel, who's still staring at me. Her smile widens, obviously remembering our unconventional first meeting.

"Oh, so you met at the gym." Dellah is still trying to put the pieces together.

Hazel finally speaks up, breaking us out of our connection and turning to her friend. "Not exactly. I literally ran into him leaving the gym while he was entering. He helped me pick up the contents of my purse when they spilled on the floor at his feet. I told you about it, remember?" I see the recollection on her face remembering the story. She spoke to her friend about me. I guess I made as much of an impression on her as she made on me.

Scotty comes over to our end of the bar to check on us.

65

"Ladies, can I get you some refills? How about you, Nix, another beer and a shot?" Dellah and Hazel both nod at Scotty then he turns to me.

"Care if I join you, Angel, or is this a ladies-only evening?" She turns to Dellah. There's an unspoken conversation between them before she turns back to me.

"Stools all yours if you're brave enough to join us?" I can see the spark in her eyes.

I nod to Scotty before turning my attention back to Hazel. I lean in close to her, my lips barely brushing the shell of her ear. "I'm always up for a challenge." I see the shiver run up her spine and the goosebumps form on her arms as she inhales a sharp breath.

I pull back and give her a half smile. Her cheeks are flushed, and I can see the rapid rise and fall of her chest. The motion calling for my eyes to slide down to her cleavage. I'm at a much better advantage to see more of the luscious swells of her breasts. I don't linger too long but just long enough that someone catches me looking.

"You might need to buy her a drink before you can handle the merchandise, Nix." She called me Nix. I just realized I hadn't introduced myself, so she must have gotten the nickname when Scotty spoke to me.

"Fair point. You have one hell of a wing woman there, Angel." I yell down the bar, "Scotty, make this gorgeous lady's drink a double." He nods and raises the glass he has in his hand to acknowledge he heard me.

Turning back towards them, I see they are in a heated whisper discussion. Arms are flailing around. I finally take a seat next to Hazel and sit back and watch the entertainment. I hear phrases like, "How could you," "Put out," and "condom."

That last one piqued my interest. Clearing my throat, they whip their heads to me like they'd forgotten I was there. Hazel has this adorable deer-in-headlights look, and I almost get lost in her hazel green eyes again.

I know I have a cocky grin on my face, but I can't help it. "Let me know if I can help settle this disagreement, ladies." Hazel puts her elbows on the bar and plants her face in her hands. I can't tell if she's groaning or mumbling into her hands, but her friend is definitely laughing at her expense.

"Don't mind her. She hasn't gotten laid in a whi-"

"DELLAH!" Hazel's hands fly to her friend's mouth.

"Oh, my God. Please ignore her. She's on a day pass from the mental hospital. Ewww. Did you just lick me, Bitch. Gross." She pulls her hand away from her friend's mouth and wipes it on her skirt. The same skirt that's ridden up from all the commotion and is giving me a delicious view of her upper thighs.

"Sharing is caring." Dellah shrugs. She peeks over Hazel's shoulder at me before she leans in and whispers to her, "But he's all yours." Pulling back, she winks at me.

Scotty has impeccable timing and drops off our drinks.

"That's my cue!" Dellah exclaims as she hops off her stool, taking her drink. Grabbing Hazel's shoulders, she tells her, "You're a hot ass bitch." Turning to me, she points a finger at my chest. "No glove, no love." Then she leans closer and whispers, "She likes it a little rough." Turning back to Hazel, she winks and walks to the other end of the room, stopping to talk to another group of women.

Hazel picks her jaw up off the floor. The redness on her cheeks has now spread to her neck and chest, leaving me wondering how far down it might go.

"I don't know her. I have no words. I'm so sorry. Oh my god, I can't believe she said all that to you. RIP, my best friend." She is rambling into the bartop, clearly nervous.

I place a hand on her arm. She's so lost in her embarrassment she doesn't even notice and continues talking. I trail my hand up her arm until I reach her shoulder. There seems to be no getting her out of her humiliated rant. I lift my other hand and plant them on either side of her cheeks. Her eyes lock with mine briefly before I crush my lips to hers. That got her to stop rambling. I smirk into the kiss at my success. Her hands meet the tops of mine, and she kisses me back with fervor.

I slowly slide off the bar stool so our bodies can get closer. Her hands move from mine to reach up and wrap around my neck. I slide my hands slowly down her body to her hips. Her hips that have been running through my mind for weeks. She moans into our kiss, and I push my hips closer toward her. Close enough that she can feel how much I'm enjoying this kiss pressing into her stomach.

She quickly pulls away and places her forehead against mine while we both catch our breath.

"Holy shit," I hear her whisper between breaths.

"My sentiments exactly, Angel."

She turns her head slightly and starts to laugh. I look in the same direction and find Dellah giving two enthusiastic thumbs up at her. She mouths, "Get it, girl," and we laugh.

Hazel pulls back to look deeply into my eyes. "What the hell," she says. "Take me somewhere."

"With pleasure, Angel." I give her hips a gentle squeeze before helping her off the stool.

16

Hazel

oly Fuck! What has Dellah gotten me into? I just told this guy, who I've spent no more than an hour with, to "take me somewhere." I'm doing this. I just told Dellah recently that I don't put out on the first date, and here I am about to have another one night stand. Have I learned nothing?

He helps me off the stool and walks us to the end of the bar, where the bartender is standing. "Scotty, I'm tabbing out for me and the two ladies. Put it all on my card." Then he leans in and whispers into Scotty's ear. The bartender's eyes flash to mine. I can feel my cheeks heating even redder, and I look away. What is he saying to him? Scotty nods and slaps Nix on the back before running his card and handing over two slips of paper. He signs one and writes on the other. I hear Scotty say, "Thanks, man. Don't make too much of a mess." He winks at me and goes back to the register. I feel a tug on my hand, and we start to walk toward the back of the bar.

"What was that all about?" He doesn't answer, and I'm not sure if he heard me over the noise in the bar. Suddenly we are standing next to Dellah, and he hands her the other piece of paper he had written on and whispers into her ear. Dellah looks down at the paper, and then up at me. A huge smile appears on her face, and she leans into me and says, "Have fun. You better call me tomorrow."

I'm still baffled when he continues to lead us toward the back of the bar near the bathrooms. I really hope he isn't planning on having sex in the bathroom because I didn't even do that in my teens.

"Please tell me you aren't some creepy guy about to throw me into the back of a van and kidnap me." I think about that for a moment. "On second thought, some of my favorite romance novels involve kidnappings. Carry on."

He heard me that time because he turned and smiled at me while shaking his head in amusement. We start walking down the hallway towards the bathrooms when we abruptly stop. He spins around on his heels and pushes me up against the wall. His arms encased on either side of me, caging me into his warmth, and I can smell the cinnamon on his lips from the fireball, mixed with a metallic scent. He looks deep into my eye before using his nose to nudge my head to the side. His mouth finds the sensitive spot behind my ear. He trails soft, chaste kisses down my neck and across my collarbone. I let out a small whimper at his caresses. Then he starts back up the other side of my neck until he reaches my opposite ear.

Whispering in a deep throaty voice full of lust, he speaks. "Behind you is the door to the office with a couch inside." Oh, thank god he wasn't planning on the bathrooms, which are the doors in front of me. He must see that my eyes had shifted towards the bathroom doors because he grabbed my chin to bring my attention back to him.

"No, Angel. While I know there's no way I can make it out of here without having myself inside you, I would never disrespect you by taking you in a public restroom." He smirks. "Unless that's some dirty little fantasy of yours, then, by all means let's go."

I shake my head because I don't trust my voice right now.

"Okay then." He continues peppering my neck with kisses, and all I can do is hold onto the front of his shirt and try not to melt into a puddle in front of him. "So, behind us is a room with a lock and a couch, or I have a truck outside that has a large back seat. Or if neither of those work for you, I can walk you back to your friend and go home with a raging case of blue balls. The choice is yours, Angel."

My mind clears for a moment from its lust induced-fog. "Before I decide, tell me what all that was about back there."

"All what was about?" He arches one brow, trying to figure out what I'm referring to.

"With the bartender and with Dellah. The whispers and the notes." His eyes light up with amusement when he realizes what I'm asking about.

"Scotty and I are old friends. I asked him if I could borrow the office behind you. I told him I'd give him an extra tip for the time."

"So you bought us a room? Wait, do you do this a lot?" I start to panic. My insecurities are getting the best of me. I don't know this man. I could be just another notch in his belt. I try to push him away, but he doesn't budge. His large frame is too overpowering compared to mine.

"Shhh, Angel." His knuckles caress my cheek in an attempt to calm me down. "Never. I've never brought anyone back here before. Like I said, Scotty and I are old friends. That's how I know there's a couch back here. I've slept off a few too many drinks and spent some nights hanging out with him after his shift in the office. I've never been back here with a woman."

"Okay." I nod. I have no reason to believe him other than his words, but I do. "And the note to Dellah?"

He smiled sheepishly. "The note had my name and phone number on it. I told her that I was a teacher at the high school and I'd make sure you got home safe. And if she needed anyone to vouch for me, she could talk to Scotty."

"You did all that for a quickie in a back room?"

"I'd like to hope it will be a little more than a quickie," he winks, "if it's still happening." His cocky grin is back. "Did I earn myself some brownie points with the note?" Why have I heard that phrase recently?

"I choose the office." And with those words, he opens the door to my left, and we stumble inside. I hear the lock click, and we are immediately a tornado of tongues.

I'm walking backward until my knees bump into what I assume is the couch. He gently leads me down onto my back, never breaking our kiss. He's hovering on his elbows to not put too much weight on me, and I feel his hand drift down the side of my body until he reaches the bare part of my legs below my skirt.

"This fucking skirt. Every move you made tonight made it inch higher and higher. All I could think about was what was under it." His hand explores further up my skirt on the outside of my thigh until he reaches my bare hip. "Jesus fuck."

He buries his head into the crook of my neck and growls. "Or *not* under it. You've been bare this entire time?" I bite my lip and nod.

He removes his hands from my skirt and sits up on his knees above me. He puts his hand behind his head and pulls off his shirt. Why is that simple move so impossibly hot? My eyes almost bug out of my head.

"Wow. You sure were hiding a lot under that shirt." His chest and shoulders are decorated in swirls of black ink leading to his back, which I imagine is also covered. He has six pack abs like they talk about in my books. They do exist! And are those nipple piercings? My hands are involuntarily roaming over the adonis in front of me. My thumb swipes over one of his nipples, and he moans. Damn, that was sexy. I've got to make him do that again.

I swipe my thumb across his other nipple. "Fuck, Angel," he hissed through his teeth. "Like what you see?" His fucking pecs jumped. If I were wearing any panties, they would have just melted off. As it is, I'm sure I will leave a wet spot on this couch.

I bite my bottom lip and look up into his green eyes, which look as dark as a forest. I nod in response, hands still roaming over his expansive chest.

"My turn." His turn? Before I can think about what he means, his hands are snaking under my shirt and rubbing circles over my nipples. They instantly harden at his touch, and a moan escapes my lips without permission as my hips buck up slightly.

"So responsive to my touch, Angel." His hands find the hem of my shirt. When he begins to lift it, I stiffen, and he immediately removes his hands and cups my cheeks.

"If you've changed your mind, it's okay, you can tell me, and we can stop right now." God, I hate this part. He's so perfectly beautiful.

"No, it's not that." His thumbs caress my cheeks, encouraging me to continue. "I just... well, look at you. It's like I ripped you out of a magazine and hung you up on my wall."

"'Me? Look at you. You're impossibly gorgeous, Angel. I'm barely restraining myself from diving between these pillowy soft thighs and drinking you until I drown." He drives his point home by grabbing a thigh and squeezing it. My hips buck again at his touch.

I let out a slow, steady breath before revealing what I'm about to say.

"Okay, so I don't ever do one night stands, so this never comes up so quickly." I pause, taking another shaky breath.

"Tell me." He leans down and gives me a soft kiss on the corner of my mouth.

I close my eyes. If what I say next ends the night, I don't want to see his face change into disgust. I want to remember the lust in his eyes aimed at me, because of me. "I have a scar."

"Angel, I'm not afraid of a scar. I have plenty–" I cut him off.

"From a cesarean section, a c-section. I have a daughter. I'm a mother, and I have a mother's body. There's more flab than fit when it comes to what's under my clothes."

I feel him shift off of me, and I know he's about to leave. He moves to the end of the couch, and I feel his hands lightly glide up my legs. My eyes pop open at the unexpected touch. He reaches for the button on my skirt. "Show me." I blink at him several times. Is he serious? "Show me," he repeats softer.

"You want to see... my scar?" That can't actually be what he's asking me. Why would he want to see my scar?

"I want to see the battle trophy on the body that was so strong it created a life." My brain is sputtering. He wants to see my scar. He's staring intently into my eyes, waiting for permission to take off my skirt. I nod, not trusting any words to be able to come out of my mouth right now.

Slowly he unbuttons and then unzips my skirt. I arch my hips to give him more room to shimmy it down my legs. Realizing my top is still covering me more than he'd like, he extends his hand to help me sit up. His hands go to the hem of my shirt, silently asking permission to remove it. I nod, and he lifts my black lace shirt over my head. He leans into me and wraps his hands around my back.

"May I?" He whispers into my ear as his hand clasps the back of my bra. Still unable to speak, I nod again. "I knew this would be lace to match your shirt. Beautiful." The last word came out in a barely there breath as he unclipped my bra. He stops to kiss my shoulder before he leans back to take me all in. The look on his face takes my breath away. I was unprepared to see the pure lust in his eyes. His green eyes have become hooded and impossibly darker.

"Hazel, you are absolutely stunning, and if any man in your life has ever told you otherwise, I hope he spends the rest of his life impotent and without ever feeling a woman's touch again. Your body was meant to be worshiped. Will you let me worship you?"

I'm dead. RIP me, right next to Dellah, for getting me into this situation. "Pinch me."

"What?" He chuckles.

"Pinch me. You're too damn good to be true. I must be

dreaming. Pinch me."

"How about this instead of a pinch?" He leans down and takes my nipple in his mouth. I intake a sharp breath at the intense sensation. His other hand gently pushes me to lie back on the couch before finding my other nipple. He's pinching one while he licks and nibbles on the other. It's a heady mix of both pain and pleasure.

"Still think you're dreaming?" He asks while continuing to flick my nipple with his tongue.

"Okay, I believe you're real." I somehow manage to form words between my panting and moaning. "Oh, my god. I could come from what you're doing right now. How are you so good at that?"

He smiles into my nipple. "Is that a challenge? Because you know, I said I like a challenge." He switches his mouth to my other nipple, and his other hand follows, rolling the opposite nipple between his thumb and forefinger.

"Fuuuuuuck." I'm having trouble with brain function right now.

"Now that one sounded like an offer. Is that what you want, Angel?" The hand on my nipple leaves and takes a torturously slow trail down my body until it reaches the apex of my thighs. He gives me a gentle nudge, encouraging me to shift them open. I do, and he easily slides a finger through my wet folds. "Because if that's what you want, it's yours, but I'd like to taste you before I fuck you, if that's alright?"

I nod because that's all I'm capable of doing. I feel like a bobblehead toy at this point.

"Words, Angel. I need your words to know what you want." His fingers are still sliding up and down, brushing over my clit. "Do you want me to fuck you right now, or do I get to have dessert first and feast on this delicious pussy?" His hand stops and grabs my core.

"T-taste me… then fu-fuck me."

"At your request."

17

Phoenix

I sink down the couch to position myself between her thighs. I grab her one leg and place it on top of the back of the couch to give myself better access. She's stunning and glistening for me. I am about to get lost in this perfectly pink pussy. "Your pussy is already so wet. Is this all for me?" She nods in response.

I undo my pants to give my growing cock more room. As I trail kisses up her inner thigh, I watch her eyes flutter shut. Taking a deep breath, I inhale her peach scent. It brings back the memory of the first time we met. I watch her chest rise and fall rapidly, anticipating my mouth on her. Leaning in, I give her clit a light flick. Her hips buck at my touch, and I lose my restraint. I dive in and start to devour her with my mouth.

"Angel, you taste like heaven. I might never leave." I continue licking and sucking on her clit while listening to her noises to see what drives her wild. I insert one finger inside her, and her hands land in my hair, tugging my messy locks. I moan into her pussy which causes her to pull harder on my hair. "God, that feels amazing. *You* feel amazing."

She mewls at my praise. I insert a second finger and massage the sensitive bundle of nerves inside her. Her hips start to go wild.

"That's right, Angel. Ride my face. Take your pleasure. Come for me." I suck hard on her clit, and she explodes the sweetest taste of honey with my name falling out of her mouth. *Nix, Nix, Nix*. It feels like my fingers are in a vice grip as her orgasm washes over her body. She's panting and groaning and pulling at my hair. I don't ever want to stop. But more than my want to stay buried between her thighs, my cock needs to be inside her.

"Good girl," I purr in her ear after I crawl back up her body. She pulls me to her. She's so eager to kiss me, not caring that she can taste herself on my lips and in my mouth. That thought makes me feral, and I moan a deep gravelly moan. Her hands move to my pants, and she pushes them down along with my boxer briefs.

"Are you that hungry to have my cock inside you?" Chuckling, I couldn't help but tease her eagerness.

"Yes, please. I need you inside me now. Condom?" I reach into the back pocket of my jeans and grab the condom out of my wallet.

"No glove, no love. Your friend had some sound advice." I look down and give her a half smirk.

"Could we maybe not talk about my best friend when you're naked and about to be inside me?" She pauses, and her eyes go wide. "And oh my god, how is that thing going to fit?" She's staring down at my cock. I start to laugh out loud. I know

I'm big, but I've never had someone make such an outward statement like that. I give my length a few strokes and she licks her lips.

"Angel, look at me." I position myself on top of her, sliding my cock back and forth between her dripping lips, making sure I have her attention. "In a moment, I'm going to slowly slide my cock into this gorgeous pussy of yours, and you're going to feel exactly how perfectly it's going to fit. You're going to feel every inch of me sliding in and out of you until you're coming so hard you'll see stars. And then I'm going to make you come again just to make sure you remember me in the morning." Her mouth drops open, and she's speechless. I sit up and roll on the condom before repositioning myself at her entrance. "Are you ready?"

She nods. "Words." I remind her.

"Yes, please. I'm ready."

I slowly push into her heat. She's so wet and warm. There's barely any resistance, and her body is accepting me so well. Her eyes roll into the back of her head, and we collectively moan as I become fully seated inside her. I stay still so she can adjust to me.

Kissing her neck and the swell of her breasts, I ask, "You feel so perfect taking my cock. Are you alright, Angel?"

"God fucking dammit. I'm so full. You feel so amazing. Please move. I need to feel you. I believe you promised me two mind-blowing orgasms." Oh, this woman.

"Just for that sass, we're going to make it three." I nip at her neck, and she shutters with desire.

"Mmm. Tempt me with a good time, Nix. Now move, and let's get this show on the road."

I start to pump slowly in and out of her. I lean into her ear and whisper, "Someone's asking for a spanking." Before she can sass me again, I pull back and slam into her. I continue at that pace until her first orgasm rips through her.

"That's one." I pull out, flip her over so she's on all fours, and slam back into her. I can already feel her inner walls fluttering. The new, deeper angle and the fact that she hasn't fully come down from her last orgasm has another one building up quickly. I push her shoulders down so I can go even deeper, and I start to rub her clit in circles with my finger.

"Come for me again, Angel. I can feel your body wanting to release." My hips sputter as her pussy tries to suck me in when her next orgasm crests. "Such a good fucking girl, that's two."

Shifting us again, I sit on the couch so she can straddle me, and I slowly guide her hips till she sinks on top of me. "This last orgasm is yours to own. Take it however you want it, but I want to go at the same time as you, so use your words and let me know when you're close. Alright?"

She nods as she rocks her hips back and forth. I squint my eyes at her in warning. "Yes. Yes. I'll let you know." She places both hands behind my head to use the top of the couch as leverage, and she starts bouncing on my cock.

"You're amazing. You look so beautiful. You keep bouncing on me like that, and I'm going to come before you do. What can I do to help get you there?"

"I need... I need..."

"What do you need, Angel? Tell me, and I'll make it happen."

"More. I need more." She's so lost in her ecstasy that she probably doesn't know what she wants more of.

"More. Do you need me to play with these gloriously perky nipples?" I swirl my tongue around her nipple to see if it's what she needs. Unintelligible sounds pour from her lips.

I remove my mouth and slide my hand down her body until my finger swirls circles over her clit. "Do you need me here?" Her panting increases. "Or maybe like this?" I continue to circle her clit with one hand, and I take a nipple in my other. The double stimulation is driving her wild.

She slams her mouth into mine. Her hips are bobbing on my cock and my fingers are circling her clit and pinching her nipple all at the same time. Her mumbled words start pouring out of her lips, barely audible. "Oh fug, yeth, righ there, so close." That last one I heard loud and clear.

Releasing her mouth, I tightly grip her hips, and start meeting her thrusts. She will probably have bruises in the morning but, I can't stop myself, and she doesn't seem to care. Her screams get louder, and I feel her orgasm start. Her walls are squeezing my cock hard. I continue to slam into her until I feel her start to come down, and I finally release my own orgasm. I come with a roar and bury my face into her neck. *Holy fucking shit, that was intense.*

"Yeah." I looked up at her, confused. "That was intense." Oh, I guess I said that out loud.

I lightly tap her butt. "Let's get cleaned up and get you home. That door is a private bathroom." I gesture to a door off to the side of the room. "I'll get you a warm cloth."

We clean up and walk back into the bar to leave. It's late but not yet closing time. We start towards the front door, and I see a flash out of the corner of my eye. A very drunk, bouncing blonde comes rushing towards us, almost tackling Hazel.

"Oh my god, Dellah. What are you still doing here? And why are you so drunk?" There's concern etched on Hazel's face for her friend.

"Hazy! You're here. You won't believe it. I have a flat tire. I called Collin, and he's coming to pick me up. Isn't that great!"

"Sure is. I know you've missed him on this last work trip." The girls almost stumble together, and I brace myself, ready to react if needed. "And the drunk part?"

"Oh, that's easy. It's Scotty's fault. He told me I should be drinking if I wasn't driving." I glare over at Scotty, who gives me an unashamed shrug. "He made me several blue drinks. They were scrumdiddlyumptious!"

Okay, she's drunk, and who's this Collin guy? "Flat tire? Do you ladies need a ride? I can take you both home."

"No, it's okay, thank you. Collin is her husband." She turns towards Dellah. "Are you sure he's on his way? I thought he was still out of town."

"Oh yeah. He was, but he was coming home tonight. When I called, he was about an hour away. He should be here soon. See." She shoves a cell phone in Hazel's face. Hazel pulls the phone away to a respectable reading distance, and reads whatever Dellah is trying to show her.

Turning to me, "He should be here in about 10 minutes based on the text."

"Okay. I'll let Scotty know about her car, and wait with you until he arrives. She looks like a handful."

"She usually is, thanks." By the time I finish talking to Scotty, I see Dellah and Hazel heading toward the front door.

"Everything alright?" The door opens, and a tall red-headed guy in half a suit walks in.

"We're good." She passes off her drunk friend to the redhead. "That's her husband. I'm going to catch a ride with them. Will the car be okay here overnight?"

"Yeah. It will fit right in with all the other people's cars that were too drunk to drive home."

She laughs, and it's so beautiful. I see her cheeks tinge pink as she looks up into my eyes.

"So," she starts, "Thanks for a great time." She punches my shoulder in an adorably awkward gesture. I grab her wrist and pull her into my chest.

"Thank *you* for a mind-blowing evening. It was my honor to worship you the way you deserved." I leaned in and devoured her mouth with mine. Pulling away, I look into her eyes. "Maybe I'll see you at the gym."

Looking dazed, she smiles and nods. "Maybe I'll see you at the gym. Bye, Nix."

"Goodbye, Angel."

I watch as she walks away and gets into a car. I'll check on her friend's tire before I leave and return in the morning and fix it for her.

18

Hazel

Rolling over in my bed, I stretch and realize I am sore in all the right places this morning. I grab my cell phone and check the time, 7:45 AM. I listen into the apartment and don't hear anything, so Wynnie must still be sleeping. When I came in last night, she was sound asleep, with her music blasting into her earbuds. I have no idea how she could be sleeping through all that noise.

I head into the kitchen to start the coffee pot and decide to make pancakes. Let me text Dellah and see if she wants to join us.

Me: Proof of life needed woman.

15 minutes pass. While I wait for a response, I make my coffee and get the supplies ready for the pancakes. It looks like I'm going to have to take some action. I check in on Wynnie before I leave and see she's still asleep. Throwing a jacket

over my PJs, I walk across the driveway and let myself in the back door. Collin sits at the kitchen counter, drinking coffee and working on his laptop.

"Morning, Hazel. Coffee?" He raises his mug in offering.

"Thanks, but I already have a pot going at home. I've come to collect your wife. How was your work trip?"

"Same shit, different day. She's still passed out upstairs. What happened last night? She hasn't been that rough since college." He lowers his head and chuckles. Probably remembering some crazy college days if the stories she told me back then compare to his thoughts.

"Yeah, sorry about that, Collin. I might have left her unsupervised." I raise my hands in surrender and give him an apologetic smile.

"Well, good luck with that snoring beauty up there. Last night she told me I was her white knight, and her duty was to reward me for my valiant rescue."

I sour my face. "Eww, Collin. Please keep your sexcapades to yourself. Besides, it's too early, and I'm sure she will give me all the details anyway after her coffee."

"There's nothing to tell, Hazel." He bursts out laughing. "She walked into her closet to 'put on something a sexy princess would wear,' and I found her a few minutes later asleep on the floor. She was using a purse as a pillow. I put her to bed, and she hasn't woken up since."

I roll my eyes. "Only Dellah. I'll be back."

Walking into her bedroom, I see my friend sprawled out like a starfish in the middle of the king-sized bed, tangled in sheets. At least she's dressed. That's one less step for me. I crawl up on the bed and stand above her straddling her hips. I start jumping up and down, yelling, "Wake up! Wake up! It's pancake party time!"

"What the fucking hell?" She sits up with a start, swatting at my legs and almost knocking me off the bed. I drop down next to her and fall over in a hysterical fit.

"Morning, sunshine. Let's make pancakes." She gives me the look of death.

"My mouth tastes like ass, my head is pounding, and why are you in my bedroom? Where's Collin?"

"Go brush your teeth, I'll get you some painkillers, and he's downstairs in your kitchen. But we're going back to my place for a good old-fashioned pancake party. Come on. It will be fun. I'll meet you downstairs."

She drops her head back to her pillow and groans loudly. "Ugh. I hate you. Fine, I'll be right down," she concedes.

I'm about to walk out the door when she shoots back up in bed and yells, "Wait, Bitch. You got laid by mister tall, dark, and hottie, last night didn't you?" I turn around and wink at her.

"See you downstairs." I wiggle my fingers in a wave, turn and walk toward the kitchen.

"You will tell me everything." I hear her yell down the hallway.

"She's up." I smile at Collin as I walk into his pantry. "Do you have chocolate chips?"

"Top left shelf. Making pancakes?"

"You know it. Wanna join us?" Collin is well-versed in our after drinking pancake parties. Dellah and I may not have gone to college together, where she met Collin, but that didn't stop us from drowning our morning-after alcoholic woes in pancake batter over the phone or Facetime.

"No thanks. I'm not stepping foot in that hen house this

morning." Hearing Dellah coming down the steps, he asks, "Do you have orange juice?"

"Yeah, why?"

"Good. I'm grabbing the champagne. I'm too hungover, and we have to celebrate." Dellah walks over to the wine fridge, and grabs a bottle of champagne.

"What are we celebrating? You surviving drinking like a teenager in your 30's?" She whips her head around and scowls at me.

"Owe." She rubs at her temples. "Don't make me move that fast again. I am 31, not 30's, with an 'S'. I won't be in my 30's until at least 34. And haha, but no. We are celebrating the reincarnation of your pussy. You got laid, and that's something to celebrate."

I see Collin standing up from his chair. "I came for the coffee, but I'm not staying for the show. Have fun, ladies, but maybe not as much as last night." Shaking his head at our ridiculousness, he walks over, kisses Dellah on her forehead, then leaves the kitchen.

"His loss." Dellah shrugs. Linking my arm in hers, she heads us to the back door. "Let's get this pancake party started."

Walking into my apartment, I head to the kitchen with my newly acquired chocolate chips while Dellah heads toward Wynnie's room. I hear the bed creak as she climbs on it and gives Wynnie the same rude awakening by jumping on the bed and yelling as I had just done to her. "Pancake party!"

"Moooom! Stop letting strays in the house! Oomph. Aunt Dellah, stop throwing pillows at me. I thought I was your favorite niece?" They exit the room, and all three of us are hysterical.

We work together to make several varieties of pancakes

and stuff ourselves full.

"How's school, Wynnie?" Dellah asks, sipping her mimosa. "What's the latest gossip? Spill the tea."

Wynnie rolls her eyes at her aunt's absurdity. "Spill the tea? School's good, Aunt Dells." She shifts her eyes to me. "I've decided I'm going to try out for the softball team."

"That's great. When are tryouts?" I'm so excited she's decided to try out. I know how much she loves to play.

"They're this Thursday right after school, and we will know by Monday if we've made the team."

"We can get your equipment out of storage today. This is my last week of training before my schedule switches, so I can come to watch the tryouts if you'd like."

"Um, yeah. Sure. They should be from 4 till about 7."

"I can't wait to watch you play again." Yes, I am that embarrassing mom at sporting events. I can't help it. I'm proud of my kid.

Turning my attention to Dellah, "You ready to go deal with your car? I'll drive you back to the Tipsy Penny, and we can wait for a tow truck." I turn to Wynnie, "We can head to storage when we return. Sounds good?"

Wynnie nods, cleans her space at the table, and retreats into her room.

"Oh, that's code for gossip. I'll go get dressed and be right back." Dellah clears her plate and heads back to her house.

I tell her all about my evening on the way to her car. She couldn't help but ooh and awe at all the details.

"All. The. Consent, Hazy. I thought you were just getting a fun roll in the hay. A wham, bam, thank you, ma'am. Hell, you got the royal package, girl. I still have his number. Let me find it."

She starts rummaging through her purse, and I stop her hands. "No. If you find it, toss it."

"Are you crazy? Why?" She looks at me in utter horror.

"Because if he wanted me to have his number, he would have given it to me. It was a one night stand. Besides, I probably won't see him again. I was so embarrassed I didn't join that gym, so we have no reason to cross paths."

"If you're sure?"

"I am. Here's your car." We climb out, and I walk around to assess the damage. "Um, Dells. How drunk were you last night?"

She gives me a curious look. "Pretty drunk, why? What's up?" She walks around the car to see what I'm looking at. Nothing. I'm looking at nothing.

"You don't have a flat tire." We both take another lap around the car, inspecting each tire.

"It was 100 percent flat last night. This back driver-side tire was on the ground. I know I drank a lot, but I didn't imagine a flat tire. Hold on. I even sent a picture to Collin." She digs out her phone from her purse and scrolls through a few screens. "See." She shows me the picture, and it's definitely her tire, flat.

"Is there some magical tire fairy in this parking lot?" I'm staring at the suspicious tire when I hear Dellah gasp. "What's wrong?"

"There *is* a tire fairy. Look." She hands me a note.

Dellah, thanks for being a great wing woman last night.
I felt like I owed you a favor in return. Your tire has been fixed.
Please give Hazel my phone number if she'd like it. I hope you
ladies had a good evening and got home safe.

90

HAZEL

Nix

19

Jude

Me: I hope you're having a great week, Little Dove. Would you like to have dinner with me this weekend?

"Am I interrupting?" I whip my head up towards Phoenix. We were talking about tryouts. Get your head back in the game, man.

"What? Shit, sorry, man. No, my mind just wandered away for a minute."

"I see that. Into your phone, apparently. Something you want to share with the class?" He takes a swig of his beer, shuffling around the papers in front of us.

"Nah, it's all good. Just the woman I went out with last week. I'm trying to set up another date, but we've been playing phone tag."

"Maybe she wasn't impressed by your little Target date." He smirks behind his beer bottle. I gave him a quick rundown before I left of what I had planned that night.

"Say what you will, but she had a great time. She has a new job and a kid. I'm sure she's just busy."

"A kid. Go, Daddy Jude." He clinks our beers and I roll my eyes.

"You're a caveman sometimes. Anyway, back to business. So, it looks like we have 15 girls signed up for tryouts." My phone buzzes. I pick it up, and it's a text from Hazel.

"Yeah, back to business," Phoenix mumbles.

Little Dove: That sounds great. Saturday?

Me: Saturday works perfectly. How about you come to my house and I'll cook for us?

Little Dove: You cook. I'm intrigued. I can't wait!

Me: See you Saturday at 6 Little Dove. I'll send you my address. Bring dessert? ;)

"Dude, that's a goofy grin on your face. Better be careful. Wouldn't want to catch anything." He's laughing at me.

"Don't be a dick, Phoenix. Tell me you have somewhere better to be on Saturday night because I just invited her over for dinner."

He's tapping his chin and looking up in the air, pretending he's deep in thought. "I can be scarce."

Little Dove: Why excuse me Sir, is dessert a euphemism for something dirty? I know how you like to be bad sometimes.

Little Dove: Just messing around. I'll bring something sweet and yummy. Besides myself.

"Damn. On second thought, maybe I'll stick around. I might

need to meet this woman that puts *that* look on your face."
He's pointing at my head, making a circle around my face.

I adjust myself in my pants because her text has my mind
wandering to dirty thoughts that made my dick come alive.
Phoenix notices my shifting.

"Should we take a break?" He gives me a knowing smirk.

"Just give me a minute, man. I'll go grab us some more
beers."

Sitting back in the living room with cold beers in hand,
we review this season's potential roster based on the players'
bios.

"Who's this? I don't recognize this name from last year.
Rowyn Gibson, 7th grader, shortstop."

"She's a new transfer. I spoke to the coach at her old school.
He said she has some good potential." I take her bio back
from him and add it to our stack of this year's potential team.

"You think she'll make the cut? Have you seen her play?"

"Not yet. She's stopped by the practices, but hasn't partici-
pated. She's pretty shy, but I've got a good feeling. You can let
me know what you think. I have to leave no later than 4:45
to make it home for my online class, but you know I'll trust
your judgment."

"Sounds like a plan. Wanna grab drinks Friday night to
discuss the final lineup?" He stands and collects our empty
beer bottles.

"I think that's the perfect end to the week." I collect all
the papers to put back in my folder. Rowyn's bio grabs my
attention when I see something familiar. 'Mother: Hazel
Gibson.' Hazel. Not a very common name but not uncommon
either. My Little Dove said her daughter's name is Wynnie.
I'm sure I'm still just a little lust fogged from our text earlier.

People all over the world share names.

"Night, Jude," Phoenix calls over my shoulder, and I hear the door close.

20

Hazel

I'm so late! I didn't even have a chance to change out of my scrubs. I hope Wynnie forgives me. She was so nervous this morning. I know how much of a big deal it is. She doesn't know these girls, and can be shy until you get to know her. My phone rings through the speakers.

"Hello." I say curtly. It's Dellah, and I'm still upset with her.

"Hey. How's tryouts going?"

"God, Dellah. I'm not even there yet. I got held up at work. It's almost 5 o'clock. It's so late!"

"Okay, relax, chick. It's only 4:40. I know you can't be far. Wynnie will understand. It's not like you're missing the entire tryouts. Breathe." I know she's right, but I hate being late. I don't want to disappoint her.

"I'm pulling in. Gotta go." I hang up before she can say anything else. I park my car in the lot closest to the field and pause a moment when I get out. I look at the sign in front of me, Mountain Pine Fields. This is the same middle and high

96

school I attended. It's been over a decade since I've been on campus. I take a deep breath, head towards the field, and take a seat on the bleachers.

I spotted her right away out on the field. She looks so natural out there. I watch the coach hit balls out into different parts of the field, testing the girls' reactions and throwing ability.

I catch myself lingering a little too long on the ass of the coach when he bends down to pick up balls. He's wearing black athletic pants with a baseball T sporting the school mascot. His backward baseball hat and dark sunglasses give him a deliciously mysterious look. "Hey, Coach Graves!" Someone calls from the dugout, and I get a view of his profile. He looks familiar. Probably just someone I knew from high school coming back to coach.

I watch the rest of the tryouts, and Wynnie played great. I think she has a good chance of making the team. The coach calls everyone in from the field, signaling the ending of tryouts. The girls huddle around him, and he takes his sunglasses off to talk to them.

"Holy shit." I gasp into my hands. It's Nix. What is he doing here? I thought he said he was a high school teacher. This is middle school softball.

They break their huddle, and Wynnie comes jogging toward me. I meet her at the bottom of the bleachers.

"You played great, kiddo. Sorry, I was late. How do you feel?" I do my best to keep my back to the field and avoid her coach.

"I feel good. It felt awesome to get back out there. I think I'll make the team." I love the big smile she has on her face. "I have to run to the locker room. I left my school stuff there."

97

"Okay, I'll meet you back at the car. Take your time." She heads toward the locker room, and I make my way to the car.

"Angel?" Oh no. No. Oh no. Oh no. This can't be happening. I turn around and Nix is right behind me.

"Hey." I give him a shy smile.

"I thought that was you. What are you doing here?" He reaches up, removes his baseball hat with one hand, and runs his fingers through his hair with the other.

"I could ask you the same question."

A broad smile crosses his face as he looks me up and down. "Well, I work here. Based on your choice of clothing, I can't say the same for you." Ugh, my unflattering scrubs.

"Um, yeah. You got me there." I let out a nervous laugh. Guess it's time to rip off this band aid. I inhale a deep breath and let the words fall out of my mouth on the exhale. "My daughter was trying out."

"For softball, here?" He looks back at the now deserted field with furrowed brows, clearly trying to figure out who my daughter is. I see it on his face the moment it clicks. "Rowyn?"

The ground looks interesting right now. "Yeah, she's mine."

"Okay. Yeah, okay. I knew you had a daughter, but I never imagined a *daughter*. I pictured a little kid." Suddenly the ground seems interesting to him as well.

"Teen mom. Surprise." I wiggle my fingers in front of me in a surprise gesture. "Well, I was 18 but still technically a teen. Don't worry. Most people assume the same." There's a long awkward pause in the conversation. "Oh, thank you for fixing Dellah's car. You didn't have to do that."

"You didn't call." My eyes snap up to meet his.

"I- Dellah." I say her name as a sigh. "She was so drunk that night. She lost your number."

"Oh, that makes sense. I was hoping to hear from you, but I understood if you didn't want to. It was an intense night."

"I did," I reassure him quickly. "I was thinking of stopping back at the Tipsy Penny this weekend and leaving my number with the bartender to give to you."

"I could save you the trip and give it to you now if you'd like." He smiles, pulls his phone out of his pocket, unlocks it, and offers it to me. I take it and enter my number and call myself so I have his. "Thank you, Angel."

"I should get to my car. My daughter's probably waiting for me. It was good to see you again, Nix. I hope that our… history, doesn't hurt her chances of making the team."

"Not in the slightest. Rowyn played really well." He puts his hands in his pockets. "Would you like to go out Saturday night?"

"Oh, I already have plans. And that's not "a line" I promise." I make air quotes with my fingers. "I really do have plans. Tomorrow night?" I offer.

He laughs. "Tomorrow night, I "have plans" also." He teases me by using his own air quotes. "I might be a teacher, but I don't mind going out on a school night. Maybe we can try for sometime next week?" He flashes me a boyish grin.

"Next week sounds great. Text me. I gotta go. Bye, Nix. It was great not running into you again." I'm smiling and walking backward away from the temptation in front of me. He's so damn hot. When I get to the car, Wynnie is already waiting for me.

"What took you so long?" She looks at me skeptically. I can feel the slight blush on my cheeks.

"Oh, sorry. I ran into a friend. You know how that can be."

"Only you, Mom. Let's go home. I'm starving." Only me is

right.

"Let me just shoot a quick text to your aunt, and we'll head home." I grab my phone from my purse, see the missed call from Nix's unknown number, and smile.

Me: S.O.S.

Immediately the three bubbles start bouncing.

Bestie: Wine or Vodka
    Work, kid or guy/s

This woman gets me.

Me: Wine AND ice cream.
    Guy
    Home In 10. Come over in 30.
    Bestie: On it! <eggplant emoji>

She might get it, but she's crazy.

"Stop for pizza?" I turn and ask Wynnie.

"That's fine." She doesn't even bother to look up from her phone to answer me.

20 minutes later, we are pulling into the driveway. Dellah sees us and comes rushing out her back door, supplies in hand. So much for "come over in 30."

"I got the goods." She lifts an arm carrying a bag with more than wine and ice cream.

"Dells, you gotta give me a minute to change out of these clothes." I head towards my bedroom when we make it upstairs.

"No problem, I'll just hang out with my favorite niece." Wynnie shoots me a "Thanks, Mom" look.

"Sorry, Aunt Dellah. I have homework then bed. Maybe next time." Damn, she's good at being that elusive preteen. She grabs two slices of pizza and disappears into her room.

" 'Yes, Aunt Dellah. I'd love to hang out with my favorite Aunt.' Brat!" She mocks Wynnie across the apartment as she puts the ice cream away. I return to the room dressed in a comfy sweatshirt and sleep shorts.

Handing me a glass of wine, she lowers her voice and asks, "Is this a one or a two eggplant problem?" I take several gulps of my wine, trying to wash away some of the day.

"Why am I still friends with you?" I grab a slice of pizza and stuff my face while gesturing the box towards Dellah in offering.

"Because I got you laid." She says so nonchalantly.

"Speaking of getting laid. Guess who Wynnie's softball coach is?"

Her hand stops mid-air holding her slice of pizza. "No. Which one?"

I drop my head to the counter with a loud groan. "The fact that you have to ask 'which one' is part of the problem." I turn my head to look at her, forehead still on the counter. "Nix."

"Wow. Okay. I thought he was a high school teacher?" She takes a bite of her pizza.

"That's what I said."

"Well, what happened? P.S. You know I still feel terrible about losing his number."

"Yeah, yeah. So, I noticed him looking absolutely edible in a backward hat during tryouts."

"Why is a backward hat so hot?" She tops off my glass of

wine.

"I know, right? Thanks." I gesture towards the wine. "As I was leaving, he spotted me and called my name. I had no choice but to acknowledge him. Then, of course, the awkward conversation about Wynnie happened."

"And?" She's at the edge of her seat.

"He was shocked, to say the least. It's not every day you end up coaching the daughter of your one night stand. And, like usual, he was even more shocked to realize that she was older. I thanked him for your tire, and he asked why I didn't call. I blamed it on you, of course, and we exchanged numbers. He asked me out on Saturday night, but I already have a date."

"You do?"

"Yeah, with Jude. What is wrong with me? Am I actually dating two guys at once? This conversation might require more than just wine." She reaches into her bag and pulls out a bottle of vodka. I knew that bag had more.

"Technically, you're dating one, and you fucked the other."

"Semantics, Dells." I watch as she reaches for the shot glasses and pours us each one.

"It's been one date and one romp in the hay. Did either one ask to be exclusive? I already know the answer to that, no. So don't worry about it. Live a little. You deserve it."

"You're a bad influence." We clink glasses and take our shots.

"And that's why you keep me around."

21

Jude

"Alright, I'm getting out of your hair, man. I'm gonna go hang out with Scotty at the bar. Leave a sock on the door if you need me to stay out longer." He winks at me and looks me up and down. Hmm did he just check me out? A smirk starts to work at the edge of my lips. No. I shake that thought out of my head. "Nice apron, by the way." He's laughing as he heads to the front door.

"Oh, you got jokes now, Phoenix? Very funny. I wanted to keep my shirt clean." I look down at my crisp white button up shirt and then at the offending red pasta sauce I'm stirring. That's a disaster waiting to happen without the apron.

"If that's what you need to tell yourself. Have a good night, and remember, don't be a fool; cover your tool."

"Phoenix."

"What? It's sound advice. Don't be silly; wrap your willy. Love is cleaner with a packaged wiener." He's standing at the front door laughing so hard he can barely breathe.

"Get out."

"Alright, alright, I'm gone. But remember, don't make a mistake; wrap your snake." I hear the front door slam as his loud laughter continues down the walkway. Who needs enemies when you have friends like that?

Right around 6 o'clock, my doorbell rings, and I open the door to a smiling Hazel. Her beauty always astounds me, but I'm almost struck speechless by the goddess in front of me.

"Little Dove, you look incredible." She's wearing black skinny jeans and a dark red top that hangs off one shoulder. But it's the confidence in the smile she's wearing that makes her stunning.

"Thank you." Her eyes look me up and down. "You look… brave."

"Brave. Care to explain? And what's in the bag?" I step aside and gesture for her to come inside.

"Brave because you're wearing white." She stops in front of me and runs her hands up and down the buttons of my shirt. "I learned very quickly that white and kids don't mix. And the bag is dessert. Well, the ingredients for dessert. Since you cooked for me, I thought we could make dessert together."

"What are we making?" I inspect the bag's contents and see lemon cake mix, cool whip, powdered sugar, and an egg wrapped in a bag to keep it safe.

"Cookies. Crinkle cookies, to be exact." She has a proud look on her face.

"Cookies with only these four ingredients? What else do you need from me?"

"Just a sheet pan and some cooking spray."

"That's it?" I'm skeptical.

"That's it. I promise." There's a hint of mischief in her eyes.

"Okay, I'll take your word for it. Are you ready to eat? Can I get you something to drink?"

"Yes, and yes, please."

We spend the next hour eating and laughing, specifically laughing at me. Mid-conversation, Hazel laughed so hard she snorted. It was the most adorable thing I've ever heard, but it caught me so off guard that I dropped my fork on my plate, causing pasta sauce to splash onto my white shirt.

"Who needs to worry about wearing white around kids when a grown man can't keep himself clean." Every time her eyes drifted to the splash stains, she would snort again.

"Let me go get changed, and we can get started on the cookies." I clear our plates and then head to my bedroom to change. A navy henley seems like a safe bet. At least it isn't white.

Back in the kitchen, I find Hazel preparing all the ingredients. "I'll preheat the oven. What temp do you need?" She assesses my new shirt and smiles.

"375* and a sheet pan, two bowls, and cooking spray, please." She looks so good in my kitchen. Her hips sway to the music I put on in the background for dinner. I grab everything and place it on the counter next to her.

"I like your new shirt. Our favorite color, nice choice." I didn't think about the color when I put on the shirt. This is a happy coincidence.

"Well, thank you. Glad you approve. Now, how can I help? I am at your service, my lady." I give a little bow, and she giggles. The sound is music to my ears.

"Wanna mix after I have everything in the bowl? I can get the next step ready while you do that."

"Anything for you." Oh boy, does that statement hold a lot

more weight than just about making cookies. She hands me the bowl after she's dumped three of the four ingredients into it, and I start mixing. She pours the powdered sugar into the second bowl and gives me a devilish look.

"What's that look for?" I have a feeling whatever comes next is going to be trouble.

"Oh, nothing," she sings. Yep, definitely trouble.

She dips her finger into the powdered sugar and walks up to me. She rubs her finger across my bottom lip and leans in to lick the powder off. Too quickly, she pulls away.

"You had something on your lip."

"Did I now? Well, thank you for helping me out. Apparently, I've been very messy this evening." I set the bowl down and take my turn to stick my finger in the powdered sugar. I swipe a little on her exposed shoulder, then lick it off, trailing kisses along the hollow of her neck. A low moan escapes from her throat.

"You had a little something there." I swipe my finger on her lips and kiss her lightly. "And there," I whisper.

She throws her arms around my neck and deepens the kiss. Turning her to the side so her back is against the counter, I lift her and place her next to the ingredients.

She pulls away and gasps. "You just… lifted me up here."

"I did. I'm sorry, would you like to get down." I look back and forth between her eyes, trying to assess her feelings–shock, embarrassment, disbelief.

"I've never had anyone lift me before. I'm not exactly the tiniest person." Her eyes shift down to the floor. I grab her chin and lift it lightly.

"Look at me, Little Dove." She looks into my eyes. "You are every bit of the woman I want in my kitchen right now. All of you. You ate my food and drank my wine. We are making cookies, and we are going to eat them as well. You're beautiful to me, and I don't care what the scale says or what the tag might say on your clothes. I wanted you on my counter, and I put you there. And now, I want to continue kissing you. Is that alright with you?" I run my hand up and down her thighs, giving a little squeeze at the top to accentuate my point.

"Maybe." Maybe? I thought we were on the same page. I felt her shift under my palms as she placed her hand on my chest. Is she going to push me away? She erupts into a fit of giggles.

"What?" Her giggles burst into full-on laughter.

She looks down at her hand on my chest and pulls it away. "You… should have… stuck… with the white… shirt." She manages to get out between beats of laughter. I look down and see a perfectly formed handprint in powdered sugar on my navy shirt."

"Oh, Little Dove, you're in trouble now." I lean forward, caging her in between my arms and the counter. I reach for the powdered sugar and grab a pinch in my fingers. I dangle it above her head.

"No. No, please, Jude. I'm sorry." She's attempting to wiggle away from me but I have her pinned with my hips.

"That smile doesn't look very sorry. Do you like snow?" She looks up at my fingers shaking her head. Her arms come up to cover her face just as I release the sprinkling of sugar. She squeals in delight.

She leans forward, puts her hands on my cheeks, and catches my mouth with hers. "I'm," *kiss,* "really," *kiss,* "Sorry," *kiss.*

"I'm beginning to believe you." I'm not. "Let's get finished with these cookies." I help lift her back to the floor. She turns around to grab the batter bowl, and I take my opportunity to strike. I quickly dip my hands into the powdered sugar and then plant both flat on each ass cheek of her black jeans.

She whips around, jaw on the floor. "Did you just do what I think you did?"

I throw my powdered-covered hands up in the "I don't know" position and smile wide. She looks over her shoulder to see my artwork on her pants.

"I can't believe you. You know this means war, right?" She squints her eyes and bends her knees, ready to pounce.

"Oh no. Truce, Little Dove? Phoenix will kill me if I trash the kitchen. It's his week for kitchen duty." I grab the bowl of powdered sugar and move it a safe distance from her.

She straightens up. "Who's Phoenix?"

"He's my roommate, my best friend. We rotate the household chores. I know we're adults, but it's how we've done it since college, and it works for us."

"I had no idea you had a roommate. Is he here right now?" Her head swivels to look around the house.

"No, I told him to find somewhere else to be tonight. I wanted you alone. He'll text before he comes back, though. Should we finish the cookies?"

"Sure. Although maybe we should clean up a little first." She looks around the room at the streaks of powdered sugar all over the floor and counter.

I wrap my arms around her back, trailing my hands down until they are seated over my powder hands on her ass, and I squeeze. "I think I like it when you're a little dirty." I nibble on the shell of her ear.

"At this rate, we'll never get the cookies done."

"You're right." I stopped kissing her abruptly. "Let's focus and finish our dessert." I give her ass another squeeze and back away so we can complete our task.

We finished making our cookies which were as sweet and yummy as she promised.

"I should get going. I need to wash this powdered sugar out of my hair tonight, or I might attract ants into my bed." Laughing, we walk towards the door. "Once again, you've been a perfect gentleman, Jude."

"And I always will be. There's only room for one naughty person in this relationship, and you do a fine job with that title." Her eyes flash up to mine. Crap, did the 'relationship' word scare her? I didn't mean anything by it. She quickly gives me a smile and shrugs.

"I don't know. I like it when you're a little naughty, too."

"Oh yeah? How about this?" I pause for a moment to look deeply into her hazel green eyes. I can see the lust shining back. I don't make us wait a moment longer before I crash into her mouth. Our lips entwine, and I nip at her lower lip, asking permission to enter her mouth. She slides her tongue over my upper lip, and I dive in.

I reach a hand around her back, and under her shirt until I feel her warm, silky skin. My other hand finds its way to her hair, and I give it a little tug as I trail kisses down her neck, and she moans.

"Your skin feels and smells so amazing." I nip and then lick the top of her shoulder. She moans. "Here." I trail my kisses back up her neck to the skin below her ear and nip again. "Here." I rub my hands on her back towards her hips. "And here."

Her hips flex, and she rubs against the thickening length of my cock, forcing a moan out of me. I momentarily lose my restraint and pull her hips closer to mine, grinding into her. Our kiss deepens. When she lifts her leg around my hip to gain more friction, I grab her upper thigh and return to my senses. I pull away and rest my forehead against hers.

"I've been naughty enough for tonight, Little Dove."

She pulls away from my forehead and peppers kisses along the base of my neck. "Are you sure you've had enough?" She grinds her hips into mine again.

"No, not at all." I squeeze her thigh in my hand. "I'm definitely sure I *haven't* had enough. But that doesn't mean we shouldn't stop before we can't." I reluctantly released her thigh. She slowly slides her leg down my hip until it reaches the floor.

She places another kiss on my lips and then whispers, "I'll corrupt you soon enough, naughty boy."

"Fuck, Little Dove. You can't say things like that and expect me to let you walk out of this house." I thrust my hips into hers again. "Do you feel what you just did to me?" My cock is impossibly hard. "Now, you better go home and dream about me because you sure gave me plenty to dream about tonight."

I kiss her one more time and spin her around by the shoulders. I open the door and smack her ass to move her along. "Thank you for another amazing evening, Little Dove."

"Thank *you*, Jude. I hope your roommate enjoys the extra cookies." She gives me one last peck on the lips and bounces away.

I watch her until her tail lights disappear down the road. Shower. Cold. Right now.

Walking into my room, stripping my clothes, I can't get the feel of her skin out of my mind. She's such a temptress. I've never wanted to take a woman into my bedroom so badly.

Turning on the water, I step in before it has a chance to warm up. I need to calm down. I grab the shampoo and start washing my hair. My mind roams to my hands in her hair. The way her smell of peaches intoxicated my senses.

My hand drops from my hair and grabs my hard cock. I need relief, and a cold shower hasn't helped me. Stroking myself hard, I remember the way it felt having her grind against me. How easily I could have wrapped my arm around her other thigh and pinned her to the wall. She was willing to give herself to me right there in the foyer, and I was almost ready to give it all up to her.

I lean forward and brace my hand against the cool tile. My strokes become more frantic as my tip turns purple, yearning for release. I feel the familiar tingle build up at the base of my spine, and I continue to think of what it could feel like to have her thick thighs wrapped around my hips, my head.

My orgasm rips through me with a loud groan. Come bursts onto the tile, and I finally feel some relief.

22

Hazel

Wynnie: Mom, I got a letter from the softball coach. I'm not allowed to open it until I leave school.

Me: A letter? I hope that's a good sign. Can you wait until I get home to open it together? If not, I understand.

Wynnie: Still planning to get home around 7:15?

Me: I am, unless I'm stopping somewhere for takeout?

Wynnie: No, come straight home. I'll wait. Love ya.

Me: Love you too, kid.

I stumble through the door at 7:13. "I'm here!"

"Geez, Mom. Way to make an entrance."

"I'm excited for you to see what's in the letter. I appreciate you waiting for me." I give her a side hug and sit down at the counter. "Okay. Let's see what it says."

I watch as she opens the envelope and reads it over. It looks like a single sheet of paper and a Post-it.

"I made the team! I'm the new shortstop." I jump up from

my seat, and we both start bouncing up and down.

"I knew you could do it. What's the Post-it say?"

She picks it up and reads it, then passes it in my direction. "It's for you."

-Ms. Gibson

We are so excited to have Rowyn join the team this year. As a new team member, we have some forms for you to sign. Could you please come to the coach's office Wednesday evening after practice around 7:30.

Thanks

Coach S

Coach S? I thought Nix's last name was Grove... Grave. Something with a G.

"Hey, Wynnie, how many coaches do you have?"

"We have two coaches. Coach Graves and Mr-Coach S. Coach S had to leave tryouts early for a class."

"Ah, okay. I guess I'll get to meet your other coach on Wednesday." I give her another big hug. "I'm so proud of you."

Wednesday comes quickly, and I find myself walking the familiar halls of the middle school toward the coach's offices. Faded lockers still line the walls on either side of me, and several bulletin boards are decorated with posters about the spring musical. I walk through the double doors leading to the school's athletic section, and I'm hit with the pungent odor of middle school boys and too much body spray. I find the office marked for the softball coach ajar and knock on the door. I hear a faint "Come in," and I enter the room and close the door behind me. I see a man looking down at the papers on his desk. The brim of a baseball hat covers his face.

"Hi, Coach S. I'm Rowyn's mother-

His head snaps up. "Little Dove?" The look of shock on his face matches mine.

"Jude? What are you doing here?" I look around the room to make sure I'm in the right office. "I'm looking for the girl's softball coach. Coach S."

"That's me. Jude Sanders. Coach S." He pauses for a heartbeat. "Wait, did you say you were Rowyn's mother? I thought you said your daughter's name was Wynnie?"

"Oh, well yeah. Wynnie is my nickname for Rowyn. I thought you were a school counselor?"

"Rowyn. Wynnie. Okay, that makes sense. And I am. I'm the school counselor at the middle school, and one of the softball coaches." Oh no. Oh shit. *One of.* That means...no, no, no.

As if he was summoned, the office door opens.

"Hey man, sorry I'm late. These cookies are amazing. You gotta get your woman to make more of these for us." I let out a small groan because this can't be my life right now. It draws his attention.

He looks up, finally seeing me. "Angel, what are you doing here?" He walks up to me, wraps a gentle arm around my waist, and kisses me on the forehead in greeting. He steps back, and my eyes snap to Jude's.

"Phoenix," Jude says apprehensively. "This is Rowyn's mother." Jude introduces me. Phoenix. Phoenix. Nix. I give myself a mental forehead slap.

As if it's no big deal, he responds, "Yeah, I know she's Rowyn's mom. I found out at tryouts."

I look back at Phoenix. "Phoe-NIX. I get it now."

114

"Sorry, Angel. It's an old nickname. I should have corrected you at the bar that night, but there were more pressing matters at hand." He gives me a mischievous grin and a wink.

"Phoenix, that cookie you're enjoying right now was made by Hazel, Rowyn's mother. At our house. On Saturday." *Our house.* Oh god. I forgot.

I look at Jude. "This is… Phoenix. Your roommate, your best friend, Phoenix." I need the floor to open up right now and swallow me whole.

"Yes, Little Dove. Phoenix and I are roommates."

"Oh shit. Hold on." Phoenix looks at me. "You made these cookies?" I nod. "That means…" He looks at Jude. "I had no idea, man. I'm so sorry."

"No idea of what?" Jude asks. This is so bad. I sit down in the chair off to the side of the room. I should leave, but I came here for Wynnie. To sign paperwork.

"Remember I told you about the tire I changed at the Tipsy Penny? And I mentioned that I had hooked up with the friend of the girl whose tire I changed. This is the friend." Jude stands up, leans forward, and puts his hands on his desk. I can't even look at him. I'm completely mortified.

"So, let me get all this straight." He looks at Phoenix. "You know Hazel."

"Yeah. We actually met over winter break at the gym. Well, in the gym doorway. Story for another time."

"Okay. And you know Hazel is Rowyn's mother because you found out at tryouts."

"Correct." Phoenix isn't showing any emotion to this absurd situation.

Jude turns his attention to me. "And the two of you hooked up at the Tipsy Penny about two weeks ago. Which was after

115

our first date." Those were statements, not questions. He hates me. They are both going to hate me. I've ruined my daughter's softball career.

"Okay. Okay." He's nodding in thought, blinking several times as he sits back down.

"This is obviously *really* awkward. If I could just sign the paperwork you needed, I'll leave and go find a ditch somewhere to hide in." I'm utterly embarrassed.

My comment snaps Jude out of his daze. He stands and rounds the desk. Crouching in front of me he places his hand on my cheeks.

"Little Dove. No. You haven't done anything wrong. I'm just processing. You didn't know." He looks over at Phoenix. "None of us knew."

Phoenix walks over and takes my hand in his. "Angel, it's alright. I promise. I'm not mad. Jude isn't mad, either. We've just found ourselves in an interesting position. Why don't we get the paperwork for Rowyn out of the way, and then we can talk." Jude nods in agreement.

"Okay, Let's get that taken care of." One thing at a time. The paperwork is the top priority. I can handle that. Then maybe I can leave before things can get even more awkward.

Jude hands me a stack of papers: liability, travel requirements, and medical forms. I sign them all while Phoenix and Jude have a quiet discussion together. When I finish, I stand up and hand the papers to Jude, hoping to make a quick exit.

"Please don't run out. We'd like to discuss something with you." Jude sounds so sincere.

"Okay. I guess."

Phoenix walks closer to me. "We have a proposition for you."

"A proposition?"

"Yes," Jude says, standing next to Phoenix.

"What kind of proposition?"

"Give us six weeks." I'm not sure what Phoenix is asking for. Are they asking me to give them each six weeks to decide which one I like better?

"Six weeks for what? You two are friends, roommates. I can't choose between you. I won't break up a friendship."

"What if you didn't have to choose?" I stare in shock into Jude's cinnamon eyes.

"Well, now I know you're messing with me, Jude. Life isn't a romance novel. Especially mine." The absurdity of thinking that I could have a relationship with these two sexy as fuck men is tempting and amusing. Dellah and I will have a good laugh about this later over a bottle of wine.

"We are completely serious, Angel. We aren't messing with you. We've never done anything like this before, so we don't know what the rules are, but we'd like to try it if you do."

"Okay, hold on. So you both want to date me, together. At the same time. The three of us?"

"Yes, Little Dove. The three of us."

"And what happens at the end of six weeks?" I can't believe I'm even considering this. I went from the longest dry spell to two unbelievably gorgeous men wanting to date me... together.

"At the end of six weeks, we decide if it's working or not. If it's working, we will continue." Phoenix is so matter-of-fact about it.

"And if it's not working?" I feel like I'm getting whiplash from this ping-pong of a conversation.

"Well, like you said, Angel. We're best friends. If it's not working we walk away from you together, and our friendship stays intact.

"You make it sound so simple." Can it really be that simple? Having the attention of these two men sounds tempting, but is it feasible? I guess unofficially, I've already been doing it.

"It's as simple as we make it. We can go at your pace. No pressure or rush for anything. Well, unlike our first meeting." He winks at the memory of our office romp.

"What about Wynnie? You're both her coaches. I don't want this to affect anything for her."

"Please don't think for a second that there would ever be any negative impact on her. Jude and I are very fair coaches and would never treat her differently, even if you told us no and walked out right now. She's earned her position, and she keeps that spot as long as she continues to play to her potential."

"Okay. This is a lot." I rub my temples thinking. "Do I need to fill out any more paperwork for softball?"

Jude checks over the papers I signed. "No. You're all set."

"Alright, good. Could I take the night and think about this? There's so much sexy testosterone in this room right now I'm not sure I can think straight for much longer." They both have a good little laugh at that.

"Of course, Little Dove. Take all the time you need."

"Just the night. If I don't give myself a deadline, I'll overthink it and probably talk myself out of it completely."

"Okay. Just the night. You have our numbers. You can text or call us for anything." I nod at Phoenix and give him a small smile. He steps forward, slides his hand to the back of my neck, and grabs my hip. He pulls me flush to his chest with a gentle tug and captures me in a sensual kiss. Our lips dance together as if it's the only thing in the world he needs to be doing right now. I feel warmth on my back and the smell of citrus. Jude moves my hair, pressing gentle kisses along my neck and jaw while Phoenix continues to invade my lips. This is...indescribable. I get lost in the moment, and a moan escapes me. Phoenix smiles against my lips before pulling away. Jude pulls away as well, but not before whispering in my ear, "Just a little something to help you decide. Have a good evening, Little Dove."

"Goodbye, Angel. Talk to you soon." Phoenix opens the office door for me, and I walk out in a daze.

I reach my car and grab my keys and cell phone from my purse. Collapsing into my seat, I shoot off a text to Dellah.

Me: S.O.S. S.O.S. Vodka <two eggplant emojis>

Bestie: Oh fuck. Sure you don't want tequila?

Me: And THAT is the exact reason you're my best friend. Be home soon.

23

Hazel

My mind has been in a fog all week. I've woken up every morning with both men's sweet good morning texts. I've seen them all three times I've picked Wynnie up from softball practice, and every time I've needed new panties from the lust in their eyes that they gave me across the field. I learned my lesson after the first night to stay in my car and wait for Wynnie to come to me.

"Hey, beautiful Angel. You look absolutely edible. When do we get to have you over again for dinner so you can be our main course?"

"Yes, Little Dove. Phoenix is rather jealous that he missed out on the first time you were here."

After my evening with tequila and Dellah, and yes, tequila was a very present "person" in the room with us, I texted them both the following day with a clear head and let them know I'd like to give it a try...together. After all, it's only six weeks, and I can walk away after that if it's not working.

When I got home from the proposition in their office that night, the tequila was flowing, and Dellah got all the details of what happened. She was a big cheerleader in giving it a go.

"You had a baby at 18. You didn't get to do your sexual experimentation in college. What a better time than at 30."

"Bitch, you need a good dicking."

"I wonder if I could convince Collin to let another dick in our bed? Or do you need another pussy in your little menage a trois? Wait, I guess then that would be a foursome. Is there a French term for a foursome?"

Needless to say, the tequila did all the talking that night, and most of the thinking. But I felt solid in my decision when I texted them my answer. You only live once, right?

They had tried to get me to come over last weekend, but I wanted to wrap my head around things. So instead, I spent the weekend with Wynnie and Dellah in our pajamas, reading and watching trash TV. We ate too many pancakes and devoured too much ice cream, but it was just what the three of us needed.

Now, I'm driving to their house more nervous than before my c-section with Wynnie.

At Dellah's insistence, I'm wearing my sexiest bra and panties set in red. A dress and heels, of course, for easy access. But not just any dress. The "every girl needs a little black dress" dress. My overly large purse is filled with condoms, lube, and extra panties because, apparently, all the hottest guys are just ripping them off nowadays. Maybe we shouldn't have read those spicy romance novels last weekend. I'm convinced Dellah is trying to live out her wildest fantasies vicariously through me, and if I'm being completely honest with myself, I'm totally here for it.

I'm hit with another wave of nervousness as I pull into their driveway.

Me: Need words of encouragement.

Bestie: You're a badass bitch. They are lucky as fuck. Thick thighs save lives! Come back and give me all the deets. Love ya.

Me: Thank you bestie! Love you too.

I rolled my eyes because she knew exactly what I needed to hear. Climbing out of my car, I head towards their front door, which opens as soon as I step on the porch.

"Hello, Little Dove. Come on in." He steps back and gestures for me to go inside. "Let's take off your coat." I pause a moment and look into his cinnamon eyes. I'm inside. There's no turning back now. I can do this.

I shrug off my coat with my back towards Jude and place it on the chair next to me. I hear the moment he takes in my entire outfit. His sharp intake of breath comes only a moment before I hear his growl.

Warm hands encase my hips from behind, and I feel the length of his hard body against mine.

"Fuck, Hazel." My name slips from his lips like a prayer. "What are you wearing?"

I smile and internally thank Dellah for convincing me to wear this outfit. I feel confident in it, and Jude also seems to be enjoying it. I turn around in his arms, trail my hands up his shoulders and wrap them around the back of his neck.

"Do you like my dress?" The lust in his eyes tells me he likes it too much. His hands move down to the swells of my ass cheeks and he pulls me closer to him.

"Do you feel how much I like your dress, Little Dove?" Yes, I absolutely can. The prominent bulge in his khaki pants is unmistakably hard against my stomach. I lean in for a kiss, and as our lips meet, I feel the butterflies in my stomach swarm. He lets a moan escape from the back of his throat as I pull at the hair on the nape of his neck. He responds by pushing further into me with his hips and giving my ass a firm squeeze.

He pulls away from the kiss, both of us breathless. I run one hand down his neck to the front of his shirt and smile.

"I see you've learned your lesson?" I tap on his pec.

"That you look sexy in anything you wear?" He rubs his hands up and down the sides of my dress with his hungry eyes. Oh, this man. Flattery will get him everywhere.

"That white isn't a safe color around me." I look at his light green polo shirt, and we both chuckle. I hear a door open behind me and I look down the hallway over Jude's shoulder. "Holy fuck."

Jude turns around at my reaction and groans. "Come on, dude. Foul play." Down the hall is a very wet Phoenix, wearing only a towel.

"Sorry, man. I needed to clean up." He starts walking to his room. "I was helping a buddy with his truck and lost track of time." He finally turns his attention to me and pauses. He spins and starts walking back down the hall towards us. "Angel…" The word is barely a whisper.

Jude shields me from Phoenix's eyes with his body. "Don't you dare Phoenix. Turn your ass back around and put some clothes on."

"Yeah, yeah. Party pooper. Be right back." He winks at me over Jude's shoulder, then retreats to his room. I watch him until his door shuts. I look back to Jude, whose eyes are lingering on Phoenix's closed door. Interesting.

I smile. "Who knew dinner would come with a show?"

Jude turns back around and offers me his hand. "Ready for dinner, Little Dove. Are you hungry?"

"Hmmm, I'm ravenous.

24

Phoenix

Damn alternator was giving Mac and me problems causing me to run late for my date with my Angel. I hoped I'd be out of the shower before she arrived, but I heard Jude talking to her as I stepped out. I just needed to slip down the hallway unseen and-

"Holy Fuck." Shit. So much for going unseen. I didn't realize they were still in the doorway, and Hazel spotted me.

"Come on, dude. Foul play." I smile inwardly. I never said I played fair, but being seen in only a towel wasn't my plan for how to start the evening either.

I start to retreat to my room. "Sorry, man. I needed to clean up. I was helping a buddy with his truck, and lost track of time." I turn back around and finally get a good look at her–my vixen.

"Angel." I didn't even realize I started walking back in their direction. She looks breathtaking in a little black dress. And those heels. Those fuck me heels need to be wrapped around my waist right now.

"Don't you dare Phoenix. Turn your ass back around and put some clothes on." My attention turns back to Jude. His eyes seem to be roaming over me. I rub my hands up and down my chest and watch his eyes follow the movement as they flash with heat for a brief moment. If I wasn't paying attention, I would have missed it. Am I putting on this show for Hazel, or Jude? *Clothes.* I need clothes. Right. I'm basically naked.

"Yeah, yeah. Party pooper. Be right back."

I go to my room and grab a pair of gray sweatpants from my drawer. Nope. I don't intend to play fair. Not after seeing her in that sexy as sin dress. I throw a black shirt over my sweats and stroll into the kitchen to find Jude and Hazel sitting down with their plates of chicken and vegetables. Jude sees my outfit, huffs, and rolls his eyes.

"Starting without me, Angel?" Leaning over, I kiss her forehead, her peach smell lingering around her. She turns her head and finds herself at eye level with the growing bulge in my pants. Her eyes widen, roaming my body until they meet my green eyes. She shrugs.

"I figured the quicker we eat dinner, the quicker we can get to dessert." This girl is naughty, and I love it.

Across the table, Jude chokes on her comment. "Damn, Little Dove. I know where your mind is at tonight."

A sly smile crosses her face. "Wynnie is having a sleepover with her Aunt Dellah tonight, so I don't have a curfew." Her hungry eyes pass between us, and then she returns to eating her chicken like she didn't just drop that bomb.

"Naughty, naughty girl." She shivers as I run my fingers lightly down her arm, leaving a trail of goosebumps behind them. I smile at her body's reaction as I go and make my plate.

Hazel sat at the head of the table with Jude and me flanking either side. It was the perfect position to have an easy conversation. Finishing our dinner, we clean up and head to the three-season porch. I grabbed a bottle of wine and some glasses while Jude grabbed a blanket. It's a mild February evening, and Jude lit the gas fireplace to keep us warm. I sat on the sofa and motioned for Hazel to sit beside me. Jude sat on her other side.

"Well, isn't this cozy? Your porch is beautiful." Her eyes scan the room, noticing the flat-screen TV and wet bar, and our indoor grill that gets frequent use. But what lies on the right side, taking up almost an entire porch wall, piqued her curiosity.

"Is that a giant bean bag chair?" Her smile widens like she's a kid in a candy store.

"Go ahead, Angel."

She looks up at me. Eyes alight with joy. "Go ahead, what?"

"I know you want to go over there and jump on top of it." She starts to shake her head in mock protest. I whisper in her ear, "Do it."

She stands up and takes her heels off. Damn, I'm gonna need her to put those back on later. Taking a few tentative steps forward, she turns and looks back at us, then takes a running leap, spinning at the last second so she lands on her back in a fit of laughter. It's the most beautiful thing I've ever seen. That is until I notice that her little leap has made her dress ride up her creamy thighs, exposing more flesh than she probably realizes.

Jude and I look at each other, stand up and walk over. Peering down at her, he asks, "Can we join you, Little Dove."

She pats both sides of her, and we each lay down, propping our heads in our hands and facing her. Jude looks her deep in the eyes. They lick their lips, and their mouths crash together as if being attracted like magnets. She rolls towards him to deepen the kiss, and I'm graced with a peek at a pair of red lacy panties poking out from her hiked-up dress. Running my hands up her thigh towards the lace, I watch them as their tongues find each other's mouths.

"We have another proposition for you, Angel." Jude smiles into their kiss while a low hum comes from Hazel.

"Look at me, Angel." Jude pulls away and tilts her chin towards me, so I have her attention. "Jude tells me he hasn't shared his dirty little secret with you."

Her eyes narrow, and she turns back to Jude. He has a slight pink tint to his cheeks, likely from embarrassment.

"Jude, what kind of dirty little secret are you keeping?" She gently caresses his cheek, and I wish I could feel her touch, too.

I look to Jude, silently asking for permission to answer her question. We had already discussed telling her, but I wanted to ensure he was still comfortable. He nods. I grab Hazel's chin and turn her back to face me again.

"Jude told you why he calls you Little Dove, correct?" She nods. "About how he came from a very religious background." She nods again, turning for a brief moment to look back at Jude.

I open my mouth to reveal Jude's truth, and he raises a hand to stop me. This is a touchy subject for him, but it seems he has found the courage to tell her himself.

"Little Dove, while I'm not a completely innocent man," he pauses, and a look of concern washed over Hazel's face. "No."

He puts a hand on her cheek. "Whatever you're thinking, I promise it's not that." She looks relieved. After another pause, he signs and looks deep into her hazel green eyes.

"Hazel, I'm a virgin." His face flushed, and his eyes closed tight. He's bracing himself for whatever her reaction might be.

Being 27 and not having had sex with a woman has put a damper on his previous relationships. Sure, he's had other experiences before, hence his "not innocent" comment, but he's never pulled the plug. He spent most of his life believing he had to save himself for marriage, and while he no longer believes that, he just hasn't found anyone he's wanted to give that last piece of himself to.

He admitted to me that he feels a different type of connection to Hazel, and I can honestly say I understand where he's coming from. I feel that link, too, which is why we came to this agreement. This arrangement between the two of us. The three of us.

He finally opens his eyes and explores hers for any answers. Hazel grabs both of his cheeks and rolls so she's half on top of him. She gently kisses him, and I can see his muscles relax at her touch.

"Jude, I don't care how much experience you do or don't have. We can take everything at your pace. I'd never rush or pressure you to do anything." She looks down at his chest, and her face falls. "So you know about Phoenix and me. Does it bother you that we…"

It's his turn to roll them. Hazel ends up with her back half on top of me while Jude is half on top of her. We may be stretching the limit of this giant bean bag.

"No, Little Dove. What you and Phoenix have done doesn't

affect us as a whole. I want to learn and explore things with you."

"Hence our proposition, Angel. Jude had a suggestion, and I'm happy to oblige, but it's ultimately up to you."

She looks at Jude, who has a mischievous smile on his face. "What's your suggestion, naughty boy?"

"My experiences are minor compared to Phoenix's. I propose, for your enjoyment and in the name of education," he winks, "that Phoenix helps me learn how to pleasure you."

"Hmm. Are we roleplaying teacher, student, Jude?" She smiles up at him with eagerness in her voice.

"Oh, naughty, Angel." I reach over and place my hand around her neck. She gasps at the pressure and grinds her butt back into me. Mmm, she likes that. Into her ear, I rasp, "Do you want to play games? You want to be our good girl?" She shudders. This woman is fantastic. She's taking all of this with such ease.

Sharing a woman is not something that Jude and I have ever done before. We don't generally even talk about women together, which is how we got into the predicament of both dating Hazel and not knowing. However, that has seemingly changed in the last week.

"So, Mr. Graves, what's the first lesson?" She's such a little minx. I slide out from under her and stand. Being outside and on this bean bag chair isn't the best choice to start our activities.

"Come with me Ms. Gibson, and we can start our lesson inside."

25

Jude

Phoenix takes Hazel's hand and helps her off the oversize bean bag. They walk inside and sit on the couch while I turn off the fireplace and grab the forgotten wine and glasses.

"Would anyone like some wine?" I offer.

"Got anything harder?" She looks up at me and bats her eyelashes. I nod. I could use something to take the edge off myself.

"Vodka, tequila, whiskey?" We have a fully stocked bar and probably have whatever she would like.

"Lime and salt?" Hmm, I wonder if tequila makes her clothes come off.

"Coming right up, Little Dove." Grabbing the tequila, salt, limes, and three shot glasses, I can hear their murmurs and her giggles, and even a few snorts come floating into the room. I smile at how easily she seems to fit with us, which gives me some confidence for the events that will hopefully occur. I return, place everything on the table, and pour three shots. She tries to grab the salt, and Phoenix stops her.

"Jude, come sit down." He pats the couch next to Hazel, and I obey. This is his show, and I'm going to follow directions. He grabs my chin and tilts it to the side. A sigh escapes my lips. "Lick, Angel," he instructs her.

Her hazel greens meet my cinnamon browns, and she smirks. Leaning over, she flattens her tongue and makes a long stroke on my neck. I bite my lip to hold in the groan. Phoenix sprinkles salt on my neck, grabs a lime, and hands her the filled shot glass.

"Bottoms up," he says before placing the lime in his mouth. With lust in her eyes, she licks the salt off my neck, throws back the shot, and grabs the lime from Phoenix's mouth with her teeth. She drops the lime and dives for him. "Tsk, tsk, naughty girl. You know the rules. It's our turn now." It seems they've played a similar game before.

He tilts her chin back so her head is resting on the back of the couch. Grabbing for the salt, we lick lines across the pulse points of her neck. Phoenix situates two limes in her mouth and hands me a shot. We clink our glasses, lick, drink, and dive for the limes simultaneously. The three of our lips brush together. A long breathy moan escapes her mouth, and the sound goes right to my increasingly hard cock. Based on the heat in Phoenix's eyes, it's affecting him just as much.

"Another, Angel?" She nods at him in response. "Do you think Jude is wearing too many clothes?" Her eyes widen as she nods again.

My eyes flash to him. While we didn't discuss specifics, we had a general game plan for the evening. Mostly I would follow his lead. I can talk a big game, but I have no experience with follow-through. When women would hear I'm a virgin, there was one of two reactions. Either they wanted to immediately get me in bed to devirginize me, or my lack of experience completely turned them off. I'm putting all of my trust in my best friend, and this woman who has seemed to accept me for exactly who I am.

"Well, go ahead. Take Jude's shirt off." With a feather-light touch, she reaches for the bottom hem of my shirt and lifts it up and over my head. Her hands roam over my smooth, rippled stomach. I have a light smattering of hair along the top of my chest, but it's blond and not incredibly noticeable. She finds it and runs her fingers through it, and I close my eyes and relish in the warmth of her touch.

"Shall we?" I hear Phoenix ask her. My eyes are still closed as I hear shuffling around. Then I feel the heat of two tongues across my pecs. My eyes pop open to see both Phoenix and Hazel licking lines across me. I watch as Phoenix sprinkles salt on both wet spots. He looks at me and places two limes in my mouth as he had just done to Hazel.

My eyes ping pong between them as they lick the salt off my chest, drink their shots and come towards me to get their limes. *Jesus fucking Christ.* They start to make out in front of my face, and all I can do is stare, frozen in arousal. My dick is as hard as steel over their little show.

"I...you...that..." I can't even complete a thought. I flop my head back on the couch in a long sigh, trying to compose myself.

Through Hazel's giggles, Phoenix says, "I think we broke him, Angel."

"Naughty boy, did we break you? How can we fix it?" She's leaning over my body, assumingly trying to look into my eyes, but they are still closed. The feel of her breasts rubbing against my chest does nothing to tamp down my erection. With a growl, I slam my mouth into hers. She grabs two fistfuls of my hair in an attempt not to fall off the couch. I pick her up and adjust her so she's straddling my waist, and I pull away from her mouth.

"How can you fix me? I think *you're* wearing too many clothes, Little Dove. What do you think, Phoenix?" I look at him over Hazel's shoulder.

In a moment of hesitation, she stiffens. "I think I need another drink before I'm ready for that. What do you think, Jude? Is it *our* turn?"

"Okay, Little Dove. No rush. But I agree with you. I think it is our turn. Grab the salt." We turn to Phoenix. "Fair is fair. Shirt off, man." A slow grin forms on his face as he reaches behind him and pulls his shirt off. His gray sweatpants are doing nothing to hide his thickening cock. I don't think he even bothered to put on any boxers based on the tent in his pants. Something I probably shouldn't be noticing.

"Where shall we do it?" I ask. Her eyes roam up and down his decorated chest.

"Right here." She flicks one of his nipple piercings, and he groans at the sensation. I hesitate at her choice and glance at Phoenix.

"You good, man?" Am I really asking my best friend for permission to lick his nipple ring right now?

"Really fucking good. Hand me the limes." Well okay. Fuck me. This is so hot. Or did the room get hot? What is this woman doing to us? Whatever it is, I'm here for it, 100 percent. And it would seem so is Phoenix.

Salt in Hazel's hand, we both lean down and lick over his

nipples. Hazel lingers and swirls her tongue around a few times. Phoenix's hips flex from the sensation, and a moan, almost like a growl, comes from deep in his throat.

"Angel," he warns. She smiles a devilish smile, and shakes salt on both of his nipples for us. Hazel and I lock eyes before we descend to lick off the salt. His hips flex again, and he sighs a throaty "fuck me" when we chug the shots and then lean in to get our limes.

This is absolutely not how I saw this evening going. The sounds Phoenix makes seem to affect me just as much as Hazel. His raging erection proves he's enjoying this as much as mine does–something to explore for another day. Right now, we have a beautiful woman to worship.

"You ready to take this dress off now, so we can start our next lesson?" Phoenix gives me a knowing smile, and I wonder what he has on his mind next.

26

Hazel

Phoenix and Jude. Jude and Phoenix. Two men. A sex god and a virgin. A virgin. My sweet cinnamon roll Jude is a virgin. That explains so much. Now I understand why he was always trying to be such a gentleman. Oh my god, and I told him I was going to corrupt him. Mental forehead slap, Hazel. But he didn't shy away from me, and he's certainly not shying away from Phoenix's instruction. They discussed this, so I have to assume Phoenix knows what Jude is comfortable with. Deep breaths, Hazel. Deep breaths. I wonder what they have in store for me next.

"Angel, will you stand up for us?" He's standing over me, offering his hand. I take it and stand. He offers his other hand to Jude, who does the same. I'm not sure what kind of dynamic these two men have, but I'm ready to explore it. To explore them. Together.

"Are you ready to let us take this dress off of you? The peeks I've been getting of your red lacy panties is driving me wild, and I'm ready to see the entire picture." His words make me feel sexy.

Nodding, I turn towards Jude. "Phoenix, will you unzip me?"

"With pleasure." Slowly he unzips my dress. His fingers trace down my spine as he goes, and I shiver from his touch.

"Jude, why don't you unwrap our woman like the gorgeous gift that she is." *Our.* Our woman. Well, I guess for tonight, at least, that's what I am. I'm at their mercy.

I watch Jude's nostrils flair, and his chest expands with his deep inhale. He crouches down and grabs the hem of my dress looking into my eyes. He slowly peels it up and over my arms, only losing eye contact when the dress crosses my face.

"Fuck, Angel. You really were sent from heaven just for me with this body." I can feel the heat from his eyes on my back as he roams over the matching red lace barely covering me.

"Just for *us*. She was sent for us both. Spin for us, Little Dove. Let us get a good look at all of you." I slowly spin between them, locking my eyes with Phoenix when I turn. His green eyes are almost black. His pupils are blown wide with lust. Finishing my spin, I come face to face with Jude's matching lust-blown eyes. Both men are muttering low curses and omitting growls of approval.

Looking over my shoulder, "What's the next lesson, Mr. Graves?"

"Oh, Jude, it seems we may have a teacher's pet on our hands. And to think, I thought she was a brat." He hums, brushing my hair aside to run his lips over my shoulder. "So eager to learn. Only this lesson is for Jude. Not for you, Angel. This lesson was his request."

I look up at Jude, rubbing my hands over his chest that's

heaving with barely restrained desire. "What is it that you want Phoenix to teach you?"

He places his hands on my hips, and Phoenix presses closer against my back. "I want to taste you, and I want Phoenix to teach me to make you scream. I want you to see stars. I want you to come so hard that you forget your name and only remember mine and his." I'm a fucking goner. If I weren't sandwiched between these two men, I'd be on the floor right now because my knees just gave out.

"What do you think about that, Angel? Can you be our good girl and let me teach Jude how to worship you?" Hot kisses and nips run over both sides of my neck. A noise comes out of me that can only be described as a purr.

Jude's mouth trails across my jaw and claims my lips. "Would you like that, Little Dove? Would you like both of us between your luscious thighs exploring every inch of your delectable pussy? I want to learn what makes you moan and squirm and gasp. I want so badly to hear my name on your lips when you come."

"Jude?" He hums in response. "I don't know who taught you how to talk dirty, but I hope they gave you an A+ because you just made me flood my panties."

Both men chuckle in response. "Is that a yes, Angel?"

"Take me to a bed and worship me... Holy shit! Put me down!" Phoenix spun me around and threw me over his shoulder like a rag doll. Damn. I could get used to being manhandled. Realizing that this angle has me staring directly a his butt, "On second thought, I like the view here. Carry on, Jeeves." Phoenix lightly pops me on my ass and laughs.

Jude follows us down the hall, intently watching me massage and smack Phoenix's ass. Is he watching my hands, or is he also checking out his ass? Hmm?

We walk into a bedroom, and there's no doubt it belongs to Phoenix. It's decorated in black, gray and metal. He throws me unceremoniously onto his black comforter, and I can't stop a giggle from escaping.

"Let's make her do that again." There's pure hunger in Jude's eyes.

"Do what again? Make her giggle?" Jude nods in response to Phoenix's question. "As beautiful as that sound was, I'd rather make her moan." Oh fuck yes, please do. I'm so ready to be ravished by these two men in front of me.

I sit up on the bed and gesture with my finger for Phoenix to come closer. He smiles and walks towards me, stopping when his legs hit the end of the bed. I crawl to him and lift on my knees to examine the art on his body. It's so beautiful.

"Will you turn around for me?" I haven't gotten a good look at his back tattoos yet.

"Only if you promise that won't be the last time you ever crawl for me."

I smile and nod and he turns his back to me, and it's just as impressive as his front. "You're beautiful. Why do you hide these? You can barely notice them unless your shirt is off." Not that I mind his shirt being off.

"Because I'm a teacher, even if it is just Auto Shop. I never want anyone to doubt my skills in a classroom. Officially I'm certified to teach math...but I've always preferred to work with my hands." That smirk. I hear your innuendo loud and clear, Phoenix.

"Will you lay down for us so we can get this lesson on the way?" He doesn't have to ask me twice. I crawl to the middle of the bed and lay on my back.

"Angel, will you let Jude remove your red lacy lingerie?" I look at Jude as he's licking his lips in anticipation.

"Yes, please." The bed dips on either side as they crawl toward me. Jude leans down and encases my lips with his as his hands drift to the swell of my breasts. He gives a firm squeeze, and my back arches to meet his touch.

"I want to smother myself in your glorious tits. They fit so perfectly in my hands." He gives them another squeeze before his hand's snake to the clasp on the back of my bra. I sit up slightly to give him better access, and he peels my bra off my shoulders.

Phoenix's hot mouth engulfs one of my nipples, and I moan into Jude's mouth.

"Mmm, peaches are my new favorite fruit." His tongue continues to swirl my nipple, making it pebble in his mouth.

"Phoenix?" I must have misheard him.

Jude releases my mouth and tilts my chin to face him. "Little Dove, you always smell like the most delicious peaches. It makes me want to sink my teeth into you. In fact…"

A slight jolt of pain flashes over my nipple before the pleasure of his licking tongue washes it away. It's all too much and not enough at the same time.

"Someone touch me." I don't care that I'm practically begging. I want to feel them all over me.

"Show him, Angel. Take Jude's hand and use his fingers to pleasure yourself. Show him how to rub your clit to make yourself come. Teach him."

I gently grab Jude's hand. I look deep into his eyes to ensure he wants this, too. There's no denying what he wants by the lust I see. He starts to pull our hands towards my thighs.

"Show me. Teach me, Little Dove. Give me your pleasure."

I part my legs and bring our hands lower. I gently slide his fingers through my slick folds and rub them up and down my sex. Phoenix shifts closer to my legs on the bed to watch our hands.

"Jude, she's so wet right now. Can you feel how warm and wet she is for us?"

"I can feel it." He closes his eyes and soaks in the sensation. I guide two fingers to make small circles around my clit, and we collectively moan.

"Come down here and watch what you're doing to her. It's an incredible sight." I look down and see Phoenix rubbing himself over his sweatpants.

Jude's hand leaves mine, and he positions himself lower around my legs. Once seated, he brings his hand back to mine.

"That really is an incredible sight. Let me do it, Little Dove." I remove my hand, and his fingers take over, circling my clit.

"Tongue or fingers, Angel?"

I'm so lost in the feeling of Jude's fingers I barely register Phoenix's question. "Hmm?"

"For your first orgasm. Do you want Jude's tongue or his fingers?" *Oh.*

"First?"

"Oh yes, Angel, first. There are two of us, so always expect at least two." Oh, god. Two orgasms at all times. That's a lot of pleasure.

"Jude?" I look up into his eyes. He's staring at the motion of his fingers, completely lost in his lust.

"Little Dove, I want to taste you on my lips." He licks his lips, and I almost climax right then.

"Would you like me to show you what she likes, Jude?"

141

Phoenix is as entranced as Jude is at the site of my spread open legs and the motion of Jude's fingers.

"Fuck. Goddammit. Yes." He removes his fingers from my clit, and I whimper at the chill he leaves behind.

Jude sits back and lets Phoenix position himself between my legs. My eyes roll into the back of my head at the first swipe of his tongue.

"Hooooly fuck!" When his tongue reaches my clit, sparks fly. I'm already so close from only Jude's fingers.

Pulling his mouth away and replacing it with his hands, he turns to Jude. "She likes slow circles around her clit like you did with her fingers." He demonstrated the movement to Jude with his tongue, and I groaned. "She loves it when you hum into her pussy. Suction her clit into your mouth and hum. Like this." My hips buck off the bed when he hums.

"Phoenix." My moan is breathy and needy.

"Shh, Angel. Not yet. Be our good girl, and don't come until Jude has his lips around your pretty pussy." He looks back at Jude. "She enjoys being licked like an ice cream cone from her core to her clit. That's my favorite because I get to enjoy a mouthful of her heavenly taste. But I think her favorite is when you flick her clit rapidly."

"Fuck, fuck, fuck." Between the licking and the flicking, if he doesn't stop, I will tip over the edge. He sits back on his knees and gestures to my spread legs like an offering.

"Are you ready to taste heaven?" I look at Jude and find him sitting in his gray boxer briefs, palming his massive erection. I wonder if he will let me help him out with that.

"I'm more than ready."

Phoenix moves over to give Jude room between my thighs. He starts kissing up my inner thighs until his mouth reaches my core. In one smooth move, he licks a long line up my pussy. When he reaches the top, he swirls his tongue around my clit. A feral sound erupts deep in my throat, and my hips lift off the mattress, searching for more friction.

"You're a quick fucking study, Jude. Keep that up, and she'll be coming on your tongue in no time."

He smiles and lifts away for just a moment. "That's the plan. And I was always an A+ student in school."

"Well, then, let me help you out." Jude hums, and my eyes roll into the back of my head. Phoenix leans on top of me and takes a nipple in his mouth. His hand engulfs my other breast, and he assaults my nipples again with pleasure and pain. Pinching and licking. Nipping and sucking.

"I'm gonna…I'm…I'm so close." I manage to stammer out. I grab handfuls of Phoenix and Jude's hair, encouraging them to continue what their mouths are doing.

"Jude, take two fingers and slide them inside her. Pump gently in and out and flick her clit with your tongue. That'll throw her over the edge."

Jude does as Phoenix has instructed, and I feel two thick fingers slide inside me without any resistance. I'm so wet and ready to explode. He starts to flick his tongue, and my orgasm detonates. My fingers and toes are tingling with the sensation. I can't stop my hips from riding his face as he laps up my arousal.

"Oh fuck, Jude." His name comes out as a moan, just like he wanted to hear. I pull at his hair when I become too sensitive, encouraging him to stop. As he sits up with a smug smile, Phoenix grabs his wrist.

"Can't waste any of this." He brings Jude's fingers to his mouth and sucks my come off until they are clean.

"Holy. Shit," slips through Jude's lips as his eyes roll back into his head.

"That's one, Angel. You ready to let Jude learn where your g-spot is?"

"I think I need a minute. I can't feel my legs." I laugh and stare at the ceiling. There is so much to process about what just happened. They both had their mouths on me at the same time. My breasts. My pussy. Wait. Popping up, I look at these two sexy men in front of me. I've got an idea.

I look between the two of them. "My turn?"

27

Jude

"My turn?" she says. The mischievous smile on her face has me wondering what she's thinking until her eyes roam over both of our erections, straining our respective bottoms. My cock jumps in response to her attention.

"Angel, tonight is all about you, not us. We can handle ourselves."

"Well, if it's all about me, what if *I* want to suck your cocks? Shouldn't I get to do what I want to do?"

I look at Phoenix because I'm in uncharted waters. She's made a valid point. This very sexy, confident woman lying before us is asking to suck our cocks. While we absolutely can take care of ourselves, what if we didn't have to?

"Well, boys. What do you say? Will you let me have my turn to worship you?" She's sitting in the middle of the bed, looking at us like we're her next meal. Her index finger is dragging along her bottom lip, drawing my attention to her mouth. I imagine her full, swollen pink lips would feel like nirvana wrapped around my dick. I can almost see the damp spot on my boxers where I'm leaking pre-cum.

"Alright, naughty girl. If that's what you want." He pauses to look at me. "Jude, stand up. Angel, get on your knees and take Jude's boxers off."

"Yes, Mr. Graves." She says in her most seductive voice. Phoenix growls at her. Lost in thought with what's about to happen, I'm frozen to my spot on the bed.

"Jude. Stand up." Phoenix's tone leaves no room for disobedience.

"Yes, Mr. Graves." I mimic back to him what I just heard Hazel say. His eyes snap to mine, and I see a flash of heat before he turns his attention back to Hazel. I swear I hear him mutter "brats" under his breath.

Standing in front of my goddess on her knees, she grabs the elastic on my boxers and slowly peels them off me. My cock springs free and bounces off my stomach. Hazel gasps, and I look down to see her eyes wide and hands clasped over her mouth.

"Jude, you've been keeping even more secrets." Hazel takes hold of me and gives my cock one long stroke from root to tip, stopping when her hand reaches my Prince Albert. She swirls my pre-cum around my piercing with her thumb, and I let out a throaty groan. Her small hands feel euphoric wrapped around me.

"This is a very pleasant surprise, naughty boy. Care to explain yourself." My mind is blank as she continues to stroke me.

Phoenix laughs under his breath before speaking up. "He lost a bet in college. But that's a story for another time."

"Okay, another time then. It's my turn to taste you, Jude." That's the only warning I get before she dives onto my cock, taking half of me in her mouth at once. She hums along my shaft as her tongue teases the head of my cock. I jerk my hips back and pull out of her mouth.

"Little Dove, if I have any chance of enjoying this and not blowing my load down your throat in 10 seconds, I'm going to need you to slow down." I hear Phoenix chuckling again at my expense.

"No." No? One word. That's all she said. With one hand at the base of my shaft and the other sliding up my thigh to cup my balls, she puts me back in her mouth, somehow deeper than the first time. I feel my piercing hit the back of her throat and moan out in pleasure. Her mouth is hot and the pressure she's using to suck me is making my toes curl.

"God fucking dammit. Phoenix, help me out here. Distract her or something. Give me a second to breathe." Hazel is relentlessly bobbing on my cock and tugging my balls. I can feel the tingling begin at the base of my spine.

"Sorry, Jude. You're on your own. I'm enjoying the show." Asshole.

Placing my hands in her hair I give a little tug at her roots, eliciting a moan. "FUCK! Little Dove, please just slow down for one minute. Please. I want to enjoy your talented mouth. Just one minute." I'm begging, and I'm unashamed. Her mouth is incredible.

"You have 30 seconds." Finally, she continues to slide her hands up and down my shaft, but I have a moment to breathe.

A few deep breaths later she exclaims, "Times up," and her hot mouth surrounds me again. I only last another two minutes before my balls start to draw in.

"Little Dove, I'm about to come. If you don't want to swallow, you better let go now." With a long suck and a hum, she seals her fate. Hot ropes of my come fill her mouth. She swallows it all as I moan my pleasure, her name on my lips. When she starts to stand, Phoenix grabs her by the shoulders and spins her to face him.

He gets inches from her mouth and growls, "Good girl," before dipping his tongue into her mouth for a kiss. A kiss that undoubtedly still tastes like my come, and he doesn't care. It almost looks like he's trying to taste me through her. My semi-erect cock twitches at the sight.

"Your turn," she breathes into his mouth. Once again, she sinks to her knees, and it's such a beautiful sight. This woman wants to please us for her own pleasure. She removes his sweatpants, and he steps out of them. He's long and thick, and she looks up at him through her eyelashes as she slowly licks up one side of his shaft and then the other. She swirls her tongue around his tip and then up and down his slit. I notice her thighs rub together as she takes him fully in her mouth. I drop down next to her.

"Open your knees for me, Little Dove, and let me give your pussy the attention it's yearning for." She spreads her knees, and I trail my fingers down the front of her body until they slide between her soaked pussy. I make lazy circles around her clit while she licks and sucks at Phoenix's cock. Their eyes are locked as he moans with pleasure. Threading his hands through her hair, he guides her mouth to move how he likes it. His eyes shift to mine, and he catches me watching their exchange.

"Do you want another lesson, naughty boy? Do you want to learn?" Hazel stops her actions and releases him with a pop. Her eyes find mine, both of us with shocked expressions from his question.

He grabs my chin to look back up at him. "Be a good boy and answer my question, Jude. There's no wrong answer."

Jesus fuck. He just called me a good boy, making my stomach flutter and my cock twitch. I look into his eyes, trying to find the answer to his question. Do I want to put my mouth on my best friend's dick? I look into Hazel's eyes, feeling like I need her permission. She gives me the slightest nod of encouragement or acceptance. Either way, it was the push I needed.

Looking back into Phoenix's eyes, I nod slowly, "Yes, Mr. Graves, I'd like to learn." A growl comes from deep in his throat at my response. He runs his hand through my hair and turns my head to face Hazel.

"Teach him, Angel." There's a command in his tone and it sends a shiver up my spine.

Hazel takes my wrist from her pussy and guides my hand to his shaft. Wrapping it around, she places her small hand around mine, pumping us up and down his length.

"Let me show you how to please him." My cheeks heat, and she repeats her earlier ministries. Using her tongue, she licks one side of his cock, encouraging me to do the same on the other. I hesitate, and she drops a hand to my chest.

"You don't have to do anything you aren't comfortable with, Jude." But that's just it. I'm not uncomfortable. This feels right, but I'm expecting it to feel wrong. I'm waiting for a feeling that doesn't come.

I look up at Phoenix. My hand never stopped stroking his cock. I lean in and take my first tentative swipe with my tongue. He feels velvety smooth. I explore his length with my mouth. Phoenix's eyes never leave me as I take him fully in my mouth for the first time. I take him in until my face is flush with his pubic bone and I'm forced to breathe through my nose. I pull back and swallow him in again.

"Holy fucking shit, you can deep throat." Hazel's voice drips with enthusiasm and awe.

Phoenix grabs my hair with a groan and starts pumping into my mouth. "Good. Fucking. Boy." Every word is pronounced by a thrust of his hips. Fuck, those words do things to me and I want to pleasure him more to hear his praise.

Next to me, Hazel whimpers. She's squirming with desire. I reach down and start rubbing her clit again and let Phoenix take complete control of his pleasure from me. The room is a cacophony of moaning and panting.

"Fuck Jude, I'm about to come. What do you want me to do?" I reach up and squeeze his balls how I like it. "Okay then. Get ready." A few more pumps and he comes with a roar down my throat. He tastes thick and salty, and I swallow it all, basking in my accomplishment of making Phoenix come. When I pull away from him, Hazel grabs my cheeks and pulls me in for a soul-crushing kiss, devouring me and undoubtedly tasting Phoenix.

"Move to the bed," Phoenix commands into our ears. All three of us move into the middle of the bed. "Let's teach you your final lesson, Jude. Let's find her G-spot."

With Hazel lying between us, Phoenix starts rubbing her clit and tells me to insert my middle finger inside her.

"What am I looking for?" I know she feels warm and tight and her noises tell me she's enjoying what we are doing, but I want to give her maximum pleasure.

"I'll show you." He reaches his opposite hand down and

slips his middle finger inside with mine, both of our palm facing up.

Hazel gasps. "Are you both inside me?"

"We are, Angel." He smiles at her.

"Jude, do you feel this spot right under your finger that's a little different? Maybe a little rougher than the silkiness of the rest of her inner walls?"

"I do." I feel what he's talking about, and Hazel's breath changes in response to our touch.

"Good. We're going to scissor that spot together with our fingers, and I want you to suck on her clit. Let's make Hazel scream.

Within minutes she's panting, telling us she was going to come and chanting our names. Not only did she come, but she squirted, leaving our hands dripping with her arousal.

"Holy shit, Little Dove. That was beautiful. Did you know you could do that?"

Shaking her head, "I didn't do that, you both did."

"And that's two." Phoenix kisses her on the forehead, telling her what a good girl she is, and praises her while I get a warm cloth to clean all of us up. This is definitely a night I won't forget.

28

Hazel

"…what do you think, Mom?"

"Hmm?" Oh right. "Sorry, Wynnie. I was lost in thought there for a second." Lost would be an understatement. I hope my cheeks aren't flushed. I've spent the last week in continuous flashbacks of the best night of my entire life. Two men, two orgasms, piercings, blowjobs. *Sigh.* There's no doubt my cheeks are pink now.

"You okay there, bestie?" Bitch. She knows I'm not okay. I want to wipe that knowing grin off her face.

"Yeah, I'm good. What were you asking, Wynnie?" *Get your brain out of the gutter. You're out with your kid.*

"I was hoping we could spend the weekend at Grandma and Grandpa's house soon. I really miss Nora. Maybe I could even spend spring break there?" She's looking at me with such hope and a longing that I remember all too well from my late teenage years.

I'm sure she misses her friend. We've been here about two

months now and haven't been back to the place she called home for her entire life.

"Of course. We can look at our schedules and see when we can make time. Your games start soon, so making a weekend trip might be a little difficult, but I'll talk to them about spring break."

"Where are we going for lunch?" Dellah asks over her coffee cup. The three of us decided we needed a girl's day. We are currently sitting at a mismatched table and chairs in The Book Beanery. They love it as much as I did when Jude first brought me here. Like me, Wynnie loves the smell of books, but Dellah gravitated toward the coffee bar and the myriad of delicious looking pastries.

"Aunt Dellah, we're having breakfast, and you're already thinking of lunch?"

She puts her hand on Wynnie's shoulder. "Oh, my darling niece. You have so much to learn about your Aunt Dellah. Where we eat lunch determines what I can order to drink. What I can drink determines whether I shop more before or after lunch. Uncle Collin made me promise I wouldn't swipe my card if I had more than two drinks. Buuuut, if we have Mexican for lunch, I can order two margaritas that are the size of my head and still be within his shopping stipulations."

She wiggles her eyes at Wynnie, and Wynnie returns it with an eye roll. "You skate along the lines, Aunt Dells."

"It's the best way to live! Can we have Mexican for lunch, Mommy dearest?" She's looking at me with puppy dog eyes batting her eyelashes. Now it's my turn to give Dellah an eye roll.

"Eat your muffin, *child*. Be on your best behavior, and maybe you can get a reward at lunch." We all laugh as she pouts like the petulant adult child that she is.

"Fine." She takes another look around, taking in all the quirks that make this store absolutely adorable. "This place is great. I can't believe Jude found it and took you here."

"Who's Jude?" *Don't panic, don't panic. Don't. Panic.* Dellah has a deer in headlights look on her face when she realizes her slip-up. I haven't told Wynnie about dating one of her softball coaches, let alone both. Does she know Coach S's first name is Jude?

"Oh, um. He's an old friend who took me here for coffee a few weeks ago." Quick, I need a subject change. Shopping. "Where do you want to start first today? Didn't you need a new pair of sneakers?"

She gives me a skeptical look. I am not playing this off well. "Sure, Mom, let's go to the shoe store first."

"Yay, shoes." Dellah squeals loudly and starts clapping and bouncing in her seat. Thank goodness for embarrassing best friends because she's distracted Wynnie from the topic of Jude.

The next several hours were spent shopping, drinking giant margaritas, and more shopping. By early afternoon my preteen is tired of our antics and asks to go home.

"Are you suuuuure you don't want to get a pedicure with your favorite aunt?" Dellah whines at Wynnie.

"Dells, let the girl have some time away from your crazy ass. Don't you think you've scarred her enough for one day?" She scoffs at me.

"I'll have you know I'm awesome to hang out with, but fine, let's take her home. But I still want my pedicure."

Snickering, I side-eye her. "Yes, dear, you've been a good girl and can get your reward." She smacks my shoulder.

"Ouch! Always so violent. I'm driving, Bitch."

"And you both wonder why I'm ready to go home." An exasperated huff leaves Wynnie's lips, followed by an eye roll.

"Damn!"

"What's up?" Dellah looks concerned about my outburst.

"My oil light just came on."

"Oh, Collin is home. If you want to switch cars when we drop off Wynnie, he can check it out for you."

"It's okay. I can just call Ph…actually, that sounds great." I check the rearview mirror. It's a good thing Wynnie has her headphones in. Two slip-ups in one day would definitely make her even more suspicious.

"I'll text him and let him know."

We drop off Wynnie and switch cars, and with a wave and a promise from Collin that he will check on my car and keep an ear out if Wynnie needs anything, we're off to get pedicures. We end up at one of the fancy nail salons that serve wine, and since I'm not driving, Dellah tells me to indulge myself. Who am I to argue?

"You're my favorite bestie, bestie." My window is rolled down, and my hand is surfing in the wind. I may have had several glasses of wine during our pedicure, but they kept offering, and Dellah kept telling them yes. "My toes are sooooo pretty."

"Bitch, I better be your only bestie. Don't make me go all Xena Warrior Princess on another woman. I don't like to share my favorite people." I love when she gets possessive of our friendship.

"Awe, you know I love you." I lean across the center console to give her a sloppy kiss on the cheek. She intercepts me and pushes me away, swerving the wheel a bit in the process.

"Okay, Hazy Dazy, it's time to tuck you in bed. You're getting a little too handsy for me." We both burst into laughter, that quickly fades when we see flashing red and blue lights behind us.

"Ohhhh, you're in trouble now, Dells."

"Be quiet, sit there, and act sober before you get us arrested." I smash my lips together and suppress a giggle. She pulls over, and we patiently wait for the officer to approach her car.

"Good evening, ladies. License and registration, please." Dellah hands him her documents. "Do you know why I pulled you over... Ms. McLain?" He reads her last name off her license.

"Not sure, Officer."

"Ms. McLain, I observed you swerve over the lines about a mile back. Is everything alright?" He's checking over her cards as he's speaking to her. I'm sitting quietly, trying to be one with the seat.

"Oh, I'm sorry, Officer..." He leans in a bit so she can read his name tag. "Harmon. We were just having a little too much fun on our girl's day. I laughed too hard, and my hand slipped on the wheel. It was an accident. I'm so sorry."

He leans his hands into the open window frame to look in my direction. "Everything okay, Miss?"

My intoxicated paranoia has me staring at my hands, and I start rambling. "Yes, Officer. Everything is fine. My wonderful friend is driving us home. I had a little too much to drink. She didn't have anything. I promise. I'm the one who drank too much. We were joking around—" I abruptly stopped talking.

All the air leaves my lungs when I take my first look at the man standing at Dellah's window. Not just the man but specifically his forearm. The blood drains from my face, my heart beats out of my chest, and my stomach bottoms out. I'm suddenly very sober. My chin drops to my chest, and I slump lower into my seat. I can't say another word through the lump in my throat. Dellah shoots me a quizzical glance.

"Alright, ladies, you be more careful, please, and have a nice night." He leaves us and Dellah puts her hands on top of mine. My hands shake, and my clasped knuckles are white from my tight grasp. My chest is heaving up and down forcefully. I feel like I can't breathe.

"Hazel, what's wrong?" Her voice is laced with concern.

"Just drive." I manage to get out in a barely there whisper. This can't be happening. I saw it wrong. It's been so long that I must not remember it right. But there's no way I forgot.

Despite her questioning looks and attempts to talk to me, I stay silent the rest of the drive home. She parks in the driveway and turns off the car. Turning her body to me and grabbing my hands again, she waits until I look at her.

"Okay, Hazel. Tell me what's wrong. What happened back there?"

My voice was barely a whisper. "Did you see his arm? His tattoo?"

Her brows furrow. "His tattoo? No. Why, what was it? What spooked you so badly?"

"Hatter." One word. That's all that could escape my lips before I felt like the world was caving in on me. My vision starts to darken around me, and the air feels thick.

"Breathe, Hazel. BREATHE!" Dellah's voice sounds like it's coming through a tunnel in my ears. No matter how hard I inhale, I can't get any air into my lungs.

I rip my hands from hers and get out of the car. The cool

night air hits me, and I'm able to take my first deep breath. I'm leaned over with my hands on my knees when Dellah comes behind me and starts rubbing my back.

"That's it. Keep taking deep breaths. Did you say what I think you said? Are you sure? It's been almost 13 years. Could you be wrong?"

Wrong. Oh, god, how I wish I were wrong. Plain as day on his forearm, just as it had been that night, was the Mad Hatter's hat, a playing card, and a pocket watch.

"It was him, Dellah. It... it was..." I can't even say it out loud.

"Officer Harmon is Wynnie's father," she finishes for me.

"What am I going to do? He's a police officer in this town. There's no way I can avoid him for the rest of her life."

Oh god. I've always been honest with Wynnie about the circumstances of her conception. When she was little, I told her she was made from love. When she was old enough to understand, which has only been a few years, I told her about the dashing young man who swept me off my feet for one night and the wonderful miracle I received from that night. Her. It's never been a big deal for her not to have a father. My dad was involved and has always been enough of a male presence for her. But now, he's here. My Hatter, Wynnie's father, is here. The college that Dellah went to, that he went to, is only an hour away, so it's not unreasonable for him to be here. But it's not something I even considered when moving back.

She grabs my shoulders and straightens me up. Looking me square in the eyes, she says, "What are we going to do, you ask? We will do what our female DNA has taught us to do. We will be internet sleuths and find every possible piece of information we can find online about Officer Harmon, starting with his first name. And then we will go from there. One step at a time." I nod in response.

Okay, I can do that. One step at a time. He's here, and I will have to do something about that, but not this second. First research, then panic.

29

Hazel

Malcolm Harmon. Better known as Mac. 33 years old. Unmarried. Seemingly single. At least there's no mention of another woman on any of his social medias. It appears he's been a police officer since he graduated college.

I've had this overwhelming feeling of guilt since seeing him. I thought the panic would come, but instead, it's this lead brick in my stomach. For 12 years, I've kept this man from knowing his daughter. I've kept my daughter from knowing her father. I'm such a terrible parent. It was a one night stand with a guy I never expected to see again.

Dellah keeps reassuring me that I've done nothing wrong, but I have. I could have gone back to the house where the party was. I could have asked around. He has a memorable tattoo. Someone would have known him. But I didn't. I chose to have and raise this baby, our baby, my beautiful Rowyn, alone.

I'm struggling. The guys have asked me several times over the past week to get together, and I keep making excuses. I'm sure they think I'm avoiding them after our amazing night together. I've even been staying in the car when I've picked Wynnie up from practice. Unfortunately, that isn't the case tonight. Tonight, Friday, a non-practice day, there is a mandatory parent meeting before the official start of games for the season.

I reluctantly leave my car and head to the bleachers to find a place to sit among the other parents. I waited until the last minute so they couldn't corner me before it started. They've done nothing wrong. I can't shake the terrible feelings that have washed over me, and I don't want to bring them down with me.

They spot me as soon as I arrive, and when I find a seat, I feel my phone buzz in my pocket. Two texts in our group chat.

Jude: Little Dove, you look beautiful.

Phoenix: Angel, I'm so glad to see you. I've missed your sexy face.

If I'm completely honest with myself, I've missed them, too. Their morning texts still make me smile every day, but my responses have been dwindling, and it's just another thing for me to feel guilty about. I look up and see them gazing at me. I give them a smile and a small nod. Phoenix picks up his phone, and I see him texting before my phone vibrates again.

Phoenix: Please talk to us, Angel. Come over. Meet us for coffee. Whatever you'd like. We want to fix whatever we did wrong.

Fix what they did wrong? Ugh. I really am terrible. How could I let them think they've done something to upset me? It's the complete opposite. I know they could make me feel better, but I don't deserve it for what I've done to Mac and Wynnie. I could confide in them. Or I could get lost in them and let them take these feelings away for a little while.

Me: I'm so sorry. You haven't done anything wrong. My life has been a little crazy. I can come over.

Jude and Phoenix have already started the meeting, but I see Jude check his phone quickly, and he glances my way and smiles.

The meeting ends, and under the guise of needing to speak to the coaches, I hang around until the crowd of parents clears. Approaching them, I ask, "Can I speak to you in your office?"

"Of course, Ms. Gibson. Follow us." Jude's warm voice is like a soothing balm to the raging storm in my stomach. I have really missed them.

I follow them to the office, and their hands are on me as soon as the door closes. Jude grabs my cheeks, and Phoenix comes up behind me and takes my hips in his hands. My eyes close as I take in the warmth of their embraces and their combined scents of citrus and metal.

"Oh, Little Dove. What's going on in that pretty little head of yours? It's been two weeks since we've seen you. You've had us worried."

"Were we too much for you, Angel? Things got a little intense. We're so sorry."

162

"No. No, I promise it wasn't you. Either of you." I can't get into this right now. Not in their office, but I need to reassure them we are okay. I lean back into Phoenix, and he wraps his arms around me.

"Come over. Come talk to us. Please." Jude seals his request with a gentle kiss. It's just a brush of his lips—almost a plea to accept his invitation. Behind me, Phoenix is nuzzling his nose into my hair. I already feel better.

"Let me text Wynnie and Dellah to confirm everyone is okay if I go out."

"Whatever you need to do, Angel." They release me, and I grab my phone to send my texts.

Me: Hey kiddo. Meeting went well. Can't wait for the season to start. You good if I go out with some friends for a couple of hours?

Wynnie: Yes Mom, I'm not your mother. <eye roll emoji> Have fun. Use protection ;) Love ya.

Me: Oh god. You're grounded from hanging out with your Aunt. Love you, too.

Me: Dellah! You're grounded from seeing your niece. She just told me to use protection. I'm going out with the guys. Keep an ear out for Wynnie for me, please.

Bestie: Sounds like good advice to me. <shrugging emoji> Have fun. Bring the rain gear ;)

Me: OMG. You're dead to me. Love ya and thanks.

"Okay, I'm free. I'll meet you at your house?" They respond with smiles.

Arriving at their house, I'm much less nervous than the last time I was here. The guys haven't arrived yet. They texted me and said they would stop and grab us some Chinese food. I'm glad to have these few minutes to sit and decide how much I'll share with them. We haven't been together long, but I feel a connection with them that I've never felt before.

All the things that we've done together. The things that *they* did together. Wow. They told me they'd never done anything like this before, but they are so comfortable together that I wonder if there's something between them.

Oh my god, we should probably have a conversation about things like birth control and limits. It's been so long since I've had to think about this kind of stuff. *One thing at a time, Hazel. You're spiraling.* They might not even want to see you after they hear about your baby daddy drama. And bring on the guilt again.

Deep breaths. You can only fix one thing at a time. I close my eyes and lean my head back on the headrest. A few minutes later, Phoenix's truck pulls up. Before I can do it myself, Jude opens my door and extends his hand.

"I was worried you might not have been here, Little Dove. I'm so glad I was wrong." He pulls me into his and wraps his arms around me. I lean into his chest and embrace the warmth of his hug. Once again, I feel the stress melt away a little.

"Are you hungry? We picked up a little of everything." Phoenix rounds his truck and approaches us with two bags stuffed with boxes and containers of food."

"Starved." And I am. Physically and emotionally. I've put my emotions through the blender this week, and I'm ready to float away with them and escape for a few hours. I can be a terrible mess tomorrow. Right now I want to be a goddess, worshiped by these two sexy men.

"Good. Let's sit and eat, and maybe we can talk about what's on your mind. You've had us concerned, Angel."

Phoenix wasn't kidding when he said they got a little of everything. As we spread the boxes across the table, I sigh in contentment with all of the comfort foods I'm about to consume.

"Will you talk to us? We want to help you however we can." Jude has a crease between his eyebrows, accentuating his concern.

I'm not even sure where to start. How far back should I go? Do I just rip off the band aid, reader's digest version, start from the very beginning?

I close my eyes. "It's been a roller coaster of a week. Last weekend…" Just do it, Hazel. I open my eyes and look at each of them before continuing. "How much do you want to know?"

"Whatever you're willing to share. We don't want you to feel uncomfortable, but we want to be here for you." Phoenix passes me a box with noodles, and I shake my head.

"Okay, how does the beginning sound?"

"Sounds wonderful, Angel."

I gave them quick details about my one night stand at Dellah's college and how I didn't know his name or any other information about him. Finding out I was pregnant and moving away to my aunt's house. How I worked up to my LPN license, and what brought Wynnie and me back here. They listen in silence and let me give them as much or as little details as I feel comfortable with.

"Then last weekend." What I say next will probably change everything. Jude grabs my hands, sensing my hesitation.

"What are you worried about? I can see the turmoil in your

165

eyes." He rubs small comforting circles on the palm of my hands.

"What I say next might make you see me differently. I'm afraid to lose whatever this is that's starting between us." I gesture between the three of us. "I haven't felt this safe and cherished...ever." Jude squeezes my hand, and Phoenix gives me a warm smile. Moving his chair closer, Phoenix takes one hand from Jude so they each hold onto me.

"Hazel, look at me." I turn to face Phoenix.

"We won't judge you. Yes, what we have is new, but we both feel the connection with you. What we did last time you were here takes trust. Trust that you gave us. Trust that we would do anything within our power not to break."

"About that." I look sheepishly between them. "What the two of you did. Together. Is that something you do often?"

They exchange a glance. "Never. We've never done anything like that before. But we can discuss that after you tell us what's bothering you. What happened, Angel?"

Nodding, I start again. "Last weekend Dellah and I got pulled over." They both squeeze my hands but don't say anything. "I had too much wine, and she was driving us home. We were goofing off, and she swerved a little. The officer came to the car, and I didn't notice at first, but then I did." I stopped to take a much needed breath, trying to tamp down the panic that wanted to rise.

"Noticed what, Little Dove." Okay, here goes.

"The cop. It was... he was, is...Wynnie's father. The guy from the college party."

I can't stop it. The tears start to fall. I pulled my hands from theirs and covered my face. The guilt and shame rush in again like a tidal wave pulling me back into the ocean.

166

"Hazel?" No Phoenix. Please don't use my name. Call me Angel. I'm your Angel. Here it comes.

I give him a muffled "yes" through my hands.

"How do you know it was her father? You said you didn't get his name. You were drinking. Could you be wrong?"

Unconsciously I drop my hands and start rubbing my forearm, shaking my head in response.

"No. It was him. He has a very distinct tattoo. I'd never forget it." Hands back on my face, I start rambling. "I'm such a terrible person. How could I do such a horrible thing? I've ruined their lives. God, I'm such a mess."

Someone's hands come up to mine, gently pulling them away from my face and placing them on my lap. Jude cups my cheeks while Phoenix makes small circles on my wrists.

"Shh, Little Dove. It's alright. It's going to be okay." They haven't kicked me out yet. That's a good sign so far.

"I've made such a mess of this situation. Do you want me to leave? I'll understand if you do. This is a lot, and you don't have to be involved."

"Hey, let us help you figure it out. We are here for you. Please don't leave," Jude pleads. He looks to Phoenix, who nods in reassurance, squeezing my hands. "What can we do?"

30

Hazel

"Can you...distract me? I want to forget about this for just a little while. I want to not feel this consuming guilt."

The edge of Phoenix's lip curls up. "Oh, naughty girl, you want us to distract you from your thoughts?" His fingers slowly slide up my arms. I stare deeply into his green eyes, trying to convey how much I want their distraction right now.

"Please." The temperature in the room heats up from my single word. Still cupping my cheeks, Jude brings me in for a fierce kiss. His tongue dances on my lips, needing to be inside my mouth. I open to allow him entrance, and he consumes me.

"Let's move to the couch." Phoenix purrs in my ear. His hands move to my hips and squeeze to get me to stand. Guiding him backward, Jude doesn't release his lips from mine until his legs hit the couch. He breaks away to sit down, taking me with him to straddle his lap before returning to our kissing. Phoenix sits beside us on the couch, touching his thigh to mine. I feel someone's hands brush the hem of my shirt to remove it.

"Wait." All movement stops. "I want answers first."

"Answers to what, naughty girl?" I look down at Phoenix's hand rubbing my thigh, brushing Jude's leg at the same time.

"That. That, right there." I point to his roaming hands on our legs. "You said you've never done anything like that before, but you act so naturally about it. So casual as if you've always done it."

"We were roommates our freshman year of college, and we've been best friends ever since. It's been almost ten years of knowing each other. We aren't strangers to seeing each other's bodies." Phoenix shoots Jude a look laced with heat.

"I told you I grew up in a very religious family, Little Dove. I was never allowed to explore myself sexually and was taught not to lie with another man. As I got older, I lost faith in the things I was taught to believe, so I went off on my own to college. My parents weren't happy but understood I needed to make my own decisions. Phoenix helped me a lot in college to break the religious bonds I had learned and seek out the life I wanted. I think deep down that I've always wanted to test all aspects of my sexuality, but a small part of me carried that guilt from what I was taught growing up. When we were exploring you, when I was learning what you liked, I wanted to see what I liked, too."

I cupped one hand to his cheek and the other over his heart. "Thank you for sharing that part of you, Jude. That was beautiful."

"It was the piercings for me," came Phoenix's gruff voice

over my shoulder.

"Piercings? Oh, the bet. You definitely owe me that explanation, too."

"The bet." Phoenix chuckles and shakes his head. Jude closes his eyes, cheeks turning pink.

"Tell me." I'm eager to hear how my cinnamon roll virgin has a Prince Albert piercing. "Wait, piercings. With an S? As in plural. Did I miss something?" I look between the two men.

"No, Angel. Did you already forget my nipple piercings that you seem to love so much?"

"Oh, right. I didn't realize they were a part of the same bet. I just figured my sexy, tattooed man liked his metal." I wink and run my hands across his shirt, swiping a nipple.

He growls and grabs my wrist. "Careful, Angel, or you won't get all the answers you're looking for."

"Okay. Piercings. Tell me." I hear Jude groan as he drops his head to the back of the couch.

"Pretty, please." I grind my hips a little on Jude's lap. His hands grab my waist, and he groans again for a completely different reason.

Phoenix grabs the back of my neck and turns my face towards him. "Are you trying to be a brat and earn yourself a spanking?"

Biting my lower lip, I shake my head, "No, Mr. Graves." He drops his mouth to mine and bites my lower lip.

"Naughty girl, this is your last warning. If you want your answers, you better stop taunting me and grinding on Jude's cock. Do you understand? And before you answer, don't be sassy. Just nod yes or no. Do you understand?" I nod.

"Good girl." Oh god, what those two words do to me.

Still laying with his eyes closed, head on the couch Jude begins. "It was a bet and then a double down." I hear him mutter "so stupid" under his breath. "Beginning of junior year of college, Phoenix got a little wild. He was drinking a lot. His grades were suffering, and I was getting worried about him. One night, things…got out of hand. Bets were always our thing. I'll bet you a pizza if you pass the Comm test. I'll bet you a tank of gas if you can get that girl's phone number. It was how we incentivized ourselves and had some fun. I knew I had to do something extreme to get him to focus and quit all his bullshit.

"So you bet him a dick piercing?" I ask in shock.

Phoenix jumps in. "No, actually that was the double down part. He bet me that if I could stay sober for the rest of the fall semester, he would get his nipples pierced. I doubled down and said that if I stayed sober for the rest of the *school year*, I'd pierce my nipples, and he would get to pick the dick piercing of his choice."

"Of course, I agreed because who would have thought this guy could go eight months without a drink? Christmas, New Year, both of our birthdays, nothing. He drank nothing until the day Junior year ended. After our final exams, he took me straight to a tattoo parlor, and we conceded to our bets. Then, with our fresh piercings, we went to the bar and got shitfaced."

"Wow, Phoenix, that's some dedication to the cause." He shrugs.

"It was his fault." Phoenix shoots Jude a look that I can't describe, and Jude looks back in shock.

"My fault. What did I do?"

"You kissed me," Phoenix says plainly. Jude's eyes go wide,

and he stops breathing.

"Wait, what? I thought you had never done anything before. I want details. Jude, give me details."

He looks at Phoenix, and his voice is a whisper. "I thought you were too drunk to remember." Phoenix brushes a piece of Jude's messy blonde hair off his forehead. It's such a tender move.

"I thought you wanted to forget. So I never brought it up. I assumed you took advantage of the opportunity because you didn't think I'd remember it. I always thought you'd ask me about it, but you never did."

"Oh my god, you guys. That's so amazingly sweet. But I'm gonna be selfish. You're going to make me cry, and that's not exactly the distraction I need. But, I need to know what made you choose a Prince Albert, Jude."

"When I realized that this asshole was probably going to win the bet, I did my research. Studies say Prince Alberts give a woman the most pleasure." My mouth forms an "O" shape, and my eyes trail down to his bulge growing under me.

"I was in the room when he had it done." Phoenix looks Jude in the eyes. "He made me hold his hand. When he screamed like a girl," Jude punches him in the shoulder, and he smiles, "something inside me stirred a little. I felt protective of him but I brushed it off. Thought maybe it was just indigestion." He laughs, and Jude punches him again.

"You brought it out in us, Little Dove. Now if you don't have any more questions, I'd like to ravish you." He flexes the hands on my waist, and I shift a little to rub against him.

"I'll allow it."

"Oh, you'll do more than allow it," Phoenix growls. "You'll take what we give you, and you'll enjoy the fuck out of it." He sinks his teeth into the spot where my shoulder meets my neck. It's the most delicious pleasure, and it shoots a spark of desire right to my clit. He follows it with a lick to soothe the pain. "Can we remove this shirt now?"

"Only if you remove yours as well." Both men do the sexy 'one hand behind their head' move to take off their shirts. How can taking off a shirt be so hot? "Have I told you lately I love when you're topless?"

"The feeling is mutual, Little Dove." He slowly removed my shirt, and Phoenix made quick work of my bra.

Jude palms both of my breasts, thumbs grazing over my nipples. Phoenix grabs my hair at the base of my skull, pulling. My back arches into Jude's hand, and he squeezes my breasts harder.

"Stand," Phoenix commands, accentuating it with a tug of my hair. I fulfill his request, and he slowly removes my shoes, leggings, and panties, leaving them in the growing discarded clothes pile on the floor.

"You remember the rule of orgasms, right, Angel?" Oh god. Who could forget? Two of them means two orgasms for me, always.

"Two for two," I breathe out.

"Good girl. Now, take off Jude's pants. Leave his boxers on. He's not ready for all of you yet." I kneel on the ground and do as I'm told. "Now, sit back down on top of him." I sit down, relishing in the feel of Jude's hard cock nestled between my thighs. All that stands between him and me is a thin piece of fabric.

"Now, I want you to ride him. Give him a taste of what it will be like when he finally gets to sink inside your sweet pussy." His dirty words commanding us around make me impossibly wet.

"Oh fuck yes," Jude murmurs beneath me. His hands are guiding my hips back and forth, slowly drawing out his pleasure using my body. A wet spot forms on his boxers, and I have a feeling it's not just from me.

Phoenix moves closer to us on the couch and kisses my neck. He smooths a hand gently across my collarbone, between my breasts, across my stomach and lands on my engorged clit. He starts making slow circles, and Jude and I both moan in pleasure. Looking down at his hand, I see the reasoning for Jude's reaction. The circles Phoenix's fingers are making on my clit, are also rubbing Jude's cock. He's pleasuring both of us at the same time.

The sight of Jude's pleasure and the feeling of Phoenix's hand, combined with my rocking hips between both men, has me dancing on the edge of an orgasm already.

"I'm close. Don't stop." I'm panting as we continue to grind against each other.

Phoenix leans into Jude's ear. "Are you going to be our good boy and come for us, too?"

Jude turns his head to face Phoenix. Their faces are inches apart. Both of their eyes are hooded, pupils blown with lust. I see the silent war going on in their minds.

"Do it," I whisper. As if my two words were the permission they were waiting for, they closed the gap between their mouths. Their tongues battle for dominance, and the sight of them kissing is the last push I need before I scream their names in an earth-shattering orgasm. My spasming sets off Jude. He pulls away from Phoenix's mouth and buries his face into my neck, muttering fuck into my hair.

"Angel, you just made Jude come in his pants like a 15 year

old boy," he teases.

Leaning in to kiss him, "I'm pretty sure you had something to do with that as well." He smiles into our kiss, humming his approval.

"Can we teach Jude another lesson? I need you to trust me, though."

"If Jude is up for it. I trust you." He has a glint of mischief in his eyes.

"Good girl. I need you to climb off the couch so Jude can lie on his back." I love how he conducts us like we are his puppets, and he's our master.

"Now, here's where your trust comes in. I want you to sit on his face." I open my mouth to speak up, and he silences me with a finger to my lips. "Before you object, I promise you he can handle it. And don't talk down about yourself. I can see the apprehension in your eyes."

"But I don't want to suffocate him. And not talking down about myself, just a fact, these thighs aren't exactly made to be earmuffs." That earns me a chuckle.

"Jude, are you worried about suffocating?"

"No, but I hope I drown," Jude smirks and licks his lips.

"Trust us. If you don't like it, or you aren't comfortable, you can stop. It's always your choice." Phoenix's words are calming and reassuring.

"Okay, but Jude, tap my thighs three times if you need me to get off of you, alright?"

"Alright, Little Dove. Tap three times. Now get that sweet pussy over here and sit on my face." Climbing onto his chest, he hooks his arms around my knees and hauls me over his shoulders so my core is above his face.

Phoenix comes to the arm of the couch. "Hold onto my

shoulders and sit." I relax a bit and feel Jude's tongue take a long swipe from my entrance to my already sensitive clit. He hums his approval. "Angel. Sit. Down." He slightly pushes down my shoulders, and I fall the rest of the way onto Jude's face.

I lose myself in the feel of his hot tongue on my wet pussy when I gasp and lift up a little.

"Oh, my god. Are you okay?"

"I am wonderful. Now get back down here. I was enjoying the taste of honey and the smell of peaches." He grabs a handful of both ass cheeks and pulls me back down on his.

"See, he's completely fine. Now do you think you could suck my cock while he devours your pussy?"

"Oh god, yes, please." I release his shoulders and slide down his torso. He undoes his jeans and pulls himself free for me. I lean my hands on the arm of the couch and open my mouth for Phoenix to slide his cock into. The taste of his salty pre-cum hits my tongue in a little flavor explosion.

While I suck and bob, Jude licks and nips. The room heats up from our panting and moaning. Phoenix growls with his hands in my hair.

"I'm gonna come. Are you ready to come with me, Angel?" I hum on his cock, the only response I can give with my mouth full.

Jude reaches up and cups Phoenix's balls. At the same time, he bites down on my clit, and we both shout his name as our orgasms detonate. I'm riding Jude's face, and Phoenix has slammed his cock as far into the back of my throat as he can go. I swallow everything he gives me, and when my orgasm subsides, I lift off Jude's face and sit back on his chest. Phoenix leans over the couch and devours Jude in a kiss. His tongue is licking every inch of the inside of Jude's mouth. When he pulls away, he looks at us and shrugs.

"I wanted a taste of you, Angel, so I took it from Jude. Let's get you cleaned up and let the teenager shower."

31

Hazel

"Honey, I'm home!"

"You live above our garage. Aren't you technically always home?"

"Haha, Collin. You're so funny. Thanks for inviting me over for dinner. Where's your better half?" I look around their open-concept main floor, and she's nowhere to be seen.

"Around here somewhere. Where's yours?" He shoots me a glance.

"Man, you got jokes today. She wasn't feeling a hundred percent. With her first softball game this weekend, I told her to stay home and make sure she's well-rested and isn't coming down with something.

"Ah, so it's just us adults tonight. I don't know if that makes you or me the 3rd wheel in this party?"

"Hey, I'm dating two guys. Who needs a circle when you can have a triangle?" He gives me a look that's part curiosity and part horror.

"Right. Please don't give that woman any more ideas than she already has. Ever since you girls read Fifty Shades in college, our bedroom life has been...eclectic."

"And you love every rope and vibrator I bring into the bedroom." Dellah makes her grand entrance. "Hey, bestie. Where's the mini-me?"

"Home, sick. She's fine. She just needed some extra rest." She squeals, making Collin and I both jump. "What?"

"That means we can have adult time and talk about all your sexcapades."

Looking at Collin, "How much has she told you?"

"More than you or I probably both want to know."

"Collin McLain." An angry Dellah stands before him with her hands on her hips.

"Ohhhh, you're in trouble," I tease.

"You know damn well that every night you're like the high school gossip asking for the latest details of Hazel's boy toys."

Looking sheepish, "Can't a man hope for some pointers? Oomph." Collin rubs the side of his head.

"Dellah! Did you just throw your flip-flop at Collin? I swear, woman. Always so violent."

"It's okay, Hazel. She can think she wears the pants around the house, but behind our bedroom door, she knows who's really in charge. Isn't that right, Bunny?" He crouches down on his side of the counter like he's stalking his prey. She tries to run, and they circle the counter a few times before he grabs her from behind, picks her up, and tosses her onto a bar stool.

"Oh, goodie, dinner and a show." I roll my eyes at their antics.

"Hush, you love us. Now tell us about what's going on with your men." The oven timer beeps, and she sticks her tongue

179

out at Collin before jumping off the stool and walking over to it. I hear him mumble, "Promises, promises."

"I told them about Mac." She puts the lasagna on the counter and spins around slack-jawed.

"No way. What did they say? I didn't get an S.O.S tequila text, so that must be a good sign."

"They were oddly calm about it. Although, I didn't give them much of an opportunity to think about it. I asked them to *distract* me, and they were happy to oblige."

"Oh, girl. Now I want all those details." She leans up close to me with her elbows on the counter and head in her hands.

Collin scoffs. "And I just got a flip-flop to the head for asking the same question."

She jokingly glowers at him. "It's different."

The three of us have the type of relationship where we share everything, so I am fine giving them all the details.

"You know Hazel, I've always admired your confidence. You've always done what's best for you and Wynnie, no matter what." Collin has a proud dad face on despite only being a few years older than me.

"Thanks, Collin. Honestly, it hasn't always been easy. Having a baby at 18 changed me a lot. After everything, I've come to the conclusion that this is just me, like it or not. This is my body. It created and housed an entire person. I'm only going to live this one life, so I'm going to do it for me."

"I really respect that. That's an awesome way to view life."

"Duh. That's because my bestie is the absolute best! Let's eat."

After dinner, I check on Wynnie to see how she's feeling. I knock quietly on her door and see that she's drawing and on Facetime with Nora.

"Hey. My mom's here. I'll talk to you later." She disconnects and smiles at me. "Hey, Mom."

"Hey, kiddo, how are you feeling?"

"Better. I think I just overworked myself at practice today. How was dinner?" She wanders over to her desk to put her sketchbook away.

"It was fun. I brought you back a plate. It's in the microwave. Aunt Dellah made lasagna and garlic bread. I'll put it in the fridge if you aren't hungry."

"Thanks, Mom. Dinner sounds good." We walk into the kitchen, and I grab the plate and get her a fork. Sitting down at the counter, I decide it's time we have a talk.

"Hey, can I chat with you about something?"

"Sure, what's up?" She takes a big bite of her lasagna.

"I'm sure you've noticed I've been going out more than usual lately. I wanted to let you know I've been seeing…someone."

"I kind of figured." She shrugs and scoops another forkful of food from her plate.

"How do you feel about that?" She seems so nonchalant about it. Internally I'm freaking out. I'll respect her if she doesn't like the idea of me dating. It's always been me and her. I wouldn't let a guy, or guys, get between us.

She looks into my eyes, "Are you happy?" Is she 12 or 32? Such a sophisticated question.

"Yeah, I'm happy." She smiles at me.

"Then I'm cool with it." Well, okay. That went way easier than I expected. Although, it's only step one in a complicated web of steps.

"Okay, good." And that's that. "Are you excited for your first game this weekend?"

"Yeah, everyone on the team is." She takes her last bite,

walks to the sink to rinse her plate, and loads it into the dishwasher. "I'm headed to bed. Thanks, Mom. Love you."

"Love you, too. Night, Wynnie."

A few days later, Dellah, Collin, and I are bundled up in the bleachers on a cold March morning, eagerly waiting for the game to start.

"I bet you're wishing now you let me spike that coffee in your hands." Dellah takes a big whiff of her boozy drink while I attempt to wrap my blanket tighter around my legs. "It's warming me from the inside out. Mmm."

"Shush, woman. Do you see that security guard over there? Why don't you announce a little louder that you're drinking at 9 AM at a kid's sporting event." I give her a warning look, and her eyes suddenly light up.

"Oh, think he'd arrest me and use his handcuffs?"

Looking past Dellah, I lean towards Collin. "Hey, tame your woman before she intentionally flashes the security guard or something. She saw his handcuffs and got "that look" in her eyes." I emphasize the words by using air quotes. He knows what look I'm referring to. The one that gets her, or us, in trouble.

"I'll grab her a pretzel to soak up some of the *coffee* she's drinking. Be right back."

He heads to the concession stand, leaving me with my half-drunk, half-horny best friend. This exact situation has happened many times before.

Huffing out a sigh, "I swear, woman, you're worse than my own kid sometimes. How many of her do you see out there between 2nd and 3rd base?" She sticks her tongue out at me. We're giggling together and having a good time waiting for the game to start when I glimpse something over her shoulder.

Or should I say, someone?

"Oh fuck no. Fuck, fuck, fuuuuuck." I can only imagine the look of panic that washed over my face. Dellah snaps into action.

"What's wrong? What happened?" She's looking around trying to see what spooked me. I could feel all the blood drain from my face, and I started twisting and turning in my seat, pulling the collar up on my jacket. Anything to make myself smaller. Invisible.

"What. Is. Wrong?" Freezing in my spot, standing not far from us in the dugout, I spot three men having a conversation. Dellah looks in the same direction as I am, and I can tell she still doesn't see it.

"What? Are you shocked to see the two coaches together?" She knows damn well what she's asking, but at least she covered up her actual question.

"Do you see who the *coaches* are talking to?" His back is slightly to hers, but I saw the start of the interaction before he turned.

"The security guard? Duh, Hazel. We were just talking about him when he was near the other field." Yeah, when he was too far away to get a good view of him. When all you could tell was that he was tall, dark-haired, and built. But he's closer now. Closer and interacting with Jude and Phoenix in the dugout. They're laughing together like they know each other.

"Oh, god." *Do* they know each other?

"Bitch, what? You're starting to freak me out." I am freaking out.

"Dellah, the security guard. It's…It's Mac." Her face starts to resemble mine: shock and disbelief.

"But he's talking to -your coaches-." The last two words are whispered into my ear.

"I know," my voice barely rasps out.

This has to be a joke. His jacket says security, but he pulled us over in a police uniform. And how do they know each other? Mac gives a manly back slap to the guys and continues rounding the ball fields.

Dellah fills in Collin when he gets back with her pretzel. I watched the game in a daze. I faked my interactions entirely on autopilot until the end. They won. Everyone was excited. My body was present, but my mind wasn't.

After the game, Wynnie asked to get pizza for lunch, and we all said yes.

I have to get to the bottom of this. I need to know how they know each other. I text the group chat before we head to my car.

Me: I need to see you guys. Tonight if possible. Please.

Phoenix: Tonight is great. Everything okay?

Jude: Let us know when, Little Dove. I hope you're alright.

Me: See you tonight around 7.

Is everything okay? Am I alright? No. And I can't answer those questions through text right now. We will have to have another big conversation tonight.

32

Phoenix

I didn't like the tone of Hazel's text. It made me anxious. It's obvious something upset her recently. We were exchanging dirty texts in the group chat last night, and all was well.

Something changed this morning. She wasn't acting like herself. Our usual over-the-top cheerleader, Hazel, seemed reserved and nervous. Jude and I tried to keep our heads in the game, but I could tell it was nagging in the back of his mind, too.

The girls played well and won their first game of the season. We watched Hazel celebrate on the field with Rowyn before they all left. She never sent a glance in our direction.

"Any thoughts on why Hazel needs to see us tonight? Not that she needs an excuse. I'll see her every chance we can get. But, there was something off in her text, and it worries me." Jude's staring out the passenger window of my truck as we head home from the game.

I notice him suck in his lower lip, moving his jaw back and forth in concentration. I reach over my center console and pull it out from between his teeth. He side-eyes me and smiles. I've noticed things between us lately. Little things that may have already been there, but seem to be making more of an impact since our talk with Hazel. Like that smile, how he makes me a travel mug of coffee every day before work. He noticed a stain on my shirt one morning and went and got me a new one. Things that seem so mundane for us because it's just how we are, but it feels like more now.

We were strangers put together our freshman year in college and became unlikely friends. Despite his preppiness and my 'don't fuck with me attitude' back then, we hit it off. In retrospect, there were probably signs that we both missed. Neither of us woke up one day and said, "I'm going to suck my best friend's dick today." We've had a mutual respect and love for each other for the majority of our friendship. We fell into this comfortable pattern of sharing life together, and now we want to share it with Hazel.

Over the years, I've had my suspicion that Jude might be a little bi-curious. He can be a little loose-lipped when drunk, and other than our Junior year of college, we've had a healthy relationship with alcohol. He's flirted with me before, and I half believed he was just drunk. And then, of course, the kiss we shared and never spoke about. I've never glanced in another man's direction. What we did together in the comfort of Hazel's presence felt right, and maybe all along, when he flirted, I flirted back unknowingly. I'm interested to see where this will go from here.

Jude and I have yet to talk about it after the first night we all shared between us. Neither of us was embarrassed, but it felt natural, and there wasn't any reason to discuss it. When she asked us for answers, we shared our truths. Nothing has happened between us outside of our time with Hazel, but I'm unsure if it will stay that way. I'm unsure if I want it to stay that way.

"I don't know, but I felt it, too. Think there's been a development with Rowyn's father?" He sucks his lip back in again but quickly releases it when he sees me start to lift my hand toward him.

Jude and I discussed our feelings about Rowyn's potential father after Hazel left that night. We brought out the shot glasses and vodka and honestly discussed how to move forward. Our immediate response was that we didn't want to let her go. But knowing we weren't in a traditional relationship, we understood that things might not work the same as a normal couple. Also, add that we already know Rowyn personally, but she doesn't know about our relationship with her mother, and we find ourselves in a precarious situation. Ultimately we decided that all decisions revert to Hazel and what's comfortable for her and Rowyn. Her daughter is her number one priority, and we would never come between their happiness.

"Maybe. Whatever it is, at least she's coming to us right away, and we can work it out together." He takes a deep breath and lets it out slowly.

"Agreed." Together. As long as we can talk about things, we can work them out. Always together.

We spend the rest of the day working on random tasks around the house to pass the time. Jude's anxiety has increased since he sent a text telling Hazel he couldn't wait to see her, and she never responded. Just before 7 o'clock, we find ourselves sitting on the couch together. I reach my hand over and place it on Jude's knee, stopping it from anxiously bobbing.

"Relax, or you'll shake the house off its foundation. She will be here soon, and we'll talk everything out." His knee starts to bob again under my hand. Grabbing his chin, I pulled his face towards me. "Hey, look at me. What's up?"

His cinnamon eyes are warring within themselves. "She's special."

"I know she is." He stands up and starts pacing the room.

"No, you don't understand. She's *special*. I've never felt this way about anyone before." I feel the same way. He stops pacing and looks down at the floor. "I think I'm ready, Phoenix. No, I know I'm ready." He looks back up at me, grabbing the back of his neck.

"Yeah? Are you sure?"

"I'm sure. I've been thinking about it since she was last here. When you told her to leave my boxers on because 'I wasn't ready for her.' "

"Hey man, I didn't mean it like-"

"No, please don't be upset. I'm not. You were right. At that moment, I was so lost in my desires I would have done it then and there. But you stopped it before it could even start, and I'm thankful." A big smile crosses his face. "It gave me time to think about it with a clear head, the right head. I'm ready and can know I made the decision consciously." He starts pacing again.

"That's awesome. I'm proud of you." I grabbed his wrist as he paced by me. "But what's really wrong?"

"Why does she need to talk to us? No good conversation ever starts with 'I need to talk to you.' " He's not wrong.

"I don't know, man. We just have to wait and see what she says." I stand up and pull him into a hug, and he wraps his arms around me. I can feel the anxious vibrations of his body start to relax when we hear her car pull into the driveway. He pulls away, and his eyes are wild. Taking his cheeks in my hands, I look directly into his eyes.

"Stop. Relax. She's here now, and we will get answers." I give his lips a firm, lingering kiss and walk to the door to let Hazel in.

I open the door, and Hazel's usual breathtaking body looks stressed. She momentarily relaxes when she looks up at me, but her rigid posture quickly returns. What's wrong with my Angel?

"Come in. Jude's in the-" Turning around after I closed the door, Jude's standing in front of us. "Right here." He's on edge. It's written all over his face.

He embraces her and buries his face into her hair, inhaling deeply. "Little Dove." There's so much emotion behind those two words. Her shoulders release their tension in his arms, giving me hope for whatever is about to come.

I join them in their embrace and feel her melt into us. Sweeping her hair to the side, I nuzzle in her ear, "You're here now, Angel. Will you talk to us? We've been a little on edge all day waiting."

Pulling his head from her hair, Jude looks her in the eyes. "Do I need to get the tequila?"

"Tempting, but no. I should probably keep a clear head." She looks between the two of us. "I need more answers." She guides us to the couch and motions for us to sit, taking her position on the coffee table.

Reaching in and grabbing each of our hands, she laces our

fingers together. She closes her eyes and begins.

"Today at the game, you guys talked to a security guard." She pauses, waiting for us to respond, but neither of us says anything, so she continues. "How do you know him?" She opens her eyes and they dart between us.

"Mac? He's a buddy of ours. He usually works security for the sporting events at school. It's easy side-money for him." Her hands start to tremble.

"Little Dove, did he do something to you?"

A low laugh starts in the back of her throat which turns into hysterical laughter. She's out of breath, and tears are streaming down her face. Jude and I sit and stare at her in utter confusion. It takes her several minutes before she calms down enough to speak.

"Did he do something to me? Yeah, yeah, he did. He knocked me up 13 years ago at a college party." Jude freezes, obviously understanding before I can comprehend her statement.

"Angel, I don't understand. Knocked you up? Is he..."

No. This can't be possible. How?

"Mac is Wynnie- Rowyn's biological father. And apparently, he's your friend." She releases our hands, stands up, and begins pacing the room, running her fingers through her hair.

Jude is still frozen where he sits. I'm overwhelmed and conflicted. My heart is breaking in two right now. Half is panicking with Hazel over this new development of who Rowyn's father is. The other half is upset and angry for Mac, knowing what he's already been through, and now he has this fantastic daughter and has no idea who she is.

"Please, someone say something." I can understand how

frazzled her nerves are right now because I feel the same.

"Are you planning to tell him?" Jude has come out of his trance.

"Of course I am." Sitting back on the coffee table, she retakes our hands. "I just don't know what that means for us, and it scares me."

Inhaling a deep breath, I look into her hazel green eyes. "This isn't an 'us' situation. We are here to support you, but the decisions about you, Rowyn, and Mac's future is up to you. I know you were already feeling guilty about not trying to look for him when you found out you were pregnant. You have an opportunity to make things right."

Jude takes over. "I can tell you that Mac is a great guy. He works on the town's police force and helps at the schools. That's how we met him. He's a bit of a loner and can be a little rough around the edges at first. Life's been a little tough on him." He looks off to the side, deep in thought. "I have a suggestion."

"I'm all ears. I'm not sure I've ever felt more like a fish out of water." Will she let us be her life raft?

Jude glances at me with an apprehensive look. "What if we invited him over for dinner? You could sit down and talk with him one-on-one, on neutral ground. Or, if you'd like, we could all sit down together."

"I...that's." Her face scrunches in confusion, trying to digest everything Jude just said.

"I think it sounds like a solid idea. If that's what you decide." I close my eyes because I'm about to be vulnerable, and I don't want to see her face when I give away my insecurities. "Unless you don't want us there. Unless you feel this is too hard to continue with everything else going on. You have some big decisions to make. I'll support you even if that doesn't include me, us."

"Phoenix, no. That's the opposite of what I want." She drops to her knees before us, placing her head in my lap. I stroked her hair in an effort to comfort her. "I need you both. I need your strength. I know I have no right to ask either of you to help me. It's a lot to ask of anyone, and we are just getting started in an already complicated relationship.

"Little Dove, you don't need our strength. You are one of the strongest women I know. You took a potentially bad situation at 18 and turned it around. You created a great life for yourself and Rowyn. You've raised an amazing young lady that you should be proud of. I know we're proud of her and you. Just like Phoenix said, we will be here for you. Whatever role you need us to play. We aren't going anywhere if you don't want us to."

She jumps up off the floor and throws herself in our laps. One arm wrapped around each of our necks, she swivels her head back and forth, kissing us both.

"I don't deserve your generosity. You're both too good to me. You'd really do this? You'd sit down with me while I tell Mac about the worst mistake I've made in my entire life?" Unshed tears are brimming in her eyes.

"You know we would." There's no room for question in Jude's statement. We would do anything for her, even walk away if that's what she really wanted. It would be the most challenging thing either of us ever did, but we would do it for Hazel.

The three of us relax on the couch and discuss the details of the arranged dinner. Mindlessly stroking Hazel's hair, I'm pondering how easy everything feels right now but how quickly this could all change. Telling Mac about Rowyn will alter all of our lives. Then another thought comes to mind.

"Hey, Angel?" She responds with a hmm. "Rowyn doesn't know about us, does she?"

"She knows I'm dating someone, but none of the particulars. She asked if I was happy, and I told her yes. That's all that mattered to her. She hasn't brought it up since."

Hazel shifts and lays between us, putting her head in Jude's lap and her legs in mine. I smile in contentment and watch, mesmerized, as Jude now runs his fingers through Hazel's soft, auburn hair. Heat flares in my stomach as I continue to watch their interaction. Occasionally she lets out a soft moan when he massages her scalp. I can't help my hands that rub up and down her jean-clad thighs. She starts to wiggle at my touch, and Jude glances at me with the same heat in his eyes that I'm feeling.

"Hey, Little Dove, want to watch a movie?"

"I'd rather lay here and continue to be stroked by my boyfriends."

Boyfriends. Is that what we are? It seems like such a juvenile label for what we have. Based on Jude's current expression, he's also rolling around the term in his head.

"Angel, did you just ask us to go steady?"

She peeks up at me through her dark lashes with a smirk on her lips. "Yep, but these are playground rules. I licked it, so it's mine. Well, you're both mine. Deal with it." She sticks out her tongue to punctuate her statement.

"Playground rules, huh? Okay, naughty girl, if you insist." I stand up from under her legs, dip down to her stomach and lift her over my shoulder.

"What are you doing, caveman? Put me down." There's no

conviction as her words come out through laughter.

I nod at Jude in the direction of the bedrooms. "You said playground rules, Angel. So, finders keepers.

33

Jude

Walking down the hall to Phoenix's room, I take my time to peruse both of their bodies. The globes of Hazel's round ass peeking just over his shoulder. The bulge of Phoenix's biceps as he holds her. Mine. She said we were hers, and we are, just as much as she belongs to us. This woman has captivated both of us.

Before Phoenix takes her off his shoulder, I crouch down and nibble on Hazel's ear. "You belong to us. Finders keepers, naughty girl."

I don't know how to tell this fascinating woman before me that I want to give her all of me without sounding like a teenager. "Hey Hazel, wanna take my V-card?" That's not exactly romantic, or mature. Hazel and Phoenix haven't been intimate since their one night stand, and I believe he's done that for my benefit. Tonight that's going to change.

"Hey Phoenix, why don't we show our beautiful woman a good time with no holding back." He locks eyes with me confirming I'm ready for what I just suggested. A quick nod is all the approval he needs.

He drags her down the front of his body until her feet hit the floor. She looks at me over his shoulder and extends her hand in offering. Taking her invitation, I erased the distance between us. I suppress a groan when my hands encase her lush hips from behind, and I pull her body flush with my chest. I bring my mouth to the sensitive skin where her neck meets her shoulder and suck until she melts into me. Phoenix steps closer and takes her lips in his. She suddenly giggles into his mouth.

"What's so funny, Angel?" She rotates her hips in a circle brushing over the bulge in my pants that's trying to break through. Phoenix moans, also feeling the effect of her hips.

"It's a Hazel-NUT sandwich." She swirled her hips again on the word 'nut.'

"You did this to us with your siren ways. What are you going to do about it now?" I press my growing cock into her back.

She steps out of our embrace and makes a slow circle around us. Tapping her lips with her finger, she assesses the situation. "Hmm. There are so many options."

"Yes to them all." I don't hesitate with my answer. Whatever, she might suggest I'll do it. We'll do it. This woman has me hypnotized.

"Strip." The firm command has us shedding our clothes into a heap on the floor. Standing before her, naked and wanting, she takes in our physiques. We are both tall and lean but Phoenix's build is larger than mine, earned by all the hours he spends in the gym. Our shafts stand at attention, waiting to obey her next command. "You're both so pretty." I preen at her compliment.

Hazel runs her finger down Phoenix's chest and he vibrates with excitement. Continuing to tease him, she trails her finger through his abs, over his hips, and down his inner thigh. He inhales a sharp breath when she passes where he longs to be touched. She brushes a feather-light kiss over his lips and pulls away before he can indulge in her. His fists are clenched at his sides, barely restraining himself.

With a sly smile, she turns her attention to me. "Turn around." I spin on my feet as two warm hands caress my shoulders and down my back until they land on my ass. I flex in her hands, and she gives me a firm squeeze. Her fingers continue to roam across my lower back, around my hips, and thighs, and then I'm graced with one long, slow tug on my cock. I release a groaning sigh and she removes her hands from me. We are at her mercy, and she knows it.

"Face each other." Turning our bodies inward, we look to her for the next instructions. "Will you kiss each other?" This time it's a whispered request.

Phoenix's lip curls up before he grabs my shoulders and pulls us together. This kiss is different from the ones we've exchanged before. His lips are hard, but his tongue is soft in its perusal to taste all of me. His hard chest against mine starkly contrasts the softness I'm used to with Hazel. I grab his hips in an effort to keep myself steady. This consuming kiss has my knees threatening to give out. Hazel gasps and says on a whimper, "That's so hot."

I need to tell her, and I need to tell her now. I want her to take me to places of ecstasy that I've only ever imagined. I want to feel her hot, wet heat wrapped around my 8 inches of pierced steel. To make her come with my thrusting hips.

My lips release from Phoenix, and I reach out to pull her into a kiss.

"Little Dove, I want to give all of me to all of you. I want to be inside you. Please let me worship your body inside and out." She pulls away from our kiss and searches my eyes for answers. All she will find are truths. I'm ready.

"Are you sure? We don't have to do anything you aren't ready for." I love her effort to make sure I'm comfortable with my decision.

"I'm positive. I'm giving my pleasure over to you mind, body, and soul." She drops to her knees, and before I can register what she's doing, she swallows my cock down her throat as far as it will go before she gags. "Fuck, fuck, *fuck*." I dive my hands into her hair and grab two fist fulls. Phoenix leans over her and begins kissing me again. I'm overwhelmed with sensations, and I take a step away from them. My chest is panting, gasping for air, but I'm unable to take a full breath.

A hand brushes my cheek, and Phoenix stares into my eyes. "Let us both take care of you, Jude." His green eyes are cloaked in lust and swimming with sincerity. I couldn't imagine a more perfect scenario for this to take place. "Get on the bed."

Hazel, who had remained fully clothed until now, strips naked while I sit in the middle of the bed. Phoenix sits next to me, and we watch as our temptress crawls up and sits in front of us.

"We need some ground rules. Things we probably should have already discussed prior to right now." We both nod at her. "Contraceptives. I have an IUD, and I'm clean. I get tested regularly at work. How about the two of you?"

"I'm clean. I got tested at my annual visit over winter break and haven't been with anyone but you since the bar." He shoots her a wink.

"I've never been with anyone, so that answer is pretty easy for me. But I also get tested annually; the last time was in January." That was easy and simple to get out of the way. "What else, Little Dove?"

"Okay, good. A safe word. We shouldn't need it right now, but it's a good thing to have in place for when we do. Thoughts?"

"Should we keep it simple with red, yellow, and green?" I nod in agreement, and so does Hazel. We will divert to Phoenix's experience on this one.

He explains, "Red means stop, no questions asked. Whatever we are doing at the moment, if someone says red, it ends. Yellow means someone needs to pause and think about the situation, and green means everything is good.

"Okay, one final thing." She hesitates for a moment." There are two of you and obviously just one of me. I don't have much experience, but I'm open to anal play, although today is not the day for exploring."

At her admission, Phoenix drags his index finger from the top of her spine all the way to the top of her ass cheeks, causing her to shudder. "Sounds good to me, Angel. Are we ready to please our naughty boy?" This time it's my turn to shudder.

"I think our goddess needs an orgasm first. I want to taste her." She licks her lips and smiles in response. "Lay down." With my hand in the middle of her chest, I gently ease her down until she's splayed out flat with her legs open for us. Phoenix reaches over and drags a finger through her slit.

"She's so wet and ready for you, Jude." His fingers make lazy circles around her clit as I place kisses at her ankles. She mewls at our touches. When I reach the top of her thigh, I grab Phoenix's fingers and suck them into my mouth, tasting her arousal. Humming in appreciation, I pull his fingers out of my mouth with a pop and reach for the back of his neck. I pull him in for a kiss, our tongues tangling, and he moans into my mouth.

"Doesn't our girl taste delicious, Phoenix?"

"God, that's still so hot," Hazel whispers in awe.

"You want hot? How about this?" I plunge my mouth onto her pussy, and with a flat tongue, I swipe from her entrance to her clit. I take a long pull on her already sensitive nub, and she arches off the bed, her mouth opening in a silent scream. Phoenix starts flicking his tongue on her rosy nipples, and it doesn't take long until she's a writhing mess of arousal between us. The sweetest burst of honey mixed with her peach scent assaults my taste buds when she orgasms. She looks so beautiful from this angle, her face flushed, eyes rolled back, gripping the sheets in her fists as she rides out her pleasure.

"I need you inside me, Jude. Please." At her pleading, I lose what's left of my resolve. I sit up on my knees, chin still glistening, and take in all the beauty of her post-orgasm glow. She sits up and places a palm on my chest. "Let me take care of you. Lay back for me."

I do as I'm told, and she rewards me by crawling up my body until she's fully on top of me. She kisses me tenderly, and my hands roam up and down her thighs while I mentally prepare to be inside her. She shifts slightly until my cock is nestled between her folds, and she starts stroking me with her wet pussy.

"Are you sure you're ready?" She's checking in with me one final time, and I love her for that. That realization strikes me like a bat to the head because it's true. I'm in love with her. I'm about to lose my virginity to the woman that I'm in love with. A sense of peace washes over me, and I'm eager to make this union between us.

Reaching up, I take her cheeks. "Green," I whisper on her lips. She smiles and grasps my length in her hand, teasing my piercing at her entrance.

"Jude, I want you to know that I have no expectations for this first time. I understand that you probably won't last long, and that's completely normal and okay. But you *will* owe me a round two." She winks at me with her Cheshire cat smile, and I give a quick upward thrust of my hips, pushing a few inches inside of her. She slowly sits back, and my senses go into overdrive once she's fully seated on top of me. She's hot and wet and tight. Her pussy walls fit me like a glove, stretching to accommodate my length. I hold tightly onto her hips, giving myself a moment to clear my head so I don't come in two pumps. Phoenix groans next to us, and I look over to find him stroking his erection, eyes focused on where we are connected.

"Move for him, Angel. Show him what heaven feels like."

She splays her hands on my chest, then rises a few inches and slowly slides back down. The remnants of her orgasm give us the perfect amount of friction, and there is no resistance as she continues to ease up and down my shaft. Her name slips between my lips like a prayer. The sensation of her wrapped around me is beyond my wildest fantasies. The connection I feel as we find a rhythm between our bodies is otherworldly.

"Jude," she whines. "Your fucking piercing is hitting all the right spots inside me. Goddammit." I can't help the shit-eating grin that spreads across my face.

"I guess all that research paid off." She agrees with another long moan.

Phoenix reaches between us and starts to rub her clit. She clenches around me, and I gasp. "Oh, fuck. She somehow just got tighter." I grab her hips in an effort to slow her movements down. "I don't think I'm going to last much longer, Little Dove. Can you come with me?"

"Oh god, yes. Phoenix, keep doing that." She grabs her nipples between her fingers and pinches to give herself extra stimulation. The sight of her taking her pleasure into her own hands tips me over the edge. With one last slam upwards, I spill my come deep inside her, marking her as mine. Her inner walls flutter against me as she comes with my name slipping out of her lips.

34

Phoenix

That was one of the most memorable things I've ever seen. Watching my best friend and our girl come together for the first time has me ready to come in my hands. I need to be inside her right now, but I don't want to ruin their moment. Hazel collapsed onto his chest once her orgasm subsided, and they are now laying together chest to chest catching their breath. Jude is running his fingers up and down her spine, and she's whispering words of encouragement in his ear, turning his cheeks pink. I've heard the word 'piercing' a few times, and I can tell she enjoyed his adornment.

I watch as he finally slides out of her, his semi-erect cock glistening with their joint arousal. My already thin patience snaps like a string at the sight. I crawl around the bed and position myself between Jude's legs. Running my hands down Hazel's back, and around her waist I pull her hips back until she's up on her knees. Ass in the air and her chest still lying on Jude's body, I line up with her entrance.

"I can't wait any longer, Angel. Hold onto Jude, and you can both enjoy the ride." She flashes me a heated grin over her shoulder and wiggles her ass against my awaiting cock.

"All yours for the taking, big boy." In one quick thrust, I'm buried deep inside her to the hilt, and it's like taking the first cleaning breath after almost drowning. My nerves are on fire, and heat runs through my veins. After watching their slow, sweet lovemaking, I feel like a wild beast. My hips pump at a punishing pace, and my grip on her will surely leave bruises. The sounds of our hips slapping, and their joint moaning bounces through the room around us. My balls start to tighten, and I know I'm getting close. Leaning down, I snake an arm around her and pull her up to my chest. Slowing my pace, I glance over her shoulder to Jude.

"I want you to pull your legs out from under us and flip around onto your back. Eat her out while I finish. Let's see how much you've learned, naughty boy."

After some shifting, I can tell the moment Jude's mouth connects with her. The sharp inhale of her breath lets me know whatever he's doing she's enjoying, and so am I. As his tongue laps at her pussy he's also dipping back lower and running his tongue over my cock.

"Angel, look at our good fucking boy down there. He's doing an amazing job pleasuring both of us. Can we come for him so he can clean us up with his tongue?" Jude hums his approval, and Hazel and I both moan. She leans further into me, and locks her hands behind my neck pulling me into a kiss. With her back arched, I palm her breasts, kneading them in my hands. I feel movement below us, and a hand grabs my balls, giving them a firm tug.

"Jesus fuck, Jude. Fuck. Angel, I'm going to come. Come with me. Now." She starts to scream when I give one final pump and explode into her. Sharp bursts of light flash in my eyes as our orgasms rip around us. Jude hums as he laps up our joint arousals dripping from Hazel.

Pulling out, she falls backward onto me, her back meeting my chest. Jude rolls over and dives back into her pussy.

"Oh god, Jude. You are relentless. Phoenix, I think we created a monster." I agree with a kiss on her neck.

"Mmm, we taste so good mixed together. Oh, and Little Dove, you required a round two from me, and I'm ready to deliver." The wild look in Jude's eyes has me agreeing with Hazel's observation.

35

Hazel

"Ugh. Why did I let you convince me to go shopping, Dellah?" I hate wandering store after store shopping the tiny, boxy, less than sexy plus size sections in most stores.

"Because you love to shop." She's so matter-of-fact in her statement it's like she believes it.

"Shoe shopping. I love shoe shopping. My feet don't care if I ate an extra helping of mashed potatoes for dinner. Clothes, on the other hand, do."

"Okay, how about because you're about to have dinner with your two hot as fuck boyfriends. And you're about to meet your baby daddy after 13 years and one drunken night. You need to look like a badass with her shit together."

"I do have my shit together." She waves her hand like my comment is a fly she needs to shoo away.

I have to admit it's not a terrible idea to find something new and fresh to wear to this dreaded dinner. I've been a nervous wreck since Tuesday when Phoenix told me he invited Mac to dinner this Saturday after the game. With the dinner now two days away and no Dellah-approved outfit in my closet, I find myself in the mall—my own brand of hell. I try to go to my happy place as I stand in front of the dressing room door, waiting for Dellah to finish bringing me her outfit choices.

Dellah finally returns, shaking me from my daydream of remembering being with both guys last weekend. She puts me through the torture of trying on too many outfits until we find one she deems worthy. Fortunately, I'm allowed to pick out my own shoes, and I force her to buy me coffee for allowing her to play dress up with me. Our conversation remains casual until she asks the question I know has been burning her up inside.

"What are you going to do?" It feels like I'm about to play a game of Russian roulette, but all the chambers are full of bullets.

In two days, five lives are about to be turned upside down. I believe the guys when they say they support me and will be there for me unless I decide I can't handle it. And I know that I'll want them there to help me. But will it come to a point that it's too much for them? This is my mess and I can't expect them to want to stick around once everything is out in the open. Mac is their friend. They have no loyalty to me.

The guilt towards Mac is still significantly present. He's about to find out I kept his daughter a secret from him for 12 years. Well, I guess it's not a secret if I didn't know who or where he was, but it's still a tremendous betrayal that I didn't even try to find him.

And my Wynnie. Will she ever forgive me once she finally knows I've found him? When will we tell her? Oh god! I press my trembling hands to my lips and turn to my best friend.

"Dellah, what if Mac rejects Wynnie?" My mind went off on such a tailspin I forgot she had asked me a question first.

"Oh, Hazel. He would be the biggest asshole in the world if he rejected that little girl. Unfortunately, you won't know until you tell him." She embraces me in a hug. "We will get through this together, and it sounds like your guys are there to support you as well."

I hope she's right about the guys. I just have to take this one potential tragedy at a time. First, I tell Mac and hope it doesn't scare the guys off. Then once the dust settles, I need to tell Wynnie. If all else fails, at least I'll look my absolute best for dinner.

Driving around the lot near the softball fields, looking for a parking space, I'm grateful Dellah offered to drive us. I barely kept myself together on the ride over. As soon as we dropped Wynnie off at the field, my hands started trembling. My stomach is in knots, and my heart feels like there's a hummingbird in my chest. Somewhere, roaming around those fields, Mac is working security. Wynnie's father is about to watch her play and doesn't even know it. I drop my head into my hands and groan.

"I've got you, Bestie. I'm right here. You aren't alone." The warmth of her hand rubbing my back is soothing to my nerves.

"Thanks for driving us. My nerves are shot today." I couldn't eat this morning. I barely kept down my coffee. Wynnie could tell something was wrong, but bless her wonderful heart, she didn't ask about it. I'm not sure I could have held myself together enough for a convincing lie.

"You know I'll be at every one of her games that I'm available for, and I'm always here for you. I've said it a hundred times this week, and I'll say it a hundred more before tonight if you need it. We. Will. Get. Through. This. I love you, Hazy."

"Love you, too, Dells. Let's go watch our girl play some softball." I muster a small smile of enthusiasm.

It doesn't take us long to get through the concession stand and then find seats. It takes even less time before the first Mac sighting. As soon as we sit, I look into the dugout to see my guys, and he's there with them. He's as handsome as I remember him being. He looks a little rough around the edges, but I'm sure that's par for the course with a cop's life. But what catches me the most is his eyes, the same as Wynnie's. I had forgotten that about him. Wynnie's eyes have always been the same cornflower blue as her father's. Another block of cement lands in my stomach.

"I'll be right back. I have to use the bathroom." I fumble down the stairs, half causing a scene. I hear Dellah ask if I'm okay as I'm fleeing, and I swipe a hand in the air in response.

Reaching the communal bathroom, I fling the door open and go directly to a sink. Turning the faucet on, I splash cold water on my face. I lean against the sink, dipping my head below my shoulders, staring at the floor. I need to get my breathing under control before I hyperventilate and pass out.

I look up at myself in the mirror. A flashback of a very similar situation from 13 years ago slaps me with deja vu. Here I stand once again, assessing myself in the mirror before a life-altering event. Okay, I can do this. I can do this. I CAN DO THIS. I have to live with the massive, life-shattering consequences of my actions.

I grab a paper towel and dry off my face and hands. I swing the door handle open and take two steps outside before I slam into a very hard someone. Another wave of deja vu hits me. I met Phoenix the same way, only instead of being oblivious because my nose was in my purse, this time I was lost in thought and oblivious to my surroundings.

"I'm so sorry I wasn't paying attent...Mac." I hadn't looked into the stranger's eyes until that moment when he grabbed my shoulders to steady me from our collision. All I can see is his familiar cornflower blue eyes, the eyes he gave Wynnie. I feel fireworks exploding on my shoulder where his hands touch my body. What the fuck?

He's looking up and down, assessing me. "Do I know you?" More than you know.

"Um, I'm sorry. I have to go." I step away from him and quickly rush back to the bleachers, causing no less of a scene than when I left. I tell Dellah what happened, and she holds my hand for the rest of the game in silent support.

36

Phoenix

Mac came over to give us his usual greetings and good lucks, making his rounds before the games started. I saw when Hazel arrived with Dellah and watched her look towards the dugout, searching for us. The shock that washed over her face when she saw him standing there made my stomach drop. When the shock turned into horror, she bolted towards the bathrooms. It took everything in me not to chase after her. I wish I could take all her pain away, but I'd be lying if I didn't admit to the guilt nagging in my gut. Mac has been a good buddy for years. We work on each other's vehicles together. Standing here knowing I'm keeping this secret from him doesn't sit well with me, but tonight it will be out in the open, and we will deal with the fallout together.

Mac confirms he will see us tonight at 7 o'clock and moves on to make more rounds. Hazel still hasn't returned from the bathroom yet, and I have to physically stop myself from going in search of her. Just after the game starts, she finally appears looking more composed, but I can tell how emotionally battered she still was. She spent the rest of the game giving the appropriate emotions when needed, but her hand never left Dellah's.

I'm grateful that Hazel has such a strong, supportive friend like Dellah. That woman may be a bit unbalanced at times, but she loves Hazel fiercely and I appreciate that. I love that. I love her. I love Hazel. Why else would I be feeling so wildly protective of her emotional state? Hazel literally crashed into my life and left with remnants of my heart when she walked through that gym door.

The girls play another amazing game on the field. Hazel left as soon as it was over, leaving Dellah to collect Rowyn. She sent us a text in the group chat letting us know she'd see us at 5 o'clock, but that doesn't make this war raging inside me any calmer. Realizing that I'm in love with Hazel makes me feel like my emotions are on high alert, ready to strike at any danger.

Jude's sitting in my passenger seat, looking as tortured as I feel. We are both uneasy about tonight. Hazel still hasn't decided if she wants us to be in the room or just in the house when she tells Mac. We both want to be in the room to support her, but this isn't about what we want. She's a strong woman and can handle anything, and if she can't, then Jude and I will be there to pick up the pieces and glue her back together.

Jude's leg starts to bounce, shaking the truck as we sit at a stop light. I place my hand on his knee, giving it a squeeze. "Jude, relax." Closing his eyes and taking in a deep breath, his shoulders slump down, and he drops his head to the back of

212

the seat.

"Phoenix, I love her." He rolls his head and looks at me. Well, well, it seems I'm not the only one Hazel's caught in her net.

An involuntary smile crosses my lips. "I do, too, Jude." He places his hand over mine, lacing our fingers. "I do, too."

"Please tell me we won't lose her. Tell me we will get through tonight and become some dysfunctional party of 5 and live happily ever after." His hand squeezes mine tighter.

"I hate to say it, but I think our fairy godmother is on an extended vacation. But we *will* get through tonight. If it goes badly, she will try to push us away and retreat into herself. We can't let our little spitfire do that. We need to show a solid wall of support for her no matter how Mac reacts." Jude nods the entire time I'm speaking.

"I'm with you on that. We will get through this together. Always together." His eyes close again, ending our conversation.

At 4:45, there's a knock at the door. Hazel is never early, She's either right on time or late. Jude and I exchange a passing glance before I open the door. Standing in front of me is a very beautiful but very frazzled Hazel. She collapses into my arms, and I catch her, wrapping her body in my embrace. It's clear that the fortified walls she's built around her emotions are crumbling. Jude joins us and wraps her up from behind. She giggles.

"It's another Hazel-nut sandwich sans the nuts."

Jude hums into her hair. "That can be arranged if you'd like. Just say the word, Little Dove." He flexes his hips gently into her back and kisses the top of her head.

"Phoenix, we really did create a monster." I feel her body

ease a little tension at our light banter. I look down at what she's wearing, and I almost choke on air.

"Angel, can we talk about this fucking dress you're wearing?" I contain the growl that wants to escape, Jude, however, doesn't. He had come into the room in such a rush at Hazel's state, that he hadn't noticed what she was wearing either.

"Here's the nuts you wanted, Little Dove." He grinds his hips into her back again, this time letting her feel his appreciation. "Holy hell, let us get a better look at you." We both pull away from her so we can get a full view. "Fuck, is this dress painted on you? I love when you wear our favorite color. You look absolutely edible. Give me permission, and I'll make you my appetizer right now. Nope, fuck that. I don't need permission. I'm taking what's mine."

I chuckle as I grab his arm, stopping him from attacking her. She's laughing now, and it warms my heart. In front of us stands our goddess wearing a navy blue wrap dress that cinches at the waist, accentuating the curves of her hips. The v-shaped neckline plunges, leaving ample cleavage on display. She has on silver fuck me heels that draw my eyes directly up her legs and stop mid-thigh at the hem of her dress. I adjust myself in my pants. Jude's right, she looks completely edible, but now is not the time.

"I would love nothing more than to let you boys distract me, but that won't solve any of my problems. Jude, can I help with dinner?" She wants to stay busy, and I can understand that.

"Of course, you can. We're having meatloaf, mashed potatoes, and glazed carrots. Would you like to slice the carrots and potatoes?" Following him into the kitchen, he hands her an apron.

214

"I'd love to. Thank you."

Dinner is almost finished cooking, and our time remaining blissfully ignorant of the storm that's about to pass through our lives is dwindling. Hazel's been obsessively checking the time since about 6:50. It's now 7:03, and she's sitting on the couch wringing her hands together in her lap. The rumble of a motorcycle pulls into our driveway, and her head snaps up in the direction of the noise.

"Is that him? Does he have a motorcycle?" She's up and pacing now.

"Yes, Angel. That's most likely, Mac. He has a motorcycle and a pickup truck." I step up behind her and wrap my arms around her waist, stopping her pacing. She takes a deep, ragged breath. "Do you want to answer the door, or should I?" She steps away from my embrace and sits back on the couch, hands in her lap and legs bouncing.

"I'll wait here." Her voice is so tiny and childlike. I feel the anxiety radiating off of her.

Jude and I meet Mac at the door, and each give a handshake back slap greeting. Walking into the living room, we all glimpse a trembling Hazel sitting on the couch. Her head is down, and her eyes are closed. On a big inhale, she stands up and slowly turns towards us, facing the ground.

"What's up, guys? Who's this?" Mac looks between us. Stopping to get a better look at Hazel, a hint of recognition gleams in his eyes. "Hey, aren't you the lady I ran into this morning at the softball game? Are you okay? Did I do something to you? Are you hurt? Is that why you're here?" All of us are silent. A low snicker starts. It grows to a chuckle, and then a full-blown laugh comes out of Hazel. It takes me a moment to realize he asked her the same question Jude had that sent her into hysterics. *Did I do something to you?*

"Hazel?" I try to approach her, and she raises a hand to stop me. She clears her throat and composes herself. Lifting her head, she looks directly at Mac. Her chest rises and falls rapidly as they stare at each other. A mask of resilience washes over her face. Mac's face, however, is going through a myriad of emotions: curiosity, doubt, recognition, and shock. Does he recognize her?

"You...I thought...you had a hat on this morning. I didn't see your full face." He's slowly walking around the couch, approaching her like she's a rabid dog ready to attack. Maybe she is. "It can't be. It's you, isn't it?" He stops a few feet in front of her. She nods at his last question.

"You remember me?" I can't tell if her tone has hope or disappointment in it.

"Alice. How could I forget you?" Who's Alice? Maybe he doesn't remember who she is.

"Hatter," she says under her breath. Okay, now I'm completely confused about what's going on. Jude looks equally confused by the exchange between them.

"What are you doing here? Did you know I was coming over?" He has so many questions, and she isn't answering any of them. He looks at Jude and me, trying to figure out what's happening. There's a long pause where no one says anything.

"Okay," Jude claps his hands. "Maybe we should have dinner. Everything is ready. We should eat before it gets cold." He turns to walk away, and Mac opens his mouth to object. Before he can, Hazel speaks up.

"I agree, we should eat. Mac, I'm okay. You didn't hurt me this morning. We can talk once we've eaten." He silently concedes, and we all head towards the dining room.

Dinner was mostly silent and awkward. The only safe topics to discuss were work. Specifically, Mac's work at the police department, my work in shop class, or Hazel's work as a nurse. Jude's work and softball weren't safe because of the potential of accidentally bringing up Rowyn. As soon as the last plate was empty, Mac's patience wore out.

"What's going on? I know this can't be a coincidence, and I'm ready for answers." His cop senses must be tingling. Through conversation, he's learned her name is Hazel, and she's a nurse, but no other personal information was shared. My curiosity is still piqued as to why he called her Alice.

"I'll clear the table. Little Dove, do you want us to stay or go?" Jude's tone is soft and comforting. That's the first term of endearment that either of us let slip. We had previously decided not to tell Mac about our relationship but to let Hazel reveal as much about it as she was comfortable with. All references to her tonight have been her name.

"Little Dove? Seriously, someone needs to tell me what's going on." His anger is starting to simmer.

She ignores his question once again and stands up. "I'll help you clear the table, Jude. Phoenix, why don't you get all four of us drinks, and we will meet you in the living room." I dip my head in agreement, not missing the fact she said, "All four of us." She wants to do this together. And we will. Always together.

I grab two beers and two glasses of wine and join Mac in the living room.

"Phoenix." Mac's voice is stern and commanding. "Why am I here?"

He's kept his composure much longer than I would have been able to.

217

"Please just give Hazel a few more minutes. She'd like to talk to you." He lets out a frustrated sigh and slumps down into the armchair. Hazel and Jude walk in, and I hand her a glass of wine, giving the other to Jude. She drinks the entire glass until it's empty and hands it back to me. She shakes her head when I ask her if she'd like a refill.

The three of us sit on the couch, flanking Hazel. Her heart is racing so rapidly that I can see her pulse beating in her neck. I internally battle with myself, wanting to take her hand in mine to show her support, but I also don't want to give away our relationship.

Hazel finds strength through our presence and looks up at Mac.

"Mac, you've asked quite a few questions, and I know you're wondering why you're here." She pauses, and I lose my resilience taking her hand. I give it a light squeeze, and she returns the gesture.

Looking between the three of us, he loses whatever patience is left. "No shit. Why the fuck am I here in this obviously bizarre situation?" Hazel shrinks in on herself at his outburst.

"Mac, I'm so sorry-" He interrupts her.

"Don't apologize. Just fucking explain." He's yelling now, as he stands up. I stand up with him.

"Sit your ass down, Mac. If you want your answers, sit down, shut the fuck up, and be respectful." I will not allow him to treat her like that in our home.

We glare at each other before he concedes. "Fine. Fuck. I'm listening." He runs his hands through his hair in frustration. I sit back next to Hazel and grab her hand again. I kiss her knuckles and encourage her to continue. She signs and closes her eyes. I hear her mumble, "just rip the band aid off" to herself.

"Mac. I have a daughter."

"That's great. Congrats, it's a girl. Why the fuck am I here?" He shifts to the edge of his seat and leans his elbows on his knees.

"She's 12 years old." She stops again, waiting for him to calculate the math.

Suddenly he's on his feet, charging towards her. Jude and I jump up and create a wall between them.

Jude reaches back behind us and takes Hazel's hand. "Calm the fuck down, Mac."

"No, fuck no. Fuck you, Jude. Are you both fucking kidding me. This is some kind of a sick joke, right?"

Hazel releases Jude's hand, and steps around me to face Mac. "Her name is Rowyn. I've called her Wynnie since she was born. She plays softball. She was out there on the field this morning."

Mac walks to the other side of the room, pauses, then comes back and gets in my face. The heat radiating off his body has caused beads of sweat to form on his forehead.

"You're a real fucking prick, you know that? How did you even find this bitch?" He's poking his finger into my pec.

"Back. The fuck. Up, Mac." My blood is starting to boil. We're almost nose to nose. He has about an inch of height on me, but it could be ten inches right now, and I wouldn't back down. Jude puts his hands between us, and pushes our chests apart. Reluctantly we both take a step back.

"What the fuck is going on?" He points towards Hazel but he's talking to Jude and me. "I slept with this bitch one night in college when we were both drunk, and you expect me to believe I've had a kid for the past 12 years. After all the bullshit

I went through with Jenna, you expect me to believe this is happening again! No. Fuck you and fuck this." His attention turns to Hazel. "What the fuck do you want from me? I'm a cop. I'm not exactly rolling in the dough. I've already had one dumb slut try and rope me into being her-"

I see red, and without even a second thought, I sucker punched Mac. I will not allow him to degrade the woman I love. He stumbled back and tripped over the coffee table, landing flat on his back with a thud. I jumped on top of him, and started pummeling him with my fists. There's blood on my knuckles, and I don't know if it's his or mine, but I don't care. My ears are ringing, and I can vaguely hear Hazel screaming my name. A strong pair of arms wrap around my chest, and hauls me up. Mac lands a single punch to my left temple before I'm ripped off him. We both get back on our feet, bloody, chests heaving and rage-filled.

Hazel walks up to Mac, and with a shaking hand, she shoves her phone into his bloody face. "Look at her, you asshole. Look at your daughter and tell me she isn't yours. Look at YOUR eyes staring back at you. Fucking look at her!" Her entire body is trembling. Mac's face turns white as he stares in disbelief at her phone. Stumbling backward, he swings his arms around, trying not to bump into any furniture. We watch as he fumbles to the front door, rips it open, and walks out. We stand frozen as we hear his engine roar to life and his tires peel out.

37

Mac

It's just me and my bike on the backroads. I can ignore all my problems if I just ride. The wind in my face, the road under my feet, just me and loneliness. The way it's been for the past four years until today. Congrats, Mac. It's a girl. How fucking ironic.

That one picture of Rowyn just changed my life. One little snapshot of a daughter, my daughter, that's 12 years old. A daughter that I had no idea existed. And her eyes, the same cornflower blue as mine.

After my failed marriage with Jenna, I never thought there would be anything but a lonely future for me. Marrying right after we both graduated from Auburn University, still wet behind the ears, was one of my biggest life mistakes. I thought I had a perfect life. Young and dumb, I always knew I wanted to attend the police academy. Jenna was thrilled to be a cop's wife. She encouraged me all through the academy, and when I was placed at Mountain Pine Police Department, we moved from Alabama to Georgia and created our life. Jenna got her Realtor license, and we were a power couple.

One night, a few years into our marriage, Jenna told me she had a surprise for me, and handed me a wrapped box. Inside was a positive pregnancy test, and I was overjoyed. We were going to be parents. For nine months, I was the loving, doting daddy-to-be. The day Jenna gave birth was the most devastating day of my life. I knew the moment the baby was cleaned up and placed in her arms. She wasn't mine. It was a girl. We had waited to find out the gender. We wanted to be surprised. Jenna has blue eyes and dirty blonde hair, and I have dark brown hair with my unique blue eyes. The eyes that I share with Rowyn. The baby on Jenna's chest had brown eyes and the most beautiful olive-colored skin. When Jenna saw the devastation in my eyes, all she could say was, "I'm sorry."

I left the hospital, a shell of the man I walked in as. I went home, packed a bag, and showed up on Phoenix and Jude's doorstep. They opened their door to me, offering to stay as long as I needed.

Later that night, Jenna sent me a text telling me she would be moving back to Alabama to live with her parents. The baby was a product of a fling she had with a client. She told me she would sell the house for us and send me my half of the money. I told her to keep it. Six months later, in the divorce lawyer's office, the only time I've seen her since that day at the hospital, she handed me a check. The money has sat in a savings account untouched ever since.

I'm furious and disgusted with myself for how I just acted. I was blindsided. I walked in the door of my friend's house to see the most memorable moment of my college experience, sitting on their couch. When we ran into each other outside the bathroom, I was sure I had seen a ghost. Thirteen years changes people, but she was still as beautiful as the night I met her. My memory of that night is so vivid, not because of the sex, which was great, but because of the conversations we had. We talked about our families, our hopes for the future, and our love for *Alice In Wonderland*, which is something, as a guy, I don't get to talk about very often. Most people see my tattoo and never bridge the gap between the symbols. Phoenix and Jude have never asked about it before, and I saw their confusion when I called her Alice. Until an hour ago, I didn't know her by any other name. But even without names, we had a connection. It felt like our souls fused that night. I asked around after the party, and no one knew who she was. I was always on the lookout for my "Alice" on campus but eventually had to accept that it was just an amazing night I'd never forget.

I royally fucked shit up. My entire face hurts. Phoenix and I have never so much as gotten into an argument before tonight. I met them on the softball field one spring when they were new coaches. I had been doing security for the school's sporting events for a few years. I spotted their newness right away. I invited them to play on a local kickball team, and we hit it off. The night I showed up on their doorstep, we drank a lot of tequila, I cried over the loss of a daughter that was never mine and I put up a wall around my heart. This gruff bastard was born that night out of anger and betrayal.

I'm a father. A fucking father. I have a 12 year old daughter that has hopes and dreams. Does she know who I am? How could I have missed so much of her life already? I have to talk to Hazel. I have to make this right.

Turning my bike around, I head back to Phoenix and Jude's house. This won't be a pleasant conversation, but nothing worth having in life ever is. Jenna majorly fucked me up with her stunt, and I won't let her mistake stop me from having a relationship with my daughter. If she even wants to have one with me. Somehow, some way, I will make this right.

I want to be mad at Hazel. She kept this from me. She stopped me from being able to have a relationship with my daughter. I missed her birth, first steps, and her first day of kindergarten. I can't imagine how scared she must have been when she found out. Did she have a complicated pregnancy? Jenna's was easy. I wonder what Hazel's was like. Was she alone at night, or did she have help with her newborn?

I still have so many frustrating questions that need to be answered. Like an asshole, I stormed out. I had no right to compare what Jenna did to me to Hazel's confession. I want to, but I can't be mad at her. We didn't know each other. We had a one night stand at a college party.

I'll have to work hard to get any information from Phoenix and Jude about Hazel. I'm not even entirely sure how they know her or what the relationship is between them. What I do know is I'm going to have some major apologizing to do. But first, I have a stop to make.

38

Jude

Tonight was a total shit show. Despite our efforts to get Hazel to stay, after the roar of Mac's engine went silent in the distance, she said she was leaving. Phoenix and I watched her text Dellah, gather her things and leave with barely a goodbye to us. Giving my ethical code a big "screw you" I looked up Rowyn's school records hoping that Hazel used Dellah as an emergency contact. Luckily she had, and I texted her asking if she'd let us know when Hazel got home. We were worried about her. The text came in while Phoenix and I were in the bathroom cleaning up his injuries.

"She made it home. Hopefully, Dellah will take care of her tonight. What the fuck do we do now, Phoenix?"

"I don't know, man. I didn't expect her to run off. I knew there would be tension. I expected him to be mad, but this?" He raises his hands in the air displaying his cut and bruised knuckles. "I didn't expect this. I snapped. He may not have

225

used his fists on her, but I know his words cut her deep. I couldn't let him talk to her like that." Grabbing his shoulders, I pull him into a hug. The adrenaline rush from the fight is gone, leaving us raw and emotional.

"Why do you think she left?" She knew we were here to support her through this entire ordeal. She trusted us enough to be in the room when she told him.

"I think I might have scared her. I feel like shit about it." I pull away from the hug, squeeze his shoulders, and look him in the eyes.

"Hey, don't think like that. He got what he had coming to him. Mac had no right to treat her like that." I drop my hands to my sides and sigh. "Despite his outrage though, I feel bad for him. We should have considered what Jenna put him through and maybe approached him differently. We were here for his devastation. I know this is different, but in a way, it's also the same.

"That's bullshit, and you know it. It's not the same. Jenna was a lying, cheating bitch. Hazel was a scared teenager who made a wrong choice." He storms out of the bathroom, and I follow him.

"Phoenix, I'm not saying his reaction wasn't wrong. I'm just saying, put yourself in his shoes for 2 minutes. He wasn't completely out of line. He doesn't know Hazel like we do. He has no idea of our relationship with her. How much we trust her...love her." That realization still takes me by surprise every time I think about it. "We should have told her that we loved her."

I sit on the couch while Phoenix paces the living room, full of anxiety.

"Yeah, we should have told her. I hope it's not too late. She needs to know we aren't going anywhere, but not tonight. We'll let Dellah be her glue tonight. Tomorrow belongs to us, and every day after."

Eventually, Phoenix sits down next to me and holds my hand. We sat in silence for a while until I couldn't contain a burning question in my mind.

"Why do you think *he* left?" It's not like Mac to walk away from his problems. Being a cop, he always steps up to any situation he's confronted with.

"I've been wondering about that myself..." We both look at the front door as the rumble of a motorcycle pulls into our driveway. "He's got some fucking nerve!"

I place my hand on his chest, stopping him from getting up. "Phoenix, stop. Let me handle it. You're still too heated to deal with him. Why don't you go take a shower and get cleaned up? I'll see what he wants." I'm trying my best to avoid another confrontation. Phoenix agrees and heads to the bathroom.

I step outside before there's a knock on the door. I find Mac still sitting on his bike, rubbing his fingers into his temples with his thumb and forefinger. When he hears my footsteps approaching, he looks up. Reaching behind him, he grabs something from his saddle bag.

"A peace offering?" He extends his arm out, a bottle of tequila in his hand. I sigh, taking the bottle.

"Let's go. I'll grab the shot glasses. It's probably better if you don't come in. I'll meet you back on the porch." He follows me up the walkway, stops at the door, and sits in a rocking chair.

I walk inside and get three shot glasses from the cabinet. Hearing the shower turn off, I decided to check on Phoenix.

I knock on the bathroom door, and a puff of steam wafts over me when he opens it. He's standing in only a towel, and my eyes slowly roam down his hot, damp body, causing me to bite my lip. When my eyes reach back up to his, there's amusement and lust in them. I step inside the bathroom, put my hands on his hips and kiss him. It's a slow, deep kiss. The release of tension is physically visible in both of our bodies. We're breathless when we pull away.

"What was that for?" Phoenix asked while gently massaging my shoulders.

"I thought you might need something extra to help you relax. Did it help?" It was more for me than him. I know I'm about to have a difficult conversation with Mac, and I need some strength.

"It did. Is he gone?" I shake my head, and I feel him tense again.

"Listen, he brought tequila as a peace offering. If we are going to fix this, someone has to at least hear him out. I don't expect you to talk with him tonight. I imagine there will be enough drinking that he'll end up in the guestroom. Asshole or not, I won't let him get on his bike drunk. Alright?"

"It doesn't sound like I have much of a choice. I don't like it, but I also know you're right." He kisses me on the forehead and wishes me good luck. He walks down the hall to his room, and I walk outside with the shot glasses.

"I thought maybe you were gonna leave me out here alone." Mac is sitting in the rocking chair, rocking out his nervous energy. I put the shot glasses on the table between us and take a seat.

"I thought about it, but I didn't want the neighbors to talk in the morning."

228

"Thanks." A somber chuckle escapes from him. He looks at the table and arches a brow. "Three glasses?" I shrug.

"Just in case Phoenix decides to join us." Pouring our shots, I continue. "Here's the deal. The guest room is open to you tonight. I feel like there's going to be more drinking than talking, and I can't have your safety in my hands. Got it?" He responds by raising his shot, knocking it back, and pouring himself another. "Okay, good. So, if it wasn't already obvious, you did and said a lot of fucked up shit tonight. I hope you brought some knee pads because it's going to cost you a lot of groveling if you expect to get anywhere in Hazel's good graces."

Before he can speak, the front door slams open. Phoenix walks out wearing low-hanging sweatpants, and my instant reaction has me wanting to pin him against the wall, and see what he's wearing, or not, under them. He reaches for the tequila, pours himself a shot, and shoots it back, slamming the empty glass on the table. He stands directly in front of Mac and puts a finger to his chest, anger radiating from his body.

"You're a fucking douchebag. Drink your tequila, spill your guts to Jude tonight because he's the only one that's going to give a fuck. Sleep your ass in the guest room and make a plan to fix shit with Hazel. Whether you like it or not, you're no longer alone in this world anymore, asshole. You don't deserve Rowyn or Hazel after how you acted, but I know you're a better man than this, and you better be ready to prove it to those two." He pushed Mac in the chest, causing the rocking chair to hit the wall behind him.

Walking back to me, he leans down and gives me a quick peck on the lips. "Good night. I'll make breakfast in the morning. You two will probably need it." He grabs my full shot glass off the table and chugs it back. He refills the glass and hands it back to me. Whispering in my ear so Mac doesn't hear, "You know where to find me if you need me."

He walks back inside, and Mac and I sit in uncomfortable silence. I wonder what he's thinking of the display Phoenix just made. Was his speech or the kiss more shocking?

Mac finally finds his words. "I think we might need more tequila."

39

Phoenix

Around 3 AM, I feel my bed dip. The smell of tequila and Jude's citrus body wash engulfs me as he wraps his arm around my chest from behind. His bare chest pressed to my bare back.

"Is this okay?" He sounds half asleep and extremely drunk. I roll over and switch our positions, wrapping my arms around his chest.

"Now it is. I'm the big spoon." I feel the laugh in his chest under my hands. "How was your talk?"

He mumbles, "It sucked. Tequila sucks. Mac sucks. Tomorrow is gonna suck."

"I got you. Get some sleep, my good boy." Kissing the back of his head, he hums in response, and almost immediately, I hear soft snoring. Yep, tomorrow is gonna suck.

Walking past the guest room with coffee in hand, I see the door is closed. I know Mac is in there because his bike is still in the driveway. I open the door to my bedroom, and Jude is curled up on his stomach in the middle of my large bed. My black comforter is twisted around his legs, giving me an unobstructed view of the hard lines on his back. I bite my lip and let my eyes linger for a moment longer. I place the two steaming cups on my nightstand and crawl in next to him. Rubbing his back in an effort to gently wake him, his eyes open slightly. He gives me a small smile before realizing where he is, and he shoots up to a sitting position.

Groaning, he grabs his head. "Oh my god, that hurt." Sitting up, I pull a bottle of pain medicine from my pocket, and hand it to him along with his coffee. He takes them and smiles in appreciation.

"Thanks. And, um…sorry I ended up in here last night. We almost finished the bottle. I must have wandered in here by accident." He drinks more of his coffee, avoiding eye contact with me.

I grab his jaw and turn it towards me. "You have nothing to apologize for. It was no accident you found your way to my bed. You obviously needed the comfort, and I was more than happy to give it to you." I smile a boyish grin. "You make a great little spoon."

Over his coffee cup, he flashes me a shy smile. Gesturing to the mug he says, "Thanks for this."

"I'm about to go start some eggs and bacon. I figured you'd both need it."

His brows raise. "Is he still here? I thought he might try to high-tail it out of here early."

"Yeah, his bike's outside. You were pretty drunk last night. How did it go?" His shoulders droop and he signs.

"He talked, and I listened mostly. And we drank. A lot. He's still fucked up in the head from Jenna. I didn't realize

232

how much until he purged it all last night. He wants to make things right. He wants to be a father to Rowyn."

"Yeah, well, he has a long road ahead of him." I lean over and kiss his forehead. "Go shower, and I'll meet you in the kitchen for breakfast."

30 minutes later, Jude comes strolling in looking casual in light-washed jeans and a gray t-shirt. It's a stark contrast to my black basketball shorts and bare chest. I lick my lips at the sight of him. How had I never noticed how attracted to him I was before Hazel came into our lives? His sandy mop of hair is still wet from his shower, and I want to run my fingers through it. *Tame yourself, Phoenix. We have a guest in the house.*

Speaking of, "I'll go wake up Mac, make yourself a plate. I made another pot of coffee." He thanks me, and I head down the hall. Reaching the guest room, I bang on the door.

"Wake up, Mac. Time to face the consequences of your actions." Hearing nothing, I bang harder. "Come on, man, time to get up." I hear movement this time, and the door opens. An extremely disheveled, hungover Mac stands before me. His left eye is swollen, and a bruise forms on the right side of his jaw. I got him good last night. I take a bottle of pain medicine from my pocket and shove it into his chest. "Shower, coffee, eggs, bacon, kitchen." I walk away back to Jude and breakfast.

Jude and I are finishing up when Mac appears in the kitchen. I gesture to the food, "Eat, you look like shit, then talk to us." He grunts and nods, making himself a plate.

"Thank you, and I'm sorry." He finally speaks up after eating half of his food. He continues, speaking into his plate. "I know neither of those have any meaning right now, but they're the most honest words I have. You were right, Phoenix," he pauses and looks at me. "I don't deserve either of them, but they're my family now, and I need to take care of them. I need to make this right. I *will* make this right."

"Those are some pretty words, Mac, but how? We aren't the ones you need to convince. What are you going to do to fix this?"

His gaze passes between Jude and me. "I need your help." Against my better judgment, we will help him. We know Mac, and we know what he's been through. In the light of day and with a clear head, I can see now how things spiraled out of control last night. The man was blindsided by his worst nightmare. My outburst only exacerbated an already tense situation.

Jude speaks up in support. "We will help you, but you have to know, despite what our relationship is with you..." He looks at me, asking for permission, and I give him a quick nod. "Mac, you need to know that we are both with Hazel. Phoenix and I are both dating her. We love her, and no matter what, she comes first. We want you to have a relationship with Hazel and Rowyn, and we won't get in your way, but we're not going anywhere. Not unless she tells us otherwise.

'Well, shit. That answers some questions about last night." He looks away deep in thought, and we give him some time to process the information he's just learned. He rubs his temples with his thumbs and grunts. "So the two of you are...together?" His tone is pure curiosity, no judgment.

"We are developing," I tell him. I'm not sure what the correct answer is for what's happening between us but developing sounds like an accurate enough description. "Is that a problem?"

"Nope, not at all." He takes a long drink of his coffee. "And

Hazel, the three of you are together?"

"We are." I get up and start clearing everyone's plates. "Is *that* a problem?" I look at him over my shoulder as I rinse our dishes.

"Is she happy? Do you make her happy?"

Jude puts his hand on Mac's shoulder. "She is, and we do. She's lived life with little support for the past 12 years. She's made a wonderful life for her and Rowyn. She is strong, independent, and fiercely protective of her daughter. If Hazel didn't want us in her life, we wouldn't be here. And if she didn't want you in her life, she wouldn't have told you about Rowyn. You're basically a stranger to her. You may share DNA with her daughter, but that doesn't give you the right to be in their lives. You have to earn it." Mac places his hand over Jude's, and looks intently into his eyes.

"I will, I promise. And if I fuck up again," he looks at me, "You can beat my ass again, Phoenix."

"I'll hold you to that, Mac. Now get your shit together and get out. We need to check on our girl."

"Thanks again. I have to get to the station anyway. I have some paperwork to get done. I'll earn my place in their life. I swear to it."

40

Hazel

Sitting with my morning coffee, watching Dellah make us pancakes, I reflect on the night's events. I text Dellah 9-1-1. That's all she needed. By the time I got to my apartment, she was waiting in my living room with tequila, ice cream, chocolates, and tissues– the essential break-up items. My text gave her no details as to what the issue was, so she came prepared. She also sent Wynnie to her house for a movie night with Collin and told her to plan to spend the night in their guest room. This woman is my soulmate.

As we indulged ourselves in booze and sugar, I gave her the details of my evening. She silently listened, only making occasional noises of encouragement or disbelief and passing me tissues when needed. I was still in denial.

As heartbroken as I am for myself, I'm more heartbroken for Wynnie. She may have just lost something she never even knew she had. The Mac I saw last night was not the same man I met 13 years ago at that party. The way he exploded at me and the mention of the name Jenna led me to believe there was something more than my confession that set him off. The guys seemed to know what he was referring to, but I didn't stick around long enough to question them.

I still need to let them know I'm okay and that they didn't do anything wrong, but I was so overwhelmed last night that my flight response kicked in. I knew at that moment I needed my rock, Dellah. The woman who was here for me when it all started.

"Are we Team Revenge or Team Redemption as far as Mac is concerned?" She glances at me quickly before flipping a pancake. This is the exact type of support I need.

"Can I say both right now? While he was a complete asshole, and I want to drive his motorcycle into a lake, I'm still holding out hope that he comes to his senses, and wants to have a relationship with his daughter."

"Absolutely." She stares down into the mix of pancake batter. "Have you heard from the guys?" I shake my head. I haven't gotten a single text since I left. I hope I didn't royally mess things up. "I have."

"What? What do you mean you have? When?" I'm in utter disbelief that they text her and not me.

"They texted me shortly after you did last night. They wanted to make sure you got home safe. I let them know when you got here, and they said they'd talk to you today. I guess they wanted to give you some time to process. They're really good guys, Hazel."

"I know," and I do. "I was in shock. Mac's reactions scared me. Phoenix punching Mac shocked me." He punched Mac. Phoenix punched Mac. They were on the floor fighting, over me, for me. The guys begged me to stay and talk with them, but I couldn't. I needed to get out of there and think. It was all so overwhelming, and I needed my bestie.

Dellah nods in understanding and tops off my coffee. "I'll text Wynnie and Collin and let them know the pancakes are ready. We can all have a pancake party."

Once everyone is together and we are laughing and having fun while eating our pancakes, I feel a little lighter. No matter what happens, Wynnie has a family here. Dellah and Collin are our family. My lightheartedness quickly subsides when we hear a truck pull up into the driveway.

I cross the apartment to look out the window. I freeze and internally panic at the sight of Phoenix's pickup truck in the driveway. No, why are they here? They can't be here. Wynnie will see them. Sensing my panic, Dellah joins me at the window. Seeing the truck, she leans in so no one else hears her and asks, "Do you want me to get rid of them?"

I shake my head. "No, I have to talk to them. Try and distract Wynnie so she doesn't see." I quickly text the group chat and tell the guys I'll be right out and not to come up. I take a critical look at my clothing choice, black yoga pants, and an oversize long-sleeve T. I guess this will have to do. Changing would only raise suspicion. I throw on my shoes and quietly leave the apartment.

Walking across the driveway, I jump into the back of Phoenix's truck and tell them to drive anywhere but my driveway. With confused looks on their faces, all I say is "Wynnie," and they understand. Once parked in a nearby parking lot, they both get out and join me in the back seat. Their faces are full of apprehension and longing.

"I'm okay," is all I had to say before they embraced me in a hug. Once again, I'm giggling, and in unison. they both say-

"Hazel-nut sandwich." At least the absurdity of the word is always a tension breaker.

"How are you?" Jude asks.

"I'm processing. Last night was much more than I expected, and I didn't react well. I'm sorry." I turn towards Phoenix and examine the bruise forming on his cheekbone. Looking at his hands, I ask, "How are you?"

"A little worse for the wear, but you're our concern right now. My bruises will heal. You have nothing to apologize for. Dellah told us when you got home, and we knew you were safe. That's what mattered most to us last night." I gently touch the bruise on his cheek. I know it had to hurt, and he's more concerned about me than himself.

"Have you heard from him? From, Mac?" I don't know what answer I want to hear. Part of me hopes he just fucked off to wallow alone, and part of me hopes he reached out to the guys and they were able to knock some sense into him.

"I did," Jude swiped a loose piece of my hair off my forehead. "He came back last night, and I talked with him. And we drank a lot of tequila."

She huffs. "Seems like there was a lot of that going around last night."

"Little Dove, he acted very inappropriately last night. It's no excuse, but he has a good reason for his outburst. It's his story to tell, and I know he'd like to speak to you whenever you're ready."

"Does it have to do with... Jenna?" He dips his head in confirmation. "But you won't tell me?"

"No, Angel, you'll need to hear it from him." I understand and respect them not wanting to tell me.

"Alright, I will, when I'm ready. I have a lot to process from

239

last night." I look back and forth between them. "Are...are we okay?" This is the answer I'm dreading. They are here, and I should take that as a good sign, but my insecurities are screaming in my ear that walking away ruined everything. I hate feeling this vulnerable. It's easy to be confident and independent when you have no choice but to rely on yourself because that's all you have. Sure, I've always had Dellah, but there's a difference between relying on a best friend and relying on a partner, or partners in this case.

"We're okay." Jude strokes my cheek in reassurance. "I'll be honest, it hurt when you left without talking to us first. We want you to trust us and lean on us for support." He gently kisses the corner of my mouth, turns my face towards him, and looks deeply into my eyes. "Hazel, I love you." He loves me.

I feel Phoenix's hand squeeze my thigh. I look down at his hand then up to his green eyes. "I love you, Hazel. We love you. We are more than okay. We want to help you through this thing with Mac. However you want it to play out. We told him about us this morning. He knows that the three of us are in a relationship and that we aren't going anywhere unless you tell us to."

My head is swimming with emotions right now. They told Mac about us. They shared our relationship with him. They love me. These two sexy, sweet, generous men who are so far out of my league love me. No one outside of my family has ever loved me.

"I...I..." Jude puts his hand over my lips, stopping my stuttering.

"Shh, you don't have to say anything back. You have two hearts to worry about, not just one. Rowyn doesn't even know about us yet." I'm nodding like a bobble head again. "You have a lot you're working through right now, and we want to help you. Please let us be your support, your rocks."

I should let them help me. I want to let them help me. Even though I could do this alone, I don't have to. Asking for help has always been challenging for me, but they are here offering it. They know Mac, and I trust them. I need to trust their judgment, too.

"Okay, alright. Let's get through this Mac situation together." They squeeze me tighter between them, and I'm surrounded by citrus and metal. Phoenix kisses my neck and I rest my head on Jude's shoulder to give him more access. Jude's hand runs up and down my thigh, inching higher and higher each time. These men make my libido go from 0 to 60 with just a slight touch.

"Hey, Angel?" Phoenix purrs in my ear. I hmm, as a response. "Wanna act like teenagers and give each other hand jobs in the back of my truck? I'm still turned on from that dress that I never got to take off of you last night." I hear Jude snicker in my other ear as he nuzzles my neck. Phoenix peers over at him and smiles.

"You like the sound of that, don't you, naughty boy? Do you want to bury your fingers deep in her pussy while she uses her hands to jerk us off?" My core starts to heat with the thought of doing what he's suggesting. I watch as Jude's hips make an involuntary thrust at Phoenix's words. He seems to like his dirty talk as much as I do.

Reaching over, I rub my hand across Jude's pants, rubbing his noticeably hard bulge. "Do you want that, Jude?" I squeeze my hand over his length, and he groans a breathy, "Yes." I look around us outside the windows. We're at the back of a commuter parking lot, and it's mostly deserted since it's a weekend. Reading my thoughts, Phoenix eases my mild concern.

"The windows are tinted dark enough that you can't see inside just by driving by. I wouldn't put you in harm's way. This body belongs to us, and I wouldn't want to share it with a random passerby." I hear clicking and look down to see them undoing belts, buttons and zippers. I guess we're really doing this.

Presented before me are two extremely delicious-looking long, hard dicks just waiting for me to touch them. As I reach down to claim my prizes, Phoenix swipes his hand along the top of my yoga pants.

"Can we pull these down?" I lift my hips in acknowledgment. He pulls my pants down to my ankles and pushes my legs apart to give them access. He swipes a finger through my folds and feels how ready I am for what we are about to do. "Mmm, already wet for us, you dirty girl. Does this excite you?" He swirls my arousal around my clit, and I moan. Jude swallows the sounds with his mouth and joins Phoenix's finger to tease me.

With their hands working me up, I grab hold of both of their warm, velvety cocks. Giving them a big pull from base to tip, I swirl my thumbs around the tips spreading their pre-cum. It appears I'm not the only one excited about this.

Jude pushes two fingers inside me, and we all gasp as the intrusion causes me to give a tight squeeze on their shafts. We find a rhythm of pushing, pulling, and swirling, and soon the windows are fogged on the truck from our heavy panting. The tingling is building in the pit of my stomach, and I can feel my orgasm growing.

"I need more. Deeper, Jude." He reaches down and pulls off my shoes.

"Fuck these pants." He grabs a handful of my pants pooled at my ankles, and pulls them until they pop off my feet. Picking up each leg, he drapes one over his thigh and the other over Phoenix, leaving me spread wide between them. Diving his fingers back inside my pussy he hums. "That's much better." And it is. He hits my sweet spot at the new angle, and within minutes, I'm a writhing mess of pleasure and moans.

I give their cocks a few more tugs and I stop. I need them. I want them.

"Take me. I need you both. I need you both to come inside me now." I push Phoenix so his back is flush against the door, and I crawl between his legs. I wiggle my ass to Jude in invitation, and he takes the hint. Lowering his pants, he gets on his knees behind me on the seat and pushes inside me in one thrust as I swallow Phoenix's cock. We all moan in relief and pleasure. Jude's thrusting hips cause me to take Phoenix deeper each time, and it's not long before they are both ready to come. I reach between my legs and start to tease my clit. I'm close, and I want us to come together.

"Are you going to come with us, Angel? I nod as best as I can and mumble into his cock. He reaches under me and pinches one of my nipples, and the fireworks explode inside me. My bucking hips set off Jude, and the vibrations from my moaning sets off Phoenix. We are a sweaty mess of pheromones, and pleasure, and I didn't realize how much the truck was rocking until it stopped.

"Fuck, Little Dove." I rest my head on Phoenix's chest as Jude trails kisses along my back where my shirt rode up. "Did you know that car sex was one of my teenage fantasies?"

243

"Hmm, I'd love to fulfill more of those fantasies, Jude." Just as I lean up to kiss him, we hear the telltale "whoop, whoop" of a police car just outside.

"Shit!" We all scramble to put our clothes back on. Phoenix is the quickest since he only has to tuck himself back into his pants. He opens the back door giving us a "hurry up" look before he leaves to assess the situation. Scrambling to peel my yoga pants back on in the small space, I hear Phoenix talking to another male voice. Unfortunately, I can't make out anything they are saying. A few minutes go by, and Phoenix opens the back door. His look is apologetic. He extends his hand for me to step out of the truck.

"What's going on, Phoenix? Are we in trouble?" He shakes his head, and the corner of his lip tilts up.

"No, we aren't in any trouble. Someone wants to talk to you." Me? What's going on? I look down at myself to confirm I'm fully dressed before accepting his hand.

Stepping out, I see an unmarked police cruiser parked perpendicular behind Phoenix's truck. Someone is leaning on the trunk of the car with their head down. Phoenix stops pulling me into him, and starts speaking into my hair.

"I told him now wasn't the best time, but it's not my decision to make. He doesn't want to push you to talk, but he'd like to apologize." It's Mac, that's whose leaning against the car. Mac caught us in the back of Phoenix's truck with the windows all steamed up.

"What's he doing here? How did he find us?" I look back over at the man whose posture seems defeated. His head is still down, and his arms crossed over his chest.

Phoenix chuckles. "Someone called into the police department about a steamy, rocking truck in the parking lot. Mac

244

was there doing some paperwork and figured it was just some teenagers making out. He offered to check on it." That makes sense. I'm sure the truck was a sight to see on the outside. "If you want me to go over there and tell him you don't want to see him, I will." Do I want to talk to him? No. I'm not ready to talk, but if it's just an apology for his behavior last night, I can listen. He looks tortured standing there, and I don't want to be the cause of that if I can help it.

"I'll let him apologize." He kisses the top of my head and releases me. Walking over to him, I rub my sweaty palms on my thighs. Our last meeting went terribly. I hope I can walk away from this one without more emotional wounds. He hears me coming and looks up.

"Alice-" He shakes his head like he's trying to shake away the word or the memory. "Hazel." I stop a few feet away from him.

"Mac." I cross my arms to tighten my defenses a little more.

"I…Shit." He lifts off the back of the car and takes a step towards me. His eyes turn to the side, and he stops and steps back. Looking over my shoulder, I see Phoenix and Jude watching us intently at the back of the truck. My strength. Mac rubs his hand over his face and sighs. "Fuck. I'm sorry, Hazel. I was a goddamn asshole last night, and you didn't deserve the way I reacted or treated you. This…I. I'd like to explain it all to you some time. Soon, I hope." He pauses, taking in a big inhale. When he exhales, he looks me in the eyes. "I believe you. There's no denying that Rowyn is my daughter. I want to be in her life, your lives. I know I have a long way to go, but I just wanted you to know how sorry I am about the things I said. I didn't mean any of them, and it's not an excuse, but I was in shock, and I'm sorry." He stops and looks at me, waiting for a response.

"I understand. I accept your apology for your outburst last night. It seems you repaired whatever damage you caused with Jude and Phoenix, and their opinions mean a lot to me. We do need to talk, but I need a little more time." The brick of guilt has formed back in the pit of my stomach. "I need to apologize as well. I never meant to keep her from you. There was no malicious intent. And I'm also sorry you had to find the three of us like...this." I gesture back to Phoenix's truck, windows still steamed over.

He chuckles through a smile. I remember that smile, so warm and comforting. "I can't say it isn't the first time I've interrupted extracurriculars in a vehicle. I was a little shocked to see it was Phoenix's truck but good for you guys. Maybe next time, keep it inside the house, though." It's my turn to chuckle and smile. "And, Hazel. Thank you. Your apology means a lot. It's not needed, but I still appreciate it."

"I'll get your number from one of the guys when I'm ready to sit down and talk. Soon." His shoulders raise a bit in hope. We have a long road ahead of us, but I'm going to hold hope with him.

Pulling back into my driveway, I give each of the guys a quick peck on the cheek, and walk towards the door to my apartment. I look up and see the curtains swaying. Looks like Dellah spotted our return home. I hope she doesn't mind that I took off without letting her know.

41

Hazel

I'm exhausted. Work has been crazy this week. There's a stomach bug going around, and our schedule has been packed. Wynnie and the guys are preparing for their first away game, so they have been just as busy. On Tuesday, I asked them for Mac's number, and I texted him on Wednesday, asking if he was free this weekend to get coffee and talk. Friday worked best for him, and after running home to change, I'm sitting at The Book Beanery, waiting for him to arrive. This place gives me comfort, and I wanted to be calm when we spoke.

Hearing the rumble of a motorcycle outside, I look out the window and spot him parking. He swings his leg over his bike and takes his helmet off. I internally swoon at the sight in front of me. It's like those slow-motion scenes in the movie. The gorgeous dark, broody superstar *or villain* swoops in on his motorcycle, looking all sexy. Dark jeans, a light gray shirt, a leather jacket, and his almost black hair make the perfect backdrop to contrast his cornflower blue eyes that seem to sparkle in the evening light. It almost takes my breath away. Damn, this bookstore must be rubbing off on me.

He walks in and spots me in the back corner. I lift my cup and motion to the counter, signaling him to grab a coffee before he joins me.

"Thank you for reaching out to me." He gives me a warm smile reminding me of the night we met. "I really appreciate it."

"Mac, there was never an option where I wouldn't reach out. I just needed things to calm down. Your apology helped a lot." Some of the tension releases from his shoulders.

"So, where would you like to start?" He takes a sip of his coffee, and I can see his hands slightly shaking. He's as nervous as I am, and that grounds me. Where to start? That would be the big question. There are so many options: the party, Rowyn, Jenna, and my relationship with the guys. Maybe we should just start from the beginning.

"How about the night we met? Sounds like as good a place as any."

We talked about what we remembered from the night. It seems the later details were foggy for us both. He told me about how he looked for me after. I apologized for not looking for him. Then we moved to the topic of Jenna, what seemed to be the catalyst to his outrage last weekend. I learned about her betrayal, which put much of what he accused me of into perspective. All along the way, he was apologizing, and I kept telling him I understood, which I did.

"Can you tell me about Rowyn?"

"How about we take this outside and go for a walk? It's a nice evening." Despite the nice weather, I just needed to get

248

up and move. I was nervous telling him about Rowyn. More specifically, his reaction to realizing he's missed so much of her life. There's knowing, and then there's having it spoken out loud.

I shared details about her childhood as we leisurely walked down the dimly lit main street of town. He did better than I expected. I saw his jaw tense several times when I spoke about fun things we did together, her likes and dislikes. I watched his shoulders and eyes droop with sorrow at the loss of missing her milestones. When we talked about her softball career, he remembers seeing her out on the field these past few weeks, and I saw his chest swell with pride.

"I want to get to know my daughter, Hazel. I was robbed of being a father once, and although I may be a little behind the game now, I don't want to let another opportunity slip away." His words are so sincere, but I can hear the hint of heartbreak in the undertone. Jenna may have cheated on him, but I was truly the one who robbed him of his fatherhood.

"She's not a little kid, Mac. She's an angsty preteen that will have to be won over slowly. I haven't told her anything about you. I haven't even told her about the guys yet. She knows I'm dating someone, but that's the extent of it." We continue to stroll the streets in silence for a few minutes. It's late March, but the weather has been warmer than usual, and the trees are starting to show some green. There's new life all around us.

"Will you tell me about your relationship with Jude and Phoenix? How did you meet? How did this three-way relationship happen?"

I smile as I recount to him how I bumped into both men at different times. Jude's Target date, Dellah playing wing woman for Phoenix, and finding out about each other in the coach's office. Then I told him about the first and second times I saw him before that night at dinner. I told him that before I bumped into him outside the bathroom, I had run in there because of him. Then we laughed about how I need to pay more attention to where I'm going because bumping into people seems to be a habit of mine.

We've made a loop and are almost back to the coffee shop. I can see my car not too far ahead. There's only one topic left for us to discuss.

"So, is it serious with them?" They love me. I love them, although I'm too afraid to admit it out loud, but I do.

"Yeah, it's serious. They've been great to me. Even though Wynnie doesn't know who they are to me, she really likes them as her coaches."

"Hazel, I…" He stops walking and rakes his hand through his hair. He looks confused and conflicted. "Fuck it."

Unexpectedly I found myself pressed against the side of the building we were just passing. Mac has me pinned by his hips, one hand on my waist and the other around the front of my neck. His piercing blue eyes bore into mine and I feel like his prey. I whimper at the intensity of them.

"Shhh. Don't be afraid, my little Alice. I could never hurt you." If only he knew my whimper wasn't a scared sound but a turned-on sound. This is not okay. My body feels charged from his commanding presence. I feel my heartbeat bouncing off his hand as he gently squeezes my neck.

"W-what are you doing, Mac?"

"Alice, my Alice. I never gave up on you. I've felt a connection to you since that night. Maybe my soul always knew Rowyn was out there. I'm going to ask for forgiveness, not permission." He angles his head and seals his lips to mine. The reminders of that night, our night, come flashing back. For a moment, I forget everything else around us. I feel the brush of his tongue on my bottom lip while his hand around my neck gives a slight pulse. The smell of leather permeates the air, and I get lost in his kiss. I lace my fingers in his hair and lean closer into his firm chest. A car honks in the distance breaking the spell we were in. I freeze and he steps back removing his hands from my body. He stares at me waiting for my next move. I feel like I'm in a daze. Touching my fingers to my lips in disbelief, I push him away, and he steps back farther.

"What did you do? Jude. Phoenix. Why?" My entire body is trembling. I have to get out of here. "Please let me leave." My voice is so low I'm surprised he heard me. He leans forward and brushes his lips to my ear.

"The secret, Alice, is to surround yourself with people who make your heart smile. It's then, only then, that you'll find Wonderland." He whispers a gentle kiss on my neck and steps aside.

I speed walk the entire way to my car, my heart beating out of my chest, not from the exertion but from the event that just occurred. He kissed me and I kissed him back. Why didn't I stop him sooner? God, what does this mean? I love Phoenix and Jude. Do I have feelings for Mac? No. I don't know him. He's Wynnie's biological father. That's it, nothing more. I need to go home and shower because I can still smell the leather on my skin from our bodies pressed together.

42

Mac

I'm so fucking fucked. That kiss was everything that I remembered it to be. My soul remembers her touch, her taste. She didn't pull away when my lips touched hers. She must have felt it, too.

God, when I pulled up behind Phoenix's truck last weekend, windows fogged over, and the whole thing rocking, I knew someone was in there with him. I'm glad it was me that took the call, or they would have had a very different morning. I waited until the rocking stopped before I tapped the siren. No need to be a cock block. But when Phoenix stepped out of the truck looking flushed and sated, I wanted to punch him. He gave me a cocky smile when he saw it was me.

When he told me Hazel was in his truck, I knew I had to apologize, and that's not usually my thing. I don't make stupid mistakes. Even though she accepted my apology, I still feel terrible. And I don't regret the kiss we just shared, but I'm not looking forward to the talk I will have with Jude and Phoenix.

Knocking on their door, I attempt to put on my cop, no-bullshit mask. Phoenix opens the door, and I shove a bottle of tequila at his chest. He takes a look at it and shakes his head.

"What now?" I shove a second bottle at his chest, and his demeanor changes. "What the fuck, Mac. What the fuck did you do?" Well, his hands are full. At least he can't punch me yet.

"Jude, get your ass in here!" His boisterous voice echoes off the walls. He places the bottles on a table, crosses his arms around his chest, and waits for Jude. Phoenix points at the bottles on the table when he enters the room. Jude's face darkens. He pulls out his phone and glances at it.

"I don't have any missed calls or texts from Hazel. So, either this doesn't involve her, or you fucked up so royally again that she's retreated back into herself. If that's the case, you'll need more than tequila not to get your ass kicked by both of us." I can see the tension vibrating off him as his fists open and close.

"Can I come in and talk?"

"It's your fucking funeral." I grab the tequila bottles as Phoenix steps aside for me to pass. Walking into the kitchen, I take out three shot glasses. Pouring each one of us a drink, we chug them back. I do that two more times before Phoenix stops me.

"Enough fucking around, Mac. Talk." His voice is almost a growl. I've intentionally positioned myself with the counter between us, hoping I'd at least have a split second to react if needed. Based on the energy in the room, I'm sure it will be.

"Can I make a request first?" They're both seething with rage. "When you hit me this time, could you aim for below the neck? I had a lot of lying and explaining to do about this."

I poke at my still swollen cheek and wince.

"Fucking. Talk." Fuck. Phoenix is definitely going to punch me again.

"IkissedHazel." I mumble the words so fast they mash together.

"What did you just fucking say?" Jude is inching toward the end of the counter.

"No, you know what, fuck it. I'm not gonna be a little bitch about this. I kissed Hazel." That split second I gave myself didn't matter when Jude rounded the corner, and Phoenix launched himself over the counter to tackle me. "SHE DIDN'T STOP ME! SHE KISSED ME BACK!" We landed on the floor, and they froze for a heartbeat. I took the chance to roll out of their attack and scrambled to my feet.

"What do you mean? You have two fucking seconds to explain." Phoenix takes Jude's offered hand to stand from his crouched position.

"Listen, we went for coffee tonight and talked everything over. I still feel the connection from that night 13 years ago. There was always a piece of her still inside my soul. I had to know if she still had a piece of me, too. She's my fucking one, dammit. The one that got away. She kissed me back, and we both felt it." I dipped my head, the emotions weighing me down. That was my fatal mistake. Phoenix sucker punched me in the gut, and I went down hard, expecting more, but it didn't come. Instead, when I look up, Phoenix is handing me a shot of tequila, and Jude is extending his hand to help me up. I swallow back the shot and accept the hand.

"Fuck," is all Phoenix says before he pours another round of shots.

Grabbing one, I ask, "What now?" before downing yet

another shot, relishing in the burn. I know it's a loaded question, but it's one that needs to be asked.

"What now? Isn't that the fucking question?" Phoenix stands rigid and continues to pour amber liquid into our glasses as we empty them.

Jude places an arm around Phoenix's waist pulling him in close. "Now we get shitfaced. Tomorrow we have our first away game, and tomorrow night the four of us will come back here and figure this shit out."

"Sounds like as good a plan as any. Salud!" I tap the shot glass on the counter and then chug it back.

I leave early the next morning before the guys wake up. I need to get home and prepare for my security job at the baseball fields. Unfortunately, Rowyn and the guys are away, but I patrol all the fields, and several other games are still playing at home.

I watch as Hazel and Rowyn pull into the parking lot, and I stay on the other end of the fields. Phoenix, Jude, and the rest of the team arrive, pack up on the bus, and head to the neighboring town for their game.

Several hours later, I'm getting ready to head home. All of the games on my fields have finished, and the last of the lingering spectators have left when I see the bus pull up. I hang back as they unpack and parents come to collect their girls.

I watch as, one by one, each girl gets picked up, except Rowyn. Where's Hazel? Phoenix walks over to his truck and pulls down the hatch for Rowyn to sit. She pauses and examines his truck before hesitantly climbing on to wait. Everything in me wants to walk over and casually say hi to the guys to get closer to her. To see the blue of her eyes that match mine, that are mine. I made them. That's my daughter, my flesh and blood. But I can't go over there because I kissed her mother last night. Fuck. My only connection to Rowyn and I might have messed it up. I need to make this right.

43

Hazel

I'm completely stressed out. Mac kissed me last night, and I didn't stop him. A car horn did. I went home and cried in the shower until the water ran cold. I didn't even call Dellah for support. I allowed myself to wallow in a bottle of wine alone.

The guys texted me last night and asked if I'd come over for dinner after the game. I barely slept because I was a nervous wreck. I spent most of the morning avoiding their glances during the game because I felt guilty about my actions. After, in my frantic state, I locked my keys in the car at the school where the away game was held. I had to wait for Dellah to bring me my spare key, making me late to pick up Wynnie. Karma is really being a bitch. Then again, I feel like a terrible person. I have to tell the guys tonight at dinner.

My stomach is in knots on the way to their house. Pulling into the driveway, I see a navy blue pickup truck parked that I don't recognize. I don't dwell on it too much and knock on the door. Preparing myself for the bomb I'm about to drop on them, Jude opens the door.

"Little Dove, you know you don't need to knock and wait anymore. Our house is always open to you." He smiles a reserved smile, places his warm hand on the small of my back, and pulls me into his citrus scent. I rest my head on his chest and bask in his warmth. "I've missed you." He kisses the top of my head, and I hope of all hopes, after my confession, he still feels the same way.

Walking into the living room, I expect to see Phoenix sitting on the couch, but I see a different head of dark hair. Mac turns as we walk in and smiles at me. Frozen in shock, Jude rubs his hands on my back and whispers into my ear.

"It's okay, Hazel. Come have a seat." Hazel? I wrap my arms around my stomach to hide my trembling hands.

"I...I...I have to use the bathroom." Spinning on my heels, I rush down the hall, and try not to slam the door behind me.

I lock the door as soon as I'm alone inside and press my back against it. Taking a few deep breaths I attempt to get my breathing under control. Jude called me Hazel. That's what set off the panic. He only calls me Hazel when he's serious, and there was nothing to be serious about in that moment. Taking a step forward, I give myself a long look in the mirror. I have to think about this rationally. What are the facts?

1. Mac kissed me, and I kissed him back.
2. The guys invited me over for dinner. But that's not uncommon for a Saturday night.
3. Mac is here, and I have no idea why.
4. There's no way Mac told them about the kiss. The guys would have kicked his ass, and I didn't see any new

injuries. Then again, I also haven't seen Phoenix yet.

What if Mac did tell them, and that was just the calm before the storm? There are too many variables, and I have no answers. No, I have one answer. I came here to tell Phoenix and Jude that Mac kissed me, and I didn't stop him. I came here to confess my transgressions. Will it be harder with Mac sitting right there? Abso-fucking-lutely. I need to woman up and face the music. And apparently, when I'm internally panicking, I talk to myself in cliches.

There's a light knock on the door, and it makes me jump. I unlock it and crack it open.

"Jude, I'm okay I just-"

"Alice…" I whip around at the sound of his voice. Grabbing the front of his shirt, I pulled him into the bathroom. But let's be honest. He came willingly because there was no way I could have pulled his wall of muscles inside if he didn't want to come. Reaching around him to close the door, I give him my back.

"What are you doing here, Mac? You shouldn't be here. I need to tell the guys what we did. What I did. You can't be here. I need to tell them."

"I already did." My knees give out like jello, and I collapse to the floor. I feel like someone just punched me in the gut. All the air has left my lungs. It *was* the calm before the storm. How could I be so stupid? I can't breathe. I brace my hands in front of me on the floor. The air feels too thick. Is the room getting smaller? Is Mac talking to me? He sounds like he's in a tunnel. Breathe, Hazel. I can't breathe.

Mmm, the smell of metal sends a warm feeling of calm through my body. I can feel arms wrapped around me, and I snuggle into them.

"Angel? Are you awake?" Phoenix. I'll just snuggle here a bit longer. Another hand sweeps through my hair, and I smell citrus. Jude. Jude is here, too. I must have said his name out loud because he kisses my forehead.

"I'm right here, Little Dove." He strokes his hands in my hair again. A warmth spreads on my calf, and I realize it's another hand rubbing my leg. It feels nice. The combined smells of citrus and metal and leather are soothing me. My Jude and Phoenix and...

"Leather," I mumble as I quickly sit up on the couch. Looking around, I see the three men that my senses recognized. What am I doing on the couch?

"Shhh, it's okay, Angel. You had a panic attack and fainted. You're alright." I can hear Phoenix talking, but I'm staring at Mac. My heart starts galloping like a racehorse. We were in the bathroom together. He told them...

"You told them." I turn to face Jude and Phoenix. "You know. I'm so sorry. Please don't hate me. I don't know what happened. I didn't mean to-"

"Angel, relax. It's okay." His hands run reassuringly up and down my arm.

"Okay? How is it okay? I...we...kissed." I cover my face with my hands as I say the last word. I must have heard him wrong. It must be okay because they're just going to break it off. We've exceeded our six weeks, and can now part ways with no hard feelings. Love or not, that was the deal.

Jude grabs my wrists and it focuses my attention back to the present.

"Shh, Little Dove. It really is okay. We would like to offer you another proposition." Another proposition. They want to renegotiate terms. This could be good. I should hear them out. Although this stopped being anything but a real relationship for me a while ago.

"What kind of a proposition?" Looking between the three men, there is a myriad of emotions on their faces. Jude looks reserved, Phoenix clenches his jaw in restraint and Mac seems determined. For what? I'm not sure. No one has spoken up yet.

Mac puts his hand on my knee, and all I can do is stare at it. Why is no one talking? The silence is more nerve-wracking than the yelling last weekend.

"Angel, do you know what a hall pass is?" Um, what? I hope we have two completely different definitions of a hall pass. They can't be suggesting what I think they are.

"Sure, great movie. What about it?" My tone is even and dismissive. Mac squeezes my leg.

"That's not what he's asking you, and I think you're smart enough to know that, Alice." I stand, removing myself from Mac's grasp on my leg. Pacing the room, I'm trying to convince myself that I must have stepped into some alternate universe where my two, not one but TWO, boyfriends are trying to tell me they want to share me with yet another man. And not just any man, my baby daddy. Here we go with the cliches again. *Internal eye roll.* I laugh at the absurdity of their offer. This has to be a joke. Running my hands through my hair, I stop laughing. I make a realization and turn to Phoenix and Jude.

"Is this some self-sacrificing bullshit because he's Wynnie's father. Do you think that we should "give it a go" for her sake because we have a child together?" I use air quotes to get my point across harder.

At least Jude has the wherewithal to look a little guilty. My blood is starting to boil. I'm not some toy they get to pass around to their friends. These three bastards got together and decided they would share me with Mac. A fucking hall pass.

I walk towards the door, and all three of my nicknames pour out of their mouths. I spin around on my heels and put my hand up so they stop trying to get to me.

"Fuck the hall pass. You're all in detention." I storm out to my car, text Dellah and Wynnie that I'm stopping for Chinese and cupcakes, and we're having a girl's night. Both of their response texts were various emojis. It seems it's a night for few words.

We enjoyed our horror movie marathon and Chinese food, and when the preteen got too cool for us, she went to her room. When I heard Wynnie's music turn on, I took my first deep breath since I had gotten home. I'm able to take off the Mom mask and wallow in my girlfriend drama with my best friend. Dellah went and got the wine, and I told her not to even bother with glasses. Handing me the bottle, she gives me a shocked "O" face and plops on the couch next to me. We drank from the bottle as I told my humiliating tale of the kiss with Mac, and the hall pass idea they had all presented me with.

"Okay, before I speak, do you want bestie Dellah or practical work Dellah because they both have very different opinions right now." Sighing, I drop my head back on the couch because I already know what both Dellahs are going to say.

"Give me the bad news first, although it all seems like bad news right now."

"Okay, work Dellah wants you to know that they are

dickheads for even considering passing you around like you're their possession." She's got that right. I don't belong to anyone, although I think I've given Jude and Phoenix my heart without my permission. I haven't even told them that I loved them. For the past week, since they've confessed their love for me, they've ended every text and phone call with an "I love you." I want to tell them in return because I feel it, but something has been holding me back.

"Your bestie Dellah is screaming like a kid in a candy shop. Girl, that night in college has lived rent-free in your head for almost half your life. They are unselfishly allowing you to give Mac another test run. What are the boundaries?"

"What do you mean?"

"Like, what are the limits to what you can do with Mac? Are they going to be there? Is it just one night of sex? Give me the dirty details." She pulls her legs under her and leans closer ready for my answers.

"Um, well, I didn't get any. I was so upset about the entire thing. I didn't even ask. I just walked out." How stupid. I didn't even give them a chance to explain. I have no idea what they were even offering. Ugh. How old am I? I threw a temper tantrum and left.

"Wait. I thought you were just holding out on me. You really have no idea what they meant by a hall pass?" Raising to my feet, I walk across the room. "What are you doing?" I pick my cell phone up off the counter and wave it at her. "It's 12:45 AM, Hazy. Think they are still up?"

"The way I left them, I'd bet anything they are at the bottom of a tequila bottle by now." I start a new group chat that includes Mac and text them.

Me: I'm an idiot.

Short and sweet and straight to the point. Their replies come in all at once. As my phone pings, I look at Dellah with an "I told you so" look.

Jude: Love you, Little Dove. So sorry we bombarded you like that. Please forgive me.

Mac: Alice, please let us explain.

Phoenix: Angel, you're the smartest woman I know and I'm the dumbest man. Forgive me please.

Me: Let's talk. How much tequila is left?

Me: Nevermind, I'm sure there's plenty. See you in 15.

"Dellah."

"Go. This is huge. I'll crash here with Wynnie. Collin is out of town, so take your time. I'll sleep in your bed and have naughty dreams about you." My phone is buzzing in my pocket from their responses.

"You're insufferable, but I love you." I hand her the bottle of wine, and she pulls me in for a hug. "It's a good thing I ate all those carbs before we opened this. I'm probably about to go drown my liver in tequila.

"You better love me, Hazel. Now go get your harem." She releases me and slaps me on the ass as I leave. We really do read too many romance novels.

In my car, I check my phone to confirm they are expecting me. Their messages are filled with various degrees of: drive safe, see you soon, and love yous.

44

Mac

She's coming back. We get a chance to explain ourselves. I wish I had known earlier, and I wouldn't have taken those last two tequila shots. Who am I kidding? I probably should have stopped five shots ago. Phoenix and Jude aren't any better. At least we're on an even playing field. Responsible Jude puts on a pot of coffee to try and sober us up.

When we came up with the hall pass idea last night, it was the last thing I expected either of them to say, especially Jude. Phoenix had every right to punch me for kissing Hazel, but the shock of hearing that she didn't immediately push me away was enough to get them both thinking. She was right when she called them self-sacrificing. It was their exact reasoning. Everyone always roots for a whole family, and Hazel not pushing me away made them feel she needed to explore whatever we might have together. We had decided to discuss as a group what a "hall pass" meant for each of us

265

once we proposed it to her. What we didn't expect was her extreme reaction, or rather, lack thereof. We upset her, and it broke us all a little when she left. The guys assured me she just needed time to process. It's just how she handles difficult events in her life.

"Maybe we should have asked her to come tomorrow when we were sober." Jude blows steam off his cup of coffee.

Phoenix slams his mug on the counter. "Fuck that. I'm tired of giving her space. She needs to know we love her and that she can lean on us for support. If she hasn't figured that out yet, we need to show her harder. We have to prove to her that nothing she says or does will scare us away. Did we go about this wrong? Yeah, probably. I should have started by discussing the kiss and led up to the hall pass idea. We will fix this together, and she will trust us fully once and for all. Always together."

"Do you guys want me to be scarce so you can work this out with her first?" I don't want to get in their way. I can see their love for her and can tell she feels the same for them, just as I can see the love between Phoenix and Jude.

"No." Phoenix stares me down. "You started this, and you don't get to hide now. We will all figure this out together. But, Mac, my liver can't handle another weekend of tequila. You've exceeded your fuck ups for at least a year. "

"Got it, man." And I do. I need things to work out with Hazel so I can have a good relationship with my daughter. Would I like my relationship with Hazel to be physical, abso-fucking-lutely, but more than anything, we need a good foundation, and currently, we are on rocky ground.

When Hazel arrives, this time, she takes Jude's advice. She knocks twice and then walks in without waiting. She's changed in the few hours since we last saw her. Her hair is in a messy knot on the top of her head, and she's wearing a light blue hoodie with dark gray sweatpants. She's also removed all of her makeup, and she's never looked more beautiful.

Without greeting any of us, she walks straight to the counter, grabs the tequila bottle and a shot glass, and takes two back-to-back shots. Then she adds another shot glass, fills the four of them up, and glares at us all. Without hesitation, we all slam back our shots.

"Okay, first, I need to apologize for throwing a fit like a toddler before getting any information and jumping to conclusions." Phoenix tried to speak, but she put her hand on his mouth. "Second, your delivery sucked. I felt like a toy you wanted to pass around. Whatever you all decided doesn't matter. We will discuss this, and then I will get the final say in what happens. Got it?"

She's so strong and confident right now. She just put three grown men in their place, and none of us batted an eye at her demand. My hand is itching to wrap around her neck, and whisper my praises in her ear but it's also tingling to spank her ass until she loses the sass. She's incredible.

We all agree to her terms, and she takes one more shot for herself before we head to the living room. She points for us to sit on the couch. Jude sits in the middle, with Phoenix and me on either side. Hazel sits on the coffee table in front of us, taking the power position in the room. She's showing us who's in charge, and we are all following along like little puppies waiting for any scraps she's willing to give us. Does she realize the power she has right now?

"What did you guys decide this hall pass entailed?" She crosses her arms over her chest. Another power move that she probably doesn't realize she's done. I have to shift in my seat to discreetly adjust myself to make room for my growing dick.

"We didn't, Little Dove. We wanted to talk everything over with you. There was never a plan, just an idea. Do you have any thoughts?"

"My thought is that I can't believe this is even an option. You're both just so willing to let me what? Sleep with Mac? Go on a date? Fool around? All of us? Just the two of us? I thought you loved me? I don't understand how you're so willing to push me into the arms of another man." Oh, my dear Alice. If only she knew that I was never 'just another man.'

"Because you kissed him back. You didn't push him away." Phoenix flashes her a tortured look. "We love you and want you to be happy, even if that isn't with us. He's Rowyn's father. That means something to us. She will always come first."

Damn, he's talking about my daughter like he cares for her. A pang of jealousy swirls in my stomach. Hazel places a hand on my knee, and my eyes snap to hers.

"Are you okay? You were…growling." Was I? It hadn't been a conscious reaction. I guess I feel more protective over Rowyn than I realized. I placed my hand on top of her.

"I'm fine, Alice. We all just want you to be comfortable with whatever you decide. We can stop right now and never discuss this again if that's what you want." Please reject that offer. The longer we sit here, the more I realize how much I want this woman in front of me.

Jude touches her cheeks and looks deeply into her hazel green eyes. "I want you to close your eyes for me." She looks back into his eyes for a moment and then closes hers. "Good girl." This time I hear the growl escape from my throat. Jude looks at me and mouths "chill" with a quick head shake. "Little Dove, I'm going to ask you some questions, and I want you to give us your honest answers. Keep your eyes closed and just answer from your heart. There are no wrong answers, and we won't be upset at anything you say. Do you trust me?"

"Yes, I trust you."

"Good. Do you want to continue this conversation?" She gives him a timid nod. He brushes his thumbs across her cheek in praise. "Good. Now, are you attracted to Mac?" I watch as her body goes rigid, and he shushes her while rubbing his fingers over her cheeks again. "Remember, there are no wrong answers. Just be honest."

She squeezes her eyes tighter and gives a quick hesitant nod. "I am." I feel a squeeze on my hand. Looking down at my knee, I had forgotten that she was still holding it, and give a squeeze back.

"Would you be interested in pursuing that attraction?" There's a hesitation in her breath, and he adds, "With the blessing of Phoenix and me."

Her eyes pop open, and there's panic behind them. "I don't want to lose either of you." She releases my hand to place hers over Jude's, and I instantly feel the void.

"I promise you aren't losing us, Little Dove. Is that what you want? To see where things could go with Mac?" Her eyes roam to Phoenix. He's been quiet this entire time. I know he is having the hardest time with the whole idea. He takes a hand away from Jude's and kisses her knuckles, giving her a reassuring smile.

"We aren't going anywhere unless you tell us to. We have no ulterior motives, Angel. Tell us your truth." I take her other hand in mine, connecting the four of us through her touch. Jude whispers for her to close her eyes and answer.

"I…" She heaves a sigh. "I want to see where things go with Mac." My heart feels like it's about to burst out of my chest. Quickly she adds, "But I don't want to stop seeing any of you."

"Oh, Angel, is our naughty girl trying to have her cake and eat it too?" Fuck me. Naughty girl? I like the sound of that. Is she naughty in bed? She definitely has a fire about her. Her body seemed to like it when my hand was wrapped around her neck and her back pressed against the wall. We may have spent a night together 13 years ago, but I'm not that same, barely 20-something anymore. My appetite has changed.

Jude leans into Hazel and kisses her lips tenderly. His hands move into her hair, and she purrs when he tugs on it. Mmm, she likes that. I'm learning so many things about my Alice. Phoenix grabs her hips and drags her into his lap, taking over and kissing her. His kisses are deeper and more hungry. Jude caresses her leg while Phoenix devours her kisses. I can see their tongues dancing together. He pulls back, both of their chests heaving.

"Angel, do you want to kiss Mac?" She looks in my direction and then at each of the guys. A barely there "yes" crosses her lips. Phoenix stands and lets her slide down his body. Taking her hand, they step past Jude, and he stops her in front of me. He offers me her hand, and I greedily take it pulling her into my lap. With one hand on her hip and the other running through her hair, I guide her towards my awaiting lips. When they connect, I feel like I was a man lost in the desert getting his first drink of water. I'm so lost in the feeling of her soft lips I'm confused when she pulls away. I follow her gaze to see the guys leaving the room.

"Stay, please." They stop and hesitate, looking at me. Her eyes scan the room and land on mine, seeking permission.

"Alice, are you asking them to stay, or are you asking them to join?" I see the lust wash over her eyes. She wants all three of us. I want her any way I can but are the guys willing to include me in their activities? She dips her head down in embarrassment. Lifting her chin to look into her eyes, I reassured her. "Don't ever be afraid to ask us for what you want. We want you to be happy and satisfied."

"You know the rules, Angel. Use your words."

The slyest smile crosses her lips. "Yes, Mr. Graves... I'd like you to join us." Fucking hell. This woman has my dick so hard I'm sure she can feel it under her ass. She takes my hand. "Are you okay with that, Mac? The guys are used to sharing me." The most adorable giggle fills the room.

"You are my priority, but this is your relationship, so you need to ask them, not me, Alice." This is the make-or-break moment. They were willing to share her with me, but are they willing to share her *with* me? Jude and Phoenix have a non-verbal conversation. The air is thick in the room as we all wait for the answer. Finally, Jude breaks the silence.

"Little Dove, shall we continue this conversation in a bedroom?" She's still hesitant, waiting for Phoenix when he extends his hand to her.

"I'd love to." She takes Phoenix's hand and stands. Reaching back, she offers her hand to me, and we head down the hallway toward the bedrooms.

45

Phoenix

As we walk towards my bedroom, I'm internally assessing how I feel about the situation we find ourselves in. I'm surprised that jealousy isn't the instant emotion that I feel. I'm proud that Hazel voiced to us what she wants. Thankful that we were able to have this conversation civilly despite the amount of tequila we've consumed. Horny as hell, and that's evident by how hard my dick is straining against my jeans, but not jealous. Mac was right when he said we all want her happy and satisfied, and maybe that's why there's no jealousy. We all want to worship this stunning woman together.

Hazel sits on the end of the bed and claps her hands together, then rubs them. "Okay, before things get too hot and heavy, let's go over the ground rules so we're all on the same page. Mac, we use the "red, yellow, green" method for safe words. Does that work for you? Do you need an explanation?"

"That's good with me. Stop, slow down, and go?"

"Yellow is more of a "give me a minute to think about it" than a slow down." Mac nods at Hazel in understanding. "Good, now Jude and Phoenix have their own thing going on and have free range of touching me and each other." She turns her next question to me. "Phoenix and Jude, what are your boundaries?" Before I can answer, Mac cuts me off. Walking up to Hazel, he puts his hands on her hips and pulls her close.

"Alice, I'm only here for you. I have no interest in touching anyone but you. If bodies cross, it happens, but there won't be any intentional touching on my part." Over his shoulder, he throws out, "That okay with you guys?"

"Good with me," I tell him. Jude agrees with me.

"Next, contraception. We all know that you and I failed at this the last time. The three of us are clean, and I'm on birth control. What about you?"

"I get tested regularly for work. I'm clean."

"Good to hear. Now, Jude and I have two rules," I add. " There's two of us, so she gets no less than two orgasms. I guess that number will increase to three now." I look over to Hazel and wink as she groans at my words. "And the second rule, you heard out in the living room. She has to use her words, no nods or hmms. We need words, especially regarding consent and the colors."

"Sounds perfect. Is there anything else, my beautiful Alice? Because I'm dying to get this hoodie off of you and my hands on you." Mac knows how to read a room because I can tell we are all dying to get her naked.

Popping her hands on her hips she glares at Mac. "What if I want you boys to get naked first?" It looks like we have sassy Hazel at the moment.

"Oh, my dear sweet, Alice. I guess you haven't realized,

since the moment you stepped into this bedroom, you're no longer in control here." Her jaw drops open in shock.

"Cat got your tongue, sassy girl?" I walk over to her, grab the hem of her hoodie, pull it over her head, and toss it on the floor.

"Naughty, naughty girl," Jude tsks at her. "You've been sitting here this entire time without a bra on? You were hoping to get fucked tonight, weren't you? I bet you don't have any panties on either, do you? Mac, why don't you take off her pants and show us what's under there."

"With pleasure." Mac pushes her down to lie on the bed, removes her shoes, and practically rips her pants off. She squeaks at the quick movement. "Fucking shit, Alice. You really were naked under there." She looks breathtaking laying there naked like an offering to us.

"Sorry gentleman, but I've waited far too long to do this again." In the blink of an eye, Mac drops to his knees, pushes Hazel's thighs apart, and dives into her pussy like a starved man. Her back bows off the bed as his tongue laps at her clit. Climbing onto the bed, I take her mouth and swallow her moans. I feel Jude shift and watch as he encircles one of her nipples. Hazel is already squirming underneath all of the sensations she's receiving. Her sounds are wild and animal-like.

"Your first orgasm belongs to me, Alice." He slides a finger into her, and she gasps. Returning his mouth to suck on her clit he adds another finger. "Jesus Fuck, you taste better than I remember. Are you going to come on my fingers, naughty girl?"

I move from her mouth and kiss a trail down until I join Jude at her chest and bite her other nipple. Unintelligible words start to spill from her mouth. I see Mac enter a third finger, and she lets out a guttural moan. A sheen of sweat glistens at her hairline, and her eyes roll back into her head. She's going to explode soon.

"She's close, Mac. Are you ready to see the beautiful face she makes when she comes?" I tug at her nipple, and Mac moans to answer my question, setting her off like a bomb. Her mouth opens in a silent scream while her body convulses under us, and she squirts all over him. Her hips buck in his mouth, but he doesn't stop until she's pushing his head away.

"You taste so god damn good I don't want to stop, Alice. Fuck you're amazing. You soaked me." He pulls back, trailing kisses towards her knee, and when he takes a big bite of her thigh and then licks the spot, she makes the most delicious noise. "You liked that? Does my Alice like some pain with her pleasure?

"No, she loves it." Jude pinches one nipple while I lick at the other to show him how much she does.

Hazel lifts onto her elbows, assesses the three of us, and whines. "You are all wearing far too many clothes for my liking. Strip, now."

Jude looks at me and raises a brow. "Did anyone hear a please? It sounds like she still doesn't understand that she isn't in control right now."

"Oh, Alice, Alice, Alice." Mac huffs as he shakes his head. "Being a brat will get you a spanking. Is that what you need to understand that your pleasure belongs to us?" Hazel bites her bottom lip and shakes her head with a devilish smile.

"No, Sir." Mac's eyes turn black as she bats her eyelashes at him.

"Oh, Angel. I have a feeling you just fucked around, and

you're about to find out." The next moment, Mac had her flipped on his lap with her juicy ass in the air. She's giggling until his left hand grabs a fist full of hair at the nape of her neck. He's making soft circles across both of her ass cheeks when Jude crouches in front of Hazel's upside down face and brushes his thumb across her cheek.

"Little Dove, now is the time to remember your safewords. Even though you put yourself in this situation, you have all the power to stop it at any time. You understand that, right?" She starts to nod, and Mac's commanding voice stops her.

"Words, Brat." He squeezes one of her cheeks.

"Yes, Sir." She wiggles in his lap, trying to get friction between her thighs. She loves this. Mac notices and slides his hand down between her legs.

"Good girls get rewards." She starts to moan as he rubs her clit. He pulls his hand out, tightens his grip on her hair, and gives her a quick swat on her ass. Just enough to get her attention. "Bad girls get spankings."

"How many spankings should our naughty girl get?" My chest is heaving with the excitement of seeing Mac's handprint on her pale skin.

"How about six," Jude suggests, "two smacks for sassing each of us."

"Does six sound fair, Alice?" I can see Mac's body vibrating with anticipation.

"Yes, Sir."

"Good girl using your words. How about another little reward before we start." Her whispered yes is barely audible. "Let's give her a little of what she wants. Shirts off." We all take them off and add them to the discarded clothes pile. I unzip my pants before my dick has a zipper imprint on it from straining in my jeans. Hazel scans our bare chest and hmms her approval.

Mac rubs a few more circles around her ass cheeks, then lands two quick smacks, one on each cheek. The crack of his hand as it hit her bare skin brings tingles to my own palms. Her back is bobbing up and down in his lap as her breathing increases. Mac returns to his soothing circles, and the perfectly pink imprints of his hand begin to appear.

Jude lifts her head a bit to kiss her lips. "Color, Little Dove?"

"G...green." Two more smacks crack in the air.

"Good fucking girl," Mac praises. "Jude, come play with our pretty little pussy and give her another reward."

"She's soaked," he announces as his fingers slide over her clit. "Naughty girl, are you enjoying your punishment?" She lays there, moaning softly as Jude pushes two fingers into her.

"Answer him, or I'll add two more smacks."

"Yes, Sir...I like it." Her moans increase as Jude increases the pace with his fingers.

"Are you going to come for us, sweet Alice?"

"Yes, oh yes. I'm...so...close." She's panting about to teeter over the edge.

"Jude, stop." Mac's commanding tone has him obeying. "You don't get to come until you finish your punishment, Brat." Hazel is whimpering at the edging that Mac just caused.

"Color, Angel?" Mac is rubbing circles on her ass cheeks again.

"Yel...Green." She hesitated.

Jude grabs her chin. "Answer honestly, Hazel. We need to trust each other."

"Green. I'm okay, I promise. I'm sorry. I just need to come."

"Don't worry, Alice, we'll take care of you. You'll have plenty more chances to come before we are done with you." She coos under his massaging hand. "Last two, but I'm going to warn you. The first two sets were for the sass you gave Jude and Phoenix. These last two are for me, and they're going to be harder, and then I'm going to flip you over and fuck you. Do you think you can handle it?"

"Y-yes, Sir."

Two cracks of lightning echo through the room as his hand connects with her already-pinkened cheeks. She cries out in pain which turns into a muffled cry of desire as he flips her onto the bed face down, grabs both of her hips, and drives into her in one quick thrust. I watch as the force of his pumping tips her over the final edge, and she bursts into a sobbing orgasm. She's chanting his name through the tears streaming down her face. *Mac, Mac, Mac.* He rubs a comforting hand down her spine as her climax subsides. Pressing his chest to her back, he whispers into her ear as he slows his punishing thrusts.

"Such a good fucking girl. I've dreamed of getting you back under me for over a decade. I've wanted to reclaim you since that night of the party. Fuck you're perfect." He slips his hand around the front of her neck and pulls back until they are both upright. He flexes his hand, cutting off her air for a moment, and her eyes roll back into her head with pleasure. I climb up onto the bed, kneeling in front of her. I twist her pert nipples between my fingers, and she sobs harder.

"Check-in, Angel." Mac's hand on her neck releases slightly, giving her more air to answer.

"G...G...G."

Jude slides in beside me on the bed, palming her cheeks and looks deep into her eyes. "Green, Little Dove?"

"Yeeeeees."

"You're gonna come one more time for me, Brat. Got it?" Mac growls in her ear before taking a long lick up her neck.

"Yes, yes, yeeees." She's a mess of sweat and moaning and panting.

"Jude, play with that swollen clit of ours, and let's make her forget her own name." Jude's hand dips between her thighs and she gasps. The sight of it makes my cock turn to steel.

"Angel, while Mac paints your insides with his come, I'm gonna paint these pretty tits with mine. I can't hold out any longer." Shoving my pants down as far as my position allows, I roughly stroke my cock. Jude adjusts his position, starts rubbing Hazel's clit with his thumb, and grabs my cock out of my hand.

"Let me," he purrs, then bends down and bites my lower lip before licking away the pain.

"Fuckthatshot. Gonna...come." Hazel's words slur together, lost in the ecstasy of our tangled bodies.

"Come. Now. Alice." Mac roars as his orgasm hits him, and he pounds harder into her. Releasing her neck, she collapses into me. As the peak of her orgasm hits, she bites down on my shoulder, and I come, squirting hot ropes all over her tits and stomach.

As Mac pulls out of Hazel, Jude kisses my forehead telling me he'll get us supplies to clean up. He returns with a warm washcloth and wipes my come off of her. Once clean, I place her onto her stomach on the bed and groan as I lightly massage her ass.

"Mac, I gotta say, I'm fucking jealous, man. I've been threatening to redden her ass for a while, and you got to it first. Your handprints look like perfection on her pale skin."

"Next time, she's all yours, Phoenix. It will be worth the sore hand tomorrow." He reaches down and runs a finger up her spine, causing her to shiver. "Our good girl did a fan-fucking-tastic job." He looks over his shoulder, and then bends close to her. "Hey, Alice. You have one more man who needs some attention. I think if Jude doesn't get to come soon, his dick looks so hard it might fall off." He turns his full attention to Jude. "And fuck man, you were hiding all that metal under you're sweet and innocent khakis? I'm impressed." Jude blushes, and it's the most adorable sight.

"Angel, think you can take care of Jude?" She hums an mmhmm, and I let her get away with it this one time. "Do you want to take him in your mouth, or can this hungry pussy take more dick?" My hands slinks down into her soaking folds. She responds by wiggling her butt.

"I can take it. Claim me, Jude." She rolls over onto her back and spreads her legs open for him. She is glistening with the mix of her and Mac's orgasms and has the sweetest smile staring at Jude.

"Fuck, I have to taste you first, Little Dove." He slides between her legs, and his eyes roll into his head at the first lick. "Just like heaven." She whimpers with pleasure. I'm sure she's already sore from the beating that Mac gave her pussy and her ass. It's not long before she squirming. "Are you going to come for me already? Still so swollen and sensitive."

"Yes, Jude, yes," she moans out. Her face is awash with pleasure. He slides two fingers easily into her dripping pussy, and she clamps her thighs on his head, convulsing with her orgasm.

Peeling her thighs away, he sits up on his knees, face glistening from her come. He lifts her thighs to her chest and slowly sinks into her inch by inch. The scene in front of me is so mesmerizing my dick is coming back to life already. His rhythm is slow and deep, savoring her. I palm my cock and stroke it when an idea comes to mind.

"Angel, do you trust me?"

"Always." Her response comes immediately.

"Mac, will you open that top drawer and hand me the lube?" Her eyes go wide as he searches the drawer.

"Phoenix?" There's a slight panic in her voice. We've talked about anal before but haven't done anything yet, but that's not what I'm planning now.

"Relax, Angel, I've got you. Use your colors if you need them. I need you two to flip positions. I want you to ride Jude, Angel." As they shift around, I open the lube cap with a click and pour a generous amount straight onto my steel rod. It feels like all of the attention in the room is on me. I make my way up to Jude.

I crawl between his thighs and push Hazel down to lie on his chest. I take a moment to stare at his cock dipping in and out of her pussy. Ever so slightly, I notch the head of my dick into her entrance next to him. She gasps.

"Phoenix, you won't both fit." I shush her and caress her spine.

"Oh, but it will, Angel. You said you trusted me, so trust me." Jude moans as my tip slides in, putting pressure on his cock.

"Holy fuck, Phoenix," he groans.

"Oh, Jude, just wait until I'm fully in." I push another inch, and there's a wave of groans. "Check-in, Angel."

"Green. So much green. Keep fucking going." I pause to admire the handprints on her ass, itching to add one of my own.

"Jude, pull out just a little for me, and then we can push back in together." He does, and I'm able to push halfway in. "Angel, your pussy looks amazing stretching around our cocks." A few more pumps, and I'm almost entirely in. "Are you ready to take all of me?"

"Oh, god. Do it." I pull back a little and thrust completely in.

"Fucking hell, Jude, your piercing. Holy shit." The metal at the tip of his dick rubbed mine, and it feels incredible. "Angel, is this what you feel every time?"

"Yes, please move. I feel so full. I need you to move, please." Her begging is so sexy. Jude and I find a rhythm alternating in and out when I feel the bed shift, and Mac crawls up towards Hazel's head.

"Can you handle being a little more full, Alice?" He has his dick in his hand, stroking it close to her face. She nods and opens her mouth for him, and he slips in. "Goddamn, your puffy lips look so gorgeous wrapped around my cock. You were made to take all of us. You're such a good girl. Fuuuuk."

"I'm not gonna last much longer," Jude says from below. "It's too fucking good." I'm getting close, too. The tightness of double stuffing her, Jude's piercing giving extra friction on my head and the warmth of her pussy is the perfect trifecta for a mind-blowing orgasm that I can feel building at the base of my spine. Mac slides his hand between Hazel's legs and starts rubbing her clit.

"Give us one more, Alice. Come all over their cocks and squeeze every last drop out of them, then swallow my come like I know our naughty girl wants. Your sweet body has us all absolutely feral right now."

"Fuck, fuck, fuck." Jude's chanting and twitching, signals his orgasm. I pick up my pace and a few thrusts later, my orgasm shatters through me, finally setting off Hazel. I can barely move with the vice grip her pussy has on our cocks. Her voice starts to go horse from her screams around Mac's cock. A long guttural moan comes from Mac, and we are all lost in a nirvana of orgasms.

Once our breathing is mostly back to normal, we all slowly pull out, and I scoop Hazel into my arms. "I'll get her cleaned up." I carry her to the bathroom and set her down on the counter while I turn on the shower.

"How was your hall pass, Angel?" She's barely awake when she looks at me with an amused face.

"I think you boys need to spend some more time in detention if that's what your penance will be." I pull her off the counter and give her a quick swat on the ass.

"Keep it up, Brat, and you'll get exactly what you ask for."

"Mmm, that's what I'm hoping for."

46

Hazel

Never in my life have I been so sore, but in all the best ways. After our shower, where Phoenix thoroughly washed and massaged every body part he touched, he brought me back to his room. Mac kissed me goodnight and went to the guest room, and I slid into bed between Jude and Phoenix. I only slept for a few hours, and around 8 AM, I reluctantly crawled out of the tangle of limbs and drove home. As promised, Dellah was in my bed, and I crawled in with her and told her about my evening. I'm not sure how her jaw is still attached with the number of times it dropped to the floor.

"So what now? What does that mean for the three of you?" She asked the number one question that's been running through my mind since I left. Was it truly a one time hall pass?

"I'm not sure, Dells. We didn't do much talking after. Everything went so seamlessly. I selfishly want it to continue as the four of us, but is that even a feasible option?"

She shrugs. "It works in thousands of romance novels. Live your best single mom, why choose trope life. Just try and stay away from the third-act break up drama. That's never fun. You've already had the baby daddy drama, so you should be good."

"Speaking of baby daddy drama, I have to tell Wynnie about Mac soon, and I don't even know how to bring it up."

"Honestly, Hazy, I think that's the easiest part. Just tell her the truth; he pulled us over, and you recognized his tattoo. The question is how and when to tell her you're sleeping with her father...and two other guys." Ugh. I buried my face in my pillow because I hadn't even thought about that. I was being so selfish with Mac I didn't even think about him being Wynnie's dad.

"Dellah, I slept with my kid's dad, and I want to do it again. I'm a terrible mother. How do I tell her?"

"Do you have to tell her that part?" Of course, I do, right? Maybe she has a point?

"Don't I? That's a big piece of the puzzle to leave out."

"Not any bigger than telling her you found her long lost-father or that you're sleeping with two other guys besides him. Maybe just one-life altering confession at a time. You've kept them a secret this long. Ease her into everything."

"You're probably right. That's a lot of info for a 12 year old to process all at once. Should you and I take her to lunch today and tell her?" Please say yes. Please say yes.

"Why us?"

"Because she scares me, and there's safety in numbers. Please?" I fold my hands together and stick out my lip while fluttering my eyelashes. "You're my bestie and would put your life on the line for me, remember? Especially when it comes to your niece." I can tell I've got her on the hook. She can't say no to matters of Wynnie.

"Fiiiiiine. You're a cheater, though, using my niece against me. I get to pick the restaurant for my troubles. Let's go wake the brat up." Oh, that word. I feel my cheeks flush, and my hand involuntarily goes to my butt. Dellah notices and bursts out laughing. "Okay, maybe we won't use that word anymore to refer to your daughter."

"Please." I joined in her hysterics.

I've never seen my kid get ready quicker than when her aunt told her we were going out for tacos. After we order our food and we're sitting at the table, my nerves ramp up. Just be honest and tell her the truth. It's as simple as that.

"Mom, can I ask you-"

"Wynnie, I need to tell you-" We both speak at once. "Go ahead, kiddo. What do you need to ask me?" Her cheeks turn pink, and suddenly her napkin in her lap looks interesting. She's not the type of kid that gets embarrassed easily, so this must be big.

"Mom, are you…dating Coach Graves?" There was no time to hide my shocked face. My jaw dropped, and my eyes bugged out. I wasn't expecting that at all, and Dellah's face shows a similar reaction to mine. Do I lie or tell the truth? Her question is just as big as my news. Do I wait to tell her about Mac now? Where is the single mom, baby daddy drama handbook because I need it right now? Dellah kicks me under the table, snapping me out of my trance.

"What, uh, what makes you ask that?" Don't panic. Compose yourself, Hazel.

"Well, last weekend, I saw you get out of a black pickup truck in the driveway." That was her at the window. I assumed it was Dellah. Shit, did she see Jude, too? "And then yesterday, when you were late to pick me up, Coach Graves let me sit on the back of his pickup truck to wait. I'm pretty sure it was the same one I saw last week in the driveway. So is that who you're dating?" Crap. Crap. Crap. The napkin in my lap that I'm twisting is about to be ripped to shreds.

"I...if I was, would it be a big problem for you?" Dellah reaches under the table and holds my hand. I'm so glad I bribed her to come with me. This is not the conversation I expected to be having right now. Should I tell her about Jude, too, since we are being open? No. I still have to tell her about Mac. We agreed on one life-altering issue at a time. She just threw me a curveball.

"Well, you said the guy you were dating made you happy, and I always want you to be happy. It would definitely be awkward to have my mom dating my coach. Kids might think that's the only reason I made the team. And aren't you older than him?"

"Alright, girl, I'm only 30, and he's 27. It's not that much older."

"So you are. Dating him?" Shit, I guess I just confirmed that by accident.

"Yes, I'm dating Coach Graves, and yes, he makes me happy. And you one hundred percent earned your spot on the team. He didn't even know who you were to me until after tryouts."

"You didn't talk about me to him?" Dellah and I both laugh, and she gives us a confused look.

"Funny story. I did talk to him about you, Wynnie, but he only knows you as Rowyn. He saw me at your tryouts, and that's when he found out you were the same person. I didn't know he was your coach until I saw him on the field that day, either. It was a complete coincidence." All this information is the truth, and it feels good to not lie about anything. Not mentioning Jude or Mac as the other men I'm dating...Am I dating Mac now? *Seriously Hazel, one issue at a time.* Not mentioning them is a lie of omission, but for now, telling her about Phoenix and her father, Mac, is plenty of information.

"That's actually pretty funny. I'm glad he makes you happy. He's a great coach. But," she's looking back at her hands again. "Do you think you could continue to keep it a secret while the season is still going? I don't want it to get weird since I'm still getting to know these girls." My heart just broke a little for my sweet daughter. Making friends is hard for her, and I wouldn't want to do anything to jeopardize that.

"Of course, we can. You're our first priority, Wynnie. We would never want it to be weird or awkward for you if we could help it."

"And don't worry, little niece, if he hurts her, I'll kick his ass for the both of us."

"Aunt Dellah. He's still my coach." She leans in and whispers. "Just wait until the season is over." She winks at Dellah, and they both chuckle.

Distracted by the now light conversation, I had a moment's peace from my panic of telling her about Mac until Wynnie reminded me.

"What did you want to talk to me about, Mom?" Here goes. She has a right to know, and you need to tell her. Except I'm frozen, speechless in my seat. Dellah squeezes my hand, and I nod at her.

"A few weeks ago, your mom and I got pulled over," Dellah begins for me. Wynnie's eyes go wide. "No, it's okay. We were goofing off, and I swerved a little. No one got into any trouble.

But the officer who pulled us over, your mom...recognized him." Recognized is an understatement. "He was-"

"Wynnie, the officer was your father," I blurted out with my eyes closed. At that moment, our food arrives, giving me a moment of reprieve. She stares at me while we wait with her cornflower blue eyes, Mac's eyes, wide in shock. My heart feels like it's trying to escape from my throat, and my hands are shaking in Dellah's.

"My father? I thought you didn't know who he was. You said you didn't know him." She's getting agitated. I reach across the table and grab her hands.

"Wynnie, Rowyn, I didn't lie to you about that. I promise. He has a tattoo, an *Alice in Wonderland* tattoo that he designed himself. It's beautiful and very memorable to me. The night we were pulled over, I saw the tattoo. And then..." Has she seen him before like he has seen her?

"Then? Mom, then what?"

"Then I ran into him at one of your softball games. Actually, ran right into him, and when I looked into his eyes, they were your eyes. The same blue eyes and the same tattoo, I knew it was him.

"At one of my softball games? Is he a parent?" She's trying to connect the dots in her mind.

"No honey, he's the security guard that walks around. Have you seen him?" I don't know what answer I want her to give. Has she had any interaction with him?

"Security guard," she whispers to herself. Her brows are scrunched together as she tries to recall him. "Wait, does he know Coach Graves? Does Coach G know my father?"

I see Dellah stiffen out of the corner of my eyes. Damn, I've raised one smart girl. She put that connection together far too quickly for my liking.

"Yes, they are friends."

"I...I want to meet him. Can I meet him? Coach G is a good guy. Good enough for you and, and, if he likes my father, he can't be a bad man, right?" She's spiraling, and there's only enough room at this table for one of us to do that.

"Wynnie, calm down, honey. Yes, he's a good man, and yes, you can meet him. We can make arrangements."

"Can you tell me about him?" There's so much I could say about one of the three men that rocked my entire world not that many hours ago.

"Sure. His name is Malcolm, but he goes by Mac. He's a little older than me at 33. He's a police officer here in town."

"He's been here the entire time we have?" I had the same thought when I found out. Like mother, like daughter. She's taking this so much better than I could have expected. She really is wise beyond her years.

"He's been here since he graduated college, about ten years."

"How do you know all this?" Dellah grabs my thigh. She needs to chill. She's acting more nervous than me.

"Mac and I had coffee. I wanted to tell him before I told you." Please don't ask for specifics about that coffee date. That answer was already a small lie, and I don't want to have to tell any more.

"When can I meet him?" There's eagerness and hesitation in her question. and I can't blame her. This is a significant life event. Her father has always been a figurative person. Of course, she knew she had one, but having the physical man appear is entirely different.

"Soon, if you'd like, he's excited to meet you. He remembers watching you play these last few weeks." I must have a serious conversation with the guys before she meets Mac. Now that she knows about, Phoenix we'll need to be careful what we say and do around her. Figuring out Phoenix was the guy I was dating was too easy for her. "Maybe next weekend? After your game? I can talk to him."

"Yeah, I'd like that." She zones out for a few minutes while eating her food. Mine sits mostly untouched, having lost my appetite. Dellah's plate is empty. She's a stress eater. Wynnie must sense my uneasiness and places her fork down.

"Mom, I love you. You've been a great mother to me, and I'm not upset with you about Mac. We've had a great life. Thank you." Well fuck. Dellah hands me a napkin as she dabs at her cheeks.

"You're the best daughter I could have ever asked for. I love you, too. Now finish your food because a grown woman," I pause and look at my best friend. "Two grown women crying in public is embarrassing and awkward." I throw my napkin at her, and the three of us laugh.

47

Mac

Last night was the best night of my life. Nothing in my 33 years of living could compare to the events in the early morning hours. I thought the idea of the hall pass was ridiculous. Not in my wildest fantasies did I expect that she would want all three of us together. Watching Jude and Phoenix with her was erotic. She is a perfect specimen of a woman. But will they continue to share her with me? After one taste, I'm hooked.

I hated leaving them and going to the guest room, but it felt like the right thing to do. To give them time to discuss things if they needed to. We never talked about what would happen after our hall pass ended. I heard her leave early this morning, though. I was worried until I got a text from her a few hours later letting me know she was taking Rowyn to lunch and was planning to tell her about me. I've been on pins and needles, waiting to find out how it went.

I'm outside working on my motorcycle when my phone buzzes. Cleaning my hands off on a rag, I unlock it and see it's from Hazel in the group chat.

HAZEL: I told Wynnie about Mac...She also knows I'm dating Phoenix. We should get together soon to talk logistics.
 ME: How did it go?
 PHOENIX: Just me? How? What about Jude?
 JUDE: Anything you need, just let us know.
 HAZEL: Everything is fine. It went well. She guessed Phoenix by his truck. Please be cool at practice. She doesn't want anyone to know. Friday night?
 PHOENIX: No problem, Angel. See you Friday. Love you.
 JUDE: Friday is perfect. Love you.
 HAZEL: <3 <kiss emoji>

Everything went well? I need more than that. I open a new text window and text Hazel directly.

ME: Alice, a fine isn't good enough for me. How did it go?
 HAZEL: She's excited to meet you. She took it well. She's seen you around the field on game days.
 ME: That's all good, right?
 HAZEL: Yeah. She's seen you talking to Phoenix and decided since he's a good guy, and he's friends with you, you must be good, too. :)
 ME: I'll be so good to you both.

There's a long pause, and the little dots bounce several times on the screen, but it's 10 minutes before she responds.

HAZEL: Don't hurt us, Mac.

ME: I won't. I promise.

I thought her delayed response might have been her hesitation about our unknown relationship with the guys. Where and how do I fit in? But she's worried that I'll hurt them? I could never intentionally do that. My daughter will always be my world from now on. Nothing and no one will hurt her, even me.

Knowing that we have an impending monumental conversation with Hazel has made this week drag. It's finally Friday, and I can't wait to get home, shower, and head over to Phoenix and Jude's house. It's 7:30 PM before I walk out the door, and I send off a text in the group chat letting them know I'm on the way. Then I open my chat with Hazel and me.

ME: My beautiful Alice. I can't wait to see you soon. I want to apologize in advance if I can't keep my hands off you. My palms have been itching for a repeat of last weekend. <hand emoji> <peach emoji> <kiss face emoji>

I'm not usually someone who uses emojis, but sometimes they can be fun, and they make Hazel laugh, so I've adapted. When I pull up to the house, I see Hazel's little red sedan already in the driveway. She hadn't responded to either of the texts I sent, so I thought maybe she was stuck at work.

Knocking on the door, I walk in, not waiting to be invited. I've had an open invitation for years, and I also have their spare key. I find everyone in the kitchen and walk right up to Hazel, threading my fingers through her hair and kiss her

294

firmly on the lips, catching her off guard.

"I've been waiting to do that all week." I lift my eyes to look at Phoenix. "Am I gonna get punched again for kissing your girl?" Hazel takes a sharp inhale at my question.

"When did you punch him for kissing me?" Her head swivels between the two of us, waiting for a response.

"The night it happened. He came over and confessed what he did, and I gut-punched him. And no, I don't plan on hitting you again. We're past that now, although that probably also needs to be discussed tonight."

We all sit at the table to eat dinner. Beer and wine are passed around for this meal. It was a group decision to skip the tequila for a while. Hazel tells us about her conversation with Wynnie.

"What should I call her? Does she prefer Wynnie or Rowyn?" I want to respect whatever name she prefers. It's important to me that I make the best first impression tomorrow.

"Well, Dellah and me, and my family, are the only ones that call her Wynnie. She told Jude she prefers to be called Rowyn. I'd suggest asking her yourself. I don't want to give you the wrong answer." That's a fair point and exactly what I'll do. We have a plan for the three of us to go out to dinner tomorrow night.

"How did it come up that you're dating, Phoenix?" Jude asks over his glass of wine.

"Wynnie saw Phoenix's truck in our driveway when you dropped me back off from the... parking lot incident, and then again at the softball field the day I ran late. She asked if that's who I was dating, and I confirmed it. I wasn't expecting to discuss it with her, but she brought it up. For now, let's leave her to believe that. There will already be a lot of changes with Mac coming into her life. I don't want to add, 'Oh, by the way, I have three boyfriends' to the list."

The air goes still in the room as everyone analyzes Hazel's last sentence. She called us all her boyfriends. Three, that would include me. Does she want to include me in her relationship with Jude and Phoenix? Do they want to include me? We could all be a family together. They already have a relationship with Rowyn, and it sounds like I've been deemed a good person by association.

"Little Dove, is that what you'd like? Do you want all four of us to be together?" Her eyes widen, and her blush starts at her cheeks and flushes past the neckline of her v-neck t-shirt dress.

She places her hands on her mouth and mumbles. "I'm sorry. It just slipped out that way. I didn't mean anything by it." Based on her coloring, I'm calling bullshit.

"Angel." Phoenix grabs her hands away from her face. "You've been doing so well lately. Use your words like our good girl, and trust us." She whimpers and rubs her thighs together when he calls her a good girl. The use of the word 'our' doesn't escape me either. She shakes her head and stands quickly from the table.

"No, no. I'm not going to fall for it. Keep your Alpha, testosterone-filled, good girl ways to yourself right now. Earth shattering orgasms or not, we need to figure out what this relationship looks like without various holes being filled." She's standing in the middle of the room, her hands on her hips, wearing the most adorable scowl. I'm trying exceptionally hard not to laugh or pinch her cheeks and tell her how cute she is. I glance at Phoenix and Jude, and they have matching faces attempting to contain their laughter. Jude breaks first.

"Alpha...testosterone filled..." He's laughing so hard tears are streaming down his face. "Good girl ways?" He practically falls off his chair; barely breathing through his laughter. Phoenix has his hands covering his face trying not to laugh out loud but is about to lose based on the gasps of air he keeps inhaling. I lost the game of trying not to laugh when Jude started speaking. If looks could kill, we would all be red mist right now.

"The audacity of you men right now is astonishing. Stop laughing at me." She folds her hands over her chest and we all laugh harder. She looks like an angry kitten. "Stop it now!" She stomps her foot, and we all lose any semblance of sanity that we have left. Her angry eyes are flashing between each of us. Her 'Alpha, testosterone-filled' men, that must look like complete clowns laughing at her anger. Something flashes in her eyes. She reaches for the hem of her dress and removes it, leaving her in just a matching dark green bra and panty set. The room falls silent. "Are you all finished laughing at me now?"

"Angel, we may not be laughing anymore, but I don't think your little stunt is having the desired effort you were hoping for." She looks so smug, as if she got her way and there's nothing else to worry about.

"How so?" She places her hands back on her waist, eliciting a growl from me. She just accentuated her supple hips.

"I'm going to take a wild guess, Angel, and say that if you looked at the crotches of our pants right now, you'd probably find tents. Seeing as you were trying to calm the testosterone in the room, I'd say you failed miserably." At Phoenix's suggestion, I see her eyes roam over us, and she sees exactly what he's describing.

"Little Dove, unless you plan to be dessert, I'd suggest you put your dress back on." He licks his lips while exploring her body with his eyes.

I groan. "But I'm rather enjoying the view." I reach down and rub my hand over the straining bulge in my pants.

"Jesus fuck. You're like a bunch of kids in a candy store." She rolls her eyes at us as she redresses.

"But you're the sweetest candy, Angel."

"Ugh. Talk first, MAYBE dessert later." She collects her plate from the table and takes it to the kitchen, and we all watch her hips sway as she walks away.

"Tease," I yell at her retreating form. My phone dings in my pocket, and I check it to see it's a nonsense text from someone at the station. But that reminds me.

"Hey Alice, did you get my text earlier? You didn't respond."

"Oh um, no. I accidentally left my phone at home." Well, that explains it. At least now I know I wasn't being ignored. "Can we get back to the elephant in the room? My 'boyfriend' slip up."

"Still waiting on your answer, Little Dove. You're the one ignoring the question. Do you want all three of us to be your boyfriends? I rather enjoyed myself last weekend." She's scanning the room, searching for answers. She turns her back to us, staring into the sink.

"Okay. Ask for what I want." She whispers under her breath, giving herself a little pep talk, and I'm so proud of her. She's shifting from foot to foot. I've always called it the mother's sway, and seeing her doing it makes me think of her holding our baby while swaying. My heart both constricts and grows.

"Alright. Okay, I feel selfish saying it, but I want all three of you. I want the four of us to be together."

"Sounds good." Phoenix stands with his plate and walks up behind her. Kissing her on the top of the head he put his plate in the sink..

"That's it? I'm over here stressing and you give me a 'sounds good.' "

"Yeah, Angel, that's it. Everything worked well last weekend. Inside and outside the bedroom. We took a huge conflict between us and solved it...then had fucking amazing make-up sex. We've known Mac for years. He knows if he fucks up I'll kick his ass. Again. It's really that simple. You're our priority, and that's what you want." He says it so matter-of-factly, and she is speechless.

"Is it time for dessert now?" Jude has a huge cheeky grin on his face. She removes her dress again and huffs a big sigh.

"Yes, let's go, children." She rolls her eyes and motions down the hall with the bedrooms.

"Hmm, does that mean we get to call you Mommy?" I stifle a laugh at her expression.

"Fuck. No." She's sexy when she's stern. Amusement laces her tone. "But, maybe, if you play your cards right, Hatter, I'll call you Daddy." My jaw drops to the fucking floor. That's the hottest shit I've ever heard. I stand from the chair and strip naked right in the middle of the dining room.

"Bedroom, right fucking now, or I'm bending you over this fucking counter, Brat." Her eyes shine with anticipation and mischief. I watch as she mouths "Do it" and glares at me in challenge. "You asked for it. Remember that tomorrow."

"Oh, Angel, I'd run and hide if I were you. He's got that look in his eyes." I hope she does. Running would only make

299

this more fun. I'm already feral for her right now. She turns to run and slams into Jude.

"I don't think so. You taunted the beast. Time to get your punishment." His smile is as feral as mine.

"Jude." Her mouth drops open in mock horror. "You're supposed to be the nice one, my cinnamon roll." He laughs, and she slaps a flat hand on his chest right when I reach her and grab her hips. Pulling her towards me, I swing us toward the counter and bend her over it, pinning her in place with my hips. She places her palms flat on the counter and looks back at me. Using my feet, I knock her ankles further apart.

"I hope you didn't like these panties, Alice." I slide my finger under one side and rip them. She laughs as they slide down her legs into a tiny puddle at her feet. She steps out of them, and I bend down, pick them up, and toss them to Phoenix. "Hang on to these for me, man." Phoenix smiles and tucks them into his pocket. I graze my nose across the shell of her ear and growl. "Those are mine now. And what's so funny, Little Brat?"

"Dellah warned me that men like to rip off panties. I always keep an extra pair in my purse." I'll have to remember to thank her later.

"Angel, I thought you didn't like to talk about your best friend when we're about to be inside you?" There's humor laced in his question. Clearly, an inside joke I'm missing. I'll have to ask about it another time. I can't wait any longer.

"Enough talking." Placing my hands on both sides of her hips, I rub my throbbing cock through her soaked folds a few times before lining up and slamming into her pussy. Her mouth opens into an "O" crying a silent scream. I start pumping into her with a punishing pace, each thrust bumping

300

her hips into the counter. I'll kiss away the bruises later that I know will form both from my fingers and the counter. My movements are so rapid she barely has time to breathe between each plunge of my cock. Skimming my hand up her spine, I unclip her bra and free her gorgeous tits. Her inner walls are fluttering, ready to orgasm. I push my hand between the table and her nipple, giving it a tight squeeze and a twist. She screams as the pleasure and pain mixture causes her to peak. I ride her until she releases the vice grip on my dick and pull out, leaving her empty. Looking at the guys, I give them an offering smile.

"That's one. Who's next?" Jude's already peeling the shirt off his back with one hand while unbuckling his belt with the other. I step aside, and just as I had done, he pushes into her with one thrust.

"Color, Little Dove?" He's pumping into her rapidly.

"Green, fucking green." She loves allowing us to use her body for our pleasure. "Holy shit, Jude. You're piercing. This angle. I'm gonna…come…fuuuuuuck." That's all it took for her eyes to roll back into her head, and another orgasm consumed her.

"That's two," he tells her with an amused smile. Jude's onslaught is no less punishing than mine, and it doesn't take him long before he warns Phoenix to get ready for his turn. As he starts to spill inside her, Hazel cries out with another orgasm.

"Damn, Jude, that's three. I guess you get the bonus round, Phoenix." Phoenix and Jude share a kiss that's all tongues and passion before he pulls out, making room for Phoenix. Unlike Jude and me, he doesn't immediately sink into her sweet ass that's still on display for us. He picks her up and sits her on the edge of the counter, then drops to his knees and licks her pussy from her entrance to her still-swollen clit. She leans back, palms on the counter, as he licks and nips at her.

"The two of you taste amazing mixed together." He stands and grabs the hair at the back of her neck, pulling her into a kiss. While she's moaning into his mouth, he uses his other hand to line up and enter her. Phoenix's movements are slow and deep. He whispers into her ear what a good job she's doing and how much he loves her. His pace picks up, and as he comes close to finishing, he looks over at me and nods.

"Angel, are you ready to take care of Mac when I'm done with you? He's been waiting so patiently." She nods and throws her arms around his shoulders as they ride out their releases together. He helps her off the counter and passes her hand off to me.

"On your knees, Alice, and show me how much you love my cock in your mouth."

48

Hazel

I swear these men are going to be the death of me. I'm staring at the stairs to get up to my apartment, wondering how bad it would be to go back to my car and sleep in my back seat. I can already see the faint bruises forming on my hips from the beating they took against the counter, and my knees are sore from kneeling on the tile kitchen floor while going down on Mac. I'm trying not to think of how sore my lady parts will be in the morning.

"You are a strong independent woman. Don't wuss out because of some stairs." I groan because my pep talk isn't working. One foot in front of the other, Hazel. It's only thirteen stairs. I'm so sore and tired I can't wait to change and fall into bed.

Finally reaching the top, I breathe a big sigh of relief. I head to the kitchen, take a water bottle from the refrigerator and grab some pain meds. Preventative care is key. I mentally fist-bump myself.

I peer at Wynnie's room. It's quiet, so she must be asleep. I walk over and lightly knock on the door before opening it. Hmm, her bed is empty. She must have gone over to Dellah's for a sleepover. I bet she texted me, but I didn't have my phone. I head back to the kitchen where I last remember seeing it and text Dellah.

Me: Hey, bestie, you have my girl over there? I bet your love of scary movies finally freaked her out to be home alone.

Bestie: Ha ha. You're sooooo funny. <eye roll emoji> Are you going senile in your old age, woman? Wynnie isn't here.

She's messing with me. What a bitch. I'm too tired to deal with her.

Me: Okay, sure. Just send her back in the morning when she gets up.

A few minutes later, there's a frantic knock at my door. It's after 1 o'clock in the morning. I hope Dellah doesn't plan on hanging out long because I'm exhausted. The knocks become more urgent as I head towards the door. I unlock the deadbolt, and as soon as my hand reaches to turn the knob, Dellah is swinging the door open, pushing past me and heading straight towards Wynnie's room.

"What's going on?" I chased after her through the apartment. She walks in and then out of Wynnie's door.

"You're fucking with me, right? Where is she, Hazel?"

"Where is who? Wynnie? Is she not in your guest room?" The beginning bubbles of panic are starting in my stomach.

304

"Yes, Wynnie. Your daughter, my niece. She's not at my house. I checked after you texted me, and she's not there. She's here, right?" I stand there frozen as she walks in circles, checking every corner and cabinet. In the bathrooms, behind the couch, in the pantry. She's not here. Dellah grabs my shoulders. "Is. She. Here?"

"N-no. No. She wasn't here when I got home." I look her straight in the eyes. "You swear she isn't at your house?"

"Hazel Jane Gibson, I'm not fucking with you. Rowyn is not at my house." I take a deep breath, try to stay calm and think rationally. Panicking won't find her. What should I do? Think. Think.

"Where could she be, Dellah? God, I left my cell phone at home. What if something happened and she tried to call me." I grab my phone and frantically look through my message and call logs to see if I missed anything.

"She texted me earlier when she noticed your phone was here. If there were an emergency she would have called me." It's 1:30 in the morning. My 12 year old daughter is out somewhere in the middle of the night alone. Is she alone? She doesn't hang out with anyone outside of school. She hasn't made any real friends here yet.

"I'm calling her best friend. Maybe she knows something." Dellah grabs my hand. It's the middle of the night. You can't call a 12 year old now." I nod over and over again. She's right. I look pleading into her eyes.

"Can I text her?"

"Sure, yeah." She releases my hands so I can text.

Me: Hey Nora, have you heard from Wynnie? If you have, can you let me know, please?

305

"Okay, now what?" Dropping my phone, I plop on the couch and bury my face in my hands. I can't think straight right now to even know what to do. Dellah picks up my phone and hands it back to me.

"Now we call for help. Call the guys." She's right. I should call them. But they were heading to bed when I was leaving. Mac walked out with me and told me how excited he was to officially meet his daughter tomorrow. I'll text them.

Me: 9-1-1

Within seconds my phone is ringing with Phoenix's number. As soon as I answer, Mac is calling in. I merge the calls and put them on speaker. They all immediately start talking over each other, asking what's wrong. I can also hear Jude's voice, so I must be on speakerphone at their house. Dellah yells for them to all stop talking, and the room goes silent.

I barely manage to whisper out, "Wynnie's missing." They tell me they're on their way, and the line goes dead.

They arrive in my driveway far quicker than any of them should have. I know they broke many laws to get here in such a short amount of time. Dellah went out and directed them upstairs to me, where I'd sat staring at the floor since our call ended. They walk in, and all immediately scoop me up and embrace me.

"Talk to me." Mac has his cop voice on. Duh. He's a cop. Why didn't I think to call them first? "What do we know?"

Dellah saves me. "Hazel got home, and Wynnie's not here, and she isn't at my house. We assume she has her cell, but she isn't answering it."

"Have you tracked her cell? Do you share locations?" My

knees go weak, and if they weren't holding me up, I'd be on the ground. I didn't even think of that.

"Yeah, we do. Let me check it. I'm sorry. I don't ever need it, so I didn't even think about it," I look into Mac's eyes. "I didn't think about you. You're a cop. I should have-"

"Shhh." Jude hushes me. "You called us, and we are here now. There's nothing to be sorry about."

"Angel, we will find her. We are here to help you. Check her location on your phone, and we'll go from there." Dellah hands me my phone, and I check the app.

"It says her last known location was here at 11:34 PM, and there's been no update since."

"Okay." Mac looks deep in thought. "So either her phone is turned off, or she turned off location settings. Have you checked her room to see if anything is missing? Did she pack a bag?"

"Ugh. Why haven't I thought of any of these things?" I'm so frustrated with myself right now. I peel away from the guys to head towards Wynnie's room when Phoenix grabs my wrist. He places his hand on the side of my face and caresses my cheek.

"You're doing great. You're scared and in shock, as you should be. Let us take care of you. I'll grab you some water while you check her room. Okay?" I nod, and he kisses my forehead and walks to the kitchen. Jude walks up next to me and threads his fingers through mine.

"Lead the way." Together we walked into her room. I look around and notice all her school books are on her desk, but I don't see her bookbag. When I left, she was wearing her favorite hoodie, and I don't see it anywhere. I also don't see her cell phone charger plugged into the wall. We walk back into the living room, and Mac is on the phone.

"I'll call you right back." He hangs up and comes over to me. "Notice anything missing?" I relay the items, and he says, "Good."

"How is that good?" I try not to sound angry, but my tone comes out snippy. He replies to me in a calm tone, unbothered by my anger.

"She grabbed her cell phone charger. That means no one took her-"

"Oh my god, you think someone took her, Mac?" Did someone come into the apartment and take her? No. Nothing is out of place or broken. The door was locked when I got home.

"No. And I'm telling you why." He soothingly runs his hand along my arms. "She took her charger. She unpacked her school books and probably grabbed clothes, too. She made a conscious effort to pack and leave. There's no sign of struggle. Those are all good things. Alright?"

"Yeah, okay. But she still isn't here." Where could she have gone. "Mac, who were you on the phone with?"

"I called the station and told them to be on the lookout for her. Do you have any idea what she might be wearing? That would help them look."

"When I left, she was wearing a navy hoodie, dark ripped jeans, and her red hightops. I didn't see her shoes in her room, so she probably hadn't changed."

"Good, I'll add those details to her description." He picks up his phone to call back, and I grab his wrist to stop him.

"Add? What could you have told them already? You haven't met her yet." He rubs the back of his neck, looking toward the other guys.

"I may have gone to her practices this week." I've never seen such vulnerability in his eyes. "Please don't be upset with me. She didn't see me, but I wanted to get a closer look at her. I needed to see my daughter, Hazel." There's a desperation in his voice, momentarily letting his cop persona slip. It's my turn to console him. I wrap my arm around his broad chest and give him a big hug that he returns.

"It's alright, Mac. You're right. She's your daughter. Now, let's find her so you can get a proper introduction."

49

Jude

Phoenix and I were almost finished cleaning the house when Hazel's text came in. She usually texts us when she gets home, so it wasn't unusual for our phones to buzz in the middle of the night. Phoenix opened his phone first, and by the time I had opened mine, he was already calling her, his face white as a ghost. When she answered, there was a short pause, and then we heard Mac's voice. She must have connected the calls.

Two words. That's all it took for my blood to turn cold and a fire to start under our asses. "Wynnie's missing." We were out the door within minutes speeding through the quiet streets of town. Mac's pickup pulled in next to ours as Dellah came down to greet us.

"What happened?" Mac's voice boomed through the darkness.

"We don't know. Hazel is upstairs. She needs you all."

Mac immediately switched from boyfriend to cop mode. He asked all the appropriate questions, collecting all of the facts. When Mac told Hazel that he had come to Rowyn's practices this week, I worried how she would react. Phoenix and I knew he was there since he had asked us if he could watch. We'd told him to be scarce, and he would have to tell Hazel soon. We understood his need to see her.

"What are we missing? She couldn't have just disappeared." Hazel has taken to crying and pacing. Anytime one of us tries to console her, she brushes us off.

"Let's go over what we know." Mac's cop persona is in full effect. "She texted Dellah around 10:45 to tell her you left your phone here. She packed a bag of essentials and turned off her location at around 11:30. It's now after 2 o'clock, so she has about a three hour head start on us wherever she is." Hazel stops pacing and freezes. She walks over to the kitchen counter, picks up her phone, and starts scrolling.

Phoenix meets her in the kitchen. "What is it, Angel?"

"You all texted me tonight after I told you I was on my way." Her brows pinch, and she mindlessly scans the ceiling. "I didn't have any missed notifications when I looked at my phone earlier." She starts pacing again. "Oh god, what did she see? She had to have seen."

Dellah stands in front of Hazel, momentarily stopping her pacing. "Seen what, Hazy?"

"The texts. All of them. There were no unread texts which means she opened all of them. Our group chats, your last text about kissing the guys, Mac's spanking text." Mac's hands go up in surrender.

"I used emojis." Mac walks over and grabs Hazel's hands. "But that doesn't explain why she left.

"You..you don't understand. It's always just been the two of us. We've shared everything together. No secrets and this isn't any normal little secret. This is a secret of epic proportion. I'm not JUST dating Phoenix like I told her. I'm dating all of you. Her two softball coaches...and her father. Her father, whom she didn't know existed until a few days ago. She's feeling betrayed. I betrayed her." Hazel collapses into Mac's arms, and he brings her to the couch to sit down. It takes her a few minutes to regain her composure, but when she does, she's ready and eager to find her daughter. She stands and starts pacing again.

"What. Are. We. Missing?" She stops and spins on her heels. She heads back to the kitchen, where her phone was, and shifts through the papers on the counter. "Where is it? Where is it?" she's chanting to herself. She picks up her purse and starts rifling through it, still chanting.

"Little Dove, what are you looking for?" She jumps at my words.

"My credit card. I left it on the counter so Wynnie could order pizza for dinner. That must have been when I left my phone. But it's not here, and it's not in my purse."

"Good," Mac's gruff voice comes from across the room. "It means she has money with her, but it also means we can see where she's used the card. Hazel, can you access it online?"

"Yeah, let me grab my laptop." She sat down on the couch, and we all sat around her. We waited as she logged into her account. "There are several charges from tonight.

"Oh my god, she took a cab and bought a bus ticket." Her trembling hands came up to her mouth as she stifled a sob. Phoenix put his arms around her shoulder and pulled her into his side. I took the laptop and continued looking over the charges.

"Hazel, it looks like she bought the bus ticket to depart from Atlanta. Any idea where she would be going?" She's buried her face in Phoenix's chest, and I can see her head shake in response while she silently cries.

Mac gets up and walks across the apartment, phone in hand. He starts barking orders to whoever he called to contact the cab and bus companies. He walks back over to us and rubs a soothing hand on her back.

"Alice, my guys are on it." He grabs her chin and tilts it towards him until they look into each other's eyes. "I know this is scary, but we WILL find her. I need you to keep it together right now, though. We need all the information we can to determine where she might be going. Unfortunately, Atlanta is a major hub, and she can go almost anywhere from there. She chose Atlanta for a reason, though. It's north of us. Does she have any family or friends up north?" She inhales a sharp breath and stands, gripping her cell phone.

"Tell me who?" The commanding cop voice is back. She's fumbling with her phone. Her hands are so shaky she's having trouble pushing the screen where she wants to. Mac puts his hands over her. "Tell me who, Hazel."

"Home. Spring Ridge, South Carolina. It's where I moved when I got pregnant." Mac's jaw twitches at her words. "My parents and aunt are there, and her best friend. I already text Nora, her friend, but she hasn't responded. It's the middle of the night, though, so I wouldn't expect her to."

Mac pulls her into his chest and wraps his arms around her. "Good girl." She exhales a shaky breath. "Jude, can you look at the bus website and see how she could get to Spring Ridge from Atlanta? Alice, I'm going to need you to call your family and her friend's parents and see if any of them have heard from her. If they don't answer, I'll have the local PD knock on their doors. Let me go update my guys at the station." She nods, and he brings her to the other couch to sit with Dellah. I hear her speaking to several people while I check the different bus route options. There's no direct way to Spring Ridge as it's a small town in a rural part of the state.

"I think I've got something." Everyone comes back to my couch and sits around me. "Based on the price she paid for the ticket, it looks like she's going from Atlanta to Columbia, South Carolina. That's the closest bus depot to Spring Ridge. She'll probably have to call another car service to get to your hometown, Hazel."

"That makes sense. Columbia is about 45 minutes from there." I grab her hand and give it a firm squeeze. She looks back at me and gives a small smile. "I got in contact with everyone, and none of them have heard from her, but they will be on the lookout and call me if they do."

"I'll pack snacks." Dellah jumps off the couch and enthusiastically bounces to the kitchen. We all look at her with curious faces. "Snacks. Road food. We gotta get our girl. Who's driving?" She says it so matter-of-factly that there's no arguing. We are driving to get Rowyn.

"Okay, yeah, let's go." I look back at the bus schedule on the laptop. "The bus departs from Atlanta," I bend my wrist to look at my watch, "in 15 minutes, so she has about a two hour head start on us as far as travel time."

Phoenix put his hand on my shoulder. "You have the most roomy vehicle. Girls, pack an overnight bag. We'll head back to our house, switch out the vehicles, and grab our own bags. Mac, do you need to run home?"

"No, I always carry a change of clothes in the truck because of work. I'll call the station and let them know the new information and our plans. I will have someone come sit in the driveway in case Rowyn comes back here instead."

"No need," Dellah interjects. "Collin is home. I'll have him come over and hang out." Mac nods at her. The girls head to pack, and Mac makes his calls. I lean into Phoenix next to me on the couch.

"We need to cancel our game for tomorrow, well, today. Try to schedule a make-up game, so we don't have to forfeit."

He kisses me on the forehead. "I'll take care of it."

20 minutes later, Dellah and a half-asleep Collin walked in. Hazel is packed, and we walk out to our trucks to head to our house and switch vehicles. She's finally leaning on us for help, and I'm so proud of her. We will get through this together. Always together.

50

Wynnie

This has been a crazy week. I can't believe my mom found my father, and he lives right here in town. I've always wanted to have a dad. What little girl wouldn't, but it was easy to be okay with something I've never had. My grandpa was great growing up. He did all the father-daughter stuff with me, but now I have a dad that I'm going to get to know.

Mom went out with Coach Graves again tonight. I'm happy for her. He's great to everyone on the team, and she smiles more. I like to see her doing something for herself. I'll admit it was a little shocking when I realized that's who she was dating, but I understand why she didn't tell me at first.

I was walking past the window that morning when I saw her get out of the back of a black pickup truck. I thought it was weird she got out of the back, but there was a sun glare on the passenger seat, so I couldn't see if anyone was there. I didn't want her to think I was spying on her, so I walked away. Then after the away game, when my mom was running late, Coach G told me to hang out on his tailgate while I waited for her. I recognized the truck again. He has a thin red stripe that runs along both sides. It wasn't something I had ever seen before that morning in my driveway, and there it was again. It couldn't be a coincidence.

I'm glad she told me about them both, and now she doesn't feel like she needs to be sneaky when she goes out. She doesn't have to say she's "going to a friend's house" and can just be honest. I may only be 12, but Mom and I have always been open and truthful with each other. As a single mom, we only had each other for a long time.

I enjoy the nights mom goes out because I can blast my music through the house and not just in my earbuds. I know she feels guilty about going out a lot lately, but it doesn't bother me. Besides, Aunt Dellah is right across the driveway, or sometimes she stays and hangs out with me. Not tonight, though, It's just me. I'm jamming through the house towards the kitchen, where Mom told me she was leaving her card so I could order pizza whenever I got hungry. That's the other perk of being alone. I get to order my pizza with all the toppings I like. I hear a buzzing on the counter and turn around. Shifting through some papers, I find my mom's phone.

I swear, Mom, first you lock your keys in your car, and now you forget your phone. I roll my eyes at how forgetful she can be sometimes. I grab my phone from my hoodie pocket to text Aunt Dellah to tell her my mom forgot her phone, when my finger accidentally taps my mom's screen. It lights up, and I see she has several unread messages.

Bestie message notification.
   Phoenix message notification.
   Jude message notification.
   Mac message notification.

I stand there and stare at the phone momentarily before I realize I should text Aunt Dellah about Mom's phone before I forget. She replies with the typical "I'm here if you need me" message, and I put my phone away.

She has a message from Phoenix, which I know is Coach Graves' first name. Obviously, one from Aunt Dellah. A text from someone named Jude, who I've heard her mention before, and a text from Mac, my father. I know she's been texting with my dad. Maybe I should check it. It might be important. I swipe the screen, and it opens since neither of us has passcodes on our phones. Clicking on the message icon, I notice that several of the messages are in a group chat titled "The Guys" and she has a separate unread message from Mac. I open that one.

ME: My beautiful Alice. I can't wait to see you soon. I want to apologize in advance if I can't keep my hands off of you. My palms have been itching for a repeat of last weekend. <hand emoji> <peach emoji> <kiss face emoji>

What the actual freak is that all about? A repeat of last weekend. She told me she was out with Coach Graves last weekend. I opened the notification from Aunt Dellah.

Bestie: Hazel and Jude and Phoenix and Mac sitting in a tree K-I-S-S-I-N-G! Have fun Bitch. I'll keep an eye out for your

318

girl.

What am I reading? Kissing all three of them? Kissing my father? What does Aunt Dellah know? I hesitantly open the group chat. I read through several of the texts between "The Guys" and my mom. A recent one stands out the most.

PHOENIX: Just me? How? What about Jude?

So, my mom is dating Phoenix, and he's asking about Jude. Is she dating Phoenix AND Jude? Jude. Jude? Why do I know that name? Oh my god. That's Coach S's first name, isn't it? Jude Sanders. Crap, what are you doing Mom? Those are my coaches. But there's also something going on with Mac because those were not innocent emojis. Is she dating my dad? No. She wouldn't keep something that big from me.

I read through more of the texts and realize she's out right now with all of them. All THREE of them. My two softball coaches and my dad. This can't be right. I can't deal with this. I...I...I need to get out of here. I need my friends. I need Nora.

I spend the next 30 minutes packing a bag and looking up bus tickets. I'll definitely be buying more than pizza with my mom's card but I need to get out of here. I purchased my bus ticket and ordered a taxi to pick me up from down the street and take me to the nearest bus depot. I don't want Aunt Dellah to see me leave. I need to get to my best friend's house, and then I can digest all of the information I just learned.

I have a 90 minute taxi trip to the bus station, a four hour bus ride, then 45 minutes to Nora's house. I'll text her in the morning to let her know I'm coming and an ETA of when

I'll be there. She'll be excited to see me, but I don't want to explain to her how I'm getting there until I'm already there, and I definitely don't want anyone to warn my mom.

As I'm watching the clock so I can leave to meet the taxi on time, I have an ache in the pit of my stomach. I'm staring at the control screen on my phone to share locations with my mom. If I don't turn this off before I walk out, she'll know I left the house and can track everywhere I'm going. There's always been no secrets and total trust between us, but I'm feeling beyond betrayed right now. She broke my trust.

"I'm sorry, Mom," I say to the empty apartment as I turn off my location. I grab my backpack and turn off all the lights except the kitchen light. I always leave that one on when Mom's out, and I don't want to give any reason for Aunt Dellah to be suspicious.

I take one last look into the apartment before I leave. Closing my eyes, I whisper, "Please forgive me, Mom. I love you."

51

Hazel

This may be the worst day of my life. Not the day I found out I was pregnant at 18. Not the day I had a baby and was raising her alone. No, it's today. The day that baby decided to run away because of something I did to her. She had to have been devastated to leave without discussing anything with me. I thought I knew my daughter like the back of my hand, but do I?

It feels like we are never going to get there. Wynnie's bus left Atlanta at 3 AM and should arrive in Columbia around 7 AM. By the time we got on the road, it was 4 AM, and it's a four hour drive. Phoenix and Jude sat in the front, and I sat in the back between Mac and Dellah. I'm envious of Dellah, who's quietly snoring against the window. I'm cuddled into Mac's chest while he traces circles along my arm, sleep not even a thought. I've been periodically trying to call Wynnie, but she's still not answering, and no one else has heard from her.

Jude looks in the rearview mirror catching my eyes and giving me a warm smile. Phoenix notices the interaction and turns to face me. He gives my leg a warm squeeze. I close my eyes at the comfort it brings me.

"Angel, we will get there and find her. Try not to worry. You're going to bite a hole in your pretty little lip." I released my lip that I didn't know I was gnawing on. "Better. Now, with stopping for gas, we should be in town around 8:30 AM. Where should we go first?" I think about who she might go to see when she gets to town.

"I'm not sure. I'll call everyone when we get close if I haven't heard from them first. What time should she get to town?"

Jude responds first. "If she gets a car service right from the bus depot, she should get to town 30-45 minutes before us. Keep trying her phone. Maybe she will eventually answer." I hadn't told them her phone was going straight to voicemail now. Either it died or she blocked my calls. It's 6:50 AM, so we are more than halfway there. Wynnie should be getting off the bus anytime. I hope she's safe. She's grounded for life after I have her in my arms again.

We stopped for gas an hour later, and my nerves feel like live wires. Mac tried to get me to drink some water, but I can't think of doing anything but getting to Wynnie. We are so close. Each of them has taken turns placing their hands on my bouncing knees, and shaking legs. Wynnie's phone still goes directly to voicemail, and according to the latest texts, no one has heard from her. What if we're wrong, and this isn't where she went? We lived in this small town her entire life until three months ago. I don't know where else she would have gone.

Finally getting into town, all I can do is cry. Wynnie should be here already, but she hasn't contacted anyone. My parents and my aunt are up and waiting. Nora has tried calling her, and her phone is going straight to voicemail for everyone now. I'm convinced her phone is off. As we drive through town toward my parent's house, I'm lost in thought. We need to stop and regroup. I look out the window and see a sign on the light post.

"Pull over." My outburst startles everyone in the silent vehicle.

"Little Dove?" Jude looks at me with concerned eyes through the rearview mirror.

"Jude, pull over." He finds the closest spot and parks.

"Angel, why did we stop?"

"Look." I point at the hanging sign with a red pickup truck filled with corn and flowers.

"Oh," Dellah exclaims. "You think that's where she would go? I love this place." Dellah came to visit a few times when we lived here and we took her.

"Yeah, she always loved the monthly Farmers Market. The fresh flowers were her favorite part. This is where she will be if she's not with friends or family." I hope. Every month from spring through fall, the farmers market opens on the third weekend, and local vendors from all over the state set up and sell their handmade and grown items. "Let's split up. Dellah, you go with Jude and Phoenix since you have an idea of the layout, Mac and I will go together. Call if you find her." We set off in opposite directions to find our girl.

The market has been open for about an hour. It's not overly busy, but there's still enough of a crowd, making it difficult to see down the aisles easily. It feels like we've checked everywhere twice, even crossing paths with the others once. I'm determined she's here, and I'm not giving up. We take a third trip through the flower market section, and I spot her. She's sitting alone on a bench under a tree with a bundle of colorful flowers in her lap, her backpack on the ground next to her.

"Mac…"

"I see her." He takes my hand. "Please, let me?" His eyes are glistening, mirroring mine. I nod, and he releases my hand, slowly walking towards her. I pull out my phone to text the others our location, and walk around the crowd to get closer without being noticed. Her gaze is affixed on the flowers, and she doesn't see when he steps up.

"Excuse me, is this seat taken?" Mac gestures to the empty half of the bench. She shrugs and shakes her head without looking up. "Those are gorgeous flowers. Are they for someone special?" She runs her finger along the long petal of a yellow day lily, my favorite.

"Um, yeah, I bought them for my mom. She loves fresh flowers." I guess she never realized I bought them because I know how much she loves them.

"I know Hazel will love them." Mac has a bright smile on his face. His cornflower blue eyes match the blue irises in the bouquet she's holding.

"Yeah, my mo- How do you know her na-" She finally looks at the man sitting beside her and stops mid-thought. "You… your…" Her hand starts to lift towards his face, but stops mid-air and touches the corner of her own eye instead. Mac put his hand out to her.

"Hi, I'm Mac. I'm your father."

Warm hands come around my waist from behind, and I

smell the metallic scent and know who it is. Phoenix kisses the top of my head as Jude twines his hand with mine. Dellah stands on the other side of me with her hands over her heart as we watch the sight before us.

Wynnie timidly takes his hand, still speechless.

"I'm not sure what name I should call you, and when I asked your mom, she said I should ask you. So, what name would you like me to call you, sweetheart?" She smiles at the term of endearment.

"Well, my family has always called me Wynnie, but I go by Rowyn at school and with people in my regular life. But, um, I guess you're family. You can call me Wynnie if you'd like." A tear slips down her cheek, and he brushes it away with his thumb.

"Hi, Wynnie. It's nice to meet you finally. I've been waiting for you my entire life." She flings herself at him, throwing her arms around his neck. He wraps his arms around her, and they're both crying. I spin in Phoenix's arms and bury my face in his chest, shedding my own tears. Phoenix pulls me closer, and I feel Jude kiss my shoulder.

"We told you we'd find her. I love you, Little Dove.

"I love you, too, Angel."

I wrap an arm around Jude's waist, and pull him into a three-way hug.

"I love you both so much. Thank you. Thank you." Their arms wrap tighter around me. I feel another set of arms wrap around my back expecting it to be Dellah, but I realize they're too small for her. I hear, "I'm so sorry, Mom," mumbled into my back, and I spin around, grasping her and squeezing with everything I have.

"Oh, my god. I love you, baby. Don't you ever do that to

me, again. You're grounded until you're 50. You're doing all our laundry, and Aunt Dellah and Uncle Collin's laundry, and maybe even Jude, Phoenix and Mac's laundry." At the mention of the three guys, I realize Wynnie, and I have a lot to talk about. I pull her away and grab her by the shoulders. I look at each of my three men and then back at her. "We need to talk."

Mac rubs my arm. "We'll go update everyone and give you some time." He kisses me on the forehead, and they all head back in the direction of Jude's SUV. Wynnie and I walk back to the bench she and Mac were sitting on.

"Wynnie, I-"

"Mom, it's okay."

"But it's not." I take her hands in mine. "It's not okay because I gave you half-truths and half-lies. I've known about Mac for a couple of weeks and never said anything. Jude, Phoenix, and I have been together since school started. I promise I didn't know who they were when we met. That part wasn't a lie. And while you're only 12, we've always been open and honest with each other, and I know you could have handled it if I told you the truth–about all of them. I would have told you eventually. I wanted you to be able to process everything with Mac first. Finding your dad is a big deal, Wynnie. I thought you might need time before also finding out your mother was dating multiple men. I'm not even sure I've fully processed it myself. And then you asked me about Phoenix, and I didn't want to lie but knew I still couldn't tell you the whole truth. I feel like a terrible mother." I look down at my hands. The brick of guilt reappearing in my stomach.

"Oh, Mom." She leans forward and grabs me into a big hug. "It is a lot to process. I wanted to say I'm sorry I went through your phone. I wasn't digging for anything. I saw the text from Mac and got curious."

I groan, thinking about the text she read from Mac. "Look about what you saw…"

"Let's not talk about that. I'm not too young to understand what those emojis meant, but I'd rather not think about what my mother and her boyfriends do behind closed doors."

"Fair enough." We have a lighthearted laugh together.

"So it's true then? You're dating all three of them?" There's hesitation in her voice. I nod.

"I am. They are all really good to me, and they make me happy. But, look at me." I want to make sure she hears me and understands me. "You are my number one priority. They will never come before you. My relationship with them affects you, and if you aren't comfortable with it, it's over. You're allowed to be selfish when it comes to our life together. It always has been, and it always will be, you and me. We decide together who we let into our lives."

"Mom, that's a lot of pressure on a 12 year old." We both crack up laughing, and it feels so good. "But, Mom, you already know I like Coach S and Coach Graves."

"You might need to start calling them Jude and Phoenix outside of school." She makes a sour face.

"That's gonna be…weird, but I get it. And Mac, Dad, well, he seems pretty cool so far."

"He's going to love hearing you call him that." I can't help the big smile that takes over my face. "So we're doing this? You, me, and those three overprotective, big-hearted men."

"Yeah, Mom. I like who you are when you're with them. And I like my alone time." She winks at me, and I give her shoulder a light shove.

"You're still on laundry duty till you're married. Let's go find our crazy crew and visit your grandparents. You've got everyone in a tizzy with your disappearance. You should probably call Nora and invite her over." She reaches into her back pocket, pulls out her phone, and flashes it at me.

"It died from ignoring everyone's calls." She scrunched her nose and shrugged her shoulders in apology.

"That reminds me. Why did you come here anyway?"

"Since my phone died, I didn't have a way to call anyone. I thought I'd wander around the farmers market for a while until it was late enough to show up on someone's doorstep."

"Well, I'm glad we found you, and you're safe. I love you, kid."

"Love you, too, Mom."

52

Hazel

Lunch with my parents was interesting. When you bring home your three boyfriends, and one happens to be your baby daddy, you receive a lot of judgmental looks. Luckily there's always a Dellah to make comic relief out of any situation. Comments like:

"She'll never have to carry in her own groceries."

"They are three times more likely to fall in the toilet in the middle of the night."

"If she commits murder, she has a cop on her side to hide her crime."

Wynnie enjoyed her time with her best friend, Nora, and we made plans for her to come back in 3 weeks to spend spring break with her grandparents. We decided to leave early in the afternoon to head back home.

Dellah and Wynnie sat in the third row, Mac and me in the middle, and Jude and Phoenix in the front. The girls in the back fell asleep immediately, and I followed shortly behind them, curled into Mac's side. I must have been sleeping lightly because I heard them start to talk together.

"What do we do now?" Phoenix asks. "Rowyn knows about all of us being together. Mac's finally in the inner circle. How do we proceed?"

I feel Mac's chest rumble under my cheek as he speaks. "What does a future look like for you guys? Can you see the five of us being a family all together?"

"Maybe more than five of us eventually?" The sweet tenor of Jude's voice floats through my ears. "Hazel, is it for me. I don't see anything but her and Rowyn in my future. And you guys. I think we can all make this work together."

"More." Phoenix ponders the word. "Do you think Hazel would want more kids? I've always seen myself having kids, but Rowyn is already 12, and this isn't exactly a conventional relationship."

"Hazel does. She's always wanted more kids." I open my eyes and lock them with Phoenix. "I do." Mac rubs his hand up and down my arm.

"Hey, Alice. Were you listening in?" I nod my head. "So what do you think? Can we do it all together with maybe more of us in the future?"

"I think Wynnie would make an amazing big sister. And I think Coach S and Coach G need to ask a little lady what she prefers to be called when you guys are outside of school. Otherwise, we are going to end up with a house divided between Wynnie and Rowyn."

"A house, Little Dove. As in one house, together?" I can see the hope twinkling in his eyes.

"Well, do you expect all of our figurative future children

to float between three houses?" I give him a smirk through the rearview mirror, and he inhales a sharp breath. Phoenix reaches over and places his hand on Jude's knee.

"What are you thinking, Angel? I can hear those gears turning." I'm thinking so much. Summer BBQs outside by our pool. Any one of them shirtless, rocking their baby, or pushing a stroller. Never waking up alone again. Wynnie having good male role models in her life.

"Well, four incomes could buy a pretty nice house."

"Or we could build one. I have property." We all looked at Mac in shock. He has property?

Phoenix looks at him. "I know you have a spot of your own off the beaten path, but how much of that property is yours?"

Mac grabs the back of his neck and looks out the window. "About 45 acres, give or take."

"No shit, Mac. How'd you manage that?" Jude asks.

"The old man that used to live there had no family. When I first moved to town and started working for the PD, I had a welfare check out there. The grocery store owner used to pack up his groceries for him. He missed calling in his order one week, and she called us to check on him. When I went out there, he had fallen and been on the floor for about a day. I got him medical attention, and when he returned home, I'd check on him twice a week and bring him his groceries. He passed away five years ago and left me his property. It took a little while to get everything settled with his lawyers, and when Jenna and I divorced, it still wasn't finalized, so it didn't need to be split. It became fully mine shortly after. I also still have the money from the sale of our old house that's just been sitting collecting interest for four years. We can build a house anywhere on the property and make it ours."

I'm at a loss for words. The guys are as well. We could build a house for our family. A potentially growing family. Our own little slice of heaven.

"Can we have a pool?" All the guys laugh.

"Yes, Alice, we can have a pool. What do you guys think? Making plans and building will take a while, so there's no immediate rush." I sit up in my seat.

"Let's rush. Let's build a house. A big house with, with, seven bedrooms and a pool and a wrap-around porch with rocking chairs." The ideas are bombarding my thoughts. The possibilities seem endless.

"Okay, Angel," he laughs. "Calm down. Seven bedrooms? That's a lot. How many more babies are you wanting?"

"How many did each of you imagine having?" They each give me the standard 2-3 answers. "Okay, so let's compromise at four."

"Four kids sounds like a good number, Alice."

"Oh no, I mean four more. Maybe five, I've always wanted a big family. Being an only child was lonely, and I never wanted that for my kids. Wynnie threw that for a loop, but she's still young, and so am I. And well, I'm robbing the cradle a bit with those two up there." I wink at my two 27 year old men in the front seat.

"If that's what you want, Little Dove, you'll get a house full of babies."

"Am I gonna be a big sister?" Wynnie asked sleepily from the back seat.

"Babies? Are we having more babies? Do I get to be an aunt again?" I groan and put my face in my hands.

"Now you've done it, guys. We will never hear the end of it. Dellah has baby fever for *me*." I playfully punch Mac in the shoulder because he's the closest to reach. "Wynnie, would you want to have siblings?" I can't believe we are having this conversation. Everything about it feels right, though. My beautiful daughter is opening her heart to three father figures. We are talking about building a life together. A future with a house and more babies.

"Yeah, Mom, I'd really like to be a big sister." She gave me a genuine smile.

"Yay. Who gets to be the next baby daddy?"

"Dellah!" We all yell.

"Hey, Dells, let's not discuss that stuff in front of the kid. We don't want to scar her for life."

53

Hazel

3 weeks later

"Someone explain this to me again?" Mac is looking at the table like it's going to bite him.

"It's game night. What's so hard to understand?" Jude passes him a beer knowing full well that the box of jelly beans is an interesting "game" for game night.

"I'm with Mac on this one. A deck of cards and a box of jelly beans. Are we playing poker with snacks?" Mmmm. Phoenix looks absolutely good enough to lick with his black hair slicked back and wet from his shower. Damn him and his gray sweatpants. He does that on purpose, knowing it drives Jude and me crazy. He's about to discover how poor of a clothing choice he's just made.

"Actually…" I look over to Jude who's, mirroring my mischievous smile. We planned this night together. "We are going to play strip poker, with a twist."

"Strip poker?" Mac looks concerned.

Phoenix shoves his shoulder. "That was the concerning part of that sentence for you? What about the twist? And also, I seem to be at a disadvantage in the clothing department for strip poker."

"Too bad for you." I teasingly blow Phoenix a kiss. Jude and I join them at the table, and I unwrap the jelly beans as Jude explains the rules of the game.

"So let me get this straight," Mac has his serious cop face on. "If you lose the hand, you have the choice of stripping an article of clothing or taking your chance on a gross jelly bean?"

"A *potentially* gross jelly bean. You could get a good one." He doesn't look convinced that this will be any fun. It definitely will be.

"Let's do a practice round," Jude says as he deals everyone a hand. Mac wins and is filled with a false sense of hope. "So, everyone but Mac would have to either take off a piece of clothing or choose a jelly bean. Got it?" Everyone agrees and he deals again. Phoenix realizes his lack of clothing has put him in the position of eating some very gross jelly beans once he's lost a few hands. Everyone else has lost a few articles of clothes.

I excuse myself to use the bathroom, and on my way back, I notice my book, *The Giver*, on a side table.

"Hey Jude, are you reading my book?" He gives me a boyish smile.

"I am, and I'm enjoying it. Have you read yours?" I shake my head.

"What book, Angel?

"Jude got me *Who Moved my Cheese.*" Phoenix starts

laughing.

"What's so funny?" Mac looks utterly confused.

"It was a required reading in one of Jude's counseling classes in college. He used to buy that book for everyone's birthday. I'm not surprised he gave it to you." Well, that makes me feel a little less special. Jude must see my expression.

"No, Little Dove. Phoenix isn't wrong. I did buy that book for many people, but I had you specifically in mind when I picked it out for you. The book is about being adaptable through difficult situations. Finding strength in your weaknesses. You had just told me about Rowyn, and I was so proud of you." *Oh.* I walked over to him, sat in his lap, and gave him a passionate kiss.

"Thank you. Let's get back to our game. Next hand is stripping only. Phoenix needs to lose some clothes." I wink at him, and he scowls at me.

Phoenix does, in fact, lose his shirt in the next round. All my men are shirtless now, and I'm finding it hard to concentrate on the game.

"Next round, jelly beans only," Phoenix exclaims. Jude wins, and the rest of us each take our chances.

"Eww, what the hell is this?" Mac takes a long pull of his beer.

"If it wasn't chocolate pudding, it was canned dog food." Jude was the only one allowed to have the flavor key since he's already had all the flavors before. "Nasty. Your turn Phoenix." He grabs a light green one.

"This…tastes…like…grass. Gross. Eww. Go, Angel." He's smacking his lips while his entire face is scrunched. He looks comical. I take my chances with a white one. My options are coconut or baby wipes, and as a mother, I've had my fair taste of baby wipes. I figured it was my safest bet."

"I got coconut." A smug smile crosses my cheeks as the guys grumble at my luck. I lose the next hand and choose to strip. I'm now down to just my bra and panties, and getting lots of heated looks. I notice movement out of the corner of my eye and see Jude slip his hand onto Phoenix's thigh. They exchange a sweet smile.

"You know I'm okay with it." They both give me their attention. Questioning looks on their faces.

"Okay with what, Angel?"

"The two of you. Together. Without me." They share a look.

"We don't have to, Little Dove."

"Oh, but you want to. I see the way you look at each other. It's the same way you each look at me. I'm secure enough in our relationship that I think we can all individually explore each other. What are everyone else's thoughts?"

"I wouldn't be upset to get you one-on-one, Alice." I roll my eyes at him.

"Would anyone have a problem with me being with any of you individually?" They all shake their heads. "Then it's no different for Jude and Phoenix to be together. Not that you needed my permission, but you have it if there is any doubt. If it's something the two of you wanted to do, of course."

Phoenix grabs Jude's chin. "Is that what you want? Do you want to be my good boy? Do you want to bottom for me?" Jude whimpers, and he collides his mouth with Phoenix's. I watch them make out for a minute, then I stand and climb onto Mac's lap, straddling his chair.

"I think game night is over." Mac devours my mouth with his and makes quick work of removing my bra. Grabbing handfuls of my breasts, he kneads them between his large calloused hands as he nips at my lips.

"Couch or bed, Alice?" I peek over at Jude and Phoenix, who both have their cocks out, stroking them together as one.

"Couch. I want to enjoy the show." He wraps his hands under my ass and lifts me. Walking us to the couch, he sets me down and tells me to kneel facing the back.

"I'm going to take you from behind so you don't have to take your eyes off them." He pushes my back down so my arms are resting on the back of the couch. I feel the tug and the rip of another pair of my panties. His leather smell invades my nose as he gets close to my ear. "I'll buy you a dozen more pairs of panties just so I can continue to rip them off of you." He thrusts into me to the hilt.

"Caveman."

"You love it." He smacks my ass.

"I love you." He freezes. We hadn't shared those words yet. He grabs me by the front of my neck and pulls me up to him, chest to back.

Growling into my ear, he licks a line along my pulse point. "You don't know how long I've waited to hear those words from you, Alice. My sweet, dirty Alice. I love the fuck out of you. I want to put a baby in you and watch your belly swell with my child. I want Jude and Phoenix to put their babies in you. I want to be a family, to grow our family. All of us together."

"Always together." The guys have joined us on the couch. Phoenix has Jude bent over the arm, his ass in the air, while he strokes his cock with lube.

"Now, Alice. I want you to be our naughty girl, and watch your other boyfriends fuck each other." He pushes me back down and directs my head toward them. Mac resumes pumping into me as I listen to Phoenix talk Jude through what he's doing.

I watch Jude's face as it transitions from his brows being scrunched to wide-eyed to his eyes rolling in the back of his head with a low moan escaping from deep in his throat.

"Good boy. I'm all the way in. You're mine now." Phoenix's words, although meant for Jude, sparked something in me, and my orgasm tore through me by surprise.

"Fuck, Alice. Where the hell did that come from?"

"T-their fau-ault." I pant out. "Jude…checkin." They look so beautiful together. Seeing Phoenix take his pleasure while giving it to Jude makes me want to join them. Hmm?

"Greeeeen. Oh, God. Fuck, you feel amazing, Phoenix."

"I knew you'd like it, naughty boy. You're a perfect little bottom." With one hand on Jude's shoulder for leverage and the other on his hip, Phoenix and Mac mirror each other's pace.

"Do you guys trust me?" My idea is gonna take some rearranging.

"What's going on in that dirty mind of yours, Angel?"

"I want to make Jude feel even better. I want to suck his cock, but I don't want you or Mac to stop what you're doing."

"Okay, Alice, be the puppet master." I explain to everyone how I want them. Jude in the same position that Mac and I were in, with Jude leaning against the back of the couch and Phoenix behind him. When they got settled, I laid across the couch on my back under Jude, opened my legs for Mac and he slid back in. I grabbed Jude's cock and swirled my tongue around the cool metal at his tip, and then sucked him into my mouth.

"Oh, my Jesus Fuck. Fuck I love you guys. Holy shit." More curses fly out of Jude's mouth as I hollow my cheeks and suck deep.

"Angel, I think he likes your idea." I hummed my response which only made Jude swear more. I release his cock with a pop but continue stroking with my hand.

"I want you all to mark me. Make me yours. I want you all to come on me."

"Fuck, Alice. Keep talking like that, and I won't last much longer."

"Make me your dirty girl. Make me filthy. Claim me." Curses start to flow freely around me, and one by one, they each pull out and come on my stomach and chest with moans and roars of pleasure. I swirl my fingers through the mess on my body, thinking about how much I love these men. Mac's words about wanting to see them all put babies in me makes me think about our future. I want their babies. I have to call my doctor.

"Little Dove, you look fucking stunning with all of our come covering you." I feel incredible. All of us are here enjoying each other's bodies together.

"We still owe you more orgasms, Angel." He runs his fingers down my stomach through their come and starts rubbing circles around my clit.

"It's a good thing Wynnie is away on spring break, and we have several more days to make up for it."

54

Epilogue Phoenix

4 months later

"Let's go, or we're gonna be late." Getting five people anywhere on time is like herding cats. Add Dellah and Collin, and it's been a nightmare all week. We decided to take our first family vacation over summer break. We rented a beach house along the coast of South Carolina. Somewhere Hazel and her parents used to go when she was a kid.

Dellah insisted we go to this restaurant where the wait staff insults you and makes you big paper hats to wear. Hazel said it would be hilarious, and we should be grateful that although they have karaoke, it's not tonight. Apparently Dellah is a big fan. So, here I am, trying to get all seven of us packed into Hazel's minivan. She traded in her car when playing vehicle roulette became too aggravating for her. Now when we all go out together, we pile into her red minivan that looks out of place between our two pickup trucks and an SUV.

When we returned from Wynnie's rescue mission, we decided we would all move into our house once the school year ended. Wynnie took over the guest room. We turned the office into a bedroom for Mac, and Hazel insisted she didn't need a bedroom, and she hasn't. She floats between our three rooms every night, and we also swap rooms. Mac moved in with us because Hazel decided she liked the bones of the house Mac had inherited and wanted to remodel and build onto it. Construction started about a month ago and is going well.

The softball season ended on a high note. Although the girls didn't make it to playoffs, they played a great season, and Wynnie did fantastic. Jude and I informed the principals at both of our schools about our relationship with Hazel and Wynnie. We wanted full disclosure so there wouldn't be any issues with preferential treatment now or in two years when she is promoted to high school. They assigned Wynnie a new school counselor, and a softball coach from the high school will help with our tryouts next season. Our principals were supportive of our relationships which was a massive relief for us both because we love what we do.

After school ended and the girls moved in, Wynnie sat Jude and me down and asked us if we would call her Wynnie. That was the day we all became a full part of her inner circle. She had started calling us Jude and Phoenix shortly after we returned from South Carolina, and the day she called Mac, Dad, I swear I saw the man cry. We all thought Wynnie would have the most challenging adjustment, but she's putting us all to shame with her acceptance of our unconventional relationship.

"You've got 2 minutes to get to the van, or I'm leaving without you. Last call." As I walk to the van everyone starts pouring out of the front door. It would figure a threat of abandonment would get them all running.

We get seated at our table, and Dellah and Hazel say that they have to go to the bathroom. By the time they return, we've ordered our drinks, our server has started making our hats, and the table is in hysterics. Jude's hat says "My only friend" with an outline of his hand. Mac's says, "Easier than 3rd grade Math." Mine says, "I'm a good guy, I pull out." Collin's says, "Day 16…same underwear." And Wynnie's says, " I stalk ugly boys on Snapchat." Our server looks at the two of them and asks which one of us they belong to.

"Mine's wearing the old underwear," Dellah proudly exclaims, which has us all laughing. He makes her a hat that says, "I dye the curtains to match the drapes." The girls have a good laugh because Dellah is a natural blonde. When he looks at Hazel, she's beat red.

"Which one is yours?" He's eagerly holding the white paper hat and a black marker.

"All three of them are hers," Wynnie states without hesitation and with a big smile. I love that little girl. I'm going to tell her soon.

The server nods and turns around so we can't see what he's writing. When he places the hat on Hazel's head, I almost fall out of my seat. Our table roars with laughter. Her hat reads, "Back door wide open."

"Maybe later," I whisper in her ear, making her face turn impossibly redder. Our drinks arrived as we are ordering, including Dellah and Hazel's very large margaritas. They told us they ordered them when they went to the bathroom.

55

Epilogue Jude

We had a wonderful meal with drinks and laughter. When we finished, we decided to take a walk on the beach. Dellah, Collin, and Wynnie go in the opposite direction to give us some alone time. They told us that we could head back to the house, and they would take Wynnie to the boardwalk to play the games for a while. We haven't had much alone time this week since we're in such a small space, but we've snuck off a few times to enjoy each other individually. Tonight we should have a couple of hours to worship our goddess together.

Hazel looks incredible in a pale blue sundress whipping around in the ocean breeze. Living together for the past month has been perfect. It has had some growing pains, mostly five people and only two bathrooms, which had us adding more bathrooms to our original blueprint for the house upgrade. It truly is *our* house. Everyone had a hand in designing aspects that they wanted. Hazel is getting her porch and pool, and Mac and Phoenix wanted a heated garage space to work on their vehicles. I'm getting my library room which is just as much for Hazel, and Wynnie wanted a movie room in the basement and a bedroom with a big window so she can do her art. We're hoping that we can move in around Thanksgiving to be able to spend our first Christmas together as a family in our new house. So far, everything is on schedule.

Pulling Hazel into me, I kiss her on the forehead. "Let's head back to the house."

"Wait, I have a surprise for all of you." She looks nervous.

"Angel, the only present I need from you is under this dress you're wearing. I want to get home and unwrap you." She gives him an exaggerated huff and pushes him away.

"Alright, Alice, hurry up and give us our present so we can get home and get ours."

"You're all a bunch of pervs. You know that, right?" She squeals when I grab her around the waist and spin her. Putting her down, she giggles, my favorite sound in the world.

"Ugh, okay, close your eyes and put your hands out." I put my hand out and hear her rummaging through her purse. "Eyes closed," she scolds one of them. Placed in my hand is a metal rectangle with a chain and a loop. It's a keychain. "Alright, you can open your eyes."

There's an inscription on the rectangle. "World's Greatest Daddy." My eyes flash to hers, and she nods. I drop to my knees in the sand pressing my head to her belly. Phoenix grabs her face and starts kissing her. Mac's reaction seems to be lagging. Since he's already Wynnie's dad, he doesn't understand the meaning as quickly as Phoenix and me.

"Are you…" He places his hand on her stomach next to my

head.

"Pregnant. I'm pregnant." She has the biggest, most beautiful smile on her face. "I'm about 7 or 8 weeks, but I have a doctor's appointment next week to confirm.

"We're going." There's no question in Phoenix's voice. They are coming to my appointment.

"When, how?" I can't stop kissing her stomach.

"Shortly after spring break I had my doctor remove my IUD. I thought it would take a while, but I also didn't want to tell you because I wanted it to happen naturally, without any pressure. One of you is very fertile." She giggles, again and I melt a little.

Phoenix points at Mac, "If this one ends up being yours again, you're wearing condoms at all times." Mac throws his hands up in surrender.

"Fair enough, man. Hell, if I'm blessed enough to have two babies with this goddess, I'll get snipped to give you guys a fighting chance." He winks, and Phoenix pushes his chest playfully.

"Little Dove, can we take you home now, please?" I'm not above begging at this point. Now we have something to celebrate. I stand and offer her my hand.

"Oh yes, Angel. Jude really wants to test out your hat." We've been so busy lately, and with Wynnie just down the hall, we haven't been able to truly enjoy ourselves in a while. Our new house will have the kid's rooms at the opposite end of ours.

"Lead the way." She offers me a devilish smirk, and we link hands and return to the van.

The front door of the house closes behind me, and Hazel is already taking off her dress while walking up the stairs to the master bedroom. Next comes off her bra that she throws behind her, and by the time we reach the bedroom, her panties are slipping down her legs. She throws herself into the middle of the bed.

"Ravish me, men. I've been keeping this baby a secret for over two weeks, and these pregnancy hormones are no joke."

"Hear that, men," Mac addresses the room as we all strip. "Our little naughty girl has been keeping secrets. What are we going to do about that?"

"It sounds like she's asking for a punishment." I walk up to the bed, grab her ankles and flip her over onto her stomach. I grab her hips, dragging her down the bed until she's hanging off the edge, ass on full display for us. Phoenix walks up next to me and starts rubbing both ass cheeks as I watch Mac crawl up the side of the bed and stops at Hazel's ears.

"Do you need a spanking, Brat? Phoenix's hand looks twitchy. How many do you think you deserve for keeping this big secret from us?" Her breathing increases in anticipation of the spanking she knows she's getting.

"T-two each?"

Phoenix squeezes each cheek. "What do you guys think? Are two each satisfactory?" Mac and I agree, and without warning, Phoenix cracks a hand on both ass cheeks simultaneously. She yelps the most delicious sound that turns into a purr when he bends down, kissing and licking the red prints he left on her pale skin. "You look so fucking sexy with my marks blooming on your ass. There's my two, Angel. Jude's next." He steps aside so I can get behind her.

Spanking Hazel has always been Phoenix and Mac's thing, but I'll admit I've been intrigued. Sensing my hesitation, Phoenix comes up behind me and starts peppering kisses along my neck and shoulder.

"It can be as hard or as soft as you want, but trust me," he grabs my wrist and guides it between her legs. Our fingers easily slide through her pussy, she's soaked. "She loves it, or she wouldn't be this wet." I run my hands across the prints he already left on her, while Phoenix kisses me. Her hips are wiggling and I grab her waist with my left hand. I smack her quickly on each cheek with my right. My hand stings, but that's quickly forgotten when I hear her moan and Phoenix whispers, "Good Boy" in my ear.

"Check-in, Alice."

"Green. Fucking green, and if you don't hurry up and get your smacks in, I'm going to jump on someone's dick because I need to be filled."

"Our naughty brat needs to be filled. We can definitely arrange that, Alice." Phoenix and I lie on the bed beside Hazel while Mac stands up behind her. "You have two more, and I want you to count them. Understand?"

"Yes, Sir." We all love it when she gets sassy like that. It spurs us on, especially Mac.

He slaps his hand over her left cheek. "Count," he demands when she doesn't say anything.

"One," she says through a sob. His hand comes barreling down on her right ass cheek, and as she breathlessly says, "Two," he thrusts into her, sinking deep.

"Good fucking girl." It only takes a few pumps before she's so worked up, she's already screaming from her first orgasm. "Jude, get the lube out of the side table. You're taking this pretty red ass first. We're gonna pop another one of your cherries." I sputter at his words.

"But my piercing?" We've all talked about anal, but it's not

348

something that we have done with Hazel yet.

"She's going to fucking love it, now get the lube, and I'll get her ready for you." I hand Mac the lube, and he squirts some onto his fingers. He begins to rub around her rim, still pumping into her, and when she starts to moan, he slips a finger in. Her moaning increases, and he slips another finger in until there seems to be no resistance.

"Jude, lube up your cock. She's ready for you." He pulls out of her, lays on the bed, and pulls her up his body until she's lying on him. He pushes back inside her, and his eyes roll back into his head. "You feel so fucking good, my precious Alice. Are you gonna suck off Phoenix while I take your pussy and Jude takes your ass? Are you going to take all of us like our good fucking girl that you are?"

"Fuck...y-yes." She's already half drunk on her pleasure.

"Phoenix?" I look to him for help. I don't want to hurt her.

"I got you." He runs a hand through my hair while his other grabs my cock and lines me up. "Angel, don't forget to use your colors and relax." We hear a barely audible "yes" before he lines me up. "You're going to feel some resistance, you need to push past that ring, and it will be all pleasure after that." I push in and feel the resistance.

"Fuck. Fuck. Fuuuuuck." Hazel's words are both moans of pain and pleasure.

"She's good. Jude. She knows to use her colors. Keep going." I pushed past the resistance, and Phoenix wasn't lying.

"Holy fucking shit, she's tight." I slowly pump in until I bottom out. My hips meeting her ass cheeks. I pull out halfway and slide back in. Hazel and Mac both let out long, loud moans.

"Jesus fuck, Jude. I feel your piercing." Phoenix flashes him

349

a smile.

"Feels good, doesn't it?" He strokes Hazel's back. "You ready for me, Angel?"

"Oh god, yes." She turns her head towards him, and he places the tip of his cock in her mouth. She sucks him in, and with all of us stuffing her full, we set an even rhythm. Mac slips his hand between them and starts rubbing Hazel's clit.

"I want you to come on our cocks, strangle them." Mac's tone is almost commanding. He starts thrusting up harder, and she explodes around us. She's so tight I'm unable to move for a moment.

"I'm getting close." I can feel my balls starting to tighten. This is unlike anything I've experienced before.

"I'm close, too," Mac says from below me. "Let's ride this orgasm right into the next. You gotta give us one more, Alice. That's the rule." She starts moaning around Phoenix's cock. It sounds desperate, and I can tell she's close already. Everyone starts pumping deeper, and we all fall over the edge, one right after the other. Our orgasms are sloppy and desperate.

We fall into a heap on each other. Hazel starts laughing uncontrollably. "Now I'm a stuffed hazel-nut sandwich." We all groaned at her corny joke.

56

Epilogue Mac

4 months later

The house is officially finished, the furniture is all moved in, and we are ready to spend our first night together in a home that holds a piece of each of us. But first, we have to put the finishing touches on our surprise for Hazel.

"Put it in the crib," Jude suggests.

"I think it should be on the rocking chair. You know she loves them. There's half a dozen on the porch." Phoenix is rocking in said rocking chair.

"I agree with the crib. Opened or closed?"

"Open," they both say in unison. I place the open box in the middle of the crib in the nursery that we created for Hazel. It's been our little secret. On our blueprints, this was an extra closet. The architect made the room look smaller so she wouldn't know the actual size, and she never bothered to

351

look at it like we'd hoped. This room is right across the hall from our master, opposite the house of the other bedrooms. We didn't want to be too far from the baby at first.

Our phones all ding at the same time. Someone has come through the front gate. We had a security system installed along with the gate because we wanted our family to be safe. Dellah did her job and delayed Hazel so we could make sure everything was perfect. We kept her away the last few days, telling her the painters had to do some touchup after the furniture was moved in, and we didn't want her and the baby exposed to the fumes. We needed those few days to set up the nursery without her seeing anything before the surprise reveal. We all greet Hazel, Dellah, and Wynnie on the porch with wide grins.

"Are you ready to see your new castle, our Queen?" I extend my hand for her to take.

"Show me the way, my Kings." The girls all oh and awe as they wander around, seeing the house for the first time fully furnished. When she's about to walk back downstairs, I stop her.

"We have a surprise, Alice." Her face lights up. She loves surprises.

"Surprise me." Jude places his hands over her eyes, and we walk back down the hall to the doorway she believes is a closet. He removes his hands and she stares at the door.

"Open it," Phoenix whispers in her ear.

"The closet?" She questions. "Did you get me one of those fancy closet organizing systems?"

"Open it," I tell her. She huffs a sigh and opens the door. All three girls gasped as they walk into the beautiful nursery decorated in grays, blacks, and yellows. The decorations are woodsy with outdoor textures. The crib and rocking chair are dark gray. The rug is fluffy with a black and gray striped pattern. The pops of yellow are in the curtains and pillows around the room. We hired a decorator specifically for this room. We chose not to find out the sex of the baby. We all agreed the surprise would be incredible, so the nursery had to be neutral, and the designer did a perfect job.

Hazel turns around, and there are tears streaming down her face. We all surround her in the middle of the room, her head on a swivel taking everything in.

"You should look at everything, Little Dove." She hasn't seen the biggest surprise yet. We hear Wynnie gasp, and she quickly spins away from the crib. We asked her if it was alright but never told her when we would do it. Guess she just figured out the when.

"Are you okay? What's wrong?" She slowly untangles herself from us and walks over to the crib. Peering in, I notice the moment she sees it. Her hands snap up to her open mouth, and when she turns around, we are all kneeling. She looks absolutely stunning standing there. She's almost seven months pregnant, and has glowed this entire pregnancy. Her floral yellow long-sleeved dress flows over her beautiful baby bump. A bump carrying our child. It doesn't matter to any of us whose DNA that baby has. It's ours together. Always together. I'd be lying if I didn't admit there have been pangs of guilt over not getting to experience any of this with Wynnie, but I'm here now, and I'll be here for however many more babies she wants to grace us with.

Dellah pushes Wynnie next to Hazel. This is the part we didn't let Wynnie in on. She hands them both a chain link bracelet. One by one, we stand and give each of them a charm to add. The charms for their bracelets represent the ways each of us met them. For Hazel, a shopping cart, a barbell, and a tiny Mad Hatter's hat. For Wynnie, a box of crayons, a softball, and a flower. Dellah hands each of them a final charm, a little ring to match the engagement ring in the crib. Phoenix stands up to approach the girls first, and takes Hazel's hands.

"Hazel, Angel, from the day you ran me over in the gym door, I knew there was something special about you. You ran over my heart that day, and I couldn't get you out of my head. I truly thought I saw an angel, and told you as much when I saw you at the bar. That night after you left, I told Scotty I was going to marry you. Little did I know you had already met my best friend, who was having the same thoughts."

"Hey, don't steal my speech, man," Jude teases. Phoenix brushes him off with a chuckle and a wave of his hand.

"My best friend, who I didn't know, was also stealing my heart, and thanks to you, I have two amazing people I'm in love with." He pauses and looks over his shoulder and smiles. "And a guy I tolerate." He winks at Mac. "Angel, will you be mine forever?"

"I already am." She throws her arms around him and cries. He pulls her away and chides, "There's more of us." She giggles and lets him step away. He looks at Wynnie.

"You are just as much of a part of this relationship as any of us. We are only here with your blessing. Mac may be your father, but I consider you my daughter. Will you have me as a father figure in your life?" Just as her mother did, she throws herself at him. He lifts her off the floor and gives her a big hug.

"Yes, I'd love that."

"I love you, Wynnie girl.

"I love you too, Phoenix." Sniffles are heard around the room. He puts her down and steps back to Jude and I. Jude is up next. He approaches Wynnie first.

"You have blossomed so much from the shy, timid girl that knocked on my office door almost a year ago. Watching you grow and bloom in school, on the field, and in life has been my absolute pleasure. You're going to be the best big sister. You may not be my blood, but I already consider you my daughter if you'll have me?"

"Yes, Jude. I absolutely will." She squeezes her arms around his waist, and Jude embraces her shoulder and kisses the top of her head. "Love you, Jude."

"Love you, kid." He turns to Hazel.

"My Little Dove. My pure, innocent rebirth."

I lean into Phoenix and whisper, "So that's what that means." I hear Hazel chuckle, and Jude shoots me a look.

"You'll have to explain to us why you call her Alice at a later time. Now hush."

"As I was saying, Little Dove. Unlike Phoenix, I came crashing into *your* life. I was such a rambling idiot, and I thought for sure you were going to throw a can of tomatoes at my head if I called you ma'am one more time. I've never felt an instant connection with anyone like I felt with you. I asked you out that day because I couldn't stand the thought of never seeing you again. And today, I'm asking you to be my wife because I can't stand the thought of ever spending another day without you." There's a pause, and he's waiting for her to answer.

"Did you ask me a question because I'm still waiting?" Oh shit. Jude's eyes darken, he leans in and whispers something to Hazel. Her cheeks turn pink. "Oh, in that case, yes, I'd love to marry you...Sir." Well damn, now I have to know what he whispered to her. He embraces her with a kiss and walks back to join us with a smug smile. I open my mouth to ask, and he mouths, "Later." It's finally my turn. I feel like I've been preparing for this for 13 years. Walking up to her, I take her hands.

"My precious, beautiful, sassy Alice. I think I might do something better with my time, than waste it in asking riddles that have no answers." She gasps. I knew she would understand the reference.

"If you knew time as well as I do, you wouldn't talk about wasting it." I lift her hands and kiss her knuckles.

"I don't want to waste anymore time asking riddles. I want to spend the rest of our lives making memories and babies. And raising our babies and making more memories. Will you marry me and watch *Alice in Wonderland* on endless loops with our children?" I hear Jude whisper an "ooooh" behind me and smirk.

"Mac, I'll waste all of my time on riddles and movies with you, all of my years." I kiss her deeply, passionately, until someone clears their throat. I release her with a smile.

"Wynnie. My Rowyn Juniper. You are the best pieces of your mother and probably the worst pieces of me." We both chuckle. "I wish I could have known you sooner but, I'll spend every day for the rest of our lives getting to know you if you'll allow me." I reach into my pocket and hand both Hazel and Wynnie papers.

"What's this," Wynnie asks as she looks over the paper.

Hazel gasps. "Are you sure?"

"Absolutely. I've never been more sure of anything in my

life. Wynnie, this is an application to be added to your birth certificate. Your mother just has to sign it to start the process, and I can officially be your father in the eyes of the law."

"But you're already my dad. I don't need a piece of paper to tell me." She wraps her arms around me, and I return the embrace.

"I know, sweetheart. It's just a piece of paper. You're mine, and I want to make sure you're taken care of, always. I love you, Wynnie. The second piece of paper is just for you. It's a request for a name change. I'd love to share my name with you and make you a Harmon." Tears spill from her eyes.

"You really want me." Was there ever a doubt?

"Yes, sweetheart, I do." I look at the guys behind me. "We all do." They join me, and we smash together into a group hug–all five and a half of us. I hear clicking and turn to see Dellah taking pictures with her phone.

"What?" She shrugs. "I was capturing the moment." We all break out into laughter, and she gets pulled into our hug huddle.

57

Epilogue Hazel

3 months later

"Has it been three minutes yet?" I asked my best friend, Dellah, as I paced the bathroom.

"Hazy, that seems like an awfully deja vu-ish question." I flash her an amused grin. I knew exactly what I said. I'm trying to find humor through the pain. My doctor said to stay home until the contractions are 3 minutes apart. It's mid-day, one week before my due date. My maternity leave started a week ago, and Dellah has been hanging out with me while she does her work on my couch from her computer. All the guys and Wynnie are at work and school, and I don't want to bother them with false alarms. Dellah is currently sitting on my bed because I keep having to pee.

"How do I know if my water breaks?"

"Are you really asking the childless woman in the room a birthing question?" She looks up from her computer at my shocked face. "Um, did you pee yourself in the middle of the bathroom? Please tell me that's pee."

"Dellah, don't panic. Call the guys. It's baby time." That was the exact wrong thing to say. Telling the person who constantly walks the line of panic to *not panic* only sent her into a tailspin. "Okay, better yet. You get my bag and keys and meet me in the van. I'm going to change and make the calls. Can you handle that?"

"Bag. Keys. Van. Got it." She walks out the door, and I grab my phone. I send a text to the group chat first, which I already know is a mistake, but I need them to get into gear while I call my doctor and let her know.

Me: It's baby time.

While on the phone with my doctor, my phone is constantly buzzing. I don't even bother to look because I know they are freaking out like Dellah. The doctor asks the standard questions. How long ago did my water break? How far apart are the contractions? She tells me to head to the Emergency Room, and she will meet me in the maternity ward. By the time I hang up, I have 37 missed texts and 11 missed calls from all three guys, Wynnie and Dellah. And oddly, two gate notifications. My phone rings in my hand, and it's Mac.

"Hey, Ma-" I get cut off and bombarded with rapid-fire questions.

"Why aren't you answering? I'm heading your way. Are you still home?" I hear him grumble. "Hold on." He's back in a few seconds.

"Angel / Little Dove / Mom." They all talk over each other, obviously in someone's vehicle together.

"Oh hey, it's a party now. The gang's all here." I roll my eyes at myself.

"Answer the questions, Alice," Mac growls at my humor.

"Okay, okay. I'm still home at the mome-." A sharp contraction hits me, taking my breath away. I put the phone down and do my best to breathe through it. I hear the panicked yells coming from the speaker. "I'm back, sorry. That was a big contraction." I hear Mac turn his sirens on in the background. "Mac, what are you doing?"

"Coming to you."

"Don't be ridiculous. Dellah is waiting in the van for me. I just needed to change my clothes because my water broke." I hear an engine rev on the line.

"You're water broke?" Phoenix yells over the speaker.

"You are all being so overbearing. I'm fiiiii-." I have to pause through another contraction. Okay, maybe I'm not fine. Those were really close together and painful. I struggled to breathe through that one. "Mac, maybe you should hurry." I get the notification for the front gate a moment before I hear his sirens coming up the driveway.

2 minutes later, Mac comes barging into the room while I'm in the middle of another contraction. He takes one look at me, picks up his phone, dials 9-1-1, and barks out his orders.

"Dispatch, this is Officer Harmon. I have a 39 week pregnant woman in active labor, and I need an ambulance to my home address now."

Hanging up the phone, he rolls up his sleeves on his way to the bathroom and washes his hands. When he comes back, he tells me to lie down on the edge of the bed.

"Where the hell is Dellah? You weren't supposed to be alone."

360

"What are you doing?" I peer down at him, crouched on the floor as he tries to lift my skirt.

"I'm going to check for the baby. Your contractions are intense and close together. If I'm right, you aren't going to make it to the hospital. Do you want to have our baby in your van trying to get there or in your bed?"

"Can I choose option C? The hospital?"

"Will you just lay down, and let me check you. Spread your legs for me."

"This is some strange foreplay, Officer Harmon. Have I told you lately how sexy you look in uniform?"

"Alice," he growls. "This isn't funny."

"Okay, but it kind of is. And you aren't a doctor."

"I've delivered several babies before. On the side of the road. A bed is much more favorable than the backseat of a sedan. Now, would you let me check you, please?" His "please" is said through clenched teeth. Just as I relax and spread my legs for him, Phoenix, Jude, and Wynnie come rushing into the room.

"Mom!" Wynnie covers her eyes and spins around.

"Funny time for foreplay, asshole." Phoenix and I have the same weird sense of humor.

"Okay, not what I expected. Where's Dellah?" Jude's eyes are wide with shock.

Mac turns and growls at them all. Hmm, he's very growly. I guess something about delivering my baby, our baby, has made him very primal.

"Wynnie, go find your Aunt Dellah and stay out unless we tell you. There should be an ambulance coming. Make sure they find us up here. Guys, this baby is-" Another contraction hits me, and I have the urge to push. Mac continues his orders once the contraction subsides. "-coming now. Get a blanket and towels. Grab a pair of scissors and sterilize it in a cup of vodka. No better yet, someone run out to my cruiser and get my med bag from my trunk. It has everything I'll need." He's so sexy when he's commanding. *Not the time, Hazel.*

"Are you ready, Alice, because our little one is ready to make their appearance with or without us."

"I trust you, Mac. Let's have a baby." Phoenix returns to the room with Mac's med bag, and Jude comes in with towels and blankets. We get everything set up, and Phoenix sits behind me, straddling my body so I can lean back on his chest. Jude sits next to me, taking my hand.

"On the next contraction, if you feel the need to push, I want you to push as hard as you can." I nod, and it doesn't take long before a contraction hits. I continue to push through the next ten contractions, all three of my guys whispering praises and encouragement every time. On the 11th push, Mac tells me to stop, the baby's head is out, and he needs to clear the airway. On the next push, our baby was born just as we heard the buzzing of our phones for the gate alarm. The ambulance is here.

Mac is cleaning the baby and asks who wants to cut the cord. From the doorway, we hear, "Can I?" We all look to see Wynnie standing there.

"Of course, sweetheart. Come here." She walks over and hands her the scissors instructing her where to cut. Why don't you tell them whether you have a brother or sister first?" He lifts the blanket covering the baby, and a big smile lights up her face.

"It's a...boy." She cuts the cord as the paramedics are walking in. They check on me and the baby, our baby boy.

Mac insists we go to the hospital to get checked out. I announced that I was riding in the ambulance with Dellah, who had been suspiciously missing, before they could argue about who would accompany me. There were lots of grumbles.

My doctor checked me and our baby boy, and we were discharged to my overbearing men only a few hours later.

The four of us stand over the crib staring at our sleeping baby.

"I love you all. We made a beautiful baby." There are collective, "I love yous" back at me.

"He needs a name," Phoenix says.

"Mac, what did you say the gentleman who used to live here's name was?"

"His name was Gideon. Hmm, I like it." I snuggled into Mac's arm. Jude puts his arm around my lower back, and Phoenix weaves his arms through us from behind.

"Baby Gideon sounds wonderful, Little Dove."

"I agree, Angel."

We all stare down at the little blonde-haired, brown-eyed baby fast asleep in his crib. And I think about the future we are building together. Always together.

The End

363

About the Author

Casiddie is a single mother to 5 children living on the east coast. This is her debut novel and she is excited to produce more works of fiction for her readers to enjoy.

You can connect with me on:

https://www.facebook.com/casiddiewilliams

https://www.tiktok.com/@casiddiewilliams

Also by Casiddie Williams

Welcome to my little corner. I hope you've enjoyed reading about Hazel and her Guys. I currently have 2 books in the works before the end of the year. I hope you'll join me again to read about Annie and Dellah's adventures

Annie You're Okay

Annie is a billionaire in software development. When her dog gets loose from her backyard, she finds herself practically naked in front of a gorgeous stranger walking a dog. She's in luck because her dog walker quit, and she's in need...of more than just someone to walk her dog. Annie You're Okay is a FFM Contemporary Romance.

Dellah's Delight
We are returning to hang out with Dellah and learn more about her relationship with Collin. Dellah's book will span before and after Hazel's, so you'll get a glimpse of how Hazel and her Harem are doing—release date planned for the end of November.

Made in the USA
Middletown, DE
26 April 2025